The
LAST

The
LAST
TRADE

JAMES CONWAY

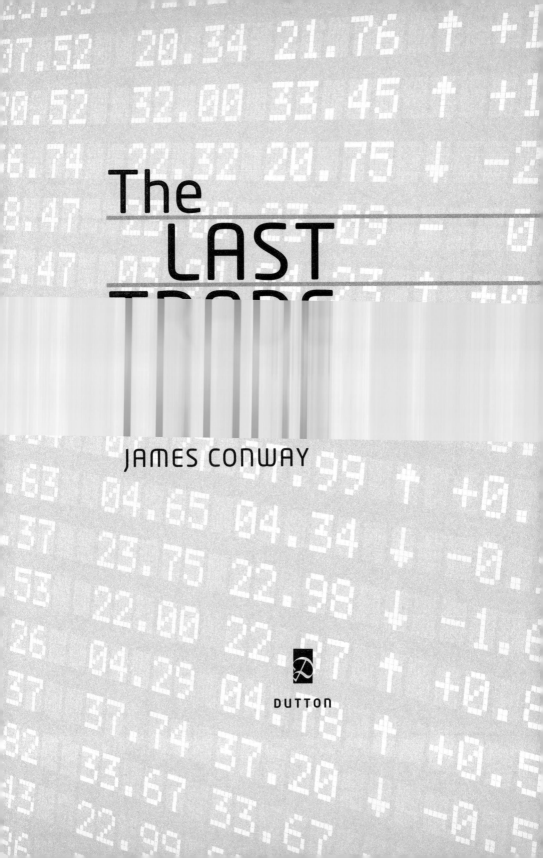

DUTTON

DUTTON
Published by Penguin Group (USA) Inc.
375 Hudson Street, New York, New York 10014, U.S.A.
Penguin Group (Canada), 90 Eglinton Avenue East, Suite 700, Toronto, Ontario M4P 2Y3,
Canada (a division of Pearson Penguin Canada Inc.); Penguin Books Ltd, 80 Strand, London
WC2R 0RL, England; Penguin Ireland, 25 St Stephen's Green, Dublin 2, Ireland (a division of
Penguin Books Ltd); Penguin Group (Australia), 250 Camberwell Road, Camberwell, Victoria
3124, Australia (a division of Pearson Australia Group Pty Ltd); Penguin Books India Pvt Ltd,
11 Community Centre, Panchsheel Park, New Delhi–110 017, India; Penguin Group (NZ), 67 Apollo
Drive, Rosedale, Auckland 0632, New Zealand (a division of Pearson New Zealand Ltd); Penguin
Books (South Africa) (Pty) Ltd, 24 Sturdee Avenue, Rosebank, Johannesburg 2196, South Africa

Penguin Books Ltd, Registered Offices: 80 Strand, London WC2R 0RL, England

Published by Dutton, a member of Penguin Group (USA) Inc.

First printing, June 2012
10   9   8   7   6   5   4   3   2   1

 REGISTERED TRADEMARK—MARCA REGISTRADA

LIBRARY OF CONGRESS CATALOGING-IN-PUBLICATION DATA
Conway, James, 1964–
    The last trade : a novel / by James Conway.
        p. cm.
    ISBN 978-0-525-95282-4
    1. International finance—Fiction.   I. Title.
    PS3603.O56476L37 2012
    813'.6—dc23   2011036278

Printed in the United States of America
Designed by Nancy Resnick
Title page photograph © Diseñador / Fotolia

PUBLISHER'S NOTE
This book is a work of fiction. Names, characters, places, and incidents either are the product of
the author's imagination or are used fictitiously, and any resemblance to actual persons, living
or dead, business establishments, events, or locales is entirely coincidental.

ALWAYS LEARNING   PEARSON

For Patricia Helen Conway

In an effort to slow or temporarily halt catastrophic financial disas-

there will be a two-hour halt of trading. In the event of a 3150-point decline in the DJIA (30 percent), regardless of the time, markets will close for the day, if not longer.

———

The *Hindenburg Omen* is a technical analysis pattern that portends a major stock market crash. It is named after the crash of the German zeppelin *Hindenburg* on May 6, 1937. The rationale is that on a given day, under "normal conditions," a substantial number of stocks on the NYSE will set new annual highs *or* annual lows. A Hindenburg Omen occurs on those rare days when there is a simultaneous presence of substantial new highs *and* lows. Soon after, according to the data, a major to catastrophic market decline is likely to follow. It is a known fact that every major U.S. stock market crash of the past seventy-five years has been preceded by a confirmed Hindenburg Omen.

"Derivatives are financial weapons of mass destruction."

The LAST

Prologue

Pissing on it. Laughing at it. Puffing thousand-dollar cigars in the white-hot center of it.

They are in a ten-thousand-square-foot mansion, the former home of a suddenly bankrupt mortgage broker, having a party, a bash, an all-American bacchanal celebrating the antithesis of bankruptcy.

Celebrating a windfall now in the billions while the country is in the midst of losing trillions.

Rick Salvado bought the mansion a week ago just for this moment. He bought it as much for the outdoor shooting range, four hot tubs, twin swimming pools, and first-floor dance club replete with two DJ booths and four stripper poles as he did for the irony. Because this "event," an exclusive gathering for the top-tier clients and executives of Salvado's hedge, the Rising Fund, was bought and paid for because The Rising was one of the few funds to see it all coming. The sub-prime mortgage debacle, the chaos at Bear and Lehman, and the collapse of the U. S. and world markets—they were one of the few to see it, bet on it, and profit from the devastating misery of many.

No one is more intimate with this fact than Drew Havens, the twenty-eight-year-old stat-arb quant who designed the elegant computer model that foretold this inelegant mess. He's the one who has made Rick Salvado an overnight multi-billionaire media darling and a lot of people, including himself, rich. Havens stands off to the side of the dance floor, sipping Diet Coke and watching the revelry. He's exhilarated and exhausted, fascinated and more than a bit mortified. Once Salvado was certain that things were going to break right, he secured the mansion, fired up the Gulfstream, and whisked dozens of them out here on a flight filled with booze and sex and coke. Havens, a happily married man with a newborn girl, was more spectator than participant. He had a few glasses of in-flight Dom Pérignon but otherwise stayed on the periphery.

When they touched down on a private strip outside Vegas, the bender continued. Salvado had a convoy of Land Rovers take them to a makeshift shooting range far out in the desert, where, armed with everything from 50-cal machine guns to a nineteenth-century Gatling gun, and provisioned by scantily clad ammo hostesses, they blasted an assortment of targets—including life-sized cutouts of everyone from Osama bin Laden and Barry Bonds to Rosie O'Donnell and the head of the SEC. For the SEC leader, Salvado had a surprise. His handlers set up the cutout inside a Toyota Corolla one hundred yards away. They then towed up a twelve-foot-long T8 90mm antitank cannon.

Havens is looking at his BlackBerry at the latest pictures his wife, Miranda, sent of their daughter, Erin, who is waving good night, when his friend Tommy Rourke approaches. While Havens is all about numbers, Rourke is all about relationships. He's the fund's top rainmaker when it comes to landing high-net-worth prospects. Rourke slaps Havens on the back. "What's up, egghead?" It's a name the staff of The Rising had taken to calling the shy and numbers-obsessed Havens, at first disparagingly and now, post-windfall, with reverence.

"The egghead is doing all right," Havens answers. "Other than having a busted eardrum from that goddamn cannon this afternoon."

Rourke laughs. "Rick's a crazy bastard. But you gotta love the guy . . . right?"

"No complaints here," Havens answers. On the dance floor Rick Salvado is bumping and grinding to Chris Brown's "Take You Down" with no fewer than three female "entertainers." Nodding at Rourke's glass of sparkling water, Havens continues, "So no strippers, coke, and single-malt for you?"

Rourke shakes his head. "Someone's got to watch over this ship while the captain lets loose." They clink nonalcoholic glasses and watch the spectacle on the dance floor and on the TV monitor hanging

Here's what happened. In the early spring of 2007, little more than a month into his new job as a desk quant in the real estate sector, Havens received a surprise cube visit from Salvado and the man who discovered him, Tommy Rourke.

"Rourke here tells me you are a freak with numbers," Salvado said. "But not exactly a people person."

"This is true."

"Fine by me," Salvado replied. "We didn't recruit you to be the face of the company. We recruited you because of your analytical skill, which I have been told is borderline genius. I say borderline because you haven't made us rich yet. Do that and you get to be called whatever kind of genius you want: Mad. Evil. Whatever."

Havens smiled. Fair enough.

Salvado continued, "So, I was impressed by your thoughts on the housing market. You really think it's gonna tank?"

"To say definitively, I'd have to dig much broader and deeper."

"But your gut tells you it's a bubble—and a big one?"

"Scary big."

"Good enough," Salvado said. "I want you to hunker down here in your quant cave and eat, breathe, and sleep the data. I want you to put together the pieces, test the hypotheses. Model the fuck out of it. Do not come back to me until you have a verdict. I wanna know the total circumference and volume of this bubble and, more importantly, the precise nanosecond it's gonna burst."

Havens dove in. He lived for that kind of work. For some in finance, numbers quantify risk and reward. For Havens, they quantified the mysteries of life. "My Quant in Captivity," Salvado began to call him, and Havens did not have a problem with it.

Three months later Havens emerged from the data cave and told his boss that his hunch was valid. The sub-prime mortgage situation in the U.S. housing market was worse than he had thought possible. Worse than anyone had imagined.

"In other words," Salvado replied that afternoon, "it's better than we ever could have hoped for."

Havens didn't have an answer. He'd never thought of it that way.

Havens checks his watch. He promised Miranda he'd call an hour ago. He wants to hear all about the baby's day and to get away from the others. He feels as if he's done more socializing in the past twenty-four hours than he's done in the previous twenty-eight years. But it's been almost impossible to get away from Salvado, Rourke, and company.

"So, this is quite the change from working in the back office for Citi out in fucking Queens, ain't it, egghead?"

On the dance floor two of the three women with Salvado have taken off their tops. The third is trying to take off Salvado's. As bizarre and excessive as this is, Havens can't help but feel proud. After a lifetime being called an antisocial nerd and an egghead, it's nice to get a bit of respect. "Yeah," he concedes. "I couldn't have predicted this in a million years."

"But the funny thing is," Rourke says, "you did."

MONDAY,

1

Even here, surrounded by beauty and green the pulse and swagger of a celebrity-studded Monday night in Manhattan, it's the numbers that make the difference, the numbers that guide and haunt and make him unlike anyone else in the room.

Drew Havens planned on quitting his job soon, perhaps within a month or so. He knew that to quit sooner, before bonuses came out, would be folly, even though he's reached the breaking point and is financially set for years and by its own high standards the fund has had an off year. An off year at a hedge like The Rising is something that 99 percent of the other funds would kill for. But thanks to nights like this, years of them, it's getting harder to stick around.

The bottle girl struts across the floor holding a sparkler with one hand and a tray of the latest round of Cristal and Grey Goose in the other. She bends at the waist and presses her breasts against the shoulder of his suit, apparently to better listen to his question. Havens always has questions and they almost always revolve around numbers. What's safe or high-risk? What circumstances created the past and what will determine what's next? What's right and wrong? What multiples can be unpacked to reveal some sort of truth (if there is such a thing)? Though his question for the bottle girl is numbers-based, this time it's merely rhetorical. Whatever she answers won't matter, because he already knows it's over. He knows he's done with finance, with excess, with the hedge life, with client parties, with the media, with the bloated ego, outlandish behavior, and out-of-control proclamations of his boss Rick Salvado. And with looking the other way when confronted with situations like this:

"Between us, 'cause I can get in trouble," explains the bottle girl in response to his question, "just for these two bottles, forty-five hundred. And you guys've had like what, seven? Then toss in another ten-k just for the table, and who knows what else you'll add on before you leave, and then you're deep into the land of six figures. Of course, gratuity not included."

"Of course." Havens nods, then looks around the corner table, an eight- by twelve-foot piece of temporary real estate that cost his firm ten thousand dollars for the night. Celebrities get these tables for free, but hedge guys, whales in money suits like them—like us, he thinks— have to pay. He considers the two other quants from the firm sitting across from him, a safe distance away from his cynicism and disgust, his burned-out soul, both relatively new, both eating it up as he once did. Then he considers the two good ole boy clients from Texas who made a fortune with them the last time around, more than a hundred million based almost entirely on his numbers, which foretold the coming sub-prime debacle, back in '08.

Finally, he looks at his boss, the street smart and chronically telegenic Rick Salvado.

Salvado and the rest of the group are surrounded by an equally large gathering of provocatively dressed young women. Their beauty ranges from just-missed runway model to girl next door to contract-girl porn star. Havens is certain that each of these young women would be miles away from here, or at least at the next-best-paying table, if they hadn't been dispatched by their VIP host/pimp and weren't bought and paid for by a bona fide Wall Street money whale like Salvado.

The numbers that the waitress just shared are disturbing, to be sure, but even more disturbing to Havens is how long he's tolerated this kind of thing. Perhaps it's because it's never been a puzzle, or a priority. They were numbers without an equation or a goal, so, until now, they were ignored. But he knows that's not true. He's always known and until now he's always looked away. "In a liquor store," Havens says to the young woman, "two bottles would run you something like a hun-

bottles of Dom Pérignon to his table and drag two of the young women of the club by their necks, without the assistance of bouncers, like rag dolls. Laslow jerks his head at the girl. Move on from the geek. There's money to be made elsewhere. As the girl leaves, Havens closes his eyes. He's tired. This morning he got into work at five, just as he always did. He checked the foreign overnights. Job numbers. Tokyo. Hong Kong. The futures. Credit swaps. European debt. Consumer confidence, or lack thereof. Housing. Then he checked his life's work, his models. A quantitative analyst designs and implements mathematical models for the pricing of derivatives, assessment of risk, or predicting market movements. There are many kinds of quant, from capital quants who analyze a bank's credit exposure, to model validation quants who ensure that their employer's financial strategies are correct, to Havens's area of expertise: statistical arbitrage quant. A stat-arb quant, most commonly found in a hedge fund, looks for pricing anomalies and future volatility in financial securities, instruments, and sectors—and conjectures their imminent success or failure.

His professional life's work has been data mining, extracting trends and patterns and answers to questions about which he's been rapidly losing interest. Some analysts will also read all the papers and industry publications that they can, the *Journal*, the *Economist*, the *Financial Times*, or the micro-trend-based ramblings of the latest financial blogger on a roll, but Havens avoids all that. He believes that opinions and words are rooted in emotion, and emotion gets in the way of the numbers.

Words have multiple meanings, manipulate behaviors and bend truths.

Numbers do not. Numbers are truth.

For instance, numbers like one hundred grand for another night on the town with a couple of high-net-worth yahoos with a fortune in the fund. The festivities started soon after the markets closed, with drinks at Salvado's table at Cipriani. Hank Paulson stopped by to slap Salvado's back. Jamie Dimon from JP Morgan Chase paid tribute with a joke. At the next table was the SEC honcho trying to bring down Raj Rajaratnam, but no one stopped by there to say hello.

They followed drinks with dinner in a private room at Del Posto in Chelsea, during which they were visited by none other than Molto Mario Batali himself. For dessert, they were served cigars and cognac while a flat screen was rolled out for the gathering to watch and gently heckle Salvado's appearance earlier this morning on CNBC's *Squawk Box*. During his cameo, Salvado's image was accompanied by the text crawl: *Salvado: Still Bullish on America*.

Of course he is. What other choice did the head of a fund called The Rising have? You don't co-opt a Springsteen song and play off the jingoism of 9/11 and then talk down the American economic future.

They kiss Salvado's ass on *Squawk Box* and just about everywhere else in the financial press these days because, thanks to Havens's numbers, he was one of the very few to have had foreknowledge (or fore-inklings) of the sub-prime mess and who had the balls to act and make a killing on it.

And because, as the crawl inferred, he's still betting all-in on an American economic recovery.

Havens's mobile device buzzes. It's Weiss again. The young quant pup Danny Weiss has been calling Havens for days, raving about the direction of the fund and some broader, potentially more duplicitous concerns that have arisen. After the phone stops buzzing, the text icon pops up. Because he's bored, and because a few crazed lines from Weiss are better than any of this, Havens opens the message. It reads:

... wilt thou not be brotherly to us?

back and alleviate his concerns and tell him that, after consideration, he can say that Rick Salvado's investment philosophy is backed by sound numbers and models and the Rising Fund is poised to have a killer fourth quarter. But instead Weiss quickly went off the deep end and insisted—without anything of substance to back it up—that things are far, far worse than Havens had thought. Havens told him to dig deeper and Weiss hasn't stopped, which is fine. But texts such as this . . .

. . . wilt thou not be brotherly to us?

. . . have Havens worried, not just about the future of the fund, but about the psychological condition of the sharp young guy he hired, and one of the few in this business he actually likes.

He lowers his head and rubs his eyes. From Del Posto ($11,600) they took two limos and Salvado's Bentley to this place. Last year they would have gone to 1Oak or Provocateur, or the less subtly named Boom

Boom Room. Tonight, at least until a more freshly decadent establishment bumps it off the Venue of the Moment map, it's this place: Elysian. On the way in, as they were led past the crowd of wannabes outside the velvet rope, Havens quipped to his group, "Welcome to Elysian, the final resting place of the heroic and virtuous," but either no one picked up on his mythological reference, or they pretended not to hear him.

For Havens the lack of response was one more piece in a mounting pile of evidence that his time with Rick Salvado has reached its expiration date. Havens has been the prized quant for Salvado's already legendary Rising Fund for four years, but as one slightly older analyst recently told him, "Four years at a hedge is like four hundred in human years."

This is the tradeoff when you are a CUNY-educated nobody, a socially challenged numbers freak who was given a chance to make millions before the age of thirty, plucked seemingly without reason from a going-nowhere back office job in Long Island City crunching derivatives for Citi, and dropped in the role of a trusted quant, an advisor to a genuine master of the universe. It's also what happens when you have a God-given gift for turning numbers into gold.

Havens's phone buzzes. He checks the screen, thinking that it might be Miranda, his former wife. But it's not. It's Danny Weiss again. When Havens made it big they moved him up, farther from the numbers and into a spotlight he does not covet. He was told to hire replacements. Protégés. The only must-hire was Weiss. Havens would like to think it was because he saw something of himself in the young, outgoing, and passionate kid. But it's really because he saw the person he wished he could be. Again he doesn't answer but again reads the text. Even Weiss's most cryptic and scatological notes are preferable to his present company.

This time the text reads:

Berlin. 12.42-6

Please, Havens thinks, keep it together for me, Weiss.

2

 A deadly and complex global conspiracy — or a string of
bizarre coincidences?

Spending three sleepless days holed up in an Upper East Side one-
bedroom apartment, hunched over a PC, piecing together a growing
web of information while consuming massive amounts of highly caf-
feinated soft drinks and an ex-girlfriend's diet pills will do that to a
mind. Yet for the first time one of his paranoid global conspiracy theories seems to be making sense. Exactly how much sense and how bad
this might be is hard to tell because the evidence is far from complete,
and he's exhausted and wired.

But still. It's not as if he's an unemployed eccentric. He's a young,
highly trained desk quant employed by one of the world's leading hedge
funds. And he's certain: The Hong Kong activity that's been coming
over the wires is not a hallucination.

If anything, coupled with the growing collection of quotes and symbols and models he's been building, gathering, and holding up against
the positions of the firm, it is a validation and a confirmation, the first

of the series of trades that he's convinced will end in catastrophe. What level of catastrophe he's not sure. But the clues and the chatter, the scatter plot results, the mean and median correlations, the linear progression, and yes, the vibe (which, he admits, very well might be speed-related) all seem to validate his operational and predictive models and portend something on a historically disastrous scale. Starting now and, best he can tell, culminating this Friday. And while he hasn't quite put together all of the pieces he's certain that somehow The Rising, the fund he works for, is directly linked to it all.

And this conclusion isn't simply deduced from the algorithm of some black box, data-crunching computer model. He employed logic, reason, and intuition, at least to the extent that any of the three exists in the financial world these days. He probed beyond margins and yields and index spread over benchmark and considered the human aspect of the questionable moves. The broader societal shifts, the management teams in place at the securities, their competitive advantage, and the political climate—he tried not just to calculate the numbers, but also to understand them. And still, they make no sense. Unless you're the sociopath behind them.

He steps away from his desktop, stretches, and looks at his phone. Havens, his boss, mentor, and only friend at the Rising Fund, still hasn't answered any of his calls or texts. This doesn't surprise him. Havens is notoriously tech-averse and hard to reach outside the office, not that that has ever stopped Weiss from trying. He's tempted to go down to Del Posto or Elysian or whatever decadent club they're at tonight and drag Havens out by his collar, but he knows such a drastic move could backfire with a low-key guy like Havens. Several times in the past he's cried wolf and been wrong with Havens, and this time he wants to be right before he makes another scene. Havens is the only person who would believe him and the only one he trusts. Plus he's the one who put him on this path, so Weiss doesn't want to blow it.

He sits back down, puts on his headphones—the neighbors shut down the big speakers months ago—and goes back to work and listening to the Clash. Lately his musical choices have been all late-seventies punk all the time. He's deemed it the official soundtrack of overthrowing institutions. The problem, he realizes, is no one hears it quite that way anymore.

He decides that the best way to get Havens to listen is to remain calm and not harass him. He tells himself he needs to chill and continue to discover the truth. He shuts down the Bloomberg software terminal and clicks on the flash drive icon on his screen. Two weeks ago he procured a proprietary piece of highly sophisticated tracking software from the hacker friend of a hacker friend. Two days ago, while

same stocks. As he watches it unfold, he name of the Hang Seng broker executing them: Patrick Lau.

His next click, prompted by the number sequence out of Berlin, takes him to another series of trades, all shorts, just like in Hong Kong, commencing out of Dubai and, curiously, also the mirror opposite of positions held by The Rising. As he leans closer, his screen blinks on and off. When it comes back up, the Dubai page is gone and a Spyware warning briefly flashes in the upper left part of the screen. Wired or not, he knows that this isn't a hallucination and that it's entirely possible that someone out there might be tracking him, tracking them.

He grabs a red flash drive on the right side of the desk and plugs it into port. Because he won't look into any of this on the office computers, everything he has is on this big, clunky desktop. In case he has to run, he wants to have some kind of backup, and to at least have a copy to give to Havens.

While the files are loading, he switches back to Bloomberg and keeps an eye on the Berlin numbers and tries to formulate a model or theory that might make sense of them. What do these transactions have to do with the Rising Fund, and who in Berlin is behind them?

He's still staring at the screen when a new message appears at the bottom of the Berlin page. He reads it, then does a search. After a few moments the software generates two slightly different variations on a response, both of which roughly translate to

kill Patrick Lau

3

and the primal roar of the dance floor below, "A toast!" He raises his just-filled flute of Cristal, and the rest of the table joins him, including the young, blond, Russian "model" who's been pawing at him since she was brought to the table. Watching the model, Havens can't help but think of Salvado's soon-to-be-ex-wife and kids and the speech that Salvado gave to him when he first started at The Rising, about the firm's unwavering commitment to fidelity and loyalty, to work and family.

"A toast to the long and the short of it. But . . . ," Salvado pauses, ". . . but this time around, especially the god damn long!"

They drink and cheer, but Salvado, not yet finished, hushes them. "This has been one of our most difficult years. Many clients who have prospered greatly from our advice in the past have begun to grow skittish. Many more have publicly doubted us. Our confidence. But we have not wavered from our path and our vision. We have not let opinion dissuade us from doing what is right and what will ultimately be beneficial for us all. We're on an epic journey, an epic tale that is still being written, and when it's all over, it will be remembered as one of the great ones. To those who have stuck with us, and are poised to reap those rewards—sooner than later, I promise!—I salute you!"

After the cheers rise and fall, Salvado raises his hand to make one last salutation. "And finally I'd like to make a special shout-out, a toast to the man who a few years back got right what 99.9 percent of the financial world got wrong. The man who immersed himself in the data and saw the potential to make billions on the sub-prime misery of the masses and walked into my office one day with the numbers to prove it. This is the man who is getting it right all over again, readying us for another major event, guiding us to zig while the rest of the street zags: the Nostradamus of Numbers, the King of the Quants, and my pal, give it up for Mister Personality, Andrew Havens!"

Havens raises his glass, fakes a sip, and grimaces more than grins along with the applause. As he bends to sit back down, he knocks over his drink and the others laugh at his social ineptitude. While he reaches for a napkin to clean up his mess, his phone buzzes again.

This text reads:

Murder @ Hang Seng

4

 October 19, 1987, and, of course, septem...

No one is more aware of this than Patrick Lau, a twenty-nine-year-old trader who lost everything and then some in the fall of 2008. He lost his client's money, his employer's money, and, of course, his own. There had been warnings, but as is the case with so many people who have only enjoyed success, even in 2008 Lau felt that he was immune to failure. After the crash, he downsized his lifestyle, sold what he could, started over, and tried to hang on.

Up until a few hours ago even that was in question. When he left for work this morning, he was fairly sure that he'd have to move out of his apartment and perhaps leave Hong Kong and the financial services industry altogether. But now that all seems to be changing for the better.

Autumn Mondays and overwhelming personal debt be damned.

It's amazing how a random phone call from a complete stranger can change everything. Lau can't move beyond this thought as he walks through the door of a seventeenth-floor condominium in the Wanchai

District of Hong Kong, a condo that he will not have to abandon after all. Amazing how one call from someone whose name he still doesn't and may never know can change a life, a career, and, in Lau's case, save the ass of a broker on the precipice of bankruptcy.

He glances out the living room window and thinks of the prospect of a born-again, amazing life as dusk falls upon the city. In the distance he can still make out the silhouette of Victoria Peak, and in every direction the rooftop lights of the towers that rim the harbor have begun flashing, illuminating the world beneath in a neon, Technicolor rainbow.

After so many bad ones, this has been a good day for Lau. Indeed, after a brutal couple of years it seems as if things are finally beginning to turn around. Of course, nothing like the millennial boom times with the coke and the raves and the spontaneous junkets to Bali and Phuket. But definitely better, especially on his small piece of real estate on the U.S. trading desk. Especially today.

Just after noon Lau received a phone call from a man at a firm called Siren Securities in Berlin, representing an American investor interested in taking a short position on a series of American-based tech stocks. Lau didn't typically take this kind of call seriously. Every day, especially since the crash, he's received similar inquiries from eccentrics and loons and amateurs without the funds or credentials to back up their claims. But there was something about this caller, the authority of the man's voice and the specificity of his intentions, that piqued Lau's curiosity.

That and the 1.1-billion-dollar price tag on the deal.

Lau fixes himself a martini, Hendrick's with a splash of olive juice, and plops down on his white leather sofa to take in the view and revel in his accomplishment. And why not? It's only Monday. Just last night he was thinking he might have to move to a more affordable apartment at a less desirable address, perhaps share something with a roommate for the first time since he graduated college, and now he's just completed the biggest deal of his twenty-nine-year-old life.

At first he had begun to tell the voice on the other end the proper procedure for executing a transaction of this nature, but within seconds the voice was telling *him*, explaining the exact protocol, the account numbers, the complex series of wire transfers, and the way in which the transactions were to be divided, each for no more than ten thousand dollars U.S., and staggered, hundreds per hour over a twenty-four-hour period.

This, Lau surmised, was to minimize the chances of the transaction showing up on whatever sophisticated tracking software the authorities ~~ing these days~~. The FSA in London. The FBI, CIA, or Department

moralize, recommend, or question. For this trade ~~...~~, the confirmation of numbers and the execution of a mandated procedure. Of course Lau had to alert his boss about a deal of this magnitude, but Emily Cheng, senior managing director, international equities, said exactly what he'd expected: "If the money comes through cleanly on the wire, and the account checks out, I don't see why not."

"Don't you wonder with something this big who it is, or even why?" Lau asked Cheng, seemingly out of curiosity but mostly to cover his ass. Because he wanted to make sure that if the deal came back to bite him, he wouldn't be the only one to take the heat. "You're not curious why someone wants to short U.S. tech stock now that it's finally starting to come back? I mean, Apple alone, with or without Jobs . . ."

Cheng shrugged. As Lau's director, she'd make a nice under-the-radar commission on this as well. When the group performed well, she did well, so she wasn't about to ask questions. "Like I said, if the transfer is good and the account is legit, for a billion-one, I don't care if he's taking a short on the Moon."

For the first time in months Lau allowed himself to flash the smile of a man about to make a killing.

A quick credentials check confirmed that the transfer was good and the account was legit. Registered to the American trading account with JP Morgan Chase of one Rondell Jameson in the city of Philadelphia in the state of Pennsylvania. Who knew? Who knows? Lau thought. Maybe the guy actually exists. Then he did something that the caller had specifically said he was not to do. "If you tell anyone besides your manager, or if you inquire into or act on any of these securities in any way, there will be serious consequences." Despite the warning, Lau went off-line almost immediately and looked into the stocks on his smart phone, linked to a personal trading account. As if they'd ever be able to find out, he thought, as he proceeded to lay down a matching series of shorts. Of course, for much less money. His credit line with this account was thirty thousand dollars U.S., thirty thousand dollars he didn't have, but his gambler's instincts told him that this was special, and if even part of it came to pass, he'd be set for years to come. So he defied the one rule his client insisted upon, and he got in on the action himself.

After placing his personal trade, he did something he hadn't done in months, something he had told himself he wouldn't do again. He called his family back on the mainland. After a dozen rings someone picked up, grunted, and hung up. Most likely his father, he surmised, but it could have been any of them.

Now, safely home with the deals in place, staring out at the first of the grand party yachts heading into the glittering harbor, Lau tries to forget about his family and manages to smile again.

As soon as he finishes the first martini, he begins to wonder if he should fix a second, or if perhaps he should call some friends to have a bit of a celebration. Even if it is a bloody Monday. Even if, technically, he hasn't yet received a cent for his effort. He doesn't have to tell them about the magnitude of the transaction or the fact that he's about to have a hell of a good week, but after months and months of lying low and avoiding almost all contact with the outside world, why not?

He gets up and decides he'll do both. He'll have that second dirty Hendrick's martini *and* celebrate. Perhaps at Nobu, or better, Hutong.

Standing at his kitchen counter, Lau calls three friends in succession, but none of them answer. He leaves the same message for each: "Call me . . . I'm ready to have fun again." Yet he can't help thinking, Do they care? Have they moved on like everyone else in my life? Screw it—he uses one hand to scroll through his smart phone for a restaurant app to find the number for Hutong—I'll celebrate alone. With the other

What do you want.

"Who else did you tell?"

"What are you talking about?"

The hand lifts his head off the stone countertop and smashes it back, cracking Lau's left jawbone and knocking loose a canine and an incisor tooth. "You were specifically told not to tell anyone. Who else?"

Lau groans, mumbles, "I told no one."

The hand raises Lau's head, poised to smash it again. "Wait!" he says, spitting blood, the uprooted teeth still floating inside his mouth. "Okay. I made some trades. I took some positions, but I didn't tell anyone, it was programmed. And my money, compared to the others' . . ."

"And who else?"

"No one. My boss. I had to, but I told you that on the—"

"Not me."

"Okay. I told *the caller* that I had to."

Pressing Lau's face against the stone: "Who . . . else?"

"No one. I called my friends. Please. Believe me."

"How can I believe someone who has failed to keep the only promise we've asked of him?"

Lau begins to weep. "I made the trade because I was desperate. I was about to lose everything."

The hand loosens its grip on the back of his neck, but the pistol is still pressed against his forehead.

"I can cancel it," Lau says, somewhat brightening. "I'll make the call, contact them right now."

"That won't be necessary. Stand up, but don't turn around."

Lau lifts his face off the counter and straightens. "I promise, I won't tell another soul."

"This is correct," the voice says. "You won't." The bullet enters through the base of Lau's skull and exits through the floor-to-ceiling harbor-view window.

His body stiffens, then goes slack all at once, and he pitches face-first toward the soon to be bloodstained white marble countertop as a squall of glass shards begins to float like snow through the Hong Kong twilight toward the warm asphalt of Harbour Street, seventeen stories below.

On the counter next to him the light on his phone flashes with a message, a text with the heading *URGENT from NYC*.

5

Wand theories written in multicolored marker

doesn't have is the type of mind that can pull it all together.

His value at the fund and in life has always been his intuition and his tenacity. He has always made up for his limited natural gifts with passion and curiosity. At the fund they call him a digger. In high school football and baseball they called him a scrapper, someone who made up for his lack of natural ability with preparation and intensity. But on the field and at work that will only get you so far. Some people are naturals, and in sports and in the financial world, he's never seen a person as naturally gifted as Drew Havens.

At this point, Weiss feels he's done enough digging and uncovered enough data to validate the hypotheses that something terrible is already happening in Hong Kong and Dubai and that something much worse is going to happen at the end of this week, to the Rising Fund and the U.S. economy. Now all he can do is assemble it all as best he can and give it to the only person he knows who can take it to the next level: Havens.

While he's watching files transfer from his desktop to his flash drive, the Spyware warning flashes again. He's already reaching to pull out the flash drive when the entire desktop flashes black and then white and then off. After two attempts to reboot the computer, he gives up. Someone sent a digital bullet his way and killed everything on his hard drive and perhaps the flash as well. He's still holding the flash when he hears the buzzer and the familiar clunk of the downstairs lobby door opening. Curious, he strides over to his front door. For a moment he considers bolting and locking it, but instead he opens it and listens. Instead of the clicking of a key through the tumblers he hears the second lobby door gently shaking in its jamb. Someone is picking the lock. As the second door creaks open, he eases out into the hall and quietly closes his door.

He takes soft steps in his stockinged feet, heading upstairs toward the steel door that leads onto the roof, while the heavier footsteps start echoing upward from below. He pauses at the roof door and listens as the steps come closer. The footsteps cease, he's sure, outside his apartment door.

He hears his door open and close. Should've locked it. Should've done a lot of things, Weiss thinks, twisting the roof doorknob and slipping into the October night. He scans the roof, most recently the scene of a barbeque with friends from college, then walks toward the shelter of an air-conditioning unit and squats. After a moment he turns and looks over the edge at the alley seven floors down. A necklace of car lights winds up the FDR. A siren bleats heading uptown. Peeking back over the edge of the unit, eyes fixed on the closed steel door, he takes out his phone, calls up Havens's name, and begins to text. He's still texting as the door to the roof begins to swing open.

6

creation myth that has been spread [...]
cial press. He looks up as the bottle girl approaches. She sidles up along-side him and places her palm on his thigh. "So I was right," she whispers, giving his quad a squeeze. "You *are* famous."

Havens removes the woman's hand from his thigh and answers, "Not for long."

He's still looking into her medicated eyes when his phone buzzes. Danny Weiss again. This time rather than simply reading and ignoring Weiss's texts, he shuts the phone off. Havens and the bottle girl watch one of the Texans pass with a girl on each arm. She asks, "How come you don't have a girl?"

He watches a chaperone open a door for the Texan and the girls. The room beyond is empty and filled with red velvet couches, flat screens, and flowers. "Is that what you call that?" he tells the bottle girl. "No thanks."

"Your boss," she says, "last week he was in there for three hours with three of them. I had the privilege of replenishing the champagne and politely declining to be number four."

Havens groans. Tommy Rourke approaches. Despite Havens's renown as a quant, Rourke is still Salvado's most valued employee, a bona fide rainmaker with a gift for bringing high-value clients, such as the Texans, into the fund and converting them into Believers. Rourke is also the person most responsible for discovering Havens, based upon the recommendation of a friend of a friend, and bringing him to Salvado's attention.

"What's wrong with the King of Quants?"

Havens smiles. Despite the fact that Rourke is all about image and has little understanding of numbers, he likes him, and sometimes wishes he had some of Rourke's social skills. In the beginning, whenever someone made a comment about Havens's antisocial, obsessive behavior, Rourke was always the first to stick up for him. Plus, during Havens's darkest time, Rourke proved to be his most loyal and caring friend.

"You know me, Rourkey."

Rourke smiles. "Good with the numbers . . . not so much with people."

Havens lifts his chin toward the room into which the Texan just vanished. "And even less so with whores."

Rourke tilts his head. "Oh, come on. I throw up in my mouth a little every time Rick pulls this shit, but you know you're a rock star to these clients. They respect you."

"They respect an old story. An *as told by* legend that you and your boy Rick tell especially well. This new stuff, this so-called investment strategy that they're being sold right now, you and I know it isn't mine, isn't close to true, and makes no sense."

Now Rourke's smile slackens. "Jesus, Drew. This again?" For the last twelve months Salvado has been loading the Rising Fund with a disproportionate amount of pro-American investment positions. Although his fund made its name shorting sub-prime real estate, he's now gone on record as being long on a broad array of American securities, specifically tech, advertising, old and new media stocks, commodities, and real estate. Almost exclusively American. Even the U.S. dollar.

Of course, on the heels of a recession, with the country's leaders at one another's throat, it's been a popular position. And why not? Salvado was one of the few, thanks to Havens, to have gotten it right in 2008. And this time it doesn't hurt that he's betting big on American success rather than widespread collapse. It was an easy story for Rourke to use while prospecting, at least at first.

One would think that Havens would be comfortable with his boss's

position on the American economy. If anything, it would

financial model.

When Havens continued to question the increasingly one-dimensional position of the fund that had made him and so many others rich, he was gradually pushed aside during key internal meetings, relegated in recent months to less strategically important tasks. Ultimately he was moved up, replaced by other analysts who were more prone to see things Salvado's way, more willing to bend their data to accommodate and promote their boss's sketchy philosophy.

If he hadn't been so instrumental in the Rising Fund's sub-prime legend, and featured so prominently in a number of bestselling books and articles about "The Crisis," Havens is sure he'd have been shit-canned a long time ago and not pidgeonholed in the position of past-tense PR poster boy, rolled out like a museum piece for this sort of client-appeasing spectacle.

But now he doesn't care. It's one thing to be right about an impending economic disaster, but even worse to predict bliss that will never happen and that the numbers just don't substantiate.

"So what are you gonna do?" Rourke asks over the music.

Havens looks around once more. "Don't worry. I'm not out to blast him in public. You guys have been too good to me. But, between us, I've got to get out."

"Now?"

"I'm fried, Tommy. You know I'm all or nothing with this stuff, and I can't . . . I know you think I'm nuts, and, yeah, the money's great, but I can't work on something I don't believe in and, worse, know is wrong."

Rourke looks at Salvado, who's clinking champagne glasses with the second Texan. "You tell the big man yet?"

Havens shakes his head. "You guys basically took me off the street and made me a rich man, and when everything went down with my—"

Rourke interrupts. "With Miranda . . . I hear you. But that was between friends. Not work. You know, I have my questions, too, and I'm far from a numbers guy. Shit, I'm a goddamn Ivy League literature major. I'd be lying if I didn't tell you that I'm ready to move on, too. Get away from the ego that ate Wall Street and go someplace with Jenny and chill for a while. But because this is a tough time for him, for the fund in general, and he has been more than generous with us, we sort of owe—"

This time Havens interrupts. "When everyone involved is rich, it's tough to say you owe anyone anything. Listen, Tom: I've made a lot the last few years, more than I ever dreamed; but I've also lost more than I'd ever wish on anyone. I'm done."

Rourke puts his hand on his friend's shoulder. "You may be done with this, Drew, but I have a feeling you're just beginning."

Havens walks away from the table and heads down the short flight of stairs to the lounge. He orders a seltzer with lime and stares at the bank of TV screens suspended over the top shelf. Baseball play-offs. Monday night football. Aussie rules football. Two men beside him are discussing a spread. One man claims to have laid ten thousand on the Cowboys, giving the 49ers four points, and the Cowboys are up three in the fourth quarter. Havens is interested for a moment—he starts to sketch a model in his head about the probability of this douche bag winning, of the Cowboys coming back and beating the spread with 6:48 and two time-outs remaining—then he's not. This is a problem. This is *his* problem, using the scalpel of mathematics to dissect the improbabilities of life. Over the course of his life it has intrigued, fascinated, and consumed him, ultimately to the brink of destruction. If not

with numbers, he would not have become rich as a direct

he

erone in charge of the Texans' VIP room.

7

New York City

Weiss ducks behind the cover of the AC unit and listens. The roof door slamming open. Steel smashing against concrete. Gravel crunching underfoot. Fast steps heading toward the west side of the roof, then doubling back. He can hear the guy's strained breaths. Now another siren, this one heading south. A car door closes on the street below.

He slips his phone into his pocket, holds his breath, and considers his options. Wait to be found, run for the stairwell, or jump. Only the stairwell holds the promise of survival. The footsteps resume, moving away again. He peeks over the unit and sees the man, large and muscular, black hair shining in the night, looking at what, his phone? Another option is reason, Weiss thinks. Explain yourself and promise no harm, to cease and desist. But this man doesn't seem to be the reasonable type.

He waits for the man to reach the farthest corner of the roof. As the man glances over the edge Weiss makes his move. On hands and knees at first, through the shadows, then into the light near the open door to the stairwell. At the threshold fear overcomes patience and he begins to rush. His knee drags through the gravel and sprays a few loose pebbles against the steel door. He turns as the man whirls and locks eyes on him.

Weiss bolts upright and lunges toward the first set of stairs. He leaps three at a time, sliding his left hand along the railing for balance. At the first landing his shoeless feet slide out from under him and he stumbles onto the linoleum. He reaches out to balance himself with his right hand and drops the flash drive. The man is already at the head of the stairs and racing toward him. Weiss grabs the flash drive and shoves it in his pocket as he rights himself. His goal is the street three flights below. At least in the street there will be witnesses. At the next landing,

8

New York City

Havens takes a frustrated breath when he sees Salvado at the head of the stairs. He came to the lounge to get away from Salvado because he knows if pressed he won't be able to hold his tongue, and Rourke is right, this isn't the time or place to quit. When he quits, he wants to do it when they're alone. He owes that much to the man who made him rich.

"What's the matter, Drew? They're looking for you up there."

"Just taking a breather. Needed some space."

"Maybe what you need is some tail."

Havens stares at his boss. At one time all he saw when he looked at Salvado was the man who took him off the street and made him rich. Now all he sees is the man who made him . . . what? Alone? Divorced? Drowning in guilt?

"Don't tell me you're back with the guilt?"

"You see it, I don't have the stomach for it anymore."

Salvado winces and glances up at his clients, where Rourke has taken over as entertainment director. He stares back at Havens. "Of course, you don't have a better alternative."

"Better, like the sub-prime? That's a once-a-century thing. So no, nothing like that. Which is part of the problem, too."

"Kind of like pitching a perfect game seven of the World Series, as a rookie."

"Pitch the perfect game, then win it with a homer in the bottom of the ninth."

"Look, you're tired. You work as hard as anyone I've ever seen. Why don't you take a break and think about it?"

"I've been thinking about . . ."

"Why don't you take a week—shit, take two—and get your head

"I need a break, and I appreciate the offer, and I publicly, until you give me the green light. You've been extremely kind and generous with me." He tries to stop here but can't help himself. "But you know me, Rick, I can't sit on my hands all day, or do this."

Salvado rolls his eyes. "*This.* You're gonna let a difference of opinion ruin how many years of . . ."

"Opinion has little to do with it," Havens says. "For me, the difference in the numbers, the data, the economic truth, means everything. That's how I function. It's easier for me to reconcile myself to this," he waves a hand back toward the clients, the champagne bottle–covered table, and the women, "than to numbers that don't make any sense."

"I'm asking you to have faith, to trust me."

"I wish I could, but my brain, it won't let me."

"This is a mistake."

Havens shakes his head. "I wish there was something to show me otherwise. You know, I've been looking around."

"Looking around?"

"To see if anyone else is seeing things the other way, my way. For my own sanity."

"And . . ."

"And while I couldn't come up with any individual fund or trend of people taking significant short puts against *all* of your longs, I found some other stuff."

Salvado scans the room, then turns his back on the table, steering the conversation to a more private place. "For instance."

"Well, apparently, at least a couple of heavy investors seem to be locking in with huge bets, one position, one security at a time, *against* you. I mean us."

Salvado nods. Havens takes this as an invitation to continue.

"For instance, I saw some activity on a bunch of our tech plays, you know Apple . . ."

"I know what the hell our tech plays are."

"Right. Anyway. Just a couple hours ago, activity coming out of Hong Kong was laying *huge* money, play for play, *against* our exact—"

Salvado shrugs. "Not everyone loves tech. Especially American tech. Especially Apple. And clearly not everyone likes me these days. Plus, how do you know it's one person, and from Hong Kong?"

"I don't, but it's all coming out of the same firm," Havens says.

"Really? And you found this out when?"

"Today. Saw some movement and then confirmed it through a fixed income guy I know from my Citi days, covers China over at HSBC."

Salvado sizes up Havens. "So you picked this movement up on our system?"

"No. I didn't want to compromise our network with something I haven't vetted. It's something Danny Weiss got his hands on."

Salvado tilts his head. Of course he has no knowledge of Weiss or any lowly quant, Havens realizes.

"Weiss, my desk quant protégé. Good kid and hard worker."

Perhaps Salvado would have known the young man's name back in

2007 when he walked the floor more often, before he became a legend, but not now. Not a chance. Finally, he mouths the name, as if committing it to memory: *Weiss*.

"What else?"

"Well, the others aren't confirmed. But there's some recent stuff in advertising and new media that Weiss is investigating. Plus other stuff he's all twisted up over that I haven't checked into yet."

"Who else knows about this?"

"Just me and Weiss." Already he wishes he'd left Weiss out of this.

tioned you publicly. In or out of the office. It's not about y me trying to find a way forward in this job. Ask Rourke."

"You know how I feel about loyalty to the fund, Drew." While Salvado states his call to loyalty, the Russian model appears and presses her hip against him. Sonya. Mischa. Something. She's putting on her best I-want-to-play face.

Havens remembers one of Salvado's loyalty speeches in particular, delivered while he paced around the conference table after the morning call, menacingly holding a Louisville Slugger, like Robert De Niro playing Capone in *The Untouchables*. "You taught me all about loyalty from day one, Rick. Fidelity and loyalty to the fund. It's people. And their families."

Salvado shrugs off the model, who then turns away, not in the least forlorn, and clippety-clops back to the table. "I called this the Rising Fund for a reason. It is an epic journey, an epic American tale about the ability to overcome adversity that is still being written, and when it's all over, it will be remembered as one of the great ones."

Havens, who has heard this all too many times, shrugs.

"I'd be disappointed to learn that you no longer want to be part of it, Drew."

"Maybe I'm not cut out to be an epic journey kind of guy. I like to know why things happen; how things end."

Salvado begins to answer, but Rourke and one of the Texas clients interrupt them. Rourke's holding a tray half-filled with tequila shots. The others were handed out at the upper table. "Herradura Seleccion Suprema," shouts the client, who couldn't have botched each word more if he'd tried. "Best in the danged world."

Havens can only imagine the jacked up club price for a bottle of the best in the danged world. Salvado takes the shot glass in his hand and considers the amber liquid. Rourke offers Havens a shot. He starts to wave him off, but Rourke steps closer. His eyes implore Havens to play along one last time. He takes the shot, but doesn't drink it as the others knock theirs back.

"Listen," Salvado says after the client wobbles away. "Just do me a favor and sleep on it. Let me think this through. Then let's talk in the morning. I want to know more about this software you're experimenting with, and I promise to give you a more succinct rationale for my position. After that, if we still agree to disagree, we'll figure something out. But I want you to know, after all we've been through, I've got your back. No matter what, I'll take care of you."

9

the same place she spe..
kicking the hell out of something or someone. ...
structors, air.

Today she's taking more than giving, squared off in a ring with a
professional Muay Thai kickboxer at Pyramid Gym on Connaught
Road. The pro needed a sparring partner, an instructor pointed to "the
pretty American," and here she is, trying but not entirely succeeding
at blocking a series of kicks and jabs. She takes a straight left to the jaw
and has her feet stripped out from under her by a sweep kick, but she
pops right back up and comes back at the pro for more. She blocks a
right and sidesteps a straight left foot, but she doesn't see the straight
right. It crashes against her headgear and rattles her brain. The pro
follows with two quick lefts, and Sobieski tips back against the rope. In
the second it takes the pro to glance at her trainer, as if to ask if she
should continue the onslaught, Sobieski bounces forward off the rope
as if it is electrified and slams a right uppercut just below the pro's ribs.
She hears the breath gush out of her opponent as she rips off two more
uppercuts with her left fist. Sobieski rears back with her left foot and

starts to bring it forward, but the pro sidesteps it and lunges forward, wrapping her in a clinch. Sobieski fights the clinch like a trapped animal, frantically trying to punch and thrust and wriggle out of it. For a moment she loses track of where she is and whom she's fighting, and she's filled with so much rage that the room dims and spins and blurs.

The pro's trainer grabs her from behind and pulls her back, "Whoa . . . whoa!" he shouts. "Time! Time!" All at once she stops. The pro says something nasty to her through her mouth guard and gestures toward the bell.

"Didn't you hear the bell?" the trainer asks, leading Sobieski to her corner. Sobieski shakes her head. "After I got hit, I lost it. Tell her I'm sorry."

The trainer nods. She looks for a stool to sit on before the next round. The trainer shakes his head. "She's done."

Sobieski shrugs, climbs out of the ring, and walks back to the heaving bag she was hitting when they approached her. "You should do this for real," the trainer tells her as she executes a flurry of punch-and-knee strike combinations. Sobieski is twenty-nine, lean, and compulsively fit. "She's nothing special," he says, meaning the pro. "But I'm telling you, the way you responded to the pain . . . you can compete."

Sobieski shakes her head and speaks without breaking the rhythm of her strikes. "I like my teeth. And this bump on my nose? Some find it funny looking, but I'm kind of fond of it, too."

"Well, if you change your mind, I'm always here." A few moments later Sobieski sees her phone flash and buzz on top of her gym bag. Usually she keeps it strapped to her arm during workouts, but she took it off before getting into the ring. Even in a gym, in the middle of a late day class in Hong Kong, she's always connected, always on. They said it would be like this when she left Treasury for the newly formed Terrorism and Financial Intelligence (TFI) task force, and they were right. She gives a final, crisp kick at an imaginary target, then steps away from the rest of the class to take the call in the hallway outside the studio.

"Sobieski."

"Sorry to interrupt your kung fu marathon, Sobes, but you know how it goes." It's her boss, Michaud, head of the Pan Asian Bureau of TFI.

Sobieski can barely hear him. The male voice in the background butchering Katy Perry's "California Gurls" is a clear giveaway that he's in a karaoke bar. "Doesn't sound like you're in an office, Chief."

"One man's office is another man's prison," Michaud replies. "What can I say, I was overcome by the urge to sing Sinatra, but now I'm not

decides the guy's a perv, to be avoided, and that she's _____ when it comes to martial arts. "And I should be interested in this because . . . ?"

"Securities trader. Twenty-nine. Single. Worked the U.S. desk at Hang Seng Bank."

"Okay . . ."

"It's a favor for a local detective. Detective Mo. Said that it looked like a professional hit, and that, combined with the nature of his job . . . Jesus, can you just check it out for me?"

Twenty-four minutes later Sobieski is standing inside Patrick Lau's condo. Hong Kong Police Department homicide detectives are scouring the rooms for clues. Lau is still facedown on the counter, blood darkening in an oval on the white marble top. Wind blasts through the opening where the floor-to-ceiling window was, lifting the drapes on a constant horizontal plane.

Staring at the kitchen counter, Sobieski tries but can't figure out how or why the rest of Lau's stiffening body is still standing. She's tempted to ask, but because this is not her purview or jurisdiction, she decides to keep her mouth shut and let HKPD Senior Tech Detective Hueng Mo initiate the talking.

It doesn't take Mo long. "Wow. Michaud said you were easy on the eyes, but—"

She cuts him off. "That's funny. Somehow he neglected to tell me you were an insecure, old-school perv."

Mo steps back. He's a short, gap-toothed man of fifty-five, with thick black-and-white hair and a face of crooked lines and crevasses. "I apologize. He also said you were the most talented, dedicated, and honest agent he had."

She stares at him with 5 percent less edge. Okay.

"So," he says, "what do you think?"

Sobieski shrugs. "Something tells me he didn't accidentally bang his head mixing a proper martini."

Mo nods. "They found the slug on the sidewalk. Long way down. Nine-millimeter. On its way to ballistics, though no one's holding their breath for a match."

"Girlfriend?"

"Gay. Neighbor said his last partner broke up with him more than a year ago and he's lived like a hermit. So the salacious sex angle, sadly, isn't likely. Nor is robbery. For example," Mo gestures with his chin toward the corpse, "they left that fake Rolex on his wrist. Plus an entire box of what in my humble opinion is extremely tacky jewelry on the nightstand." With a ballpoint pen he holds up a golden ring. "Do people still wear pinky rings in the states?"

"That's a nipple ring," Sobieski corrects him. "With all due respect." Mo drops the ring as if it's radioactive. Sobieski looks at the front door. "What about the locks? Any sign of forced entry?"

Mo shakes his head. "Door was unlocked when security came up.

Nothing out of the ordinary from the doorman, and we're already looking at the film from the lobby camera. So, no. But, again, who knows?
You don't use a crowbar to break locks today. You use data, micro-
tools. A polite knock."

"Family?"

Mo jerks his head toward a middle-aged woman being interviewed
near the front door. "Neighbor says maybe on the mainland, somewhere in Shanxi. But she says he never visited or spoke of them. I'm
guessing he was ostracized back home because of his sexuality."

Sobieski walks closer to the body. She notes the empty martini glass.

billionaire."

Mo waves her off. "I was kidding. Even I know Buffett. The Oracle
of Omaha. Anyway, Lau may have had money at one point, but not
lately. Building manager says he barely made his rent the past three
months."

"You speak to his boss?"

Mo nods. "Next stop on my journey. Waiting for legal reps from their
bank to okay it. Expecting a stonewall from them, but you're welcome
to come."

Sobieski watches two cops tracking large strips of yellow tape across
the open window space. One of the drapes blows into the face of the
second cop and he freaks, drops to the floor several feet from the window frame. "This is fascinating and all," she says to Mo. "And it's a hell
of a lot more interesting than spending eight hours breaking down
funky natural gas numbers out of Chechnya, but really, I still don't get
why I'm here."

"Okay, this is why I called Michaud: A nobody trader is executed by a pro. I thought perhaps something might have shown up in the wires. The tracking programs. You know, the chatter."

"And how do you know Michaud?" Sobieski asks, thinking, Please don't say karaoke.

"Friend of a friend. Once I gave him something he needed."

Sobieski looks down and shifts her feet. This is a tricky subject. Chatter. Wire movement. Electronic surveillance. TFI agents are not allowed to discuss the existence or findings of their tracking software. Especially with foreigners, even with cops to whom your boss owes a favor. Most insiders know that someone in an agency such as TFI or the U.S. Department of Treasury has access to amazingly intuitive software that can track trades and communiqués and predict market shifts in real time—presumably the best of its kind. But the topic has been off-limits for agents to discuss ever since the post-9/11 debacle with the Promis software. Back then it was revealed that, rather than the software being used exclusively to fight terrorism, bootleg copies of Promis were turning up on the black market and being used *against* American interests, to facilitate terrorism.

"I know what you're thinking," Mo says. "I've already spoken to agents at the Hong Kong Monetary Authority. I imagine their stuff's not bad either, but they only find what *they're* looking for and don't play especially well with others. And unless the integrity of the exchange is threatened, I doubt they give a shit about the likes of me or Patrick Lau."

"What bank was he at again?"

"Hang Seng. So far, to the extent that we can, we're seeing nothing out of the ordinary, no big moves. But who knows."

"Any PCs in the house?" Sobieski asks.

Mo points at a small device on the counter. "Just his CrackBerry. We'll scan it as soon as they're done."

Sobieski bends and looks closely at the phone's LED screen. Not a BlackBerry but the latest Motorola Droid. She sees the home page for

Hutong. Hutong is one of the finest restaurants in all of Hong Kong. She knows this because the date who took her there two months ago made a point of telling her. Several times. And he was right. The food was amazing. But the date, like all of her dates these days, was a disaster.

Mo bends down next to her, points at the device. "Think he traded on that?"

She shrugs. Who knows? The data, if anything comes up, won't lie. That's easy. But the part that doesn't really involve her, the nuts and bolts of the homicide, is what has her thinking. "Forgive me if this sounds naïve, but is it normal for someone to go through this seem-

Small batch bourbon. Single malt scotch.

you the truth, if it's good I don't care if they serve it in a sippy cup."

"Have you ever been to Hutong?"

Mo whistles. "Hutong on Peking Road? That's some good eating. I went once, two years ago in July."

"What for?"

"Well, you eat at Hutong either if you're rich or for some kind of special occasion. I took my wife for our thirtieth wedding anniversary."

She thinks of her date, who was neither rich nor special. "Did your wife like it?"

He thinks. "She liked the fact that we went more than the experience itself. She's not a fan of all that precious stuff."

Sobieski smiles. "So how do you know Michaud again?"

Mo smiles and rolls a finger near his temple. "Your boss is a unique individual."

"But . . ." A plainclothes in the hall near the bedroom door whistles for Mo. He holds up a finger to Sobieski and says, "I'll be right back."

After Mo leaves, she takes one last look at Patrick Lau, her first up-close homicide victim, before they straighten him out, put him in a bag, and strap him onto a gurney. Staring at the screen of Lau's phone, she wonders who would want to kill a twenty-nine-year-old trader on the same day that he seemed intent on celebrating something?

Two Hong Kong EMTs stand on either side of Lau's corpse, deciding how they're going to handle this. Sobieski turns away as they begin the pre-hoist three-two-one countdown in Chinese. *San. Er. Yi!* Staring out the window at the city, lights refracting an eerie spectrum off a blanket of night smog, she decides that as a favor to Michaud and Mo, who seems like a decent enough cop, and also out of an admitted fascination with the crime, she'll give this some more thought. She'll accompany Mo to Patrick Lau's bank and see where that goes.

At the very least it will keep the demons at bay.

10

To Havens the streets are a grid, a pattern, bilities waiting to be modeled. Go across the Park and down Fifth or take the subway? Is there a concert at the Garden? A visiting head of state? An accident? How far away is it? How fast can you get there?

He looks from the streets to the sky, a bigger grid, a never-ending pattern of stars and planets and galaxies, clusters of objects that defy logic but not numbers, and when he considers a fixed point in the heavens he can't help but think similar things. How far away is it? How fast can you get there?

There's a moment when he considers going back inside to Salvado and Rourke and the clients. Always the clients. But he can't do it. He passes the line of taxis and begins to walk. Because as much as he wants to get away from the club, he's in no rush to get back to his empty apartment.

After two blocks he reaches for his phone. He's forgotten that he turned it off. There are missed calls and messages from Weiss, but he ignores them as soon as he sees that he's also missed a call from Miranda. He stares at her number. Her numbers.

Once, near the end, Miranda told him that maybe they would have been able to stay together if she'd learned to communicate in numbers, rather than words. "Maybe if I'd had a Dow Jones ticker crawling cross my chest," she told him. "The latest quarterly earnings from Cisco on my forehead. The ten-year Treasury note yield reflected in my eyes. Then maybe you would have paid attention." He said it wouldn't have mattered. They would have been her numbers. And he only trusted his own.

As much as he wants to, he can't bring himself to call Miranda. Instead, as he continues walking south, he caves and decides to call Weiss. Perhaps it's because of the stress of the night, or of the last three hundred nights, or because he's lonely, or bored, or because Miranda called again. But Havens needs to talk to *someone*, and as loath as he is to admit it, sometimes he likes talking to Weiss, or at least hearing Weiss talk, because they're so different from each other.

He listens as Weiss's phone rings fourteen times. Strange. Usually, if Weiss doesn't pick up after four rings, it kicks over to his voice mail. He hangs up and tries again, but still no answer or opportunity to leave a message.

With the phone still in hand he decides that he can't go back to his apartment. When he left this morning, he felt that, as pathetic as it was, the apartment was distinctly his, the home of a wealthy but troubled loner, a divorcee with a thing for numbers.

But now it no longer feels that way; it feels like the living space of a stranger, and even the phrase "living space" is pushing it. When he's in his apartment, he feels more isolated than ever. But now, unlike most of the other times he's felt cut off from the rest of the world, he doesn't want to be. He doesn't want to be alone, or to lose himself in numbers. He wants to find himself in something else, anywhere else.

He stops and stares at the phone. At Miranda's numbers. And pushes call. What the hell.

"Thanks for returning my sixteen messages." Miranda, half-asleep.

Havens grunts. "Twenty, actually. But who's counting?"

"You're an ass."

"I am. But maybe my not calling you back the previous nineteen times was my way of showing I care, of sparing you."

"What do you want, Drew?"

He looks west toward the apartments of Hell's Kitchen and then up to find a quarter moon hanging like an apostrophe over the Hudson. "Drew?"

that I was gonna quit today. . . ."

lly. But

He pauses to frame his response. "The thing is, been finding some . . . inconsistencies."

"I never trusted that bastard."

"More illogical than illegal."

"Give it time."

"At first it was just conflicting investment philosophies, but now, I don't know. Weiss, this kid I work with . . ."

"I know Danny."

"I asked him to look into it and now he suspects all sorts of crazy things."

"You never know. What was the megalomaniac's response?"

"Rick? First he said he'd get a team together to investigate, to get to the bottom of some of my findings. Then, as weeks passed, he told me to forget about it, that it wasn't something I should be concerned with. But I can't let things like that go. You know how I am with that stuff, Mir."

She waits a few seconds before answering. "Yes. I do know. But is this why you're calling your ex-wife this late on a Monday?"

"You know it was never about the money. It was, you know, about figuring it out."

"Bullshit. Money was always part of it, and in the end, what did you ever figure out?"

"The data. The logic."

"Not every answer can be found in the data. You have a beautiful mind, and you've been wasting it serving the whims of a . . ."

"It was—"

"It was," she interrupts, "what it was."

He hears the click of another caller. He checks the number. Weiss.

"Let me guess," she says. "It's work."

"It's Weiss. He can wait."

"Go ahead. Talk to him."

"Mir, if someone would have told me how it was gonna end, I never would have put you through . . . I never would have put you through *me*."

Even over the roar of the street he can hear her take a breath and slowly exhale. A year ago, just after their divorce and more than two years after their daughter died, Miranda met him at Magnolia's for a cup of coffee and a piece of cake. It was his idea. He wanted to show her that he'd changed. That the job wasn't everything. Five minutes into the meeting his phone rang. She had arranged for his assistant to call him, to test to see if he had indeed changed. He ignored the first two rings. By the third ring he was checking the LED screen to identify the caller. When he saw that it was coming from the office, he reflexively raised a finger, pausing their talk, and answered it. Miranda was on her way out the shop door before their order was ready.

"If I'd have known . . . ," he says now.

"Really, Drew? Well, since you *have* known, how different has it been? How different have *you* been? Best I can tell, you still work day and night. You still live for the numbers. You still don't socialize, unless it's with Salvado and his money monsters."

"It's because no one . . ."

"It's because you *choose* not to. Have you been on a date since . . ."

"Since you left?"

"Yes."

"Of course not." Then, "Have you?"

She pauses, then sighs. "Drew, you've got to move on, and *engage* with the rest of the universe."

He looks for the moon. The possessive apostrophe. The official punctuation of this night. Who will own it? Who will be owned by it? Somehow it's disappeared during their conversation and is hanging over

, "

don't you g

"Because—"

"Get it," she interrupts. Then, before hanging up, she says, "The rest of your life is calling."

After she's gone, he stares at the city, but nothing registers. Not the surrounding buildings, the soft glow over the high-rises, or the darker universe above. This is how it has always been, since he was a child. One or two things mattered and everything else was an afterthought.

First it was birds. Every type in North America, then Asia, then Europe, and so on until, at age four, he had exhausted birds. Then it was Native American Indians. Every nation, every tribe, every ritual, cultural contribution, triumph, and atrocity they experienced. Then aircraft, from the Wright Brothers through the Space Shuttle. He needed to know more. He needed to know everything. He used to cry at night not because others mocked his obsessions (and they did), but because he knew he was different. The intense solitary focus, the need to know more and then everything, often at the expense of those who loved him most.

He was eleven when he discovered numbers. Mathematics. Statistics. Data. The markets. The global economy. When computers were added to the equation of his life, the change was exponential. Software enabled him to experience numbers as if they were music. He was the creator and conductor and fanatical audience of his own number music, which played out in an endless symphony. It was still a solitary obsession, but this time, because it was numbers and involved computers and, potentially, the making of money, people were more tolerant. No one thought that he was odd, or had an affliction, or suffered any kind of syndrome.

They thought he was gifted.

He redials Weiss's number, but again, no one answers. After twenty rings he clicks off and looks at his inbox. The only unopened file there is a text. Sent from Weiss, just before he shut off his phone at the club:

Help 3.338-9

11

that she can't help it. She realizes that the death of Patrick Lau transcends the demands of her job. It's a much-needed diversion, and perhaps because of his age and the dark reality of her own existence, Lau's death has taken on something of a morbid fascination.

After all, she's already done more than her part by stopping by the crime scene on Michaud's behalf. She asked all the right questions and looked at all the pertinent evidence. She's here, she decides, because right now everywhere else is worse.

As soon as Sobieski sees the lawyers, whom she expected, albeit not four of them, as well as Lau's boss Emily Cheng, she knows that Mo was correct, that the interview will reveal nothing of substance. She might not be a homicide detective, but she knows her way around the paranoid halls of a multinational bank well enough to see that no financial institution is about to open up its records simply to find the killer of one of its entirely dispensable employees. If it were money and not a life that was lost, it would be different. But for this, they won't even let them go up to Lau's floor to take a look at his workstation. Instead they're sequestered in an executive conference room and given tea in fine china cups, and repeatedly told that they will receive "the bank's full cooperation" while, repeatedly, their requests are denied.

"Was Lau happy?" Mo asks.

"Patrick was a very happy young man," answers Cheng.

"Had you noticed anything different in his performance . . . any incident with a coworker or trouble with a client?"

"Not at all."

Then, Sobieski asks, "Was he having a good year?"

"Excuse me?"

"I know the markets have been inching up, and I was wondering if, you know, performance-wise, he was having a good year."

Cheng glances at corporate legal suit number two before answering, "I'm afraid that's confidential bank information."

Mo asks, "Have you ever been to Patrick Lau's apartment?"

Cheng shakes her head. "I heard it was nice. Overlooking the harbor, correct? But Patrick and I did not socialize."

Sobieski glances at Mo, but he has nothing else to ask. Regardless, she presses on. "What about today? Was there any conversation or transaction or client interaction that involved Patrick Lau, your direct report, that seemed at all unusual?"

Cheng's eyes narrow as she considers Sobieski the inquisitor. Before Cheng can answer, legal suit number three speaks up. "Excuse me, but is this a U.S. government issue, Miss . . . Sobieski? Because as much as we'd like to . . . I don't see why or how . . ."

Sobieski waves off the attorney and stands. No problem. Not my business. Just wanted to let you know that I know you're stonewalling. "Just one last question, Miss Cheng: Do you know of anything that happened today that would have compelled Patrick Lau to want to celebrate tonight, a Monday?"

Rather than look at one of her four attorneys or at Sobieski, Cheng looks down at the conference table as she answers. "No. As I've said,

Patrick Lau is one of approximately fifty traders whom I oversee, and I make it a point to have little to no knowledge of any of their personal affairs."

As soon as they're back on the street, she mentions Cheng's downward glance. "She knows something."

"About the murder? Maybe, but if anything, it tells me they made some serious money there today. How they made it, how much, and

that's anyone's guess."

organization, but if anyone—"

She cuts him off before something is said that could get either of them in trouble, not that Mo seems to care. She decides, when she gets back to her place, she'll do some digging. Another excuse for her to stay home tonight. She tells him, "I understand . . . I'll talk to Michaud, and if he's good with it, I'll see what I can come up with."

12

New York City

He runs across Seventh and flags down a taxi.

"Upper East," he tells the cabbie. "Ninety-third and York." Then, after a pause, even though he only visited once, months ago, he sees the number of the building's address in his mind's eye. Cruising east across town on 23rd he redials Weiss. Nothing.

On First, as the cab approaches the NYU Medical Center, Havens turns from the window and looks down. This is where he rushed that night after he got the call about his daughter. Miranda was out for a rare night on the town with her teacher friends. Dinner and drinks. She needed it. She deserved it. He was out on one of many nights on the town with Salvado and clients, all of them already rich but working on more. He had arranged to have the night off, but Salvado said he needed him. Said it was huge. Everything was huge, every week, every day. Every deal. The biggest yet. The most important ever. Of course he went. Though he could take or leave the socializing, in many ways the 24/7 demands of the job fed into his obsession.

"All-consuming," Miranda called his job. Looking back, he realized the phrase could be applied to the rising importance of materialism in their life and the society in which they lived. All-consumer. All-consuming.

He was supposed to get home by eleven that night to relieve the babysitter, but things were running late—they were moving on to 1Oak for drinks—and this was an important meeting, an important client. The biggest ever that week. The babysitter, a nice enough young woman from Australia, said no problem. She'd cover.

Besides, Erin was sound asleep.

Miranda got the first call. She was walking, on her way home from ████████ two blocks away from the apartment. He was in a night-

███

Soon after that, he and Miranda were gone, too.

He doesn't look back up until the taxi rises out of the tunnel past the United Nations tower. Even after midnight there's still a group of people gathered on the sidewalk protesting something somewhere. Traffic slows to look. The cabbie curses at the delay, but Havens looks, too. He sees beauty in their anger, their outrage at human atrocity and greed, and their right to protest it. It is, he decides, the essence of his relationship with the city. It's the essence of his relationship with everything: amazed and conflicted, briefly engaged, transfixed, then detached.

Weiss's building is worse than he remembered. Certainly not the building of a hedge fund guy. The lock on glass door number one has been punched out. In the take-out menu–cluttered lobby he sees Weiss's name Scotch taped on the bank of battered mailboxes. He almost presses the buzzer but sees that it won't be necessary. Someone has left the bolt open against the jamb for door number two, so he simply opens it and heads upstairs.

Near the top of the third flight of stairs he begins to walk softly. He pauses at the half-open door to Weiss's apartment. The common hallway smells of garlic, garbage, and neglect. Human and otherwise. He clenches his fist and raises his hand to knock, but at the last moment he decides not to, though he still keeps his fist clenched.

The door glides open without a creak. Two steps into the hallway, just past a framed print for the Sex Pistols' *Pretty Vacant*, he looks to the right, into Weiss's bedroom. It's empty but disheveled. Dresser drawers open, clothing strewn on the hardwood floor. Books everywhere. On the nightstand, in stacks on the floor, piled high in the open closet. Everything from quantitative theory to video game architecture, Vonnegut to Roth to an analysis of classical Greek literature. On a white Formica desk his PC monitor flashes blue and green and orange and empty.

Havens softly calls his name. "Danny?" Even though he never calls him Danny. Always Weiss. Or Slave. Or Mulder, the guy from *The X-Files*, because for Weiss everything is a conspiracy.

The day he hired him just over a year ago, Havens asked Weiss why in the world a guy with a degree in philosophy and economics, a published poet, social activist, and allegedly recovering hacker, wanted to work for a hedge fund. This was after the fund had made its way to the top of the ratings. Every prior candidate had said something about the opportunity to work with a legend, or The Rising's impressive track record, or a number of other cloaked variations of the real reason: They wanted to get rich beyond belief. They wanted in on the exclusive money party that Rick Salvado, with an assist from Drew Havens, threw the day the rest of the global economy died.

But not Weiss. Weiss said he wanted to work for one of the world's most profitable and best-performing hedge funds because he wanted to understand it. "I want to know if it's love or money that really makes the world go round," he said. "And why."

"Weiss? You here, buddy?"

Not much of a kitchen. Cereal boxes on the narrow countertop between the sink and the stove. Cocoa Puffs. Lucky Charms. An unfinished bowl with magically delicious rainbow remnants floating in the milk. Of course he gave Weiss the job on the spot. Havens knew that Weiss would never be as good as he is with numbers, but Weiss would bring something to their work that his was lacking: emotion and empathy and, more than anything, passion. Plus, Danny Weiss was a workplace rarity for Havens: He was genuinely likeable.

. . . . is empty. No TV. Speakers with an

Maybe he got . . . .
text from someplace else.

But on the pale white wall above the futon, in between what appears to be an unframed Jules Bettencourt original and a framed photo of Bill Buckner missing Mookie Wilson's grounder in game six of the 1986 World Series, he sees a splatter pattern of still dripping blood.

"Danny," Havens says, approaching the futon. "Danny Weiss." A whisper now, and a regret. "Danny." Not for Weiss, but his own ears.

13

Hong Kong

I t's not lost on Sobieski that tonight the most important man in her life is dead, stretched out on a cold rack in an HKPD morgue.

Patrick freaking Lau. Her first and in all likelihood—she's a government financial agent, a numbers cruncher after all—her last homicide. Semi-drunk and planning a special dinner one second and facedown and dead on his countertop the next. And not just any countertop. This was gorgeous white Carerra marble in an apartment and a kitchen that put any she's lived in to shame. Not that she covets Lau's place. The truth is the only thing she ever does here in her own modest apartment is work and sleep. Or at least try to. Plus, the last time she attempted to cook a decent meal was more than a year ago. And she botched that even more than she botched the date.

Sobieski knows that she'll probably never live in a place like Patrick Lau's. Not as long as she works this job and lives this life anyway. Since she started at TFI, she's lived in five cities and tried and failed at myriad romances. In that time she's had one serious relationship. With a Brit in Budapest, a filmmaker of all things. She cared enough about him to consider declining her next assignment, a transfer to Zurich. But before she had a chance to explain, the filmmaker, Blake, flat-out refused to consider moving with her, despite the fact that he was in between projects, despite the fact that he'd once said Switzerland was one of his favorite countries. If he hadn't been so adamant about staying, or if he'd at least been in the middle of something profound and great, she might have told him she'd consider turning down her assignment to be with him. But it was clear that making a sacrifice on her behalf never entered his mind. So she dumped him. She'd thought she was in love, but her definition of love was evolving. When you were truly in love, she reasoned, you'd do anything or go anywhere to be together.

. . . faults. Because being together, theoretically, made

My . . .

there."

Rather than directly replying, Michaud gets right to business. "Anything to that thing?"

"If there is, it's buried in the data. Which the army of lawyers at Hang Seng is not in the least willing to share."

"So that's that, then."

Sobieski pauses. Either an animal has been wounded in close proximity to Michaud or someone who should be forbidden from coming within ten feet of a microphone is singing: *"I'm a cowboyyy, on a steel horse I ride . . ."*

"Obviously," Michaud says, "you're thinking there's something else."

"Well, sort of." She tells him about the martini on the counter, the restaurant page on Patrick Lau's phone, Lau's recent social and financial history, and about the way that Emily Cheng looked downward after her final question. "The guy absolutely made some money today."

"Well, those things happen in the financial industry. And even if you're right, and he made it illegally," Michaud responds, "it sounds like it's Hong Kong's problem. Mo's problem; not TFI's."

"Agreed. But Mo did ask us to take a closer look. And you wouldn't have sent me if you didn't think . . ."

"Okay, then. Run it. But you've got to promise: This is a murder investigation, big money. Who knows what level of scum. Russian mob scum. In-house bank scum. And it's not a distinctly American thing. If this becomes something more than a numbers case . . . data . . . electronic paper trail . . . anything more than that . . . if it gets danger-ous in any way, you pull back."

"Right."

"No reason to risk your life over some scumbag's money."

"Right," Sobieski answers.

"Want me to make the call?"

"No, I got it."

"Of course you do, Sobi. Always doing the right thing. Meantime, feel like coming downtown to do a little duet, maybe a little Captain and Tennille with me?"

"Who?"

"Ashford and Simpson?"

"I don't follow."

"Ike and Tina, with me as Tina?"

"Good night, Michaud." She hangs up and looks out her window at the closed stalls of Stanley Market. Not the spectacular harbor view that Patrick Lau had, but in the daytime it pulses with tourists and vendors. Sobieski likes the energy and the kinetic vibe of the human interactions happening all around her. Even if, after two years on Hong Kong Island, she doesn't know very many of the humans and a scant few of the interactions involve her.

She decides that in the morning, after she works out, she'll visit the tech center and do a secure and thorough search on any recent activity at Hang Seng Bank. But for now she is content to fix a cup of Chinese chrysanthemum tea purchased yesterday at a market stall not a hundred feet from her front door and use her own laptop to conduct an informal midnight inquiry into the life and times of Patrick Lau.

Always doing the right thing.

Why? Because it's more or less her job, and it keeps her out of trouble. But also because this stranger's death has forced her to contemplate the parallel circumstances of her own life and a world where a single, good-looking, twenty-nine-year-old, allegedly successful financial expert can die alone in a Hong Kong apartment, and no one seems

14

New York City

"Awww, shit, Weiss."

Turns out Danny Weiss wasn't a conspiracy theorist at all. Turns out he was right.

And now, as a reward for being right, he's twisted in a heap with his left shoulder against the wall on the dusty side of a Popsicle orange futon, bleeding out through a severed carotid artery.

"Shit, Weiss. Shit!" Havens punches his fist into his palm and leans down to look in Weiss's eyes. "Stay with me, Danny!" To his surprise there is a glint of recognition from Weiss. He tries to talk, but the only sound is a wet suck of air through his throat wound. Fear and adrenaline burns inside Havens like flames. Trembling, gasping for his own breath, he starts to rise, knowing that Weiss will be dead in seconds but realizing that the only hope is to call for help. But as he begins to move, Weiss reaches out and grabs his hand. He holds Weiss's fading gaze, squeezes his hand, and feels an object in the young man's still warm palm. It almost drops into the pooling blood, but Havens clasps on to it at the last second: a small red flash drive. Havens tries to speak: "Danny . . ." But Weiss shakes his head a fraction of an inch each way and then glances up toward the wall behind him. Havens follows the dying man's gaze, and his eyes settle on a large whiteboard, covered with a rainbow of symbols and letters. It's barely a glance, but the information pops out and into him, swirling through his brain as a wave of nausea rises up from the pit of his belly. He closes his eyes half-way through reading these words scrawled across the bottom in red:

> The gods may love a man, but they can't help him
> when cold death comes to lay him at his bier . . .

. . . away from the board and back at Weiss.

sirens outside . . . determines that it's the killer coming back to finish up. . . . . . . ward, turns, and leaves a set of bloody footprints as he makes his way to the window. It pops up easily, and in a moment he is out on the iron grill of the fire escape. He starts to close the window but thinks better of it when he glances at a pair of legs entering the room.

He crawls to the top rung of the rickety iron ladder, swings his hips around, and begins climbing down. Every fourth step he looks up to see if he's been discovered. It's only a matter of time before whoever it is—cop, neighbor, killer—discovers the bloody footsteps leading to the open window. Two stories down, with one to go, he stops. There is no longer a ladder. As he grabs the edge of the grate and prepares to swing his body around to the hanging position, he peeks up once more and sees movement in Weiss's window. A man's bald held thrusts out, looks right and left and then down. When his eyes lock with Havens's, there's a moment of confusion, then mutual recognition. It's Laslow, the fixer from the club last seen harassing the bottle girl.

In an instant Laslow is out the window and lunging toward the first ladder. Havens hangs from the edge of the escape and drops to the sidewalk. He falls to his hands and knees and starts scrambling, running before he's fully up. He heads east along the empty sidewalk of 93rd Street. At the corner of First Avenue he allows himself his first look back and, thinking that he might have seen the flash of a body under a distant street lamp, he begins to run even faster.

At Second Avenue he sees the first pedestrians and car traffic, but still not enough of either in which to get lost. He turns left and zigzags southward through the cross streets, between Second and Third, then Lex, Park, and Madison, finally staggering into the darkness of Central Park at the entrance at 79th and Fifth.

As he runs, he calculates. He creates several models that consider the likelihood of Laslow catching him (high), knowing him (absolutely), and/or how quickly he might get information about his address from Rick Salvado and make his way to his apartment (fifteen minutes, a half hour if he had to go back to Weiss's place to find or finish whatever prompted his return).

There is no question about whether any of this will happen. The only variable is when.

Only under the cover of trees on a silent footpath does he allow himself to slow and look back to see that no one is following him. For Havens, Central Park at night never felt so safe.

As he walks, glancing back every twenty steps, heart desperately thumping, he thinks about Weiss and can't help but feel that this is all his fault. In addition to making a fortune off the misfortune of others and losing his wife and his child, now he's brought death upon an innocent young idealist. After all, he's the one who put Weiss on the case of looking into the validity of the positions held by their own employer. He's the one who asked him to look for philosophical inconsistencies and numerical irregularities.

And he's the one who didn't object when Weiss told him about the proprietary, insanely powerful, and in all likelihood highly illegal financial tracking software he'd somehow just gotten hold of.

Yet when the young man called him yesterday, breathless and incredulous, he refused to let him tell his story. His theory. Havens told Weiss to come to him when he had facts. Confirmation. He told Weiss he wasn't interested in stories and gave him his all too familiar lecture about the danger of words, and how only numbers, only the truth of data, could reveal anything worth acting on in the financial world. Weiss begged Havens to hear him out, but he refused. He said it would only skew his read on the only thing that mattered: the data.

   as he approaches the exit on the west side of the park, near

                                        Danny Weiss's small red flash

TUESDAY,

1

soaked timbers jutting into the harbor near the ~~~~~
Halfway down the dock she turns left and strolls up a steel gangway
that takes her onto the deck of a seemingly out of commission barge.

Before she reaches the main hatch, it opens from the inside. She
steps into the dim light of a hallway, and when the door closes, a broad-
shouldered Chinese man emerges out of a shadow to address her.
"Well, well."

She shrugs.

The man takes a drag on his cigarette, then jerks his head down the
hall, beckoning her to follow. At the end of the hall she is led through
another hatch, where another man opens a door, nods at her, and leads
her down a flight of stairs. At the bottom of the stairs she stands at
the head of a large, undecorated, and sparsely furnished room that has
been transformed into a gambling hall. As she looks over the twenty-
two round tables, half of which are occupied by poker players, all but
three of whom are men, she takes off her coat without assistance and
hangs it on a wall hook. She straightens her dress, a sleek, black, snug,

silk-spun viscose number that plunges in front, revealing enough cleavage to turn the head of even the most hard-core gambler. She makes a show of walking across the floor to the banker sitting at a small table covered with a red cloth and stacks of chips.

"I can only take cash from you. No credit."

"I understand." She opens her purse and tosses him two crisp piles of Hong Kong hundred-dollar bills.

"This is not my rule. It's the rule of Mister C." C as in Cheung, as in a lieutenant in Hong Kong's powerful Sun Yee On triad.

She scoops up the chips and turns, looking for a table.

"He is on board tonight."

"Terrific," she replies over her shoulder. "Give him my regards."

Five minutes later she's sitting at a table drinking a double absinthe and staring at a lousy hand. Then another and another. Within fifteen minutes she's down three thousand U.S. and three double absinthes and staring at her rapidly vanishing stack of chips. "Maybe you should try roulette," one of the players, a young businessman from Amsterdam, tells her after she folds. "Maybe a beautiful woman like you is too dignified for a game like Texas hold 'em."

She antes up and stares at the man, the only blond in the entire room. "Maybe a handsome man like you," she replies, "should find a nice dark corner of the barge where he can go to properly and thoroughly fuck himself."

She wins the next hand, almost a thousand U.S., by calling the Dutchman's bluff and beating him with three eights. As she stacks her winnings, she sees Dominick Cheung in the back of the room, going from table to table, making the rounds.

Two hands later she sees a Londoner's raise of two thousand and follows it by raising another three. When the cards are flipped, she's staring at two pair, jacks and sevens, not enough to match his three nines.

The banker shakes his head. He can't help her. "Cash only for you."

She takes a sip of absinthe and closes her eyes as it burns down her throat and spreads across her chest. When she opens her eyes, the young, short, handsome sociopath Dominick Cheung is standing in front of her. "So, how can we help you tonight, sexy lady?"

She stares at Cheung but doesn't speak. How you can help me is no secret, she thinks: You can kill me, you can let me kill you, or you can give me some money.

Cheung smiles. "Come," he says, gesturing toward a cabin door adjacent to the bank table. On the other side is a small office cluttered with old newspapers and magazines, a stained white leather couch,

plastic desk chairs. He gestures with his right hand

"Ninety-six?"

"One twenty-two, U.S. This is quite a substantial sum."

"This is true."

"And rather than come here tonight with a plan or, call me crazy, a payment, you seek more."

She nods.

He touches the back of his hand to her cheek. "And what can you offer in return, as collateral?"

She doesn't move away or answer.

"Surely someone in your position must have access to information that could be of value to someone like me. Say, a company or security that is about to be compromised or investigated. Or another that is about to be vindicated or cleared. I'd say that a certain type of hard information would be worth ten off your tab and ten in your pocket for spending money this evening. A bit here and a bit there and who knows maybe a long overdue winning streak, and you might be solvent by year's end."

She finishes her absinthe and stares at the wall. The wall of a ratty fucking illegal casino barge on the darkest, shittiest pier in Hong Kong Harbour. Talking to a gangster, one twenty in debt with no end in sight.

Always doing the right thing.

"What do you think, Agent Sobieski?"

She puts down her glass, takes a breath, and turns to face Cheung. "Philo; big French pharma company; word is their latest FDC approval isn't going to happen anytime soon and they're about to have major money laundering charges dropped on them by the end of the week."

Cheung smiles, then claps his hands. "Exactly what I was talking about. What else?"

"What else? Nothing now. I'm working on the murder of a trader for Hang Seng, but there's nothing there."

"For now?"

"Correct."

"But if there is something there, or involving something else, we'll stay in touch?"

Within twenty minutes she turns her ten-thousand-dollar advance into seventeen. But the more she wins, the worse she feels. Worse than losing. Worse than being alone. At one-forty-five she gets up from the table and backs away, afraid that if she stays she might win again. On her way to cash in at the bank, the blond Dutchman catches up to her. Her eyes are glassy and her thoughts are guilt- and absinthe-twisted.

"What?"

"I tried."

"Tried?"

"To go, you know, to go fuck myself. But I was not successful. Which is why I was wondering, if you're leaving, if you'd like to join me. To show me the proper way."

2

ent. Back then, they didn't prescribe Ritalin or send him to a psychiatrist or assume that he had ADD or Asperger's. Back then they stuck him in what was technically known as the special ed class, but more commonly known to his fellow students and even some teachers as the retard room.

After a while he taught himself to control his outbursts by imagining that he was in a spacecraft coursing through the heavens. This was a by-product of his fixation on aeronautics. He calculated travel to distant galaxies in light-years, earth years, dog years. He gauged his changing weight depending upon the gravitational pull of the nearest celestial body. Real and make believe. And he was constantly measuring the distance to the next planet, the next star system. Always moving farther away from his own blue-green sphere. Never back toward home.

It helped. Soon he was back in honors classes, considered smart yet odd. With time, he adopted other coping mechanisms. But after Erin died and during the divorce, when nothing else worked, when he was filled with rage and frustration, it got so bad that he even tried the spaceship exercise again. But it was no use. His emotions and imagination had been grounded. So he lost himself more than ever in the numbers, even though he had grown to detest them.

Havens comes out of the park at Columbus Circle. More people, lights and traffic. Forty-three blocks from the apartment. Feeling safer but far from safe. Standing under a streetlight across from the Museum of Design he sees that there is blood smeared on the white cuff of his shirt and the sleeve of his charcoal suit jacket. Danny Weiss's blood. For the first time he thinks of calling the police, the SEC, the FBI. Miranda.

But he knows calling anyone right now would be more than complicated. He literally and figuratively has a dead man's blood on his hands and feet, and his prints are all over the apartment of the deceased. Plus his story. Or Weiss's story. Or theory. Even if true, who would believe it? Who would take his word against the word of one of the most respected and patriotic investors in the country? Accusing Rick Salvado of murder and financial terrorism is like trying to pin the Pearl Harbor attack on Warren Buffett.

Nonetheless, the quant in him continues to play out a variety of scenarios, the sequence of events that is most likely to occur if he were to come forward to name Rick Salvado as a conspirator in the death of Danny Weiss, and perhaps much more. And every one of his models ends with him dead or in jail.

Almost subconsciously, his right arm rises at the sight of an approaching cab. Forty-three blocks would take too long to walk. Once he finds the address, Laslow will surely take a cab and beat him there. "Union Square," he tells the driver.

No one's been here. Havens is sure of it. He can tell by the numbers displayed on the LED of his phone machine. The unchanged geometry of the throw pillows on his couch. The fact that the dial on the lock of his closet safe is still stopped at 28. Not that 28 is the final number in the combo. He would never leave the dial there. Leaving it on 28 is the equivalent of a poker player with an overt tell, a giveaway gesture or tic that stacks the odds in his opponent's favor, and Havens knows for a fact that when he last closed the safe, he spun the dial to the meaningless and inapplicable number 28. Twenty-five and three hash marks.

Most people wouldn't remember this sort of thing, but this is the way that Havens thinks. The way he's always thought.

Of all people, the King of the Quants should have known that there is no place for sentimentality in the world of numbers. But in this instance that's too bad.

He reaches inside the safe and fumbles through the quotidian artifacts of a life lived in quiet, recently wealthy desperation. Insurance policies, his stock and bond certificates, his brokerage licenses, his employment agreements, birth certificates, and the simplest divorce settlement known to man. They didn't want to fight. They wanted to move on. At least Miranda did.

In the back of the safe he finds a roll of a thousand dollars in twenties and his passport. Everything else is inconsequential. The numbers for his offshore accounts, his passwords and serial numbers, they're all in his head.

Before he stands, he decides to get on his knees and take one last look. Inside, tucked against the back wall, is a blank five-by-eight piece of paper. He reaches in and pulls it out, the photo of Erin, the 08/17/06 girl herself, taken just a month before the worst day of his life,

03/27/09: the day he lost her. He slips the photo into the nylon messenger bag on his shoulder and makes his way back into the living room.

As he conducts a final sweep of the premises, to comfort himself, he listens to his old messages. All variations on the same theme, from Miranda. All so familiar that he mouths her words as they play. Nineteen left over the span of the past several months. Each in a different way says that she is just checking in, that she is worried about him. Each has an emotional component and a cumulative numerical significance. While he's never responded to any of them, neither has he been able to bring himself to delete them.

> I haven't heard from you in what, a month? Just checking in!

From the center throw pillow on the couch he unzips the casing, removes a pad of hundred-dollar bills from inside, and slips it into his bag.

> It's me. It's your birthday. I hope you're well and enjoying it with other wonderful humans.

Across the room he stops at the bookshelves above his desk. Inside a hollowed-out copy of *Crime and Punishment* are two more pads of hundreds.

> I'll pretend you're getting these and I'm not talking to the air. You know that despite our . . . differences, I blame you for nothing. There's nothing that you could have done.

Inside a picture book called *The Universe* is another stack exactly where he left it: on page 184, at the head of a chapter on black holes.

You know, not every day is a picnic for me either. I understand not calling. Not e-mailing. But if you're there, I hope you'll pick up, but if you choose not to, then I hope life is good anyway.

In a kitchen cabinet, buried in the powder of a tub of Swiss Miss hot chocolate mix, are three more stacks of hundreds. He puts them in the bag and walks back to the phone.

I've been doing a lot of reading and, you know, there's a

"Listen," he says, heading back into the bedroom, happening. Bad work things."

"That son of a bitch. What did he do?"

He grabs a black leather duffel from his closet and starts shoving clothes inside. Underwear, jeans, polo shirts, a dress shirt. He doesn't have long before someone arrives. He can feel it. "I don't know. It has to do with the hedge, and with Weiss."

"Danny? He . . ."

In the bathroom now, shoving deodorant, toothpaste, and a toothbrush into a side pouch. "Yeah. Danny Weiss. I just found him. Dead, in his apartment."

She pulls away from the phone for a second. He checks his watch, continues to hustle through the apartment. "Oh my God, Drew. You have to tell the—"

Opening and closing drawers, looking for what? A gun? Hah! "I can't, Mir. Not now. If I tell anyone right now, I know that he'll set me up and take me down. He knows too many people."

"You sure it's him?"

"I saw the guy . . . the killer. He's a Salvado guy."

"What are you gonna . . ."

"I've got to go away until . . ."

"What?"

"Until I figure it out."

"My God. Then come up here."

"I won't do that to you. He'll try to blame Danny on me, I know it."

"But you didn't . . ."

"Which is why, if someone comes poking around, you have to absolutely deny having had any contact with me."

"Come up here. I'll hide you."

"Even if they find out we've spoken, say it was a fight. Say it was over money and I never return your calls—there's proof right here on my machine—and, as hard as it may be, pretend you no longer have intimate feelings for me."

"What did you find?"

He decides not to get specific with Miranda. The less she knows, the better. Plus, at this point, he's not exactly sure. Whatever it is, it's enough to piss off the CEO and founder of the second best performing hedge fund in the world and, apparently, to get someone killed. "Hard to tell."

"But you think he did this and would do this to you? Jesus, Drew, it was your research that . . . If not for you, he'd still be . . ."

"I know, which is what frightens me."

"Please, Drew. Come up here."

"I can't. I don't want to get you involved."

He's at the front door, adjusting his duffel and shoulder bag.

"But you have to."

He closes the door and doesn't bother locking it. "Why?" he asks, flabbergasted. "Why, Mir?"

"Because a few minutes after you and I spoke earlier, Danny Weiss called me."

3

sleep.

But run she must. She finds that an early morning run is the best way to forget the night and transition between her conflicting selves. Sometimes it's a reward, other times a punishment.

Most days, she starts outside her apartment in Stanley Market, but this morning she decides to change things up and drives to the Wanchai District for a loop along Victoria Harbour. Predawn light tints the eastern horizon a surreal metallic blue as she breaks into her stride. No stretching, no visualizing. Just dive in and get it over with. Usually she listens to music while she runs. Most recently the Black Keys, Spoon, and the Felice Brothers, but her head is in no condition to listen to anything this morning.

The tide is in, and the brightening sky looks as if it will soon be relatively blue. Later, the tide will recede and the sun will rise up and bake the teeming streets, and the heat and smog and noise of Hong Kong will change everything. She rounds a bend in the path and sees the Star ferry chugging out for an early morning commuter run. The ferry reminds her of the ferry to Macau. When she first arrived in Hong Kong, she'd take the night ferry to the casinos in Macau, but now that she's found the barge, and several other local games, she doesn't have to travel. There's a moment while she's thinking about Macau and the barge and the Dutchman when she feels that she might lose her stomach, but after a while it passes and she's able to keep a decent pace. She's not far from the barge, and Patrick Lau's condominium is within sight, when her phone buzzes. She slows to a stop and looks at her watch, incredulously, before answering.

"Five oh-nine A.M.," she says. "Just getting home?"

Michaud laughs. "If anyone else answered their phone breathing so heavily, at this time of day, I'd assume the most impure and obscene of scenarios were going down. But not my Sobieski."

"Only obscenity I'm feeling right now is the fact that my morning run has once again been rudely interrupted."

"How's the crowd at the market?"

"Changed it up," she explains. "Doing the Harbourfront."

"Patrick Lau's old stomping grounds."

"Why not?"

"Thoughts?"

Sobieski pauses. In between gambling and screwing, her late night/early morning research into the life of Patrick Lau didn't reveal any single case-breaking discovery. But she did uncover enough bits and pieces to keep her intrigued.

"Nothing major. But a couple things I saw about his personal matters up to but not including whatever he did yesterday are worth looking into."

"For instance?"

"Well, I did a secure credit check using the basic software on my laptop. Turns out Lau was in a lot worse shape than his coworkers or neighbors thought or were willing to admit."

"Who isn't?

"Well," she continues, "in addition to having problems making his monthly condo rent, Lau was more than two hundred and fifty thousand dollars deep in debt, mostly the result of bad real estate deals and personal trades, overextended credit cards, and another thirty thousand dropped over the past twelve months on weekend junkets to Bangkok."

"No doubt on sex vacations."

"Homosexuals do all kinds of interesting things, Boss. Just like normal people. Except solitaire karaoke. That's too gay even for them."

"So," Michaud replies, "Lau had some debt issues."

who owes you a large sum of money? Wouldn't killing the guy who owes you money guarantee that you'd never see a cent of it?"

"I don't know," replies Michaud. "No one's ever owed me a large sum of money. Listen, Sobes, it sounds like a funky homicide, but our job at TFI is—"

She cuts him off and completes the sentence, her departmental mission statement, for him. ". . . Terrorism and Financial Intelligence's twin aims are safeguarding the financial system against illicit use and combating rogue nations, terrorist facilitators, weapons of mass destruction proliferators, money launderers, drug kingpins, and other national security threats."

"None of which seems to fit the profile of the murder of Patrick Lau."

"You didn't let me finish."

"You sounded like you were."

"It's five something in the morning. Pardon me if my PowerPoint skills aren't razor sharp."

"What else?"

"From a TFI perspective, it's worth noting that Lau's group was responsible for buying up an inordinate amount of short paper yesterday. This came up in a basic at-home search. Not in one transaction, but most if not all for tech stocks."

"Okay," Michaud says. Now his voice is all business, no longer collegial. "What kind of tech?"

"Well, Apple, Dell, Cisco, and about a dozen others."

"All American-based?"

"I don't have the list in the waistband of my shorts, but on first glance, yep . . ."

Michaud sighs. One thing that raises a red flag for Americans working in the prevention of financial terrorism is a massive short position, especially on American securities. Throw a murdered broker into the equation and the flag gets twice as big and red and flies five times higher. "Why didn't you call me sooner?"

Sobieski watches three small fishing boats head out for the waters of the South China Sea. She considers saying something about the fact that she didn't discover this until a little more than an hour ago, that it didn't seem particularly conclusive, and that she didn't immediately contact him because she imagined he was passed out or still in a bar, but she resists. "You're right," she answers. "I should have."

"How much of a short?"

"Hard to tell without getting on our system, but the best I could tell with the tools on hand is that Lau or someone in his group tried to Smurf it, executing a ton of shorts, none more than ten thousand dollars to stay under the tracking radar, totaling in the area of a billion dollars. Thousands of individual transactions. Micro-transactions. Whatever. Over a period of many hours."

"Did you . . . ?"

Again, Sobieski finishes her boss's thought. "Was I able to discover in my bedroom at four-twenty-six this morning if any external, real-world circumstances may have triggered the position? No, not on the newswires or market trends or the individual company news feeds. If anything, whoever did this, they're in the distinct minority, betting so aggressively against this kind of blue chip tech. And no, I have no clue at this point about the identity of the investor or investors or if there's a deeper U.S. connection."

"How long would it take you to get in here?"

Sobieski looks at her outfit. Black tights beneath a pair of charcoal running shorts and a Chicago Cubs T-shirt. "You're already in?"

"Just completed a solitaire version of the walk of shame."

She sighs. "You know, it would be nice to be able to go to work in big

in a while."

4

Dubai

nobody walks outside in Dubai, which is why Nasseem Al Mar enjoys it so much.

He's heard all the jokes about mad dogs and Englishmen, and the warnings about the risks of exposure to the desert heat but, unlike mad dogs and Englishmen, he doesn't come out in the midday sun. He walks at dawn or, like today, after work, at dusk.

Al Mar, a forty-four-year-old broker who landed on his post-Lehman, post-collapse feet at Zayed Capital, no longer cares what the others think. In the past five years he's seen more excess and financial devastation than in the previous twenty. He's watched friends, clients, and family members make millions, spend more, then lose everything. He's seen this city and this country rise and soar and crash in a matter of months. All he cares about these days is surviving, and today was a good day, a day that makes walking through the desert on the outskirts of Dubailand doubly satisfying because of a complex yet lucrative series of trades he just finished executing.

Precisely at 9 A.M., just as the exchange opened for the day, he received a call from someone in Berlin representing an investor in the United States. The caller wanted to take a number of short positions on

a series of predominantly U.S.-based media stocks and funds special-
izing in broadcast, film, music, and print. TV networks. Newspaper,
book, and magazine publishing. Major motion picture studios. And
music. Nothing unusual. After all, each of these so-called old-media
industries is facing a series of technological, cultural, and economic
challenges threatening its future. Indeed, every day someone seems to
be predicting the death of one industry or another, so the aggressive
short positions were nothing out of the ordinary.

However, what was unusual was the sheer volume of trades and the
which the caller wanted to execute them. Rather than going

semi-anonymous client, whose transfers and credentials
out a hitch, would know the sum of the trades, which cumulatively
totaled just under a billion dollars.

So it's a screen-weary yet soon-to-be well-compensated Nasseem Al
Mar who is walking away from the ghost town periphery of his city in
101-degree, 6 P.M. desert heat. He's left his black suit jacket on the front
seat of the car and loosened his red tie, each part of the corporate uniform he and his fellow brokers wear every day. Even though they rarely
if ever have face-to-face interactions with clients, the new MD insists
on the formal dress code, says it reflects integrity and creates solidarity
within the ranks, and puts their Western clientele at ease. Al Mar
thinks, in addition to being bloody hot, the matching suits make them
look like members of a football club. But whatever. He's a survivor. And
if wearing a corporate uniform is part of the deal, so be it.

He thinks about his wife. Maybe this windfall will relax her, because
steady employment hasn't been enough. She's seen too many others
fail. His brother. Her brothers, and her brother-in-law who disappeared

after the crash and left her sister alone to raise four children. She wants a return to the golden times. This deal won't quite do that, but it's something. It's a decent start.

Briefly, he considered defying the client's request and putting some of his own money on some mirror shorts on a personal account, but he didn't. Couldn't. Not because he is afraid of retaliation, but because he has no money to invest. But, because he thought it would make his wife happy, just before leaving the office, Al Mar dialed his brother-in-law, who has some liquidity, and told him about his last trade. Not surprisingly, his brother-in-law, who is something of a gambler, jumped all over his information.

He walks to the burned-out wreck of a Mercedes. Stolen or abandoned, he thinks. Once the property of a fool, now owned by the desert. He turns around to begin his walk back to his car. Not a long walk, but a good walk. Enough to get the blood flowing, to clear the head. As he nears his car, he sees the shine of another vehicle approaching. In this stretch of the desert, when the light is right, one can see for miles. It takes more than a minute for the car to reach him. Another black Mercedes, same model as the wreck down the road.

When it's twenty yards away, Al Mar steps off the edge of the road. It's rare that one sees a pedestrian out here, plus the light is fading, so why take a chance? When the driver spots him, the car slows, almost to a stop. There is a moment when driver and pedestrian make eye contact, and it sends a shiver up Al Mar's spine. He's filled with the sensation that something is about to go terribly wrong, that he's made a mistake coming out here to this same spot day after day, that sooner or later he will be robbed or worse.

But then the driver, a middle-aged man with a mustache not unlike Al Mar's, turns back to the road and floors the gas. Al Mar stops and watches the car shrink in the twilight and the despair passes. The survivor lives another day.

5

train to ...
drunken concert- and club-goers and a handful of glassy-e-
men in suits for whom the demands of work have overtaken the importance of almost everything else. He sits on a cramped and stiff rear-
facing jumper seat at the back of the car and attempts to prioritize
what's happened and what he needs to do.

First, always first, Miranda. She told him she didn't pick up when
Weiss called because she didn't recognize the number. She said his message was short and harried. He was upset that Havens had not returned
his calls; he feared for his life; and he was certain that something horrible was about to happen. He said that the fund was involved, and that
Havens was his last best hope to figure it out. When she called him back
five minutes later, there was no answer.

Next, Weiss. Weiss was right. Havens had begun to ignore his
messages. They'd joked about it several times. Weiss knew that Havens
wasn't a great communicator, especially when it came to text messag-
ing. The way Havens saw it, if he replied to one, it would open the flood-
gates. And Weiss, who Havens once said did not have an off button,

would strive for constant contact. He looks around the train, then scrolls back through Weiss's messages, starting chronologically with two he read but chose to ignore while he was at the club:

- . . . wilt thou not be brotherly to us?
-Berlin. 12.42-6

After considering the first two, which still make no sense, he opens two more:

-Murder @ Hang Seng
-Help 3.338-9

Of course Havens is familiar with an institution the size of Hang Seng. But he has no relationship with the Hong Kong HQ'd bank or its employees. *Help* he clearly understands. That must have come soon after he walked away from Salvado at Elysian, just before Laslow got to Weiss. However, he has no idea what to make of the second part of Weiss's text: *3.338-9*. All that he can theorize is that Weiss knew he was in danger and had begun an information dump on him, one cryptic text at a time. The next and final text, sent less than a minute after *Help*, says:

This time: 7 Trades. Not 28.

Havens wonders what was going on when Weiss sent this, and why he's now seeing it for the first time. Was he hiding? Had he heard Laslow coming? Or was he simply jamming the night away, trying to find answers, scribbling explanations for his confounding world on a whiteboard and then dispatching them one text at a time, like messages in a bottle? In the end, it's obvious that he hid. What else could he do? Weiss had neither the skills nor the temperament of a fighter. At least not a physical fighter. But for an idea or a cause, he was as tenacious as they come, and Havens realizes that this message was Weiss's last punch in a fight whose outcome is yet to be determined.

As they come out of the tunnels of Manhattan and creep across the bridge over the East River, Havens thinks of a conversation he had with Salvado and Rourke back in 2007. They had just realized, based upon Havens's findings, that they would make a killing by shorting the U.S. sub-prime mortgage market. They were talking in Salvado's office while he was being fitted by a tailor from Milan he'd had flown in on the Gulfstream VI.

"Why?" Havens asked. "Why can't we simply go forward to the

models. The numbers. The inevitable result of the whole big equation. Give people a chance to make the connections, recognize the deviations, and you know, unwind some of their most volatile positions. We'd be rich *and* heroes."

Salvado's initial reaction was to laugh. Rourke didn't laugh. Rourke looked at Havens with enlightened, admiring eyes, then turned to Salvado. "You know, he has a point, Rick. I don't see why—"

Salvado cut Rourke off, dismissed him by addressing Havens only. "This is why I love you, Havens. And why you are going to need me to stop you from hearting away your hard-won money."

Rourke couldn't help himself. "There's gonna be plenty to go around, regardless."

Salvado stopped smiling. "Enough, Tommy. Please. In fact, do me a favor and get the fuck out of here. You are a words guy, a goddamn classical lit major, and because it involves something called numbers, this is way beyond your tiny, liberal arts–polluted intellect." Rourke, humbled, stepped back, a symbolic departure, and remained silent. The tailor looked up. "And you," Salvado told the tailor, "if you tell a soul about this conversation I will make a suit out of your fucking skin." Finally he turned to Havens. "Our primary obligation is to our clients. We are here to maximize the return on their—and our—investments. Second, if we did tell those assholes, it wouldn't matter. None of them would understand. Certainly not the regulators. They understand law, not the machinery of the markets. And the ratings people? Hah! Might as well alert a hot dog vendor. You think they'd bite the hand that feeds them? The first ratings service to tell the truth about this shit is the first to see its market share plummet. Do you think people go to them for truth, or to validate their agenda? And the banks? I've told the heads of some of the biggest institutions in the world, and they are in complete, utter denial. Because they don't want to believe or don't have a clue. Screw them. Let 'em fail. And this: Why not us? Why not have the handful of hardworking people smart enough to figure it out be the ones to cash in on it?"

Havens replied, "I don't care about the banks either, Rick. But if these senior sub-prime tranches go to smithereens millions of innocent people . . . if we're even one quarter right, the global economy is going to go down with them."

Salvado's response: a wink. Then, "No one's innocent. They all knew what they were getting into and didn't believe it would end. They all thought their 401(k)s were gonna double every year, and that they could day trade as well in 2008 as they could while the Internet bubble swelled. They thought they could buy homes twenty times their annual incomes and take vacations and buy flat screens with no assets and shit jobs. They aren't innocent. The banks aren't innocent. Paulson and the feds aren't innocent. The fools rating and insuring all of this aren't innocent. They all chose to ride it out and milk every last cent out of the system. Fuck them, Havens. Every last greedy one of them."

Right then and there, Havens tells himself, just as he has told himself many times since that day, *You should have known.* You should have walked away. But you stayed because of the money, and because you stayed, your life changed all at once and then forever. Because you stayed, you lost your soul, your wife, your daughter, and now your friend and protégé. An idealistic young man is dead, all because you didn't walk away.

This time: 7 Trades. Not 28.

Which seven? Havens thinks. And to what end? The conductor ̲ ̲ ̲ ̲ ̲ ̲ ̲ ̲ ̲ ̲ and punching tickets, announcing the next stop of

purpose of playing it back to Weiss once he sobered up, because he sounded out of it. On Saturday, frustrated by Havens's lack of a serious response, Weiss sent Havens a long e-mail on his personal account under the heading "28 Trades." The e-mail was a more concise and linear version of the previous day's semi-hysterical phone message.

It began with the contention that a number of unknown individuals with precise foreknowledge of the September 11, 2001, attacks on the World Trade Center had purchased an unusually large number of "put" options on a number of American holdings, including United and American Airlines. Weiss's theory, which he supported with confirmation from everyone from the Israeli Herzliya Institute for Counterterrorism to the Drudge Report, purported that there were twenty-eight such stocks, including insurance companies and U.S. financial institution holdings, in addition to the airline puts. Their bet, essentially, was that when the towers came down, the stocks would fall as well.

Havens got that far into the e-mail before stopping and hitting delete. The theory was too outrageous for him to take seriously. It reeked too much of the unsubstantiated cable news–brainwashed, rumor-mongering lunatic fringe that had hijacked the culture. He preferred the logic of facts and numbers to accusation and innuendo. The hypothetical made his brain hurt, and the theories that dealt with the fall of mankind made him want to curl up in a ball.

The next day, Sunday, Weiss called four times. On the fifth Havens picked up and agreed to meet him over drinks at Cipriani. Weiss showed up late, unshaven and dressed in a T-shirt, shredded jeans, and sandals. The hostess had to be coaxed into allowing him in. At the bar, sipping a neat Macallan, Havens said to Weiss, "I'm worried about you, Danny. All this *X-Files* stuff, what does any of this have to do with the current holdings of the Rising Fund?"

"You didn't finish the e-mail?"

"No."

"Everything and nothing."

"You're saying that Salvado had something to do with 9/11? The man who *Forbes* says paints his hedge red, white, and blue?"

"I'm saying . . ."

"Shit, in 2001 The Rising didn't even exist."

"I'm saying that my findings tell me there's something similar going on. Another twenty-eight trade–type scenario that somehow involves, well, us."

"Us?"

"Our boss. Our place of business."

"Why would a billionaire risk throwing it all away for what . . . a few more billion?"

Weiss moved his face two inches from Havens's. As Weiss began to speak, Havens wasn't thinking conspiracy theory, but nervous breakdown. "Some, like you, only see numbers. Others only see stories. I see both. And as much as you refuse to recognize it, Drew, there's a narrative in the numbers. In fact there's a narrative to every trade. The world isn't a logical place. It operates on emotions; its stories are filled with greed and revenge as well as love and redemption. I don't know all of the components for his story, his true and absolute motive, but the parts that I've been exposed to so far are the stuff of tragedy. A real one."

"I think you need to speak with someone, Danny."

"The makeup of The Rising is just the beginning. For all I know it's a goddamn red herring."

Havens grabbed Weiss by his narrow shoulders. "What do you want me to do, Danny? Go to the cops? Have 'em bust Rick, for what? Why don't you just follow me and quit?"

"I wish it was that easy. I don't know the answer yet, but I'm gonna ~~figure it out, but I do, I want~~ you to believe me."

minutes for the software to load. The program appears with no or name or audio mnemonic. After a moment a search box appears. He types "The Rising" into the box and hits enter, but nothing happens because the Internet signal on the train fades in and out. Weiss recently mentioned that he'd gotten hold of an illegal, turbocharged piece of tracking/hacking software. Havens imagines that this is what he used to discover the clues that validated his theory and led to his death, and that Weiss wanted Havens to have it. He slips the drive into his sock and goes back to the last text message from Danny Weiss. This time he notices an icon attached to it. A tiny illustration of a camera, denoting a photo attachment.

He clicks on the icon and watches the photograph begin to appear, first as a pixilated blur and then more sharply defined and perfectly framed. He recognizes that it's the whiteboard from Danny Weiss's wall, but he can't enlarge it on the small screen. As he strains to read the tiny, blurred letters, he resolves himself, in honor of Danny Weiss, to figure this out. To validate the young man's life and hopefully save some others. To make order from chaos. And to teach himself something his brain is not programmed to do: to craft a narrative out of numbers. Staring at the postage stamp–sized picture of the board he saw in the dead man's apartment less than two hours ago he thinks, I believe you now, Danny.

6

board Colonial home close to the embassies on Garden Road. From the street it looks like the home of the consul general of any one of several dozen nations that have residences in the area, and not the hub of an elite global counterterrorism task force.

A small sign on the outer door reads: DR. ROBERT MICHAUD, PODIATRIST.

Beneath it reads another: CLOSED.

Inside, beyond the faux reception area, the entire first floor is open-plan, not unlike the layout of a San Francisco digital start-up. In the center of what was once the great room of a diplomat's home are four eight-foot-long farm-style tables covered with wires and cables that merge and snake down through a hole in the center and stretch along the floor down the hall to an air-conditioned pantry that now houses four decks of the world's most powerful servers.

Sobieski stands alone at the tables, unpacking her knapsack. Michaud comes out of the kitchen. He's holding two mugs of hot tea. He offers one to Sobieski. "Oolong," he says proudly.

"Oh, boy," she answers, accepting one of the mugs. "Oolong tea. How fancy. And rare. Being that we're in China and everything."

Michaud smiles. His eyes are a mass of intersecting red lines, the cluttered flow charts of failing conglomerates. He's forty-five going on ninety, handsome in a past tense, post-divorce, pre-alcoholic kind of way. Sobieski catches a whiff of booze on his breath that the Mentos can't conceal. Sort of pathetic, but she knows she's in no position to judge, and can't help but admire the guy for coming straight to work from the karaoke bar. "Come," Michaud says, jerking his neck toward the small parlor that has been transformed into his office.

"Check this out," he says, leaning over the paper ruins of his desk and tapping the fingerprint-smudged screen of his computer monitor. He scrolls through a blur of screens, each filled with the data for more than a hundred transactions, each of which includes the call letters of the same dozen technology stocks. "Thousands of orders for the same handful of stocks. All short positions."

Sobieski sips the tea, tries to hide the fact that it tastes surprisingly good. "Hang Seng Bank?"

Michaud nods. "Your boy Patrick Lau's trading account. Disturbingly easy to hack."

"Did he have any similar action, any big positions on anything, before or after these?"

"Nothing. Over the past twelve months the guy was losing money in 3-D. Most of his real clients walked after the last crash. Or next to last. Hard to keep track. To tell you the truth, considering his overall lack of assets, clients, and trades, I don't know why they were letting the dude in the building."

"Anything on the buyer? Mr. Short?"

Michaud sips his tea and doesn't hide his distaste for it. He spits it back, puts the mug on his desk, and pushes it far away. "Nothing on the individual Mr. Short, but it looks like the order for all this stuff came out of, or at least passed through, some bullshit firm in Berlin."

"What firm?"

"Siren Securities. Most likely a false front for some bad guys. We're looking into it."

"Any news on the performance or outlook for those tech companies that would indicate why someone would lay down this heavy of a bet on their failures?"

"Other than the fact that everything I've read from the top tech analysts in the world leads me to believe that our mystery investor is absolutely nuts to short an entire sector that is all about digital content and technology, essentially the future of everything . . ."

Michaud cuts her off. "Not happening."

She mock frowns. She knows there must be more. He must know something else; otherwise he wouldn't have called her in at this hour. "Then what?"

Michaud bangs his thick fingers on the keyboard then squints, awkwardly over-scrolling and over-correcting. "Here," he says, jutting his chin at the monitor.

Sobieski leans forward. He drag and clicks the mouse several times, and the monitor flashes blue with a page of numerical transaction text, not unlike the pages they just viewed in Lau's account. "Starting yesterday morning, Dubai time, and continuing through late afternoon, a trader named Nasseem Al Mar went on a bit of a roll. In just over nine hours he booked more transactions, moved more money, and presumably made more money than he had in any one *month* since he started at this firm, Sayed Capital."

"Shorts?"

"Yup," Michaud answers. "Close to a billion U.S."

"Tech?"

Michaud shakes his head. "No, nothing on tech, which I take as a bit of relief, like, you know, maybe they're just planning on a widespread market dip."

"What, then?"

"Well his client went short on a bunch of media plays, mostly old, traditional media. Broadcast. TV and newspapers. Publishing."

"American?"

"Yup. Grade-A red, white, and blue."

"So," Sobieski responds, "someone isn't sky-high on the future of American old media, which doesn't exactly make him unique in the investment world."

"But assuming it's the same person, you'd think if he's betting against old media, he'd have a more favorable take on the future, the tech sector that's supposed to be killing it."

Sobieski says, "Yet he or she is equally bearish."

"Assuming it's the same he or she."

"Is Al Mar still alive?"

"So far, nothing has turned up that says he isn't."

Sobieski stares at the screen. "Why kill Lau and not Al Mar?"

Michaud shrugs. "Why kill anyone, unless they represent, or did something to become too much of, a risk? Unless someone somewhere compromised their plan and they decided to eliminate further damage." He picks up a single-page printout. "Here's his story: Nasseem Al Mar. Forty-four. Born wealthy, raised wealthy, slowly working his way to poverty. Wharton Grad. Usual financial services suspects, all in the Middle East. USB. Deutsche. And, fairly recently, Lehman, before . . ."

Sobieski bobs her head impatiently. She knows all too well about the demise of Lehman Brothers. The demise of all of them. Plus, she has to use the bathroom.

". . . before Lehman blew up."

"Right."

"Then in '09, right after . . ."

"I know . . ."

Michaud continues, ". . . right after 'The Crisis,' he moved to the seemingly legit Sayed Capital in Dubai, where he proceeded to have a career that, trade for trade, disgruntled client for disgruntled client, was like the mirror image of Patrick Lau's."

"Gay?"

"No. Married with two teenage boys."

"Just throwing it out there. Did—what's his name, Al Mar?—did he have a debt problem, too?"

". . . His hobbies are all about nice cars and prostitutes. He

Michaud answers with another series of mouse clicks. The page for a firm called Siren Securities appears on the screen. "The orders for Patrick Lau's last trade and Nasseem Al Mar's last trade were both initiated electronically from the same server in Berlin, which at one time was linked to this same bullshit financial services company, Siren."

He taps the screen. Sobieski looks more closely at the home page staff photo for Siren Securities, which is basically the default photo for every financial institution's home page, newsletter, and annual report: rich men in suits forcing smiles in front of a fountain at the base of a glass-and-steel tower. Beneath the logo is the phrase:

> Square in your ship's path are Seirenes, crying
> beauty to bewitch men coasting by;
> woe to the innocent who hears that sound.

"*The Iliad*," Michaud says.

"No. *The Odyssey.* Ulysses had his men strap him to the sail to resist the Sirens' temptation. Any other activity coming out of their Berlin server?"

Michaud stands and rolls his neck. "Nah."

"Do you know who placed the orders with Siren? Where the trades initiated?"

"Yes and no. I saw that they came out of the U.S., but I can't be sure until my guy in D.C. gets in."

Sobieski stares at him, waiting for an explanation.

"Here's the thing: Soon after I hacked into it, they went dark. I got what I could, but it's like its tracking software picked up on ours and shut down at the first sign of a breach. Which means whoever this is may have a version of ours . . . or something better."

Sobieski starts to leave, then turns. "So, we're onto this because some Hong Kong PD pal of yours needed a favor?"

Michaud shrugs.

"And this pal, this ordinary Detective Mo, initiated contact? He sniffed out a potential global financial plot and just happened to ring you up?"

"Stranger things have happened, Sobes," he replies, avoiding eye contact and pretending to call up a new screen.

7

the walk, he drove to the Festival City Mall and met his brother-in-law and a friend from his Lehman days for a drink on the top floor of the Intercontinental. One drink led to three, but he called his wife and she understood. Supper could wait. After the third drink he told both men everything he knew about the trades he made earlier in the day. Before he left the table, they were on their BlackBerrys, placing shorts of their own.

He gets out of his Mercedes and takes three steps toward the elevator before clicking the key remote to lock the door. A hand grabs his and twists his arm behind his back. The keys drop to the concrete. He bends forward as his wrist is shoved up the ridge of his spine between his shoulder blades. He doesn't resist.

"Come," the man says in Arabic. Saudi, Al Mar surmises. The man turns him back toward the cars, then stops to pick up Al Mar's keys. As they walk, the man says, "Of course I have a gun, so . . ." Al Mar nods. No need to say more.

A second man, with a mustache, in a wrinkled black suit, is

standing on the driver's side of Al Mar's Mercedes. The locks click open. Al Mar is shoved into the front passenger seat; the man who had grabbed him first, the one with the gun, gets in behind him. Al Mar closes his eyes. When he opens them, he sees the elevator doors to the garage begin to open. It's his daughter Risi. Most nights she watches for his car from their living room window, and lately his wife has allowed the six-year-old to come down to greet him on the elevator. Her eyes widen when she sees his car. When she doesn't see him driving, she tilts her head, confused. His heart feels as if it will burst. He checks to see if the others have seen Risi, but they are too busy watching him and settling into the unfamiliar car. As they begin to pull away, the girl steps forward. Al Mar looks at her, unsmiling, grim, his eyes wide and filled with tragic urgency. He stops her in her tracks with a glare and the slightest shake of his head. As only a father can with a daughter when he knows her life is at stake.

Within minutes they are away from the lights of the towers and the harbor, cruising slowly on an empty road. "Where are we going?"

From the back: "You know this road."

Al Mar looks out the window. He does know this road. Oasis, the road on which he takes his walks. Then he looks at the driver. Of course, it's the man in the Mercedes that slowed as it passed him this afternoon. His instincts were right, only his timing was off.

"What do you want with me?"

"We would like to know if you've told anyone about your interaction with the Berlin client today."

Al Mar blinks. "No. I was asked not to and I honored the request. I'm not—"

"Where were you this evening?"

"After my walk? I met friends at the Intercontinental."

"What did you tell them?"

"Nothing. I said that business is picking up."

They pull over soon after the highway lights end. Al Mar recognizes the burned out frame of the deserted car. His turn-around marker. The man in the back gets out and opens Al Mar's door. The gun is out in the open now. A Sig Sauer P226 nine-millimeter.

It's clear to Al Mar that he is about to die. "If I kept my word, I don't understand . . ."

"I believe you." The man with the gun guides him to the shell of the abandoned car. His hands rest on the chalky black sheet metal of the vehicle's roof. Things not meant to burn always smell the worst.

"Then why now as opposed to when you drove past me this after-

. . . . . know you existed has dis-

Al Mar presses against the can reach and lays his left cheek upon the charred roof, still warm from the afternoon sun. He's looking down the road, farther than he's yet walked, and thinking of the most profound joys and failures of his life, all of his own making, and of Risi, if she made it back to the flat, when the bullet tears into the flesh behind his right ear and exits through his left temple. His splayed arms rise once in a flapping motion, his legs spasm and then go slack. A jet of blood sprays from the notch behind his ear, then his legs give and he slides down the side of the car, folding over upon himself, onto the sand.

The shooter holsters the gun, then turns to the driver and motions him forward. He leans in through the nonexistent driver's side window of the abandoned car, pushes a button, and to his surprise the trunk clicks open. "Imagine that," he says. "German engineering."

He bends and stretches Al Mar's arms over his head. The driver grabs him by the shoes and they lift him up and drop him into what is left of the trunk.

8

Katonah, New York

The Rick Salvado that hired Drew Havens four years ago was a bombastic, megalomaniacal ass, but not a killer.

That Salvado was aggressive and cunning, heartless and demanding. But he demanded as much from himself. He worked long hours—coming in most days before dawn and leaving long after the U.S. markets closed—and he expected the same of his employees. Sure, everyone at The Rising, including Salvado, conceded that he was a publicity whore. Indeed he loved it when, after he named the fund The Rising, the media had a field day, calling him "The Boss" and a number of other bad Springsteen puns. But billions in profits later, after 2008, no one was laughing. After that, when they played Springsteen's song as he took the stage, it was without irony or mockery. Because of his success, coupled with undeniable skills and an addiction to self-promotion, he became a fixture of the Street and a warm, fuzzy mascot for the American business psyche. He was especially appreciated by the sales force charged with championing The Rising's vision to new clients. Havens's pal the rainmaker Tommy Rourke has often said that selling Rick Salvado to the financial world was the easiest job on the Street, even now, as his positions are beginning to be challenged once again. Ultimately Salvado's frequent media appearances are for the good of the fund. And what is good for the fund is good for all of them.

By the time Havens came on board, the $15 billion Rising Fund was already considered "hot," its rankings were rising, and Salvado had already, once again, become quite wealthy. In those days, when Havens was Salvado's fledgling "Quant in the Cave" and Rourke was transforming the new business group, there was camaraderie in the halls. The morning calls were filled with racy jokes, cocky barbs, and confident observations exchanged between analysts, quants, and traders. Often evenings entailed drinks at Cipriani followed by a dinner at the

who programmed the black boxes and dark pools of mega fund

the first time in his adult life Havens was beginning to feel comfortable in social situations. He was happy to tag along.

At first, Miranda was pleased for Havens. They'd been married for just over two years, and while she wasn't thrilled that she was responsible for caring for their young daughter, Erin, she understood and was encouraged by the fact that her husband seemed to be coming out of his shell. Also, within months, Havens's salary had doubled and he was told that if things continued to go well, the big money would come. But while she was pleased by Havens's sudden success, inwardly she was having a hard time with the fact that her shy, socially limited husband was going out on the town three nights a week when he rarely was available to go out with her. Or Erin.

Staring out the train window on the way to Katonah, it occurs to him that the one thing he never considered during his time at The Rising was how exactly Salvado had gotten back in the game after the disastrous fall of his Allegheny Fund. Was it all media bravado and hard work? Or maybe an angel investor? Someone who oversaw his transformation and salvation, and at what price?

He gets off in the dark late night silence of the village of Katonah. This is where Miranda had wanted them all to live after Erin was born and it's where she moved, alone, after they lost her.

Miranda's apartment is two blocks from the train, on the first floor of a large stone house across from the library. He walks past the music shop and the hardware store, stopping in the shade of a maple tree a hundred yards from the house. Her Prius is parked out front, and the best he can tell the building isn't being observed.

A breeze coaxes sidewalk leaves into a lazy spiral. Someone clicks a light off in an apartment on top of the dress shop. At one point before everything changed, Miranda had the three of them come up on the same train that he just got off to look at houses in the village.

He thought it was almost too perfect. Too orderly. Too entitled. He said it felt like a make believe town.

"Just because something happens to be nice," she responded, "doesn't mean it's fake."

This was when they were newly rich and Havens was becoming increasingly troubled. Conflicted. This was after his research and models had confirmed Salvado's hunch, after the markets had validated their bets and the fund had made billions on the U.S. sub-prime housing collapse. The biggest success of his professional life was going to be directly tied to the crushing failure of millions, and unlike his boss he was having a hard time with it. "So quit," Miranda told him during more than one of his prolonged sulks. "We have enough money to keep us happy. You're talented. We'll find something else."

But he knew he'd never find a job like his job at The Rising.

The house that Miranda had taken them to see that day, across the street from her present apartment, a large yellow Victorian with wine red shutters, had gone to foreclosure since the first time they viewed it. What had been a bargain had become a steal because of the collapse he'd predicted and exploited. The last thing Drew Havens wanted at that point in life was a house that was a steal and a constant reminder of the circumstances that led to its acquisition. Everywhere they went, even in posh Westchester, FOR SALE signs dotted the lawns and many homes were flat-out abandoned. Havens had become rich, but he couldn't help but feel responsible for the scores of devalued and deserted homes in this small village, and everywhere.

Back in their Manhattan apartment he continued to sulk. He rededicated himself to his work, but this time his obsession was to find a pattern in the numbers that foretold something good. In theory, this was what Salvado was doing. But Havens's numbers never jibed with

enough to go on the record against Salvado. He asked his friend Rourke what he thought. What did the rainmaker and his clients think about Salvado's rah-rah shtick? They went out to dinner. After Erin died, Rourke had taken it upon himself to take Havens out once a week to talk. "You were a hermit when you got here," Rourke told him. "Unless you fight it, you'll go to a darker cave and never come out." Rourke, to Havens's surprise, agreed with him. He couldn't figure out Salvado either, but he said he was going to give it time. Rourke said he didn't understand Salvado, but he believed in him. "What about you?" Rourke asked. "Are you getting out? Seeing anyone? Happy?"

"Happy," he answered. "Define 'happy.'"

Within a week, despite his misgivings, Miranda had made an offer on the Victorian in Katonah. Twenty-two days before the closing, Erin died. Since then Havens has made a point of blocking many things, but he never allows himself to block out thoughts of Erin. Even the most painful ones make him feel closer to her than none at all.

He sees Miranda through the first floor window from across the street. His ex and always. She is wearing navy blue yoga pants and a sleeveless gray T-shirt, and she looks thinner than the last time he saw her. Already he feels sick to his stomach, filled with anxiety and regret and a wan sort of desire. The same he's felt every time he's seen her since the divorce. There's been no sign of movement from the cars parked along the road outside her place, but it's hard to see inside the cars from this distance. He crosses the street and walks along the sidewalk until he comes to the back wall of Miranda's apartment house. He steps out of the streetlight and into the shadows of a narrow alley that separates the side of a pizza parlor and the five-foot-high stone wall that borders the apartment house. Wide joints in the stone provide sound footholds, and in an instant he is over the wall and standing amid the shoots of the forsythia hedge that rims her backyard. He's tempted to let himself in through the basement hatch, the red steel Bilco doors that he remembers from when he helped her move in, but decides against it. Instead he waits until she appears in her kitchen window. But rather than approach, he watches her a moment more, transfixed and sickened by the sight of the woman he loves going about her life in a world that does not include him.

When he taps on the window, she looks up from the sink, surprised but far from startled. She's been expecting him.

He raises his right forefinger to his lips, then points down with the same finger at the hatch to the basement.

A few moments later one of the steel doors opens. She doesn't speak until he comes down the last step and the hatch closes. She whispers, "How nice of you to finally visit."

Miranda leads. Up the darkened stairs to the edge of her living room. He stands to the side as she closes the curtains facing the street and pulls down the shade in her bedroom. Then she shuts off the kitchen light, the entry hall light, and a torch lamp in the living room.

She turns on the adult contemporary music channel on her TV, Kings of Leon, then stands in front of him, arms crossed, eyes beginning to well with tears. When he reaches out to soothe her she smacks him across the cheek. He stares at her with his hands at his side. "If you're going to tell me anything," she tells him, "then I want to know everything. No half truths or holding back for my benefit. Because once again, this is my life, too."

"Okay," he answers. "What do you know so far?" He sits on an antique couch to the right of the front window, slouches down, and stares at her.

"For starters, I know that someone has murdered Danny Weiss, who apparently discovered incriminating information about the fund.

wouldn't have come here unless you thought

husband, on the run, involved in a global financial conspiracy, least one homicide, sitting in her living room. He tells her about the voice mails, the texts, the photo of the board from Weiss's apartment that he wasn't able to clearly view, and the flash drive, which he tried to access on the train.

When he's finished, Miranda says, "We should go to the police."

"We should. But right now it would end up with me in jail."

"Better than dead."

"Who's to say that won't happen first? It would take no time to show that I'm linked to phone calls to and from Weiss the night he was murdered. I'm sure my prints are in his place. My DNA. I took his hand, Mir. I took his flash drive and climbed down his fire escape. His blood is on my damned clothes! And what do I have on them?"

"The truth?"

"I wish. All I have is a half-baked version of someone else's conspiracy theory that I haven't figured out and don't necessarily believe, that contends that one of America's most supportive and patriotic and beloved investors is somehow reverse gaming the financial markets, messing with some of the most powerful securities on the planet."

"What about Weiss's theory?"

"If I went forward with that as my story, *I'd* arrest me. Then I'd stick me in a mental hospital."

"So what are you going to do, disappear?"

He leans forward and rests his forearms on his thighs. "I'm going to do the thing I know best. I'm a quant. I'm going to put together the pieces—the data, the personal stuff, the global stuff—and figure out what he's up to."

"Then?"

"Then I'm going to bring him down."

"You really think that Salvado is killing people in, where did you say, China?"

"And Weiss hinted at maybe something in Berlin."

"Because?"

"I don't know. But Weiss had a theory, and obviously knew something, and thought something very bad was about to happen, otherwise he'd still be alive."

Miranda rises and walks to his side of the room to straighten a folk art watercolor of an African-American man building a stone wall.

"Weiss and now me, what we did, stumbling upon this stuff at this precise moment, was a fluke."

"You've said it a million times, Drew. There are no flukes in the financial world."

He stares at her. "Danny pointed me here. All I did was doubt the direction the fund had taken. I gave Danny the job of digging deeper. Not with the intention of uncovering some kind of deadly global plot. All I wanted to do was what every middle manager with an ego wants to do."

"What's that?"

"Prove his arrogant boss wrong."

Miranda tilts her head back and squints at a spot on the ceiling. "I don't understand. Why would Danny give you such cryptic notes?"

"It's all he had. If he had answers, he'd have told me. I think he sensed he was in danger and unloaded these clues on me in hopes that I'd figure them out."

"Do you think he knew he was going to die?"

"Not at first. Because I wasn't responding, he used what he had to tease me, because he knew I couldn't resist a puzzle."

She shakes her head.

"What?"

in the morning. "Let's check out the picture he sent you on my monitor. Then let's see what that software's all about."

9

Hong Kong

S obieski meets Detective Mo in the lobby of the Commercial Crime Bureau at HKPD headquarters on Arsenal Street in Wanchai. Michaud asked her to give Mo an update of sorts. Said he was too hungover to have a face-to-face with him. Plus, she thinks, Michaud prefers working from the shadows.

Sobieski doesn't mind. Her flight to Berlin doesn't leave until 4 P.M., and Mo's a good contact for a foreign agent in Hong Kong.

"You drive?"

She shakes her head, looks down at her clothes. She's still in her jogging tights, T-shirt, and shorts. "I walked from our place. Michaud called me in the middle of my morning run. I haven't had a chance to change."

Mo gives her a look. "No complaints here."

"Better me than you in black tights, right?"

Mo has no answer for this. He starts to walk and she follows. "So," he says, "what do you have for me?"

Sobieski looks around. "We were right. Lau was in a celebratory mood for a reason. He moved a ton of paper throughout the day. After sucking for the better part of a year."

Mo leads her into a small, windowless conference room with a round table, four chairs, and a twenty-seven-inch video monitor. "What else?"

She sits in one of the chairs. "Well, as I'm sure you've discovered, he was in deep debt. Credit cards, landlord, the works."

"What security was he moving?"

Sobieski pauses.

Mo tilts his head toward the video monitor. "Let me guess: tech stocks."

"Shorts?"

"A bet that the security will fail."

He scratches his chin. "So Lau and his client are betting, essentially, that technology will fail?"

"Right, at least these particular securities, short-term."

"And that's what it is, right? Betting. Gambling. Only the casino is more dignified."

Sobieski looks at Mo. She's heard the casino analogy dozens of times, but it never fails to unnerve her. "You say more dignified; but a lot of gamblers would beg to differ."

Mo asks, "Anything on the buyer?"

"Not really. Other than the initial request and this other thing that came out of a middle man in Germany."

Mo squints and raises one brow. "What other thing?"

She sighs. Okay, why not? "A second, similar series of puts—different securities but a similar sequence of shorts—middle man also out of Germany. Berlin. Executed by a firm out of Dubai."

"Did they kill the trader there, too?"

"Dubai? No. Not that we can tell."

Mo tries to whistle. "Wow."

"Of course," she says. "We're investigating to see if there's a connection. We're tracking big shorts, serial shorts that add up to big shorts, major movement on any U.S.-based stock, and of course, we're looking to see if any other dead brokers turn up anywhere."

Mo clears his throat. "Why so many trades? Why not one big play?"

"My guess," Sobieski answers, "is it's a form of what we call Smurfing. That's when, if say a terrorist organization is transferring money into the states, or executing some kind of deal they don't want the authorities to know about, they go just under the minimum currency total that shows up on our radar—TFI, Interpol, the FBI. In this case, they did it a lot."

"And got caught anyway," Mo replies. "Why kill the broker?"

"With Lau? My guess is maybe he blabbed in some way and someone didn't like the breach. The risk he posed. Or maybe whoever's behind this doesn't want to even risk the possibility of a leak."

"Seems awfully extreme."

Sobieski half-nods. "Billion-dollar bets are awfully extreme, too."

"So this guy in Dubai, maybe he didn't blab?"

Sobieski thinks. "Sure, maybe."

"But if they know that we know about him, isn't that the same thing? Same exposure? Same risk?"

"*If* they know? Sure. But who's to say anyone knows?"

Mo switches tack: "So, if someone's betting so big on the failure of a security, or securities, what makes them so sure it's going to fail?"

"For starters," Sobieski answers, "for every *put* there has to be someone on the other side of the bet, willing to take it. A market-maker. But with this, either the investor has a hunch, has data that shows that something is likely or inevitable, or they may be intent on gaming the market."

"How so?"

"By breaking the law. Misleading investors. Sabotaging the technology, like the trading software or using some sort of Spyware. Or creating an inciting incident that can make the security or the markets go kerplooey."

"Kerplooey?"

She smiles. "I don't think I need to translate. So what else do *you* have?"

Mo pushes the on button on the monitor, revealing color bars and a monotone. "No match from ballistics, which, as I said, is not a surprise. . . . . in the lobby, the elevators, anywhere. No one even . . . . .

the elevator.

Sobieski leans closer and says, "Doesn't look like they're talking."

Mo shifts his chair toward to the monitor, adjusts his glasses. The footage, maybe seven seconds long, is looped and has started again. "No. I'd say they did not know each other, never saw each other before. One of our guys took a still photo, such as it is, over to the condo. So far no one in the building recognizes him either, which isn't surprising since his head's down and his face is turned away from the camera, a detail that I'm guessing he was aware of."

"Also," Sobieski adds, "notice that he goes out of his way to avoid touching the door."

They watch the two men entering twice more, once in slow motion, before they see the image of the man in the suit exiting the lobby with his head down and facing the other way. "Five minutes and twenty-nine seconds later," Mo observes.

Looks to be about six-foot, she thinks. Anglo. European cut to the suit but hard to tell exactly, or what brand.

On the third pass of the alleged killer's exit from the lobby, Sobieski leans in from the other side of the monitor. "Do me a favor and pause when I tell you." When the man comes closest to the camera, she says, "Now!"

Mo hits fast forward by mistake. Then misses the frame. On the third try he stops on the image she's requested. "Still can't see his face."

"I know," Sobieski says. "I'm looking at his shoulder bag. There's some kind of logo stamped on the leather. Can you zoom?"

Mo surprises even himself by being able to do just that. He racks the image up and to the right and zooms in on the brown leather bag. At a certain point when he gets too close, the image becomes pixilated and breaks up altogether, so he pulls back to the last spot where it's viewable.

"Looks like a drawing of a woman. A goddess or something."

Mo puts on his glasses and steps back to look from a different angle. "Ancient. Some kind of god maybe."

"And . . . is that the letter S in a sort of Greek typeface?"

Mo shrugs. "We'll look. Anything else?"

Sobieski stands staring at the man who took the life of Patrick Lau. She's thinking, What else?, when her phone buzzes. Michaud.

"Yeah?"

"Anything there?"

She steps away from Mo. "Yeah. Sort of. I'll tell you in a bit. What about you?"

"I'm watching Johannesburg. Shorts. Media."

"More media?"

"Yeah. But different. This time new."

"U.S.?"

"Baseball. Hot dogs. New media. American as it gets. Initiated from guess where?"

Sobieski looks at Mo, who is doing a bad job of pretending not to listen. "The birthplace of the Nazi party and my next stop?"

"Exactly. Berlin. Just a different IP address."

"What about the trader?"

"In Johannesburg? It's a woman. Junior player at a medium-sized firm."

Sobieski takes a breath. "Alive?"

"We're checking. That's what I'm waiting to find out."

"Why don't you send me there instead?"

"We're on it. We've already assigned people who are closer than a fourteen-hour flight away."

"Because with Lau, it didn't happen until later that day . . . What time is it in Johannes—"

"Not unless he has perfected the art of time travel, Michael—"

"No way he covers that much ground—Hong Kong, Dubai, Jo'burg—in such a short period of time."

"Any word on the guy in Dubai?"

"Yeah. Not dead, or alive. Now he's missing. No one's seen him for the last four hours."

Sobieski sighs. "Shit. So, Berlin?"

"*Ja-ja wunderbar.* Unless you want to take a wild guess and go wherever in the world they're gonna strike next."

10

I n Miranda's den, they sit looking at a computer monitor on top of a secretary desk. Even blown up on the larger, higher-resolution screen, the symbols on the photo of Weiss's whiteboard are blurred and hard to comprehend. But Miranda click and drags her cursor over the faint images, a digital marker tracing over the curves and lines of the letters and numbers, turning the faint to bold and bringing the letters and numbers to life.

What emerges is a chart of seven boxes, beginning on Saturday and ending on Friday.

In the box for Saturday is the number sequence *12.42-6.*

There are two sequences for Sunday: *MSPH366259* and the words *brotherly to us?*

Under Monday are the numbers *3.340-6* and the word *Tech?*

Under Tuesday, *6.88-90.*

Under Wednesday, *18.55-57*

Thursday, *17.594-9*

Friday's numbers—*9.11*—are accompanied by two exclamation points—*!!*—written in red.

Sloppily scrawled across the middle of the board, overlapping some of the numbers, is this passage: DH—*The gods may love a man, but they can't help him when cold death comes to lay him at his bier.*

DH, Havens thinks. He's talking to me. He's passing this off on me.

When Miranda is done highlighting the faded numbers and letters, Havens says, "I have no idea what to do with these numbers. There's no sequence, no discernible pattern. The only thing I recognize is this"—he points to the box for Saturday—*12.42-6*. Weiss sent me that same note while I was at the club." He pulls out his phone. Miranda leans over while he scrolls through. "First he wrote this: *Wilt* .... *therly to us?* The next was Berlin. *12.42-6*. Then, *Help*

part of the equation." She clicks search and bends ......

words," she continues, "are some of the oldest and most profound ever written. They're from Book Three of *The Odyssey*, by Homer."

He stares at the words, then back at her, but she's typing again: "Wilt thou not be brotherly to us?" She clicks, then taps at the onscreen result and nods. "Odysseus."

Havens straightens up and closes his eyes.

She asks, "What was the number he wrote after he texted *Help?*"

With eyes still closed, he recites, "*3.338-9.*" She types. "Yup. Book Three, Lines 338 to 339." They both look at the other numbers on the chart. Then, "What's the other one that he sent you, from Saturday?"

"*12.42-46*," he answers, again without having to look at the chart or his texts.

She types, then waits. "This may not be totally accurate line for line, because there are a million versions of this, based upon the Latin and Greek translations, but the books and the general section should be close. Here:

Square in your ship's path are Seirenes, crying
Beauty to bewitch men coasting by . . .

He stares at the words. No answer for this. He thinks. "Type in this, *'Murder at Hang Seng.'* "

"Please," she says, an old issue between them.

"Yes, *please*. *"Murder at Hang Seng.'* "

Within seconds they find several news service accounts of Hang Seng trader Patrick Lau's death, but little else. After a moment he hands over the flash drive and says, "It's Danny's software. God knows how or why he got it. Let's search Lau and Hang Seng on this."

She looks at him.

"Pretty please."

Within minutes they're accessing Lau's private e-mail accounts as well as all of his accounts at Hang Seng. Havens instantly recognizes the connection between the stocks that Lau moved and the holdings in the Rising Fund. Also, this: "Berlin," which leads him to Siren Securities.

After they hack into Siren, they discover the transactions involving new media stocks out of Dubai and, this morning, old media out of Johannesburg. All through Siren, all mirroring the holdings of the Rising Fund.

"Whoever's doing these plays," Havens marvels, "it's as if they read my mind, playing the opposite—total shorts—to Salvado's longs."

"So that's a link?"

"More like an anti-link."

Miranda grunts. "Why would he publicly bet his career that something is going to be a major success and then privately bet that it will fail?"

Havens chews his lip. "Not just fail. Epic fail. For starters, if these plays do happen to fail, the people who hold the shorts stand to make much more money than those who have the much safer play on their success—including anyone associated with The Rising. The odds against this type of failure are much greater and the payoff that much higher."

"Yet, hypothetically, he holds both positions."

"One that he wants the world to know about and the other that he'd apparently kill to keep secret."

"How does he know that they will fail?"

"I'm not sure. Nothing indicates that any of those companies or plays is in any kind of trouble. Me, I wouldn't go heavily into any of ⟨...⟩ other, but especially short."

⟨...⟩ "What if," she begins, "Sal-

⟨...⟩

kind of action,⟩

Havens nods. "This, essentially, is ⟨...⟩ way that Al-Qaeda supposedly gamed the market with twenty ⟨...⟩ trades prior to 9/11, Weiss felt that Salvado was going to game it. *'This time: 7 Trades. Not 28.'* His last message to me."

"Which would imply that there's another four trades to come, and maybe four more killings to go with them."

"Right," Havens says. "But which trades, which traders, where, and what 'event' do they ramp up to?"

"And the reason that you think these transactions and these murders are happening in different countries is to dilute the focus and make them harder to link and track?"

Havens nods again, then something occurs to him. "So far he's made these trades in three separate countries, right? Each with some kind of link to Germany. Berlin, which Weiss mentioned in his last text."

Miranda squints, shakes her head less than an inch each way. She's not making the connection. "And the fact that they're all American assets, that's what the Salvado connection is all about?"

"Yeah. But no. What I mean is, because they're almost all U.S.-based, even if the market is being made overseas, they have to somehow be linked to an American trading account, opened by a genuine American human with a Social Security number and, in theory, a traceable name and address."

"I'm sorry, but I still don't get it. Why go to these extremes? Why do it at all? Why would a man worth, what, billions, risk everything to do something so criminal and horrible?"

Havens shrugs. He agrees. It makes no sense.

For another hour they look at the cryptic numbers and letters of Danny Weiss's whiteboard. They look up passages from various editions of *The Odyssey*, but no airtight narrative emerges. No absolute explanation of what was and what's next.

After one extended silence Havens points at the on-screen photo and asks, "Can you print me a few copies of this to take with me?"

"Sure. But where are you going?"

"Back to the city."

"Drew. There's not another train for hours. Why don't you get some rest?"

He stares at the closed blinds, then he sees for the first time the picture on the end table across the room. In it he's sleeping in a beach chair near the ocean's edge in Montauk and Erin is sleeping with her arms wrapped around him and her head on his chest. Best and worst picture ever.

She follows his eyes to the photo. When she looks back, she sees that his eyes are closed and that his hands are trembling. Her right hand reaches out, floats away from her almost involuntarily, and rests on top of his. She stands. Still holding one of his hands, she grabs the other, and whispers, "I want to help."

He shakes his head. A truck rumbles past. Its diesel churn rattles the windows. "I shouldn't have come. You're right. I came out of selfishness. Because I needed to . . . because I needed."

She pulls, coaxes him to rise.

"Did you ever think it was because of the money? That if we had rejected it . . ."

"It wouldn't have prevented anything."

"So many good people lost so much while we . . . It's as if . . ."

She shakes her head with conviction.

"If anything else happens to you, Mir, because of me . . ."

"Drew. Stop. Please stop."

Standing, knees weak, hands still shaking in the warmth of hers, he looks at Miranda, the only woman he's ever loved, the mother of his _____ _____ wife, and he thinks about their

sentment. Hate. ___ emotions and memories of a marriage, from when he first ___ waiting in the rain under the entrance to the Astor Place subway stop, a shy grade school English teacher in ripped jeans, with auburn hair covered by an Irish wool cap, studying for her master's at night at NYU, to the recently wealthy former grade school teacher turned not-for-profit board member with impeccable blond processed hair, wearing a two-thousand-dollar pantsuit, punching him in the chest on the sidewalk outside the hospital that night.

She kisses him while his eyes are still closed. He pulls her tight against him and she digs her fingers into his back. She cries as she kisses and claws at him, at once punishing and rewarding, resenting and caressing.

They stumble into her room and make a different kind of love, flawed and broken, bleak and raw, regretting it before it happens and while it happens, yet not being able to control themselves, and not wanting it to end. Amazed that something so primal and desperate once produced a thing as beautiful as a child.

11

Johannesburg

S awa Luhabe has an hour.

The second-year broker at Rosehall Fund Managers, a private equity firm conveniently located across from the Johannesburg Stock Exchange, taps on the wheel of her nine-year-old Toyota Celica, waiting for a light to change. Every day, while her partners sneak out to grab lunch in some upscale Sandton eatery, Luhabe hustles to her car and drives the eight kilometers back to her flat in Alexandra (Alex) township all, traffic permitting, to spend a precious half hour with her three-year-old daughter.

When she first started at Rosehall, one of Johannesburg's oldest and most respected firms, Luhabe's coworkers laughed at her for being in such a rush to leave the most affluent section of the city to visit one of its most impoverished and dangerous townships. In fact, they didn't understand why Luhabe still lived in Alex at all.

But they weren't black, female, and single. They hadn't grown up in a shantytown or had to scratch and hustle their way out of an over-crowded grammar school to a university scholarship. They hadn't worked forty-hour weeks and a series of unpaid internships at banks and brokerage houses while taking a full course load. And they had never met her daughter, Wendy. Sure, it would be easy to get a fancy condo in Sandton, and if her fortunes at the fund continue to rise, it won't be a problem at all. But still, it would be an extravagance, and in many ways a betrayal.

She is torn. She wants her girl to grow up and appreciate the heritage and culture of Alexandra, and of her family, but she doesn't want her to fall in with the wrong crowd, or worse, to die young, a victim of senseless street violence, as have so many of Luhabe's friends and extended family in Alexandra. Including her father, her brother, and

one or something will pull it all

the money. The future. Not an uncommon fear, she knows, for someone raised in a shack without a father, and whose husband was gunned down in the street three months after her wedding.

The light changes and the landscape transforms in a rush. One minute she's passing the exclusive stores and restaurants of Nelson Mandela Square, and the next she's making sure the windows are up and the door locks are down as she rolls through the crowded, trash-cluttered streets of Alex.

Plastic bags dangle from high wires like prayer flags. Men drinking home-brewed *umqombothi*, a traditional African beer, sit in front of tin-roofed squatter shanties, glaring until they see the color of her face. Then, unless they recognize her, their eyes shine with a different manner of resentment.

Luhabe is oblivious to any threat. For starters, it's daylight, and she's been passing through these neighborhoods as long as she can remember. It's not as dangerous as it would be if say, she happened to be a white, drug-seeking stock broker visiting Alex after dark.

Normally she'd be anxious, but her Tuesday morning has been better than good. After the 8 A.M. call with the analysts, she spent the rest of the morning dealing with a money manager in Berlin representing an American client who was taking a number of short positions, each chopped into almost a thousand micro-transactions, all on American new media stocks. She's never heard of some of the stocks, but then again just a couple of years ago she'd never heard of YouTube or Facebook or foursquare. Regardless, once she gets back to the office, once she checks on the progress of the ongoing transactions, she plans on looking into the numbers of the companies in play, the philosophy behind the mystery client's picks, if not the mystery client himself. Despite the fact that the client requested that she not tell anyone about the moves, she feels obligated to look into them. She's worked too hard to get here to have it all blow up over one client, no matter how wealthy he appears to be.

Plus, for Luhabe, every number tells a story, every transaction changes a life, and every moment is a new opportunity to learn.

She notices the white van trailing her when she's within ten blocks of her house. Six blocks later, she follows her instincts and takes an abrupt left without using her signal. A peek in the mirror reveals the van breaking hard and making the same sharp left. Luhabe's been followed before and robbed before, more times than she cares to remember. But never in the daylight, at lunchtime. Still, she knows that something is dangerous and odd about this van—perhaps they targeted her as a money mark coming out of Sandton?—so she responds accordingly.

At the next stop sign she taps the brakes, then races forward through another stop sign before swerving to the left. She's already decided that she won't go home for lunch this afternoon. In part because she was running late to begin with, but mostly because she'd never lead whomever this is anywhere near her home. She'll call and let her mother know not to expect her as soon as she's able to break away from the van, when she's back on safer streets.

Before her wedding, when she first started working in Sandton, her husband-to-be bought her a gun. She doesn't know what kind. Some kind of pistol. He wanted her to be able to protect herself. She responded with a tantrum, said that she would not carry a gun to work, and would not abide a gun in her house. He promised he'd take it back to the person from whom he'd bought it. But one day after his death, she found it in a bag with his soccer gear in their closet. Where it wasn't going to do her very much good at this moment.

She glances in the rearview and sees the van dropping back. Stop- ... another turn, a right down a street whose ...

will believe this ...

in Alex, so why bother mentioning it to any of them?

Mom will be worried, she thinks. And Wendy will be disappointed. She wanted to perform a dance she's been practicing. Luhabe leans across the passenger seat, reaching for her mobile with one eye trained on the light. Of course she won't mention the van to them, either. She'll simply tell them that she got caught up in the machinations of one of the biggest transactions of her career, which is true. And that perhaps as a result they'd soon be able to take a long weekend to visit Cape Town, or the relatives in Swaziland. It's been too long since she's taken them on vacation.

She's still reaching for her phone when she sees the young man in the black woolen mask rounding the corner on the passenger side of the car. She knows instantly, before he locks in on her car, that the shooter is coming for her. As he drops into a firing stance, Luhabe rams her foot down onto the accelerator. Stretched halfway across the front seat, she drives blind, from memory, for her life.

Sawa Luhabe's Toyota makes its way into the center of the intersection before the shooter locks in on his target and squeezes off a seventy-nine-bullet burst from a Tec-9 pistol on full-auto discharge.

The seemingly driverless car careers through the intersection and manages to swerve to the left onto a side street before crashing to a stop in a pile of bagged sidewalk trash. Smoke hisses from underneath the crumpled hood. Nothing else moves.

The gunman stares across the street at the silenced car for a moment, takes a half step toward it, then changes his mind. He lowers the pistol, turns, and runs back down the street from which he appeared.

Seconds later a young man on a fat-tired bicycle rolls to a stop alongside Luhabe's car, leans to look inside the front seat, then continues on. He's just curious, interested in neither the fate of the driver nor the gunman. In Alexandra, one of the worst townships in a country where more than fifty people are murdered every twenty-four hours, the scene is not out of the ordinary.

12

nize it, and decides to re furnished apartment, staring out its lone window at the stalls of Stanley Market. Five seconds after the phone stops ringing, it starts again. Same number. What the hell.

"Who is this?"

"This is your friend on the barge." She turns her back to the window and closes her eyes. Cheung.

"How'd you get—"

"How do you think? You think TFI has all the surveillance toys?"

She doesn't answer. "What?"

"Your information was not exactly proprietary. Not particularly exclusive or at all valuable."

"I see."

"In fact, I look rather foolish now, after attempting to pass this off as some kind of inside—"

"We shouldn't be discussing this. I can come—"

"No," Cheung says with force. "You will not come anywhere near here until you have something substantial. And if you don't, by the end of the week we will come to you."

"I can't do it. I'll find a way. I can't compromise myself like this."

"Too late," he answers. "You already have. On tape."

After Cheung hangs up, Sobieski turns and looks at her leather duffel, packed for Berlin, and at her computer screen, tracking the latest activity initiated by Siren in Berlin and going down in Johannesburg.

13

overpass humped up in the middle from the impact of the sheet metal of the front and rear passenger-side doors is punctured by dozens of bullet holes. The passenger windows on both sides of the car are gone, reduced to scattered blue shards on the faded seats and floor mats.

Luhabe gets out and takes inventory of her trembling body. Nothing. Then she walks to the passenger side and gasps when she sees the damage. She looks around. Cars zip past on the highway overhead. Garbage is piled against the concrete abutment, plastic bags and newspapers pressed against a chain link fence whisper in the breeze.

You still can die, she thinks. They still can kill you. She gets back in the car, which she was afraid to turn off because who knows how much longer it will last, and shifts into reverse.

Common sense tells her to drive directly to the office in Sandton, but her street instincts tell her otherwise.

She surges backward, then jerks the gearshift into drive and heads toward the streets of Alex. Back toward her house. That was not a robbery, she assures herself. That was a hit. And unless it was mistaken identity, it had to do with work. The call this morning. The client. The odd and specific set of rules. You should have known, she tells herself. Anything that easy can't be good. Anything that good can't be true.

This you, of all people, should know.

En route, she calls her office. "Hello, Lucy, it's Sawa. Have I had any calls?"

Her admin, a cheery young woman from Soweto, says, "Oh, yes, Miss Luhabe. One from your mother, who wants to know if she should still expect you. One from, believe it or not, a man in the United States. One from a man in Hong Kong and at least three from Berlin. Twice in the last five minutes."

"What did he want?"

"To know if you'd returned yet."

"Listen," Luhabe says. "If anyone else calls . . . anyone . . . do not tell them whether I've returned or have called. Tell them you don't know where I am, that you just answer the phone."

"Is everything all right, Miss Luhabe?"

"Yes. There's been . . . Some unexpected things have come up today, and I'm going to have to take some time to address them . . ."

"Yes."

"So I'm not going to be coming back to the office this afternoon, and perhaps tomorrow, as well."

She parks a half block down the street from her house and walks through a maze of narrow alleys in order to enter her lot from the back. Clean clothes hang from a nylon line stretched from the back wall of her house to a metal post in the center of the yard. A well-tended patch of vegetables—carrots and broccoli and tomatoes—runs along the length of the concrete wall that separates her house from the neighbors. She climbs the back steps and gently opens the kitchen door.

"It's about time," her mother says as she enters the kitchen. "That child has been waiting for you all day."

"Mother," Luhabe responds. "I need you to pay attention. We have to leave. Someone just tried to kill me on the way here and I believe they'll be back soon to try again."

"Jesus, girl. What have you gotten yourself involved in?"

"I haven't . . ."

"This related to your brother? Because he—"

Luhabe raises her voice. "Mother! I don't know!"

"Who, then?"

"I don't know. It was a few blocks from here. They shot at me and _____ think I'm wounded, or heading back to

To the cou___

"Cousins?"

"Yes. To your nieces and nephews back home in Swaziland. We should be safe there. And Mother . . ."

"Yes?"

"Do you remember when Tau brought home the gun ? The fight we had over it?"

Her mother nods. "What of it?"

Luhabe looks down. Her daughter calls her name from the next room. "Do we still have it?"

Her mother nods.

"Then I would like you to pack it as well."

WEDNESDAY,

1

tower that has been his life for the past four years. ... . g
Salvado, thinking about Erin and Miranda and Danny Weiss's last
seconds on earth.

Help . . .

This time: 7 Trades. Not 28.

Brotherly . . .

DH . . .

Before he left Miranda's apartment, he kissed her on the lips and left
a note on her kitchen table. The note contained the protocol for future
communication, a promise to make her happy, and a declaration of
love.

Two years ago Salvado moved The Rising's offices up from Wall
Street to a location just north of Ground Zero, into 7 World Trade
Center, the last tower to fall and the first to rise again. As if the name of
the fund wasn't heavy handed enough. The media covered the move
as if it was a great act of patriotism, reinforcing his great American
comeback investment ideology.

Sipping a cup of tea with trembling hands, he counts up to the twentieth floor, one of five occupied by The Rising and the location of Rick Salvado's executive suite. Although it's not yet 7 A.M., Havens knows that Salvado is inside. Salvado does all of his live TV remotes in a corner of his private conference room, in front of a window overlooking the Hudson, and this morning was no different. The omnipresent American flag on the stand behind Salvado's right shoulder and the bronze corporate logo, of a rising arrow with an American flag at its tip, mounted on the wall behind it was the clear giveaway. Usually for that type of gig it's just a producer and a cameraman, with questions coming from a talking head in a studio in Secaucus, or midtown, or CNN headquarters in Atlanta. Havens knows because after the sub-prime meltdown, he was often on camera alongside Salvado in that very conference room. Heroes of the disaster. Two of the few who got it right.

The lobby security guard looks up when he enters, waves as he passes holding his ID card face high. Instead of scanning his card at one of the turnstiles, he goes to the side gate, pointing to his shoulder and duffel bag. The guard nods and buzzes him through, undetected.

He gets off the elevator on twenty and stands in front of the glass doors that lead to the quant cubes. The receptionist's desk on the other side is empty and will remain that way for another hour. To gain access he has to punch in his personal password, but he knows that any activity involving his identity will alert security if they are looking for him.

He uses Danny Weiss's password instead and it works. In security's eyes, Havens was more dead than Weiss.

He walks down the hall to the right, past the vacant receptionist desk and the small kitchen area. He stops at Weiss's former cube space, which has been pillaged. His desktop computer is gone, replaced by an altogether different machine, and his filing cabinet is empty but for three empty green hanging folders. The fabric-covered cube wall has been stripped of Weiss's random photos and news clippings, mostly pertaining to family and Weiss's young friends. The only remaining evidence pinned to the cube wall is a pocket schedule for his beloved New

York Mets, whose season ended without fanfare two weeks before Weiss's life.

Havens removes the schedule and considers it. It's devoid of writing except for one mark. In the box for Friday, October 21, there's a set of red exclamation points, just as there was on the whiteboard in his apartment. Havens folds up the schedule and slips it into his pocket.

Back inside the elevator, as he stares at the panel of buttons, he can't help himself. He presses 21.

trements of massive wealth, curated to impress the

That's right, it's a real Siberian tiger skin. Yes, that is indeed Lady Gaga staring at Salvado as if *he* is the star, the sparkling pagan godlike figure of the moment that has captured the public's morbid fascination. Pics of Salvado with Kobe-Clooney-Gates-Greenspan-and-Sully, the hero pilot of the Hudson, hugging, hand-shaking, backslapping, uniformly framed and mounted on the Wall of Fawning Stars? Check.

Many months later Salvado told Havens that some wealthy people buy the time of stars to show that they, too, are stars, but he himself did it because, by buying them, by having them perform, for instance, at his wife's fortieth birthday or the end-of-year bonus party, he reduced their glow in the firmament; no matter how outlandish the price tag, it demonstrated that they could be bought, and that he was one of the few people on earth who could afford them.

Havens stops on the Moroccan tile in front of Salvado's refrigerator-sized humidor and thinks of the first Cuban, the Cohiba Behike they smoked in this very office, toasting the future: the Rising Fund's future;

America's future; Havens's future. "If you are as good as they tell me you are, we will do very well together. You will make your killing."

That night, back at their apartment, when he told Miranda about the interview, she couldn't believe it. "But you hate cigars," she responded.

"I know," he answered. "But, you know, this was different."

On the wall in the main lounge across from Salvado's desk twelve high-def video monitors are silently playing. Nikkei, London, NASDAQ, NYSE, Hong Kong, Berlin. There's one for Salvado's spotlight plays, one for CNN, one for Reuters, one for MSNBC. The last one is a wild card, chosen to fit the mood, the moment, or a desired effect it will have on visitors. For instance, one day earlier this year Salvado summoned a trader who had been having a bad run and fired him while German S&M porn was looped on the wild card monitor. Later, when word trickled back to Havens, he wasn't surprised. Salvado's behavior had become increasingly boorish, especially toward underperformers. The incident made him think of something Salvado had told him soon after he joined the firm: Reputations are built upon anecdotes, but legends are made of stories.

Havens stops in front of Salvado's gleaming onyx desk and stares at the empty chair. From this desk Salvado oversees more than two hundred analysts, traders, and managers, each of whom is acutely aware of the firm's mantra: Be great or be gone. Also known as: Produce or vanish. Or: Get rich or get lost. At this desk Salvado often sits in front of a video camera and broadcasts a constant stream of obscenity-laced visual and audio commentary to his traders. While his trades once accounted for more than 50 percent of the Rising Fund's profits, they now represent less than 20, though on any given day he may follow a hunch and make more than 75 percent of the firm's moves.

However, to the public, the Rising Fund is still all about Rick Salvado.

Behind the desk is a framed LeRoy Nieman watercolor of Salvado riding a monster wave on a short board. It's this image that was on the front of the fund's latest quarterly letter. Despite Salvado's being enormously popular and increasingly pro-American in his recent investment philosophy, the fund was underperforming. Havens believes he used the surfer image to remind the fund's increasingly skittish clientele that this was the man who had made them so many millions these last ten years not just by looking at the horizon, but by riding the top of a wave and looking past it.

The significantly thinner boy-genius rogue Stanford dropout in faded board shorts, the renegade Big Kahuna who could see the way markets lined up and played out the same way he could read distant sets of waves, knowing what to ride and what to let pass.

"You've got a bigger set than I gave you credit for." Salvado out of the bathroom in a shirt and tie and a pair of boxers. Sometimes he works without pants in the morning, even during his TV remotes, because he doesn't want to wrinkle them for personal appearances later in the day. Sometimes, if the markets are cooperating, he'll go an entire trading session without pants.

Havens takes two steps forward. "Not really. I figure you're too smart to try something here. Here, you just screw people. Outside you kill 'em."

Salvado shakes his head. "What do you want?"

"The other night, in between talking to bimbos and suckers, you told me to come stop by so you could give me a more explicit rationale for the direction the fund is headed."

"How'd you get in?"

Havens stands between Salvado and the panic button that's mounted beneath his desktop. "A ghost let me in."

Salvado frowns. "You're in some deep shit, my friend."

"Not as much as Danny Weiss, right, Rick?"

Salvado doesn't respond, so Havens continues. "You remember Danny Weiss. Twenty-six years old. Idealistic. Geeky. Always smiling. Came from a good family, Rick, good parents, a kid brother and three sisters who will never see him again."

"I know who he is. People are looking for you. I could have you arrested right now."

"For what?"

Salvado stares at him.

"You won't have me arrested because it would reflect poorly upon the fund. You don't want Danny Weiss's blood on you."

"Blood on *my* hands? What about you?"

"This is true. Anyone who's worked for you, or who's made money because of you, knowing how you did it, what you're capable of, their hands are covered in it, too."

"You know, you were a freak. A social disaster. A quant in a hole when I discovered you."

"Rourke discovered me."

Salvado waves him off. "Rourke—hah! I made you rich and you do this?"

Havens steps forward. It's work for him to get the words out. "I *was* different, you never let me forget that. But at least I could live with myself then."

"This is not a pretty business. You know how it works. For every winner there is always a loser."

"Is that what Danny was, a market loser? Another victim of bad economic times?"

"I don't know what kind of deal you had with Weiss, but he broke every rule we have. He abused his privileges and committed a series of criminal improprieties. Because he's dead I've chosen not to report him to the SEC, to pursue prosecution."

"He broke corporate policy, so why not kill him, right?"

Salvado rolls his neck. "Jesus. You're crazier than I thought."

"No one deserves what happened to him. Except maybe you."

"Calm yourself, Drew. Why are you here? To blame me for what your life has become? Shoot me? Make a citizen's arrest? Because frankly I don't understand the motivation. I know, since I'm not part of a mathematical equation, some complex algorithm, it must be difficult for you. Dealing with living, breathing human beings and all, but I've got a company to run." Salvado takes a step toward his desk, but Havens steps toward him.

"Tell me," Havens asks, inching closer. "Why are you doing this? It makes no sense."

you're running this fund into the ground.

"And you know better than anyone that a theory is nothing unless it is supported by numbers. Quantifiable, hard data."

"It's coming. All kinds of data. You know how I get when I lock in on something, the quant in the cave, right, Rick?"

Salvado pinches the bridge of his nose with a thumb and forefinger, monitoring a pressure valve. "Listen, I'll give you one more chance to . . . extricate yourself from this . . . scenario. Because you're right: I can't afford to attract undo attention to the firm. So what I'll do, if you're willing to cooperate, and by cooperate I mean go the fuck away, I will try to fix this. I can extricate you and make this extremely, mind-blowingly lucrative for you, too."

Havens clenches his fists, incredulous. "You piece of shit. I have a hard enough time living with myself over the supposedly legal things we've done in the past, but gaming the market, killing—"

"Gaming the market? My God. Who doesn't? Isn't that our job? Isn't that what we did last time, the time that made you rich?"

Havens shakes his head. "You mean the time we identified a flaw in the system and did everything in our power to put the fund in a position to capitalize on the misfortune of—"

"Please."

"When we chose to exploit the situation rather than diffuse it?"

Salvado steps back, then slides a hand down his hip, reaching for a pocket that isn't there. "Don't you think the imbeciles and criminals at the other firms would have done the same if they knew what we did? If they hadn't been so dumb? Don't you think the average Joe investor with five mortgages on his piece-of-shit house who then cried foul when it all came crashing down, don't you think he would've gone all in if he saw what we saw? If he would have known what was there for the taking?"

"It was wrong."

"Even if we told them—the feds, the ratings douche bags, the brokerages, the banks—they wouldn't have understood, and if by some fluke one of them did understand, he'd look the other way, or blame the Internet. The black boxes."

"The black boxes don't make moral decisions. We do. Why," Havens presses, "why are you taking shorts that are the opposite of your own fund's?"

"I have no idea what you're talking about."

"Why tech? Why new media? What do you know about what's coming?"

Salvado answers as if reading from a textbook: "A hedge fund is an investment typically open to a limited number of professional or high-income investors. Hedge funds often seek to hedge investment risk using a variety of methods or strategies that are often the proprietary and covert inclinations of the fund manager—"

Havens interrupts, "Why are you zeroing in on a specific set of American-based securities, and why are you killing the person who executes the trade?"

Salvado, attempting to ignore him, continues reading from the imaginary text: "Most hedge funds are exempt from many regulations that govern ordinary investment funds—"

"Why now? Why do something like this when, my God, Rick, you're rich beyond your dreams. If you don't need to kill people for money, then what?"

Salvado glares at him. "Who the hell are you? I'm the manager and CEO of one of the best-performing hedge funds of the twenty-first century, the Rising Fund. Beloved by the media, the politicians. Within a ___ ___ ___ this thing alone in my apartment in

shoves him back into the corner near the window. To the west dark clouds press down on the Hudson; beneath them giant machines sit idle on the earth of Ground Zero. "Where is this going, you son of a bitch?"

Salvado is unfazed: "In addition to making money," he continues, narrowing his eyes, smirking, "one of the fund manager's most important responsibilities is to mitigate, or hedge, risk and minimize losses."

"Danny Weiss was your hedge?"

"Forget Weiss. He was looking into things that can get a person killed. Things you seem to know more about than me."

Havens shoves himself away from Salvado, then cocks his right hand back in a fist.

From behind Havens, at the entrance to the room back near the humidor, comes a woman's voice. "Rick?" Salvado's executive assistant, Roxanne. "Everything all right in here?"

Salvado, trembling, nods. "We're fine, Roxy. Drew was just about to leave."

Havens looks at Roxanne, then back at Salvado. Roxanne half smiles, turns, and walks away. She knows something's wrong but knows enough from past experience not to question Salvado.

"Now you listen," Salvado says, regaining his bravado. "I suggest you leave and forget you ever worked here. Last chance: We can make the last few days go away and attribute your departure to a growing fundamental difference in our investment philosophies. Personal problems, and God knows you've been through a lot. You will receive a generous severance, your full bonus, and my wholehearted endorsement. But remember, there is nothing you can do to me, no way to substantiate or prove anything."

"We'll see."

"But if you try and by some fluke survive, I promise you will be the one to go away. And not to prison. I know people, at every level. People who believe in my fund and my vision."

"Your lies."

"That's subjective."

"What's gonna happen Friday?"

Salvado shakes his head. No idea. "You think you're gonna tell people about some crazy theory and the world is gonna listen to a freak like you and take action? They'd never believe you, even if by some fluke you're right, because investors never want to hear a negative truth. They never want to think that something so horrible could happen to them."

"Despite the fact that it does, every day." Havens takes three backward steps toward the door.

"Remember, you are no one. And nobody listens to no ones."

"When confronted with an overwhelmingly convincing body of evidence, they will."

"You do not know what kind of shit storm is coming your way, son."

"Weiss is dead, but he left a nice bread-crumb trail. I'm going to break down every last crumb and follow that trail right back to where you live."

Back on the elevator, heart drumming triple time against his rib cage, blood thumping in his ears like a subwoofer. He rushes out at the lobby level, past the preoccupied guard at the security desk, and back onto the street. Walking south toward the pit, toward Ground Zero, he looks up and sees his friend the rainmaker Tommy Rourke approaching, on

"It wasn't random. His murder was planned."

"What?"

"Salvado had him killed because he knew something, Tom. He . . ."

"Rick? Come on, Drew. The guy's a piece of shit, but he's no killer. Why would . . ."

"Weiss knew something about the fund. The crazy direction it's going. I put him up to it, Tom, and now he's gone."

Rourke raises his eyebrows. "What are you talking about? You sound and look like a paranoid crazy person."

"That's what I told Weiss when he tried to convince me. I didn't want to listen. Didn't believe him, but, Tommy, he *found* things."

"Like what?"

"I'm not sure, but obviously he hit a nerve."

"Shady plays are one thing, Drew, but killing?"

"I was there, Tommy. I found him when the killer was still in the apartment."

"Jesus."

"He cut his throat and left him bleeding out."

"Who?"

"Laslow. Salvado's pimp from the club, the bald guy from Elysian."

"Listen, Drew. You've been through a lot, there's no denying that, but what you're asking me to believe . . ."

"I'm not asking you, Tom. I realize no one will believe it until I prove it."

"Why don't you just go to the police and tell them what you know? Wouldn't that be best?"

Havens thinks. If it weren't for Rourke, after Erin's death, after his divorce, he doesn't know if he'd have made it. Besides Miranda, Rourke was the only one to check in on him after the funeral, the only one with the compassion to understand the link between the demands of his job, the death of his only child, and the end of his marriage. But he's thought this through. "Look, no one's been there for me like you, Tom. From everything that happened with my family to telling people to lay off the Rain Man jokes when I started. But if I go to the police without having this thing figured out, they will lock me up. A socially inept, divorced quant with a chip on his shoulder taking on an American icon. Within twenty-four hours Salvado will fix everything so that it all lands on top of me."

Rourke exhales. "Jesus. You okay?"

"I'm not okay. I'm scared shitless."

"Listen." Rourke takes a breath, tries to think. "Why don't we grab a cup of coffee and talk? I'm sure there's something we . . ."

Havens shakes his head. "Trust me, I've thought this through. Every model ends with me in jail. I don't expect you to believe me, Tommy, and I don't blame you for thinking I'm nuts."

"I don't think you're—"

"I mean," Havens interrupts, "after Erin, after Miranda . . ."

Rourke shakes his head. No need to go there. "So what can I do?"

"You've helped me enough."

"And you've helped me plenty over the years. So what?"

Havens considers his friend, then hugs him. "You can keep an eye on Salvado for me. Let me know if he does something radical."

"Done. Where you going now?"

"To a cave. To figure this shit out."

2

Hong Kong/Berlin

Flying commercial makes her feel half-human.

At one point this afternoon Michaud had tried convince Sobieski to hop on a military transport, but she talked him out of it. In theory it would get her into Germany two hours sooner, but she also knew the shorter flight time would entail being strapped into the back of a cargo plane or some speed-of-sound fighter while clutching a barf bag. She begged for commercial, got bumped up to business, is thrilled to see that it's almost empty.

She sips Sauvignon Blanc and skims the American finance rags. She opens a novel—When was the last time I read a novel?—about a fierce and seemingly senseless battle for a hill in Vietnam. She read that it took the author, a Vietnam veteran, more than thirty years to come to terms with it, to get his story right. She loves the story, rips through it the same way she attacks a training session, a case, a poker table, or anything that interests her: all in and all out. But what interests her most is the story that isn't in the book, the story of the man who wrote it.

What compels a person to dedicate his decades to the fictional recreation of a life-changing moment? Is it the hope that the end result will change things back to the way they were, or at least to something better? Or is it all about trying to make sense of the random brutality of the world?

Four hours later, when she finishes the last sentence, she closes the book and looks out at a cloud-scrimmed quarter moon, somewhere over mainland China.

"How was it?"

She looks at the smiling man in the next seat. When he sat just before takeoff, they exchanged the curt hellos of two people who'd prefer not to be bothered. Each soon got lost in a cache of carry-on media. "The book. You're pretty much devouring it."

"I started it twice at home but got nowhere before today. It's pretty compelling."

"You know," the man offers, "it took the author more than thirty years to complete the story."

Sobieski stares at the man. "You read it?"

"No. But I own it and have read about it. It's near the top of my interesting to talk about but never been read stack."

Now she smiles. "I have one of those."

"I have to admit, it's the thirty-years-to-complete part, more than the great-war-novel part, that fascinated me."

A flight attendant pauses in the aisle with a tray of warm chocolate chip cookies. They each take one. Can't get these on a C-130, Sobieski thinks. Or him. "Well," she says. "We've got about four more hours until we get to Berlin. You're more than welcome to read it."

He looks at the laptop on his tray table. "You know what, why not?" He holds out his hand and she gives him the paperback. "I'll read fast and we can have an impromptu book group, let's say in three and a half hours, thirty-seven thousand feet above western Kazakhstan."

She smiles. "Deal."

For an hour she sleeps. When she wakes up, she sees that he's well into the book. Perhaps 175 pages. She thinks of what happens at that point in the story and wonders what he thinks of it.

Sensing her gaze, he closes the book. "Amazing. I mean, I've never been to war; I'm a collectibles dealer, so I can't even imagine what it must have been like there. Firefights. Death. Fear. Bravery. The way it must change the way you look at everything when it's over."

"My dad was in Vietnam," Sobieski offers.

"Really? Mine, too."

"Mine's not around, and never spoke about his experience there, but I can understand why."

He takes a sip of bottled water and swallows before responding. "I bet your dad did some special stuff."

She tilts her head. "Why?"

"Because he never spoke about it. Isn't that how it goes, the real heroes never talk about it? My dad . . . man. I mean the guy never shut up about 'the Nam.' His stories got to the point where I began to doubt if he ever made it out of the States."

"You never know," Sobieski replies. "Maybe mine didn't talk because he had something to hide. Everyone processes conflict differently. "

The man holds the book out to her. "Here. Listen, I'm a fast reader. But not 622 pages fast."

She waves him off. "Keep it. Unless your copy's in Berlin. We'll have the book club another time."

He pulls it back. "That's kind of you." He holds out his hand. "Marco."

Sobieski shakes his hand. "Cara."

She sits up, anticipating that the conversation is about to become more intimate. But after releasing her hand, he reaches back into his carry-on for a folder and prepares to get back to work.

Sobieski tilts her head back and closes her eyes. The one time she wouldn't mind a guy getting a little aggressive on a long flight, he doesn't. She opens her eyes and stares back out the window. Her last look at the map on the seat back in front of her showed the plane cruising somewhere over Poland. Her father used to tell her that they descended from Polish royalty. That a relative, his namesake, King Jan

Sobieski, was beloved for saving Vienna from the Turks, and that he had a fairy tale love affair with his queen, and that there was a painting of him hanging in the Sistine Chapel. The painting exists—she's seen it—but he never showed her proof of their link to royalty, and she never asked for it.

She takes a breath, looks back at Marco, and goes for it. "Do you mind if I ask, what exactly is it that you collect?"

3

New York City

At the Citi branch on Ninth and 23rd he buzzes himself into the ATM chamber and dips his card. He taps Withdrawal, Cash, and the daily max, $500. The machine says no. He taps $300 and the machine says no. $100: N-O. *Insufficient Funds. See bank administrator.* At the Bank of America one block over it's the same deal. Salvado's already shut down his assets.

He crosses 23rd Street to Eighth Avenue, and halfway down the block he steps into the lobby of the Chelsea Hotel, past, present, and eternal home of writers, artists, actors, and rockers, from Dylan, Hendrix, and Joplin to Twain, Kerouac, and Tennessee Williams. This is the first hotel he and Miranda stayed at as a couple. It was Miranda's choice, not because it was chic or exclusive. She wanted to go because of its musical roots and funky, artistic vibe. When she told Havens that Arthur C. Clarke wrote one of his favorite books, *2001: A Space Odyssey,* at the Chelsea, and that Stanley Kubrick, director of the classic film of the same name, often stayed here, the outer space lover in him was smitten, with her and her seedy hotel.

He pays cash at the desk, then walks upstairs to his room and bolt and chains himself inside. Even after they bought their own place, even after they became rich, once every two or three months they returned to the Chelsea for some sort of spiritual and marital renewal. Having a night away from "parenting," from Erin, was also part of it. Of course now the thought of ever wanting to spend a night away from Erin sickens him with shame.

Another Chelsea resident of note, Havens recalls, was Sid Vicious of the Sex Pistols, one of Danny Weiss's punk rock rebel heroes, who supposedly killed his girlfriend, Nancy Spungen, in one of the rooms. It comforts Havens that Weiss would approve.

He boots up his laptop and plugs in Weiss's flash drive. While the tracking software loads, he plays an early eighties punk playlist compiled by and given to him by Weiss. The Ramones, the Stooges, the Dead Kennedys, the Misfits, the Clash, the Sex Pistols, Jim Carroll, Joe Jackson. The first song up is "Mommy's Little Monster" by Social Distortion. First he tracks the holdings of the Rising Fund, looking for any out-of-the-ordinary movement in addition to the heavy tech shorts that came out of Hong Kong. Nothing. Then he takes a closer look at the trades in Dubai. The deal there totals almost a billion in shorts, all from the same firm, in direct opposition to Salvado's Rising longs in the tech sector. They are almost exclusively American tech stocks. If Rick Salvado was Mr. Red, White, and Blue regarding U.S. tech, whoever was taking this position, in Dubai of all places, was the opposite. Insert paranoid Moslem terror conspiracy here.

He's still trying to connect Hong Kong and Dubai when he starts picking up movement coming out of South Africa. Out of Johannesburg, and Havens is watching it happen in real time. A buyer there is all over a group of U.S.-based new media stocks. The same ones that Salvado predicted would form the foundation for an American economic and innovation renaissance. But instead of one heavy short bet, the Jo'burg firm is taking a steady stream of smaller ones, just as the firms in Hong Kong and Dubai did. The only conclusion that Havens can draw is that whoever is placing the orders is "Smurfing," or executing so many small trades instead of larger, lump-sum trades to avoid detection by the authorities. He used to see this with money being wired into the States while he worked at Citi. Everyone knew those deals smelled funny, but because they were technically legal, and there were commissions to be made, they looked the other way.

He's anxious to begin constructing models around this information—Brownian motion, Black Scholes option pricing, Gaussian copulas—and indeed at least one compartment of his brain is already teasing out variables and hypotheses. But first he needs to gather as much hard information as he can. He probes "Hong Kong Hang Seng." Then: "Dubai Zayed Capital." Then: "Johannesburg Rosehall." With the abilities of a mathematical savant and the guile of a hacker, he manipulates the computing power of the software to access transactions, employee records, and their in-house trading accounts. This leads to the names of two of the brokers who executed the trades: Patrick Lau in Hong Kong and Nasseem Al Mar in Dubai.

Havens looks around. His heart rate is raging. The next song is the Misfits' "Mommy Can I Go Out and Kill Tonight?" He looks into the brokers' residences, education, credit ratings, employment. and bank accounts. He thinks of the trader Lau. Killed in his apartment within hours of completing what was surely the biggest transaction of his life. So far there is no such evidence of death for Al Mar.

He continues to try to make sense of these strange trades. He teases out a few perfunctory models, weighing risk and volatility and the law of large numbers. He looks for a fat tail in his distribution curves that may point to a surprise catastrophic "black swan" event that can only be rationalized later, but he hits a wall. He needs more information, fewer variables. He had always been frustrated in those moments when life circumstance prevented a robust sample set from which patterns might be recognized. More than anyone, he should know the biggest fallacies of data usage is a small sample size and here he is making the biggest mistake of all—trying to force a truth from a sample size of one.

As dumbfounded as he is by Salvado's unjustifiably long positions on these securities, he's equally perplexed by these moves that are the exact opposite. The only common denominator is the securities. One side predicts widespread success, the other catastrophic failure. That's not quite right: The other common denominator is dead financial guys. Lau and Danny Weiss and perhaps Al Mar.

Then, finally: What about South Africa? What about the person who is right now executing the big short on American new media stocks out of Johannesburg? Within seconds he has the name of the firm and the broker, who, it turns out, is not a he.

He's looking up information on Sawa Luhabe at Rosehall in Johannesburg when his computer screen blinks on and off. On the upper left corner of his screen a green box appears that contains the subject header "MALWARE ALERT!" Beneath the heading is the list of a New York–based Internet provider address and another IP address that originates in Germany. Berlin. He stares at the address, thinking of Weiss's second text and, of course, Siren Securities.

Berlin. 12.42-6

Maybe whoever tracked Weiss is tracking him.

He unplugs the flash drive and stands. Spooked, he walks to the window and looks out onto the mid-morning traffic of 23rd Street. There's not enough hard data. Not enough of anything to form the roughest analytical model, to construct the simplest narrative. For instance, the Gaussian copula he used to call the sub-prime crisis predicted the price correlations (or copulations) between collateralized debt variables. When X happens (a loan defaults), there's a Y chance that Z will happen (more default, and banks and economies collapse). In this case he only knows that Weiss's death and these strange trades are the X. When and if Z happens, and how catastrophic an event it may be, is unknown.

One more peek through the curtain. Autumnal morning light knifes down 23rd from the east. A man chases the crosstown bus that's stopped just short of the corner at Eighth. The bus pulls away a second before the man reaches it. Havens watches him jog in pursuit, pounding his fist on the bus door until it stops at a red light ten feet away. The man is still pounding when Havens looks away.

Holding off from calling Miranda these past few hours has been one of the hardest things he's ever done, but he doesn't want to overwhelm her or electronically implicate her. Not having anyone else to call doesn't help. This is what happens when you give up every aspect of your life to live a job that has suddenly become intent on killing you. He knew it was going to eventually kill him one way or another, but his versions usually included things such as a Black Monday coronary or a stress-related aneurism, some stranger in a downtown EMS truck applying the paddles.

Not this.

He paces. He runs numbers in his head, spitballs theories—most of which feature Salvado behind some grand comic-book-villain scheme—but nothing makes sense. Maybe what Miranda used to say is true. He can construct a rational model for everything except reality. Every few minutes he checks his watch. At 10 A.M. he turns on the small television on his dresser. The news. He pays careful attention to the headline stories and the type crawl on New York 1 to see if there is anything about the murder of Danny Weiss, the fugitive Andrew Havens, or some impending financial disaster.

Nothing.

He goes back to the laptop, eschews the flash drive, and clicks on the photo of the board in Weiss's apartment. He stares at the numbers, but his eyes keep tracking back on the words:

> The gods may love a man, but they can't help him
> when cold death comes . . .

On a hunch, he decides to run some numbers based on an obscure financial indicator he's never taken seriously. The Hindenburg Omen is a technical analysis pattern that is said to portend a major stock market crash. It's named after the crash of the German zeppelin on May 6, 1937. The rationale is that, under "normal conditions," a substantial number of stocks on the NYSE set new annual highs *or* annual lows, but not both at the same time. When there is a simultaneous presence of significantly above average new highs *and* lows, according to the Hindenburg Omen, a substantial to catastrophic market decline is likely to follow. Havens's problem with the construct is that it is at best an imperfect model and at worst the ammunition of quacks. He finds the criteria to be too random in nature and feels that with such an enormous data bank and numerous variables, any number of correlations can be found, and few really have predictive significance.

As much as he likes to discredit the Hindenburg Omen, he sits up and pays increased attention with the first result: On September 30 there were 91 and 82 fifty-two-week highs and lows on the NYSE. This would qualify as significantly more than the norm. He looks for an explanation in the news of the day—for instance a poor earnings report from Apple, a natural disaster, or geopolitical turmoil. Nothing. He moves on and within a minute is stopped in his tracks again. Last week, on October 12, there were 83 highs and 93 lows. Same deal: on the surface, no logical or numerical rhyme or reason. However, when he lays The Rising's holdings against the highs and lows of both days, he sees that a disproportionate number—more than half of its portfolio—experienced highs and lows. He cracks his knuckles, then runs his hands over his face.

He stands. On TV a gray cartoon cloud wobbles over the Northeast. Men in black masks hurl stones at unseen targets in Greece. A Cardinal pumps his fist as he rounds third on a play-off home run trot. Then the numbers. Yesterday's numbers, last night's numbers, job numbers, revealed over images of hectic Japanese traders, a North Atlantic oil platform, the six Corinthian columns of the New York Stock Exchange building topped by the triangular pedimental sculpture by John Quincy Adams titled *Integrity Protecting the Works of Man*. As if any of it matters. The building, so substantial and massive, as if to give the impression that no single thing can bring it down, except of course the on-screen numbers that are ghosted over it.

He looks back at his computer. Personal, human fear prevents him from wanting to look further, but the addictive pull of the numbers compels him to. He types and waits. The screen blinks and there it is. For the third time in the last thirty days he discovers a Hindenburg Omen, 74 highs and 102 lows. That third time was close of market yesterday.

Havens tries to come up with an explanation or model to dispel the facts in front of him. The most encouraging thing to note, he tells himself, is that not every Hindenburg Omen portends a full-blown crash. Seventy-seven percent of the time, a market dip of 5 percent occurs within thirty days of confirmed signals. Forty-one percent of the time a panic sell-off occurs. Almost one quarter of the time there's a full-blown market crash. Havens mines deeper into the data looking for instances of not one but three confirmed signal days within a month, but he can't. In the history of the NYSE, it's never happened.

Again he tries to take solace in the fact that not every Hindenburg Omen portends a crash. But then again, every major stock market crash of the past seventy-five years has been preceded by a confirmed Hindenburg Omen. Next he wonders, but doesn't bother to search, how many major crashes were preceded by the murders of brokers around the world.

He looks out his window and glimpses a section of the old Chelsea Hotel sign mounted on the building's exterior. Danny Weiss's ghost is spinning "Smash It Up" by the Damned on his player. It's been said that the ghosts of past residents such as Eugene O'Neill, Thomas Wolfe, Sid Vicious, and the poet Dylan Thomas have all been seen at the Chelsea. So why not Weiss? He certainly deserves it, Havens thinks. After binge-ing downtown at the White Horse, Thomas staggered back here and collapsed, perhaps in this very room, before finally going gently into that good night: a coma. Four days later he died at St. Vincent's on 11th Street. Perhaps, Havens thinks, he and Miranda were drawn to the

Chelsea because as much as it's associated with creativity, it's associated with death. And perhaps that's why he often came here alone after Erin's death, after the divorce, to think about the ghosts of his past. Erin was never a resident of the Chelsea Hotel, but he's done the math, and she may very well have been conceived here. He's thinking fondly of the ghosts of friends, celebrities, and loved ones when he looks back down at the street and sees Laslow's bald head get out of a taxi in front of the hotel and disappear under the awning and into the lobby.

4

Berlin

"Do you mind if I ask where you are staying?"

"Hmm. Good question." Sobieski pulls a scrap of paper out of the front flap of her carry-on. They've just come out of customs at the Berlin Brandenburg Airport and are heading out to the street, toward the ground transportation area in the pavilion in front of Terminal A. She doesn't know the name of her hotel, but if the agency booked it, she's sure it's nothing special. "Downtown," she tells Marco Nello. "Near the gate."

Nello smiles. "Perfect. I'm staying at the Ritz. Any chance you're also at the . . ."

She shakes her head. She's hesitant to tell this attractive man with whom she's had the most pleasant conversation in a long, long time that she is most likely staying in a budget hotel.

"Doesn't matter," he says. "I'm sure it's close enough that we can still share a taxi."

She checks her phone. There are four messages in her queue. Three from Michaud. Surely they can wait another half hour, but something—fear, embarrassment, or a self-destructive allegiance to her job—forces her to peek.

Nasseem Al Mar is dead. Call.

Johannesburg has gone missing.

Don't do a thing until we speak.

The fourth text is from an unknown number, but when she opens it, the identity of the sender is clear.

We eagerly await your next invaluable recommendation.

Enjoy Berlin. -C.

Cheung. She turns back to Marcus Nello. "Listen, I'd love to share a cab, but"—she holds up her phone and shrugs—"I've got to deal with some work stuff, like now."

"I can wait."

"Well, that's considerate, but . . . my boss, he's always on."

"Nothing wrong with that." Nello is still smiling, but there's a trace of disappointment in his eyes.

He thinks that I'm messing with his head, Sobieski tells herself. When in fact I'm only messing with mine. "I don't mean to be rude."

"Sure, no," Nello responds. "Some things can't wait." He holds out his hand, and they execute the handshake of business acquaintances, not of a man and a woman about to share, at the very least, a taxi. "It was a pleasure, Cara Sobieski."

"Enjoy Berlin."

"Oh," he says. "I will. I love it here. Well . . ." He half waves and turns to walk toward the taxi stand.

Way to go, loser, Sobieski tells herself as she watches him leave. Then, after four steps Nello stops, turns, and heads back toward her.

"I don't mean to be too forward," he says, reaching into his pocket. "But I like you. And unless I'm mistaken . . ."

"No, not at . . . I—"

He interrupts, "Good. Here's my card, with my mobile on it. I'm here through Friday. Once you settle in and catch up, if you have time, and feel like taking a break, I'd love to meet for a cup of tea, a drink, dinner, or part two of our mile-high book club discussion."

She tries to calibrate the time zone differences, but then decides she doesn't care. It doesn't matter with Michaud, a man who always seems to be half-asleep, but whom she's never caught in the act of sleeping.

"Since you left three messages, all while I was thirty thousand feet in the air. Do I need to call you back three times?"

"You know," Michaud answers, "with recent technological advances, it is entirely possible to maintain phone and e-mail contact with those near and dear to you even while flying halfway around the world."

She watches Nello disappear into the back of a taxi. "What's possible and what's necessary are two entirely different propositions."

"Somebody sounds cranky."

She puts Nello's card into her pocket. Now that his taxi is out of sight, she starts to approach the stand. "I am cranky. I just had the nicest conversation with a man who, believe it or not, wasn't a cop, a crook, or a finance guy."

"And now you're en route to his Berlin bachelor pad for a night of debauchery?"

"No," she says. "Now he's gone. Now I'm en route to what is likely to be based on our travel guidelines the German equivalent of a no-tell motel." She gets inside a cab and hands the driver the slip of paper on which is her hotel's name and address. Covering her mouthpiece, thinking this may be her only opportunity for tourism in Berlin, she tells the driver, "Please, take the scenic route." Then she removes her hand from the mouthpiece and says to Michaud, "So our man in Dubai."

"Bullet in the head. Dumped in the trunk of an abandoned car outside the city."

She's tempted to ask how Michaud discovered this, but knows better. She's taken to believing that somehow, half-drunk in that empty room in Hong Kong, Michaud knows everything, and only tells the world a fraction of it. "Any news on our friend in Johannesburg?"

"Well," he replies, "if she's dead, no one has found her yet. She left work at lunchtime and never went back. There was an execution-style shooting at a car that looked like hers near her home this afternoon, but the car managed to drive away."

"No body, though."

"Not yet."

"The female trader?"

"Yep."

"What else do we know about her?"

"Single mom. Black. Quite bright. Overcame a ghetto childhood, won a series of scholarships and competitions, and got herself a nice job."

"Divorced?"

"No. Her husband was murdered a few years ago. Collateral damage in a drive-by. Best as we can tell it's not at all related to this, uh, incident, though her brother is something of a boy gangster."

"What's her name?"

"Sawa Luhabe. Left work every day to visit her mother and daughter in Alexandra township, which is pretty much a ghetto and where, for some reason, despite having a solid broker's job, she still lived."

"Still lives."

"Right," Michaud answers. "There's a digital dossier on her for you to check out after you settle in."

She looks out the window as they drive along the River Spree. In the distance she sees the lights of the Fernsehturm tower. The Reichstag building. The dramatically illuminated and seemingly floating landmarks of *Museumsinsel* (Museum Island). "Anything else on the connection between Hong Kong, Dubai, and Johannesburg to this place?"

"That's what we're hoping you can help with."

"I meant a connection between who's making these trades and to what end?"

"Right. We're constructing models to see. To see if there's a number or a logic pattern that links what has happened and what might happen next."

"You think they're gaming the markets?"

Michaud laughs.

"I forgot," she says. "You think everyone's gaming the markets."

"It's just that most do it more peaceably. Most are content to ruin lives for profit. Not end them."

"I was thinking," Sobieski says. "If all three of these events revolved around U.S.-based securities, don't they each, at some level, have to be attached to U.S.-based trading accounts?"

"They do. And we're looking, but with this sort of account I'm not sure it'll lead to anything, because there's a million ways around it. For instance, all a bad guy needs is an American address and Social Security number to open an account, and it's almost impossible to police. Some underground players out of Russia and Israel have hundreds of accounts, and once you go after one of them, they just shut it down and move on to the next phony setup."

"Which, presumably," Sobieski, says, "is what my lead here in Berlin has already done."

"If they've tracked that we're tracking them, absolutely. But you never know. Maybe they've left us a bone in Berlin, or in the States, with one of those accounts. Before we can figure out where or when the next trade or the next killing is going to occur, we have to learn everything we can about the last one. Right?"

"Yes, Boss."

"Landlords, neighbors. Everything."

"Right."

"And Sobi . . ."

"Yes?"

"No crazy risks. As soon as you sense the slightest danger, the slightest funky vibe, you pull back, 'kay?"

"'kay."

"And that guy on the plane . . ."

"Uh-huh."

"You were way too good for him. I bet he had a wedding ring in his pants pocket."

After she hangs up, she closes her eyes and tries to gather her thoughts. For a moment, thinking about the flight, and Nello—with whom she discussed her father, of all people—and the money she owes Cheung, and how she ended up in the back of a cab in Berlin, without love or family, she thinks she is going to cry. But she doesn't. She reaches into her jacket and runs her fingers along Marco Nello's business card but doesn't pull it out, more for his sake than hers.

"Would you like to see more sights, miss," the driver says in broken English, "or would you like to go to your hotel?"

Sobieski looks at her phone, then back out the window. "Tell me," she finally responds, "can you recommend a nice casino here in the city?"

5

Havens cracks open the lobby door and peeks out. He always takes the stairwell in the Chelsea because it is filled with art, some modern masterpieces given to the proprietors in exchange for rent. But this time he took it because of Laslow. His hastily packed leather duffel is slung over his shoulder. He pats his front pocket to ensure that Weiss's flash drive is still there. He takes in the scene: the eclectic shapes and colors of the art, the full-time residents chatting, he imagines, about politics, art, coffee. Must be nice, he thinks.

Then he sees him.

Across the lobby, standing with his broad back to him, staring at Larry Rivers's *Dutch Masters*, to the left of the hotel's glass front doors, is the man with the shaved head who murdered Danny Weiss last night. Laslow. He's sure of it.

He steps back, eases the door closed, and continues downstairs to the basement. He wonders, How did he find me? Then he remembers the malware alert, the screen flashing off and on, and he concludes they must have tracked his IP address right back to the hotel's servers. The fire door opens on a laundry room filled with carts of soiled linens. A middle-aged Asian woman in front of a bank of washing machines stares at him with horrified eyes. If someone wanted to harm her down in this din, there's nothing she can do.

"Exit?" he asks, smiling, but the woman only stiffens and glares as he barrels past.

Coming into the light of an alley on the west side of the building, he pulls up his hood and lowers his head as he approaches the sidewalk of 23rd Street.

Zigzagging south and west with his head down, he wonders why Rick Salvado, a self-made multibillionaire, would want to kill anyone. He thinks of the Rick Salvado he'd heard of before he came to The Rising, the Rick Salvado who hired him, as compared to the man who is bent on killing him.

The Salvado he'd heard of was a fiercely independent investor, orphaned at a young age, who worked his way up from a commodities gopher to gigs at Merrill, Bear Stearns, Oppenheimer—before going out on his own. His first company, the now infamous Allegheny Fund, briefly made him a star and then, all at once, a villain, a government scapegoat for alleged trading improprieties during the NASDAQ dot-com bust and market collapse of 2001–02. His meltdown was public and the case against him was bitter and contentious. Somehow, amazingly, he didn't go to prison, but his fund went under and his reputation was seemingly destroyed.

All of which made his comeback all the more unlikely and remarkable. After paying his fines and eventually expressing his regrets, Salvado dedicated himself to helping to promote ethical and responsible trading practices. Plus, it didn't hurt that he still had a knack for making money and for self-promotion. Havens can still remember watching him on the business channels in his dark suit with the omnipresent American flag pin, dispensing wisdom, recommending winners, and cautioning against losers and market traps with the gusto of a vaudevillian, the passion of a televangelist.

Soon, instead of reading "Rick Salvado: Former Fund Manager" the title under his onscreen image began to read, "Rick Salvado: CEO, The

Rising." Not long after that Havens got the call while sitting in his windowless back office at Citi. What he remembers is that the initial call wasn't from a recruiter, or a human resources pro at The Rising.

The voice on the other end that day said, "Drew Havens, Rick Salvado at The Rising here. I've heard a helluva lot about you. How'd you like to get rich together?"

At 20th Street he climbs the stairs onto the High Line trail and walks south. At the 14th Street passage he stops in a semi-enclosed industrial space to listen to his latest favorite piece of art, a sound installation called *A Bell for Every Minute*. Every sixty seconds he hears the sound of a different bell recorded somewhere in New York City. School bells, church bells, and the New York Stock Exchange bell. It soothes him, listening not so much to sounds, but to the memories of other people and other times. As he looks westward across the roof of an abandoned meat packing plant, toward the Hudson and Jersey, the recently salvaged Coney Island Dreamland bell chimes a deep and haunting tone. He takes out his phone and pulls a scrap of paper from his pocket.

A different ringing now, a different tone. A call halfway around the world to a place he's never been, for a woman he's never met and who may very well already be dead.

"Rosehall, how may I help you?"

"Yes," he says. "Sawa Luhabe, please."

6

Wendy is asleep. Finally.

Sawa Luhabe drives east, away from the twilight. Her mother is in the passenger seat, looking out at the East Rand and mouthing the words to a prayer Luhabe has never heard. Her mother knows that something has forced them to leave, but even after Luhabe tried to explain, the older woman didn't fully understand. Nonetheless, she followed. She's seen enough in her life to know when to run, when to second-guess, and when to pray.

Even Wendy knows, Luhabe tells herself. Just three years old, but she knew that something was wrong. Something different from the normal energy of the day; a less patient type of maternal sentiment. So, of course, Wendy cried. She didn't want to go. She didn't want to stay. She cried because she knew. Luhabe thinks this is not unlike when the girl acts up, claiming to miss the father she never met. Some kind of extra sense, rooted in the heart.

If traffic on the N-17 and her mother's seldom used 1997 Daewoo Cielo cooperates, she'll cover the 430 kilometers to her cousin's house in Swaziland in less than four and a half hours. She's chosen these relatives because of the distance from Jo'burg and because, to the best of her knowledge, she's never mentioned them to anyone at work.

She's tempted to call her oldest cousin to give her some warning, but she doesn't want to use her phone. This morning she would have thought it preposterous that someone might want to track her mobile phone calls, but now she thinks it's not only possible, it's likely. Plus, today the phone has been her undoing. First the call from the mystery client out of Berlin. Then, in her post-shooting absence, calls to the office from Hong Kong, the United States, and then more calls from Berlin. The last, she reasons, was to check if to see if she is still alive.

"Did you bring this upon yourself? Out of greed?"

"No, Mother. I did nothing to invite this. If I am guilty of anything, it's believing that something good could finally come our way."

Her mother clucks her tongue. "Does this mean you will lose your job?"

"No. Unless the job brought this upon me."

After a while, her mother turns to her and says, "You know I believe you. I think you are the strongest and most decent person I know."

She crosses through the Oshoek border post, twenty-three kilometers from the Swazi capital. Abandoning the N-17, she takes a series of back roads to a small village that she has visited many times since her childhood. Her relatives—three cousins, their six children, and the home's owner, her mother's seventy-four-year-old sister—are standing in the dirt yard, as if someone alerted them to their arrival.

After they've eaten and Wendy has kissed her good night, thrilled to sleep alongside her big cousins in their bedroom, Luhabe goes out into the yard and sits on a folding chair next to her mother.

"You're leaving, aren't you?"

"Yes, Mother. It's for the best."

"And this is what I would do, too. If it were my daughter."

Driving west alone on the N-17, back into the country that she loves and hates, that amazes and repeatedly confounds her, she begins to cry. When the tears start to impede her vision, she reaches into her shoulder bag for a tissue. Before removing her hand from the bag, she extends her fingers and runs them along the barrel of her late husband's handgun.

7

Berlin

S obieski can't sleep.

Combine a type-A federal agent with a life-or-death criminal case, a seriously blown opportunity with a potentially fantastic man, a gambling/debt problem, and the opposite of jet lag, and this is what you get. This is how you feel.

The cabbie dropped her off in front of the Spielbank Berlin in Potsdamer Platz in Center City. She checked her suitcase in the lobby and walked past the slots and roulette screens of the first floor toward the elevator. On the third floor she scoped out the poker tables, observed two games for fifteen minutes, then purchased one thousand euros' worth of chips. After fifteen additional minutes a seat opened at the first table, which was filled with Chinese men. A half hour later she had lost all but fifty euros and handed over her card for another five hundred in chips. A half hour after that she had won back her losses plus another seventeen hundred euro. During a dealer change she checked her watch. Two A.M., Berlin time. Three more hours of action if she wanted. She stood up and stretched her hands over her head. One of the Chinese men said something about her to another and they laughed. She stared at them until they stopped smiling. Then, in their Cantonese dialect, she said, "I wonder how your wives would feel about your opinion of my ass." They looked away, but she didn't stop. "Now shut up and fucking play." As she began to sit back down, her head grew light and a wave of nausea fluttered from her abdomen through her chest. Heart attack? she wondered, but only for a second. Anxiety attack, coupled with a bout of acute self-loathing? More likely. Usually this sort of feeling came when she was losing. The fact that it's on the heels of winning an

the securities involved.

She looks for coincidences, common denominators, some kind of human or cultural significance or sequence, rather than the purely numerical. All the while consumed by two questions: Who's responsible? And who's next?

But as she works, as she asks the hard questions, she also asks questions of herself: Why didn't you share that cab? Why didn't you call him later to say that your night just opened up and you'd love to have that drink? Instead of the casino. *Why?*

The easy answer, the easiest lie, she knows, is the job. Duty calls. Lives and more are at stake. Etcetera. Etcetera.

Bullshit.

Sobieski knows that lives will always be at stake. Or at least livelihoods. Someone will always be manipulating the markets, bending the rules, and committing crimes, often at the expense of the innocent. She also knows that there's a big difference between dedicating your career and dedicating your life to a thing, and she crossed that line a long time ago. And the farther she gets from that line, the more she hates herself. And the more she hates herself, the more she's compelled to ruin what good remains of Jan Sobieski's daughter.

Jan Sobieski is why she majored in finance and economics with a minor in criminal justice. Jan Sobieski is why she and her mother and her younger brother lived in one of the finest houses in Cherry Hill, New Jersey, had a beach house in Cape May, and just about everything a family could ever want. He called himself King Jan, and she worshipped him and was more than happy to follow his rules, because if they worked for a self-made, handsome success like him, why not?

King Jan pushed her to get perfect grades and perfect attendance. He pushed her to compete in soccer and softball and martial arts, where she truly excelled. At times she resented his rules, his strict regimen, but she also appreciated the results. So she went along with it, and by the time she was twelve they were best friends and she, much more than her rebellious, disinterested brother Luke, was considered the heir apparent to the family business, which was all about making money for others, and themselves.

Only in retrospect, with the accumulated wisdom of a federal financial terrorism agent and the resentful heart of a child, could she begin to fathom how it all blew up.

Soon after she turned thirteen, King Jan's demeanor began to change. He still challenged her to be better, but unreasonably so. He began to accuse her of lying and seeking the easy way out. At fourteen, she witnessed him in the throes of a seemingly constant argument with her mother. That was when he hit her for the first time, a slap to the cheek. Because of her training she could have deflected or avoided the blow. In some ways she had seen it coming for months. But if he wanted to hit her, she wanted the blow to land. It would make it easier to abandon him. That was also around the time when he began to go away on long and frequent "business trips."

The end came in a disorienting rush. Just before her fifteenth birthday, a guidance counselor pulled her out of second period sophomore English class. *Lord of the Flies*. In the hallway the counselor told her that she had to go to a doctor's appointment. But by the time they reached her office, the counselor had said that something had happened with her father, who was not in any physical danger, and that her mother would soon be coming to pick her up.

But her mother never picked her up.

For three hours she sat in the guidance office, with no further updates from a teacher, counselor, or administrator. Classmates she had grown up with and would never see again passed on their way to third, fourth, fifth, and sixth period destinations. She thought of the work she was supposed to submit, the tests she was missing. Then she realized it didn't matter. She knew by the looks on the faces of the teach-

ers who passed that what was happening to her transcended grades and that degree.

Briefly she thought about her little brother, like probably in a different office close by in the junior high, and she wondered whether she was sitting there, she too filled with the anticipation of a mother that would never arrive.

Just like the thing her father used to say. But even that, even his last name, turned out to be a lie.

Sobieski returns to her notes with renewed intensity.

The traders were killed with different weapons in different cities. While the plays and the way they were executed were similar, the securities themselves were completely different.

Also, the firms at which the traders worked were all legitimate, to the extent that anyone working longs and shorts can be legit. All were small- to medium-sized. And all had some kind of contact with a client or clients here in Berlin, though using the word "client" in this regard doesn't exactly ring true. More like an accomplice. What else? While Patrick Lau in Hong Kong had significant financial woes, according to Michaud the others, though far from trading superstars, were liquid and made a decent enough living.

While she's staring at the list of securities, it occurs to her that they're almost all American companies. Which means by law the trades had to have originated from a U.S.-based account. If they're kill-ing traders to eliminate links, it's unlikely that the U.S. account would track back to an actual person, but you never know. The mere fact that she's aware of the trades and killings demonstrates that they are not as efficient or discreet as they hoped to be.

Finally, she types the name "Sawa Luhabe" into her search box. The digital dossier Michaud compiled on the young South African trader is impressive, but Sobieski wants more. She knows that Luhabe's not at work, that her bullet-pocked car was discovered on an Alexandra side street, that her corporate e-mail is frozen, and that her mobile phone is either off or she's not picking up. Which is why, on a hunch, she checks to see if Luhabe has a Facebook account. Or Twitter. Nothing, but she does have a professional profile on the LinkedIn site. Sobieski sends her a message.

> I am an agent for the United States Terrorism and Financial Intelligence task force investigating the circumstances surrounding the recent attempt on your life.
>
> I would very much like to talk with you, and to help you.
>
> We believe that other lives, perhaps many more lives, are at stake, and that your cooperation may help to prevent a tragedy.
>
> Please contact me as soon as possible at any time. If you can tell me anything about what has happened, from the description of the shooter to the name of the man who initiated the trades, please let me know, in the strictest of confidence.
>
> Sincerely,
> Cara Sobieski
> United States Dept. of Terrorism and Financial Intelligence

Soon after she hits send, an alert appears on her screen. Malware alert. While she's been tracking the moves of the dead, the presumably dead, and everyone affiliated with them, someone has been tracking her. The tech guys in TFI call it doppelgänger software. A program that, once it picks up a certain move coming from a certain source, begins to shadow and mimic every move that source makes, all the while dispatching bots into the host system, plundering and copying files until they've chronicled every move the source has ever made.

Sobieski captures the alert with a screen grab, then e-mails it to a secure and isolated holding bin for an encryption specialist at TFI to explore. Then she shuts down her computer.

8

Darien, Connecticut

The house, like their lives, is surrounded by a hedge.

In many ways, Miranda Havens tells herself, this entire town is. Towering green manicured hedges whose shining oval leaves constitute a unique and proprietary form of currency.

She's only been to Rick Salvado's country estate twice. Once for a full-blown corporate family outing and once for a luncheon with "the wives." It's hard for her to say which event was more outrageous.

The corporate family gig was all about large-scale excess: a genuine Cirque du Soleil show under a backyard big top, Arabian pony rides, a vintage carousel for the kids, and a private concert by one of that year's *American Idol* finalists.

Miranda remembers whispering to Drew in front of a giant ice sculpture replica of the Salvado estate, "What next, an ice sculpture of his manhood?" To which Drew replied, "This entire party is a tribute to his manhood." They kept telling each other that they'd soon leave, that they *should* leave. But Erin was with them and she was enjoying it. Miranda was conflicted about the possibility that the little girl might grow accustomed to the excess, but they stayed until the very end, if only to gape at the next exhibit of mercenary extravagance rolled out for their pleasure, and because it made Erin laugh. At one point near the end the three of them walked away from the rides and tents and music. At the far end of an open expanse of lawn just before the outer hedge they stopped past an herb garden and watched an elderly white man pruning an island of clustered roses. Erin pointed and said, "Flowers!" When they approached, the man smiled. "They're American Beauties," the man said by way of introduction. "Mr. Salvado's favorite." He plucked a bright red rose and gave it to Erin.

"Thank you," she said.

"Wow," Havens said as they bent to get a better look inside. "You know what the Underground Railroad is, sweetie?" he asked Erin.

"It was a hiding place to help good people stay away from bad ones," Miranda explained.

"Our hiding place," the girl replied.

The luncheon with the wives, on the other hand, was every bit the showcase of passive-aggressive, elitist, post-sorority posturing she'd anticipated. The six women, all spouses of the top earners and players at the fund, passionately discussed schools and restaurants, Pilates instructors and fashion, only deferring to the opinion of the queen, Deborah Salvado. At one point Tommy Rourke's wife actually asked Miranda, "Who are you wearing?" As if she were Joan Rivers interviewing her on the Academy Awards red carpet. As if Miranda gave a shit. She dreaded the luncheon, but because she'd seen it coming, and because she'd promised Drew that she would behave, she played along. Drew had told her about some of the wives who had preceded her and had not done so well at similar events, and the fates that soon after befell their husbands.

Despite the unnerving fog of pretense that hung over the wives' luncheon, there was an aspect of it that Miranda, to her surprise, enjoyed: Salvado's beautiful forty-five-year-old wife, Deborah. They barely exchanged words at the corporate family function, but at the wives' luncheon, they spoke quite a bit. At one point Miranda commented about how much she enjoyed a quiche recipe, and a moment later she was being led to the kitchen for an audience with the chef. While Miranda asked the chef questions, Deborah Salvado was transfixed by the industrious inquisitiveness of her guest.

Afterward, Deborah looked at Miranda and said, "You know, I've become a robot. By giving me so much, he's taken away everything. I used to love to cook, to make my mother's and grandmother's recipes: eggplant, or even something I happened to see on the Food Network. But now . . ."

Miranda tried to make her feel better. "But now you have much more important responsibilities than to—"

"Bullshit. Being Mrs. Rick Salvado may come with its responsibilities, but rarely is it accompanied by, no offense, the least amount of pleasure or fulfillment."

"Then do it."

"Excuse me?"

"Do you really think Rick would stop you from cooking something? Just go ahead and do it."

Deborah Salvado stared at Miranda for several moments before smiling. She put her arm around Miranda and led her back to the table. En route she said, "You never did say where you really got this jacket."

Miranda looked down. It was a cream-colored linen blend cut at the waist. Delicately stitched into the lapels in light pink thread were her favorite flowers, lilies. She shrugged. "I made it."

"I knew it," Deborah Salvado said, giving her a mock punch in the shoulder. "One more reason to secretly hate you."

Over the next few years they met several times outside the company circle of wives. Once they visited galleries and had lunch in a small hipster café in Williamsburg, Brooklyn. Once they went to a reading by Deborah's favorite writer at McNally Jackson and had dinner afterward on Mulberry Street. And once they even got drunk on the roof of the Hotel Gansevoort. That was the night that Deborah confided to her about her husband's chronic indiscretions with prostitutes and hostesses, young employees, and even the wife of a prominent trader at the fund.

"Did I sign up for that?" she asked, raising her cosmopolitan to her lips.

"You did not," Miranda answered.

so, the more you look away, the less you can look at the mirror.

Miranda remembers staring out beyond the hotel rooftop that night, toward the Hudson, her own head buzzing with mojitos and self-doubt, and concern about the behavior of her own absentee hedge fund husband. They were rich by then, too. Not anywhere near as rich as the Salvados, but they had made more money than she'd ever imagined they would, and while she and Drew enjoyed it, it had changed them. They were no longer as comfortable in their own skin, or with each other. As if reading her mind, Deborah Salvado said, "He told me the women meant nothing and that they all did it. Clients. Employees. Traders and quants. And when I said, 'Even Drew Havens?' he looked down, then mumbled, 'Oh, no. Havens is different.' "

Within a month, Deborah Salvado would throw her husband out of the Darien estate, banishing him to the Central Park West co-op, apparently for breaking even the most permissive bonds of their agreement. Soon after that, Erin died, and Miranda stopped having anything to do with anyone from the Rising Fund, including her sometime friend Deborah Salvado and then, of course, Drew.

9

H the photo of the board in Weiss's apartment. He enlarges the image until it begins to break apart, leans in, and squints at the symbols in the box for Sunday.

It's the only sequence on the board that has letters in addition to the numbers. He doesn't think it's a book thing, an *Odyssey* thing. Suddenly it occurs to him that it's not a clue, it's a fact. It's a trading account. MS: Morgan Stanley. PH: Philadelphia. With trades of American securities in Dubai, China, and South Africa, someone with a U.S. trading account would have to place the order to Berlin on those securities or the financial authorities in each of those countries wouldn't have allowed the trades.

He zooms out and looks at the entire board. After a moment he stops and thinks, looking back across the Hudson. He snaps open his phone and whips through the texts. He stops at the words that Weiss had sent him at the club.

Wilt thou not be brotherly to us?

"Brotherly," he thinks. Then, he looks at the sequence, specifically the letters PH. "Philly, the city of brotherly love?"

He searches the account number and Morgan Stanley, but there's no match. Perhaps, he thinks, he can ID it through his account at the Rising Fund, but he's told he's an unauthorized visitor at the company that for the past four years was his life. As a fallback he calls his friend Neil Grote at Morgan, a coworker from his back office days at Citi. Two minutes later he delivers the information Havens needs. "Dude's name's Jameson. Rondell Jameson. 1456 Pennypack Street, Northeast Philly, which, as a former resident of the city of Brotherly Love, I can without a doubt assure you is an absolute, Grade A shithole."

"Phone number?"

"Yup." He gives the number to Havens, who immediately calls, but, not surprisingly, it's no longer in service. An online search reveals a half dozen Rondell Jamesons in Philadelphia, but according to a brief mention in the Metro section of today's *Philadelphia Inquirer*, only one was murdered yesterday. Shot down outside a crack house on Pennypack Street. Survived by a brother, Charles, of Newark. There were no witnesses.

10

O shrink in Prague told her, "Gambling, promiscuity, living your
life as an act of revenge, or to avenge the way someone else lived
his life, is not healthy."

"Tell me about it," she replied.

In between sleep and dream, she wonders, If that hadn't happened,
what would you have done? If he hadn't been evil, what would you
have become? Her father's disappearance after the scandal, she reasons, left her with two choices: become a better thief than him, or the
person who punishes people like him for their actions.

It doesn't take a shrink to recognize where the gambling issues
originated.

She rolls over and sees the inbox on her laptop screen blinking. The
message came while she was sleeping. Sleeping because she gambled,
because she was too twisted to have a normal relationship with a man.

Dear Agent Sobieski,

I am the person whom you urged to contact you.

I am alive (obviously), for now. I have left my family in a safe place while I attempt to reconcile my role in this situation. I would very much like to communicate in real time, but for now, because as you say, lives are at stake, I will tell you what I know (and soon, what I hope to discover): Yesterday morning I received a call from a foreign client. A person with whom I had never done business. Male. Seemingly American. Claimed his name was Homer. He wanted to execute a series of short positions on a number of American new media securities (a list of which I can provide you as soon as I am able to safely access them). Almost a billion $US total, spread out over the course of the day.

Several hours later an attempt was made on my life in the Alexandra section of Jo'burg. Some sort of machine gun. In the afternoon, after NEVER receiving an oversees call at work, my Assistant said I had received many. From Berlin, Hong Kong. And a man in New York. Although I was asked not to contact anyone or do any research about the client or the transaction, I did (and I believe they found out and this is why they tried to kill me). Also, the man who made the initial call, who had a specific set of orders regarding the execution of his requests, was working through a trading account in the United States. Philadelfia. The first name of the person whose name was attached to the account was Rondell. Presently, I cannot think of his surname.

Cara Sobieski stares at her laptop screen. She types an immediate reply.

Can you talk NOW?

Then another.

> I apologize. I stepped away but I am here for you now.

Shit! She kicks the leg of the couch and smacks her hands together. Then, quickly, she forwards Sawa Luhabe's note to Michaud in Hong Kong. If Michaud can get in touch with someone working TFI or Treasury in Johannesburg, or at INTERPOL, then maybe someone can get in touch with Luhabe and she will have a chance.

This wouldn't have happened if I had done my job, she thinks. If I hadn't gone to the casino and had stayed in my damned room and ~~...~~ he in safe ~~...~~

~~...~~

theless.

She can't resist writing one more note to Luhabe.

> I can get you into contact with people who will protect you.
> wherever you are. Or you can go to them when you are ready.
> Be safe. Again, I am so sorry for missing your message.

For the next ten minutes she stares at her inbox, trying to will a reply from Luhabe, but nothing appears.

After rereading Luhabe's note she does a search of Philadelphia-based brokerage accounts owned by people with the first or last name of Rondell. There are seventy-nine different Rondells with open brokerage accounts in Philly. Who knew? However, this number is reduced by seventy-eight after she refines her search with the criteria that the person has to have executed recent trades overseas, specifically in Hong Kong, Dubai, or Johannesburg, with possible connections to a firm in Berlin.

The lone result:

Rondell Jameson, 1456 Pennypack Street NE, Lindenfield
Projects, Philadelphia, PA.

Her next search takes her to an article in the *Philadelphia Inquirer*.
She pick up her phone and calls Michaud.

"Frauline Sobieski, how goes it in the fader land?"

"I got an e-mail from Luhabe. She's alive and on the run. I'm
waiting to hear from her."

Michaud grunts. "She dropped her mother and kids with relatives
in Swaziland and is heading back toward Jo'burg. We're trying to
intercept."

"She mentioned a brokerage account in Philadelphia behind the
trades. Belonged to a guy named Rondell . . ."

Michaud finishes. "Jameson. Crackhead. His brother sold his identity to a bald dude from New York with a Russian accent, and now
someone has whacked the crackhead, so to speak."

Sobieski blinks. "Next time I'd appreciate a call before I spend half
the night repeating your work."

"You'd have only spent it in the arms of another, and that would
break my heart, Sobes."

"Anything else, because I've got—"

"Yeah, Hong Kong, Dubai, Philly—what they all have in common
is your boy at Siren."

11

Deborah Salvado smiles. They're having

"It's so quiet," Miranda said. "Where is everyone?"

Deborah Salvado smiles. They're having their conversation in a conservatory off the great room, surrounded by lavender-hued cattelya orchids. "I let them go. The only people left are a cleaning lady who comes once a week and a caretaker for the grounds. I'll do my laundry and cook my own meals, but I'm not quite ready to landscape seventeen acres of lawn and gardens."

"Why do any of it?" asks Miranda.

"Because I'm sick of having people live my life for me. Before I moved up here to *Hedgistan*, I was a relatively self-reliant human being and I want to get a small part of that back. If anyone should understand this, it should be you."

"Me?"

"From the first time you visited, I saw that you were determined to retain what I and the others had lost: individuality, creativity, self-reliance."

Miranda nods. "Hardly true, but thanks. If that's the case, then why still live here at all?"

"Because he won't let it go. Out of spite. Out of ego. And I'll be damned if I'll leave it and let him come back to live here with some gold-digging whore and then stonewall me on a settlement."

Miranda runs her finger along the stem of an orchid. "I'd walk. Let him have it."

Deborah lifts her chin toward the flower. "We used to have someone who was specifically in charge of the indoor plants. But you know, they never bloomed until I took over." She fixes her gaze on Miranda. "I believe you. You *would* walk. You'd let him have everything."

"But you won't?"

She shakes her head. "I won't . . . I can't." Deborah lifts the teapot and refills their cups. Miranda stares at the pot, a hand-painted blue and white eighteenth-century Chinese porcelain piece that she imagines cost more than her Prius.

"You know," Deborah continues, "you never returned my calls, and I really could've used a friend through all this."

Miranda tries to smile, but her true emotions won't allow it. The fact that she lost a child and never received a call from Deborah after the funeral is moot. It's still all about Deborah Salvado. But rather than offer an excuse or an explanation, she thinks of Drew and Danny Weiss and the real reason she's here. "This is true, Deb," she concedes. "You're absolutely right. I should have called."

In the kitchen, while she makes lunch, a chicken Caesar salad, Deborah Salvado reveals the recent developments in her life—her latest personal accomplishments and the fierce and ongoing legal battles with her husband. Rather than getting directly to her point, Miranda allows Deborah to talk. She sees her host's self-absorption as an opportunity to elicit information via a series of well-placed questions.

She wonders aloud, "How could someone so seemingly good have become such a monster? What was his childhood like, Deb?"

"His father was a bricklayer. A veteran of the Korean War who lost the use of his left arm but declined VA benefits. Told Rick he wanted to contribute to, not drain, the system.

"In the early seventies he decided to use all of his savings to build three homes on spec and promptly lost everything to the teeth of a recession.

"Finally, when the house he lived in went under, Rick's father said that the country and the system he served and believed in had abandoned him. He went back to the Veterans Administration to try to claim his war disability, but they turned him away because he'd declined help twenty years earlier.

"The day after he moved his family into a low income apartment in the center of town, Rick's father drove into the [text obscured] of Rick's [text obscured].

[several lines obscured by damage]

didn't cover suicide. And of course the banks and the regulators and the government. The press describes Rick as a patriot, but they haven't heard the things I have about corporations and the government when he is raging. I'm convinced that he's still so driven to succeed at all costs as a direct response to those events, not because of a sense of fulfillment or accomplishment."

"Kind of tragic," Miranda says, "that his being so driven because of what happened to his childhood family led to the ruination of his own, adult family."

Deborah shakes her head. "Not tragic. I'm escaping with my life and my health. He can have his goddamn hedge. Your husband . . . your ex . . . is different. For him it's an intellectual pursuit. Rick said Drew was one of the only people he knew who enjoyed the hedge business for reasons other than greed. With most of these men it goes beyond greed to obsession."

"With Rick it seems to border on vengeance."

Deborah slaps her left palm on the table. "Exactly! He attacks his work and runs his fund with a *vengeance*!"

Miranda tries to imagine how a person who once sat here

surrounded by everything money could buy would be driven to kill for more. She measures her words. "Do you think . . . with all that's happened to him, he's capable of going further . . . of doing something criminal to exact his vengeance, Deb?"

Deborah Salvado sits back and folds her arms.

"You know, harm someone?"

"Why are you here, Miranda?"

"Of course, to see . . ."

"Don't condescend. I know when someone is trying to leverage a relationship with me to get through to my husband."

Miranda sighs. "I got a rare call from Drew yesterday. Not the usual disillusion and disenchantment. He called to tell me that he'd had enough, that he was quitting The Rising."

"Interesting, but not a surprise. He'd been mortified by the spectacle of it for some time."

Miranda nods.

"Is he going somewhere else?"

"Not that I know of. He's wanted out for a while. Since Erin died. He threatened frequently, but he always stayed, I think in part because he had no idea what he'd do with the rest of his life and in part because, deep down his relationship with the numbers overshadowed his ethical and moral dilemmas. But something happened this week that made him want to leave in a hurry."

"Like what?"

Miranda shrugs. "That's really why I came here today. To try to find out. Drew and I hardly talk now, and when I pressed him the other day, he wouldn't say. And now I can't get in touch with him at all. I just thought that you might know what may have happened, if Rick said something."

"These days Rick tells me nothing."

"Has he been acting differently?"

Deborah Salvado leans forward and pushes her teacup to the side of the table. "Differently enough to commit a crime? Bigger than the crimes he's been committing with the assistance of corporate and elected masters of the universe for the past twenty-eight years? Is that what you're asking, Miranda?"

"I . . ."

"I'm not as detached as you think. Remember, sweetheart, half of everything he owns will be mine, so I make it my business to know his business."

"I'm just . . . I'm worried about . . ."

"I know someday this is all going to come crashing down, Madoff-

Deborah Salvado tilts her head and considers Miranda for a

"I meant it when I said we don't talk."

"Because, even though we're divorced . . ."

"I know. You're worried about Drew." Deborah gets out of her chair. To signal the end of the visit she begins walking out of the kitchen and into the foyer. "I'll tell you this because I do like you," she says as she walks. "When you get involved with someone like Rick Salvado, when you challenge or threaten him, you are going to a very danger-ous place, because you are dealing with someone as powerful and egomaniacal as a despot, as the corrupt sociopath head of a third world nation. He is connected to everyone, good and bad and worse, in busi-ness and politics and the illicit groups that control them.

"This is a man who has the power to do good or evil, to make something memorable or make it disappear as if it never existed with the touch of the tiniest button on his smart phone. Call it a death app.

"So no, Miranda," she continues, "I won't tell Rick that you came here, investigating him. Unless of course, he asks. Then I'll tell him everything, because while you would have chosen to walk away from all this, I obviously haven't."

"I understand, Deb."

"Good. And for your own good, whatever it is you are looking into, for yourself or your ex-husband, of all people, I suggest you cease and desist, and that he just quit and move on. Because if Rick wants to, he will find you, Miranda."

12

The cabbie takes Havens as far as Dr. Martin Luther King Boule-
vard.

"You won't take me to Springfield Avenue and Tenth?"

The cabbie looks at his surroundings, which have quickly deterio-
rated since they got off I-280. "Why not ask me to drive you to downtown Kabul?"

Havens slips five twenties through the Plexiglas barrier and
gets out.

"If you're lookin' for rock, I know some place safer. 'Cause the only
reason a white man goes to Newark is to get himself high, laid, or
killed."

He walks on crumbled sidewalks past a cinder-block pawnshop, a
discount package store, and a gated bodega. Past row houses with tat-
tered couches on front porches. Mounds of black garbage bags piled
along the sidewalk, a ghetto mountain range. A pair of African-
American boys on knockoff BMX bikes low ride in slow circles around
a pretty young girl in a tube top, chirping seduction smack. Men with
brown-bagged bottles turn his way, eyes already homing in on the
spectacle of a stopped cab in the neighborhood, a white man holding a

scrap of paper. It wasn't hard to find an address for Rondell Jameson's brother Charles. Every time he was arrested—all drug-related—it made the papers. Havens stops in front of a project to get his bearings. On a stoop sits an overweight teenage boy and a skinny kid in a throwback Iverson jersey. Havens takes a breath, preparing himself for the runaround or worse, before approaching.

"I'm looking for Charles Jameson."

The boys look at each other.

Havens checks the address. This is it. "He inside?"

The skinny kid spits. "You're too geeked to be police."

"I'll pay."

"If I want your fucking money I'll take it," says the heavy kid, who's no more than fourteen. The skinny kid gets up and walks away. Havens watches him pull out a cell phone.

"What's he doing?"

"None of your fucking business. If Sir Chuck wants to find you, he will."

The drug pusher drives a hybrid.

A brand-new, tricked-out black Cadillac Escalade hybrid. Gold rims. Blackened side windows. SIR CHUCK vanity license, just in case you didn't know.

The back door swings open, classical music wafts onto the sidewalk, and a hand emerges and motions. Get in.

Havens closes the door and nods at the man who is presumably Sir Chuck. He cocks his head as he focuses on the music, then says, "Bach."

Sir Chuck nods. "Nobody touches him. You a fan?"

"I like classical music. The notes make sense to me like math. And I'm good with numbers. This is what, Brandenburg Concerto Number Three, G major?"

The driver pulls back onto Springfield. Sir Chuck lifts his red Phillies cap off his shaved black head and smiles. "You know what, Mr. . . . ."

"Havens."

"I have no idea what concerto this is. I just like the man's music. Bach by day, to soothe the soul. Hard-core Philly rap by night, to take control. Beanie Sigel. Gillie Da Kid. Now tell me, what the fuck you doing walking on my street?"

Havens takes a breath. "I work for a hedge fund. Your brother's name came up on an account that has some issues. When he died, I saw your name as next of kin."

"Junkies have no kin. That boy died a long time ago."

How did you [illegible] up on that account? Somehow [several illegible lines, text faded/smeared]

"It's legit. You got thirty seconds to say your piece."

"The short version is someone is using the identities of people like Rondell to open trading accounts and make stock trades in exchanges around the world. Hong Kong. Johannesburg. Dubai. Then, after the trade is executed, they're killing the people who made them."

"What the fuck do I care about money people on the other side of the planet?"

Havens nods. "Probably about as much as me. But the people who are killing the money people, they also killed my friend the other day, they killed your brother, and I'm pretty sure they're gonna kill you."

Sir Chuck tilts his cap back on his head.

"Rondell was easy. The trading account with his name and vitals was directly linked to transactions where at least one broker has been killed. But you, I just did a bit of quantitative reasoning and it added up."

"We're done here."

"What did they give you for the info on the skells? Five hundred? A grand? Was it enough to sell what was left of your brother's soul?"

Chuck's eyes flare. He reaches into his jacket and wraps his fingers around a Glock. Havens takes a chance. "How much did Laslow give you? How many names did the bald man get? I hope it was a shitload, Chuck, because he used it to lay down a number with eight zeros and counting. How does that make you feel?"

Chuck stares at Havens but doesn't reply.

"You think he's gonna let a loose end like you dangle when he's got a billion on the line?"

"Don't know about any accounts. Don't know about some bald white fucker."

"Who said he was white?"

"I don't owe no one . . ."

"Actually, Chuck, you do. Because if I didn't happen to come here today and give you a solid heads-up, you probably would not be here tomorrow. You're a money guy. That's worth something."

"So what do you want?"

"Confirmation. The bald guy, Laslow, right?"

The Escalade stops at a light. Chuck nods, looks at the world outside through dark tinted glass while twisting a diamond ring on his left forefinger. "What makes them sure enough to bet a billion on something?"

"They've figured out a way to game the market, to create an event that will change everything in their favor."

"For instance?"

"Say you want to fix the World Series for your Phillies. You have Howard, Utley, Lee, and Halladay in your pocket, then you bet big on a Philly win. You've created an event that changes the odds in your favor. But, to be sure, you do something to the Yanks. Like you make sure Sabathia isn't able to pitch, or buy him, too."

Chuck tilts his head. "So you're talking terrorism?"

"Exactly. These guys aren't gangsters; they're financial terrorists, with global connections."

"And you're gonna stop them?"

Havens meets Chuck's eyes. "I've lost a child. My wife. My job. My friend. So, you know, why not?"

Chuck takes a breath. "They came down from New York. Bald guy. White guy."

"Laslow?"

"Laslow. Owns a club there. Found me through another financial wizard who thinks he's king of the world until he needs to scratch an itch at three A.M. No different from Rondell. For some time I was providing product in bulk to him. Your bald man. For his club. His clients, he called them, 'clients,' like they're any fucking different from any [illegible]"

"When did he ask for the info on the identities?"

"Month, six weeks ago. Fucking liar said it was for a phone scam."

"And you won't tell me the other names?"

"Said he'd kill me if I did."

"Like I said. He's gonna anyway. Probably a lot of others if you don't."

"So," Chuck says after a while, "you lose all that, and you still care?"

"You can dwell on what you lose. What's been taken. Or, you know, what's still there."

"I hear you." Chuck closes his eyes as the last notes of the concerto play out. "This may be my favorite. You know the name of this tune?"

"I do. Orchestral Suite Number Three, in D major."

"D major." Chuck whispers it. The car pulls back to where they started. Chuck turns to Havens and says, "Before he left, before I gave him the names I'm about to give you, you know what Laslow says? He says he'll only need one or two of them, because after this Friday, it's gonna be all over."

13

Rio de Janeiro

K leber Valverde would be willing to bet everything he owns that the name of the client on the other end of the line is not Rondell Jameson.

But if the U.S. trading account out of Philadelphia is clean and the security profile checks out, he could care less. This amount of money does not move through Trek Investimentos often, and never for one of his clients.

He drinks from a paper cup of warm black *café* and taps a soon-to-be-smoked cigarette on his desk as he listens to the specific instructions. The client wants short positions on three of the world's largest advertising holding companies, which cumulatively account for more than 75 percent of all the major agencies in the world, and more than 80 percent of total advertising-based revenue. An industry that spent more than $700 billion last year alone, selling soap, beer, and boner pills, Valverde marvels.

As he processes the information, he wonders what this guy, or at least the guy he's representing, knows to be able to so confidently foretell the death of advertising.

Some new kind of technology or medium? Perhaps a new digital ad

model, or an entirely new medium, or entertainment channel. Whatever, he thinks, as he starts activating the first of many waves of shorts.
That's for the analysts to figure out.

Under normal circumstances he'd run this by a VP, or at least
discuss the novelty and magnitude of it with one of his fellow brokers.
But last month his boss was canned along with three of his best friends
in a salary purge to make the firm look more attractive for what has
become a seemingly inevitable takeover by the Swiss at UBS. All they're
waiting on, according to hallway rumor, is the final approval of the

cash without attracting the notice of management.

By lunchtime he's programmed the transactions to the point that
they are executing themselves, rolling out in small, digitally traded
bunches. A hundred. A thousand. Five thousand. Ten thousand and
counting.

He looks out the fourth-floor window, oblivious after all these years
to the iconic image of Sugarloaf rising like a fist into the sun-blasted
azure sky from the darker blue waters of Guanabara Bay.

One of the runners brings his lunch to his desk. Cozido, a stew of
potatoes, carrots, and a sliced mango. He tips the young man ten reals,
more than twice the usual, and thanks him. Once an entry-level
runner himself, Valverde knows that the size of the tip doled out is one
of the most accurate ways to judge the kind of day a trader is having.
And a group of young runners with a pocket full of reals is a more
reliable economic indicator than the jobless numbers or the level of
the Bovespa. The boy gives him a thumbs-up with his right hand as he
pockets the note with his left.

The transactions continue to process. Ten thousand. Fifteen

thousand. He had planned on setting aside two hours this afternoon to contact existing high-end clients and cold-call leads, but he's transfixed by the accumulation of numbers, the promise of commission. For every short position, he has to find someone to make the market, to counter with a long. And today this is proving easy. Apparently more people are willing to bet on the life of advertising than on its death.

Elsewhere in Brazil the numbers are also good today. The Bovespa in Sao Paolo is up .09, and his hometown exchange, the Bolsa de Valores de Rio de Janeiro, is also up, .05. For this, Valverde thinks, you can thank the coming Olympics and World Cup, a mildly recovering U.S. economy, some good trade news out of Brazil's largest partner, China, and a surge in the prices of Brazilian billionaire Eike Batista's OGX oil conglomerate.

When he first graduated from Universidad Federal, Valverde wanted to be the next Batista. Now, so many recessions and crashes and recoveries later, he's happy to have a paycheck, a house near the beach in the Botafogo district, and his beloved red 2010 Moto Guzzi Griso 1200, a picture of which sits on his desk beside a picture of his wife and two daughters.

Out of curiosity he checks the up-to-the-second trading status of three of the top advertising holding companies. Nothing dying there. In fact, they're each up on the session, more than 2 percent.

When it's apparent that the automatic program has matters in hand, he gathers his belongings and heads for the elevator. It's only 2 P.M., but Valverde doesn't care. It's beautiful outside. His bike is waiting and he's had a good day. Why not?

He rises out of the underground garage and lifts his head toward the brilliant sun hanging over the palaces of Avenue Rio Branca. Rather than turn for home, he decides to get out on the bike for a bit and heads toward Avenue Beira Mar. At a stoplight next to the Biblioteca Nacional he takes his cell phone out of his pants pocket and calls his wife to tell her he'll be home early, and to put on a nice outfit, because he'd like to take her to dinner. Three years ago they dined out three, four nights a week. When the economy went bad, they cut back to once a week, and when the takeover rumors began to swirl, they cut back entirely.

"Are you sure?" asks his wife, Celina.

"Absolutely," he answers. "It's been a good day."

When he reaches Beira Mar, he opens up the throttle and takes an exaggerated breath of the sea air that has been a part of so many memories in his thirty-four-year life. He drives along the crescent rim of the bay until traffic begins to build. At Praca Paris he angles to his right, away from the water, and loops back toward the Catedral de São Sebastião and one of the favorite landmarks in the city.

The Lapa Arches, also known as the Carioca Aqueduct, was built in the early eighteenth century. They span 270 meters and the forty-two soaring arches connect the hills of the Santa Teresa and Santo Antônio neighborhoods. They are bold, clean, modern, and spectacular in the afternoon sun. He gets off the bike in the shade of one of the broad arches and unwraps a piece of mango leftover from lunch. When he was a child, his father would take him here and tell him about the swamps that surrounded the old city and of a great-great-grandfather who worked on the aqueduct, which brought fresh water from the Carioca into neighborhoods and fountains throughout the city. He thinks about the old city and his father and the fathers that preceded him as he eats the fruit alone beneath the great structure.

While he is wiping the mango juice off his hands, a late 1990s model white Peugeot minivan pulls up in front of him and the driver rolls down his window. Valverde approaches the Peugeot, still wiping and smiling. "Are you lost?"

"No," answers the driver, a man around the same age as Valverde, his eyes hidden behind dark lenses. "I was just looking at the aqueduct. How old?"

"Almost three hundred," Valverde answers. "Still here, while all this twenty-first-century modernity crumbles all around us."

The driver considers Valverde and the two arches directly overhead, and he smiles. "This is the truth, my friend. Today, nothing lasts as it was promised to us."

Valverde nods, says, "Good luck," and takes one last look at the aqueduct before turning back toward his motorcycle. As his fingers touch the handlebars and he is about to swing his right leg over the seat, he's distracted by the roar of an engine and the crunch of gravel. He turns, sees the van bearing down on him, and lunges away from the motorcycle. The van's right bumper hits the bike first and then the left clips Valverde in the hip. He's lifted into the air and smashes into the concrete abutment more than ten feet away. The driver shifts into reverse, points the vehicle back toward Valverde, and races forward. Valverde hears the van shift gears and start to bear down on him, but he cannot stand to run or turn to see it. He begins to crawl toward the abutment through the dust and gravel with his arms only, dragging his shattered hips and slack legs.

The driver stops short of the abutment. Valverde is halfway around the corner, bleeding from the legs and now his mouth. The driver slams his hand on the dashboard. This is not how it was supposed to happen. He grabs a meter-long length of steel pipe and opens the door. Valverde looks up and sees a dark silhouette surrounded by powerful sunshine. The driver looks at Valverde and wonders if he needs to do more. Probably not, but probably is not acceptable. He turns to make sure no one is there to see him raise the pipe.

Valverde is already dead before it crashes down on him.

14

Sobieski watches Michael as she walks through the Hackescher Markt district in Berlin Mitte. The hotel doorman told her twenty minutes to the address listed for Siren Securities, but she aims to do it in ten.

She's on Pariser Platz, in the shadow of the Brandenburg Gate, near the new Dresdner Bank and the DZ Bank building, the sweeping steel-and-glass atrium that was designed by Frank Gehry, and that she knows also functions as the central bank for Volksbanken and Raiffeisenbanken.

"How was your sleep?"

"Nonexistent. Are you going to send some—"

"Already sending agents to seek out Mr. Jameson in Philly and, yes, INTERPOL and our people are still looking for Ms. Luhabe, presumably in the Johannesburg area."

"What about . . ."

"In addition to Nasseem Al Mar dead in the trunk of a car outside Dubai City, in Rio, another broker was just found dead at the base of an aqueduct outside the city. Kleber Valverde."

Sobieski stops. "Shit." She wonders if there's a way she could have prevented Valverde's death if she hadn't gone to the casino, or been preoccupied by her debts in Hong Kong, or was simply more dedicated, more skilled. "What kind of securities?"

"Advertising holding companies. World's biggest. And yes, shorts. And yes, staggered."

She's in Gendarmenmarkt Square in front of one of the brownstone arches of KfW Banking Group, a well-preserved palace that is a rare remnant from the time of the kaisers. She doesn't know what to say.

"So, what do you think?"

"Think?"

"For starters," Michaud wonders, "I still don't see why you kill them."

"I think after Lau spoke out of school, the bad guys got spooked and wanted everyone associated with this killed. Sloppy? Yes. Unnecessary? Probably. But clearly whatever it is they're up to takes precedence over everything else, and they don't give a shit about who dies as long as they can't talk."

Michaud exhales. "Four trades in four distant parts of the world, all U.S.-based stocks, all shorts, all out of a trading account in Philadelphia with a German firm acting as some kind of middle man. But this one, in Rio, it still has a Berlin connection, but not Siren. It still originated from a Philly account, but a different one. Different name."

"They must have sensed that they were being tracked."

"Or thought they were bailing before anyone picked up on them," Michaud answers.

"Jesus," she says, slowing down to check the addresses on the passing buildings. "Do we have any kind of motive or hypothesis or clue to where this is all going, whom or what might be the next target?"

"Does it ramp up to giving us foreknowledge of something bigger?" responds Michaud. "I'm already modeling possible targets, terrorist connections, and the securities in question, but there's not a whole lot connecting at this point. Additionally, the President and the head of every U.S. security agency have been briefed, and lots of smart people all around the world are trying to connect the same dots."

"Advertising. Media. Tech," Sobieski says. "All semi-related, but there's so many variables, to be across-the-board shorting all of them."

"Maybe he's an evil genius Luddite."

Sobieski smiles. "Tell that to the President. I'm sure he and the rest of the national security task force will be impressed." She looks across the street. This is the place. A small, 1930s-era granite building just off the square. "Well," she says, "this has been fun, as always, but I've gotta go."

"Where?"

"Well, I'm a stubborn little bitch."

Michaud pauses.

"Hope."

"I don't want you to put in until we get our unit in backup."

"Backup? When?"

"This has become quite the thing, Sobes. Give me a few to pull together a team to do it right, and safely. This has taken on some scale."

She looks at her watch and wonders how much time Michaud is talking about. She thinks of the time she wasted last night and what it may have cost Sawa Luhabe and this guy in Rio, and she wonders whose life or lives may be at the mercy of her next act of selfishness.

"This isn't just a numbers investigation anymore, Sobi. It's a serial, potentially mass homicide event."

"Which means that every second counts, right?"

"Just sit tight. Keep an eye on the building and I'll get back to you in ten."

He doesn't get back to her in ten. She thinks of what a ten-minute warning might have done for Luhabe, or Lau, or the guys in Dubai and Rio.

And since Michaud has broken his end of the promise for a rapid response, and she can't bear to think about how she'd feel if her failure to act on this led to another death, or something larger, she snaps closed her phone and strides across the street and up the short flight of steps and into the once and former home of Siren Securities.

A guard sitting behind a black laminate counter looks away from his computer screen, briefly considers her, and then turns away as she strides across the empty lobby. Inside the elevator she presses nine, then closes her eyes.

The ninth floor hallway is silent and empty. There's no sign or arrow pointing her toward the offices of Siren Securities. First she walks to her left, past doors for a photographer's studio, a literary agency, and an accountant, before hitting the dead end of the emergency stairway exit.

Heading back the other way, she passes signs for an attorney and a psychic before stopping in front of the door with no words on it. Just an illustration of a godlike woman hanging high on the mast of an ancient sailing ship. The Sirens, from Homer's *Odyssey*. And also, she realizes, the exact illustration that she and Mo saw on the killer's briefcase in the lobby surveillance video of Patrick Lau's Hong Kong condo. *Sloppy.*

With an ear against the fake wood door, she takes a breath and listens. She hears nothing but the electric hum of the surrounding offices, the clicks and whirring of elevator cables rising and falling through the building's spine. But nothing on the other side of the door. No chattering people, easy listening music, or shuffling feet. No ringing phones, churning copy machines, or clattering keyboards this morning at Siren Securities.

She doesn't knock. She twists the brass knob, and to her amazement it turns. The door floats open and she takes three steps inside the small twenty- by twenty-foot unpartitioned space. It's obvious that the office has been abandoned and that no half-respectable financial services client has ever set foot here.

Despite this, as a formality, she calls, "Hello?"

Nothing.

Slowly she walks across the chipped and stained white Formica floor, looking left and right, then up at the exposed steel beams of the ceiling. All that is left of whatever operation existed here are two gray metal desks. One is against the window facing the Gate, accessorized by an open, empty one-drawer metal filing cabinet and a large, empty gray plastic garbage pail. The other desk, also stripped bare, is pressed into a corner near the door.

What tipped them off? she wonders,

Somehow they became spooked between yesterday and now, and they decided to close up the entire operation and move on. She turns the pages, looking for anything, perhaps a circled security in an agate column or news piece, or for a ripped out article the absence of which would provide a clue. But nothing.

The only way they could have found out, she surmises, is to have picked up on the fact that someone was tracking them online, perhaps Michaud or one of the agents he's placed to the case, or perhaps her. And to be able to do that, she thinks, their software must be far more sophisticated than anything we have.

She looks up and considers the clear blue Berlin sky, which is something she hadn't expected. She'd expected skies a hundred shades of gray, filled with factory particulate and drizzle. Grim men and women in trench coats traipsing through caverns of Cold War architecture. But she was wrong. The city, she thinks, is quite lovely. Of course, the fact that Marco Nello is still in it adds to its allure. For a moment she considers calling Michaud and telling him not to rush, that the place is empty. But they'll want to come anyway and take a more thorough look, and why piss him off? Why bother telling him that she's defied his orders?

What else? she thinks. What else can I do or look for in this office? This city? She's in the middle of this thought when a man's arms begin to wrap around her.

She reacts as if electrocuted. She ducks and squirms, flails her arms, and stomps hard with her left heel on the toes of his left foot before spinning to face him. Mid-twenties, blond, high cheekbones, tall, and model-thin. Not very strong or skilled at this sort of thing.

She attacks without hesitation, snapping off a left-left-right jab combination all aimed at his head, and that he manages to block. Then comes a spinning right leg kick aimed at his temple, that he does not see or block. The impact of the kick sends him careering sideways against the metal desk and onto the floor.

For an instant her survival instinct introduces the thought of running, but her competitive and responsible nature overrides and she knows that she must punish and subdue and arrest whoever this is.

He rolls twice on the floor and manages to rise to a sitting position. But she pursues, closing in on him and straight kicking him flush on the clavicle with the heel of her left foot, driving him back to the floor. Without hesitating she stabilizes her feet, regains her fighting balance, and rears back with her right foot. He rolls again and begins to rapidly crawl toward the door, this time thinking about escaping from this crazy woman rather than capturing her. But she pursues him again.

She's faster.

Her left foot connects with his right kidney and lifts him off the ground. He's collapsing face-first onto the floor, hands and legs sliding out in a palsied splay, as she sweeps her right foot around with the accumulated rage of twenty-nine frustrating years. A guttural, primal grunt accompanies the kick, directed at the young man's temple. But the instant before it lands, his right arm rises and does more than parry or deflect her foot. Through sheer luck he manages to grab her ankle as it whistles toward him. His fingers wrap tightly around the base of her shin and he rips and twists and yanks it toward his chest.

Cara Sobieski did not expect this. As her right leg is jerked away, her left comes out from under her. She's already planning her post-fall movements and the furious retaliatory combination of strikes and blocks she'll unleash upon him, when the back of her twenty-first-century head strikes the hard edge of the Cold War desk, rendering her unconscious before she hits the floor.

WEDNESDAY,
OCTOBER 19
P.M.

1

Berlin

Days, hours, or minutes, Sobieski doesn't know. She's on her stomach on the cold linoleum floor of what's left of Siren Securities. Her hands are tied
behind her back with what? A belt? No. She wriggles her fingers and
feels the soft, pliable plastic coating of wire and cables. The metallic
edge of a USB slot. She sees more wires in a clump on the floor near a
surge protector. It's starting to come back.

She closes and opens her eyes three, four times. Full minutes pass
between each transition from dark to light. Unconsciousness and
whatever this is. Pain and . . . more pain. Mumbling. A man's voice.
She listens with her eyes closed. A man speaking in German. *The* man
speaking in German. "*Ich bin Shultz.*" *Ich bin.* She thinks of Kennedy at
the wall. *Ich bin ein Berliner.*

When the thin blond man materializes and sees that she is coming
to, he pulls a chair closer, but not too close, sits and leans forward. In
his right hand is a section of aluminum window blind rolled up tightly,
grasped like a club.

"Don't try to escape."

"You're lucky I slipped."

"I am. Considering you fancy yourself some kind of cage fighter." The man speaks in perfect formal British-tinged English. As a second language, Sobieski notes, but perfect.

"You know, you're in an insane amount of trouble."

The man laughs nervously and tilts his head back. "Me?"

All at once she jerks and twists, trying to rise up to her feet. Though she's not successful, the man lurches back and scrambles away from her, holding the blinds in front of his chest in self-defense.

"Damn it!" he shouts. "Stay still. They'll be here shortly."

"Who?"

"My employers. The people you were vandalizing."

She lays her right cheek on the floor and tries to focus on him. Blue jeans. Gray pocket T-shirt. Black canvas sneakers. "Vandalizing?"

"Yes."

"What is there to vandalize here?"

He lowers the blinds. "We shut down this operation because we anticipated a threat."

"When?"

"Yester—Why should I tell you?"

She closes her eyes and takes a breath. Fine. Don't.

The man continues. "What did you mean to accomplish, breaking into our offices?"

Eyes back open. "I came here because your firm is linked to a series of highly questionable transactions that have been linked to serious crimes."

"Crimes?"

"Murders. Don't play stupid."

He walks three steps away, then turns to look down at her. "Preposterous. We are an international securities firm."

She laughs derisively. "Right. And this is your plush and luxurious worldwide headquarters."

"Tell me about the murders."

"Sure. Let me up."

He shakes his head. Not a chance.

"Okay," she begins, squinting her eyes and trying to remember the facts. "Hong Kong, Monday, October 17. An order is placed with a broker named Patrick Lau, via a trading account in Philadelphia, linked to a man named Rondell Jameson. U.S. tech stocks, all shorts, thousands of micro transactions, presumably to avoid detection, each just under the total that would catch the eye of someone in Treasury or Homeland Security, or me, totaling nearly a billion dollars. The foreign middleman in the transaction? Siren Securities. Ring a bell?"

The man cocks his head. It's clear that he is familiar with the transaction but perhaps not so much with what happened next.

"And?"

"And that evening in Hong Kong, soon after Patrick Lau got home from work, someone broke into his harbor-front condo and shot him in the head."

The man sits back down. Scratches his chin. The blinds are at his side, in his loosening grip. "How do you know this?"

"I was at the crime scene when he was still facedown on his counter, blood dripping onto the floor."

"In Hong Kong?"

"Yes. I can show you pictures if you'd like, once we get out of here."

"And there's no chance this was a coincidence?"

She begins to speak more rapidly. "Next day. Tuesday. The second trade. Media stocks. Still shorts. Still huge money. This time instead of Hong Kong it was Dubai. This time instead of Patrick Lau the murdered broker's name was Naseem Al Mar at Zayeed Capital. And of course, Siren Securities, Berlin, Germany, was in the middle of it. They found Al Mar in a car trunk yesterday."

He stares, silent, mouth open.

"I imagine your fingers were on the keyboard for that one, too."

"I . . . we simply carry out the orders of others. Clients. Institutions. There's no way that—"

"Next came Johannesburg. New media shorts. Rosehall Fund. A

woman broker named Sawa Luhabe. They riddled her car with bullets soon after."

"Are you an assassin?"

"Then, yesterday, the same brutal, despicable shit in Rio."

He paces away from, then back toward her. Dips his hands in and out of the pockets of his tight hipster jeans. "Who are you?"

"I work for the United States Terrorism and Financial Intelligence task force. I'm agent Cara Sobieski."

His eyes widen further. For the first time Sobieski thinks he might not know anything about the murders. "If you don't believe me, check my ID. It's in my back pocket."

While he hesitates, she presses. "When are your employers coming? When will they get here?"

"They're . . . on their way." He shrugs. "I don't know . . . minutes?"

"Minutes. And you didn't know about the murders?"

He shakes his head, glances at her back pocket. "The orders come through and I process them." As he speaks, he slowly bends and reaches toward her pocket. "Stay still."

"Orders from whom?"

No answer.

"Listen," Sobieski says, "what's your name?"

"My name is Heinrich." He carefully removes the leather case from her pocket, flips it open, and sighs when he sees the badge. He's never heard of TFI, but it's obvious she's legit.

"And you know nothing about these murders, Heinrich?"

He shakes his head, afraid now, still staring at her badge.

"Then we absolutely have to get out of here, Heinrich."

"But they—"

She interrupts. "They will kill us, Heinrich. When they come, of course they're going to kill me. But they're gonna kill you, too. Same as Lau in Hong Kong, Al Mar in Dubai, and whatever his name is— was—Valverde in Rio."

"What about the woman in Jo'burg?"

"Last I heard, they haven't gotten her, but they're trying. She's a loose end and they're eliminating anyone who has touched this."

As he continues to deliberate, tapping her badge against his palm, she says as convincingly as possible, "Heinrich! *You* are a loose end. They. Will. Kill. Us!"

Heinrich agonizes one more moment before deciding to believe her. He puts her badge in his back pocket, grabs her right elbow, and helps her to her feet. As they hustle toward the door, her hands still bound behind her back, he asks, "Do you have a gun?"

"Uh-uh. Not with me."

They bound into the hall and jog toward the elevator bank. As Heinrich reaches to press the down button, Sobieski bumps his hand away with her hip. "Wait." She gestures with her chin at the lights above the elevator.

He stops.

Sobieski starts walking away from the elevator, in the opposite direction of the Siren office.

. . . 4 . . .

Heinrich follows.

They're too far away from the stairwell to make it in time. She stops outside the photography studio. "Quick, try this." Heinrich rushes over and twists the knob, but it doesn't give. There's a bell to ring, but there's no time.

6 . . . 7 . . .

They scramble across the hall to the accountant's office. Heinrich twists the knob. No go.

8 . . .

Back across to the literary agency.

9 . . .

Heinrich twists.

Ding!

It opens at the same moment as the elevator doors.

2

Johannesburg

His house is a fortress.

To try to enter it in the middle of the night, unannounced, was a risk she didn't want to take. The alternative, sleeping in the car on a dark side street of a violent slum while being hunted by someone who wants to kill her, wasn't much better, but it's the choice Sawa Luhabe made.

She had driven straight through from Swaziland. Once she was back in the city, she considered calling a friend, or sleeping on the couch in her office, but she decided that the first choice unnecessarily endangered an innocent, and the second was too obvious.

Just after 2 A.M. she drove past her house in Alexandra, out of curiosity, and was not surprised to see a man standing in front of a car out front, and lights on inside. She never slowed down and never turned back. Instead she continued on to the Hillbrow slum, and the home of her brother Muntukayise, better known by his gangster name, Jolly.

Luhabe hasn't seen or spoken to Jolly in seven years. Since he left home for good at sixteen to pursue the gangster life he had courted since he was twelve. Their last conversation, on the back stoop of the family house, had not gone well. She was home from university and had found two guns and a kilo of cocaine in his closet. When she confronted him, he said, "Because crime is easy, and all that I am doing is taking back what was ours."

"*This* was ours?" she said, holding up the bag of cocaine.

"That is a means to an end. Faster and easier than what you propose."

"It's easy until you die," she answered. And she told him that if this was the life he had chosen he had to leave her parents' home because his guns and drugs under their roof had put them all in danger. He never said good-bye to his parents, but before he left, he kissed his sister and told her he loved her.

"I love Muntukaylie," she answered. "Jolly, I hate."

Muntukaylie took her hand. Then, with a smile, she crossed the sunlit yard through an alley, directly into her car. She's never been inside Muntukaylie's house before, but she's driven by it dozens of times. And besides, everyone knows where Jolly lives. The last time she drove past it was the day after her husband was murdered. If there ever had been a time when she thought she would cave and ask him to use his influence, that would have been it. It would have been for vengeance, to ask her brother to kill the man who killed her husband. But she didn't. Couldn't. She knew it would have felt good for a moment and wrong for an eternity.

Now she doesn't want anyone to kill anyone. All that she wants is refuge. A place even an assassin would fear.

As the car warms up and daylight spreads across the ruins of Pretoria Road, she continues to wipe the sleep out of her eyes and takes civic inventory of her surroundings. More than half the commercial buildings are burned out and gutted, plate glass windows long ago shattered and bricked up. Staring at sidewalk junk refrigerators and sinks, mattresses and office chairs, she thinks how odd it is that most of the buildings are closed up and vacant while people live on the streets below among their contents.

During apartheid, this street was the home of the whites-only main shopping district of Hillbrow; now it's a predominantly black slum. Progress. She rolls down her window, shifts into drive, and begins the short journey to her brother's place on Catherine Street.

Jolly's home stands out because it is something of a compound, gated, guarded, and surrounded by concrete walls. Plus there is glass beneath the iron bars in the windows and the red brick is free of graffiti, which makes the place contrast with most of the homes in the neighborhood. There are no mattresses or refrigerators in front of her brother's place. Just two armed guards standing sentry on the lawn side of the sidewalk gate.

She stands before the gate, waiting for one of them to acknowledge her. When she determines that isn't going to happen, she speaks. "Excuse me. I am here to see Muntukayise."

Both guards approach the gate. One already has raised his machine pistol poised up to his hip. "What you say, girl?"

"I am here to see Muntukayise."

Together the guards shake their heads—no one here by that name.

"Jolly."

This stops them.

"Jolly sleeping. What you want with Jolly?"

Sawa Luhabe steps closer to the gate and looks between two bars. "You call him Jolly, but to me he is Muntukayise. Wake him and tell him his sister is here."

Muntukayise opens the door in a pair of orange boxer shorts. He is a tall and muscular man, like their father. He grimaces and then, recognizing her, confirming the best and the worst, he smiles. Like their father. He bounds down the six brick steps and opens the gate. Sawa Luhabe was determined not to hug the most infamous gangster in Hillbrow, but when her baby brother reaches out for her, she can't help it.

When he pulls away, he looks her up and down and hugs her again. "Is that your car?"

She turns. Nods.

"I thought you were a big-time stockbroker?"

"Someone shot up my other car."

He tenses. "Who?" The change in his facial expression is so pronounced it unnerves her.

"I'll tell you. Can we go inside?"

While she eats her first food since leaving Swaziland, she tells him

"I will send someone to Swaziland."

"To protect. This is not about killing."

"Fine, to protect her. And Mama. Has she . . . has she mentioned . . ."

She shakes her head. "Not for some time, brother. It's the only way she can cope."

"I understand. What else?"

"I need a place to stay until I figure this out. I'm sure they will come back."

"Then you'll stay here. And we will be ready for them."

"Do you have Wi-Fi?"

"Yes."

"And a bed? A clean bed would be nice right now."

Before trying to sleep, she logs onto her brother's computer. He's given her a second-floor room with a private bath in the back of the house.

The first thing she finds is the apology from the American Agent

Cara Sobieski. Then she opens the follow-ups, which are filled with many of the same questions she's been asking herself.

Luhabe doesn't answer. She's too tired. She'll answer later, after she sleeps. But first, she decides to open the only other message in her inbox. From a stranger, SafeHavens@hotmail.com.

Dear Sawa Luhabe,

My name is Drew Havens.

I left a message in your office yesterday that arrived too late. I hope this finds you safe and well. I am an American quant whose friend was recently killed by someone I believe is linked to the people with whom you performed the short trade, and who attempted to kill you. You need to know that they have already killed stockbrokers in Hong Kong, Dubai, and Rio. They are also trying to kill me. I absolutely believe they will kill anyone who has any knowledge of or association with them. And I believe that they have something much more catastrophic planned, and that we can potentially prevent. I would very much like to hear from you in order to learn as much as I can about your contact with them.

Luhabe closes her brother's laptop, stands, and looks out the window. A guard armed with a machine pistol patrols the small walled courtyard behind the house. A neighbor's dog begins to yelp. From down the hall she hears the voice of the man who used to be her brother, ordering someone to do something. She pulls the curtains, blocking the light of the rising sun, and lies back down on the bed.

She closes her eyes and thinks of her daughter and her mother, her dead father and husband and all the iterations of the brother she has known. Child. Rebel. Criminal. Killer. Outcast. And now protector. She thinks of how he's been each of those things in distinct stages and now he is all of them at once. We all are, she thinks; only the order and the emphasis sometimes changes.

As sleep finally comes, she is thinking of the American agent Cara Sobieski and now this man Drew Havens, both of whom claim to want to help her, to protect her as well as many others.

Her last thought, which is really a whim on the edge of a dream, is: I wonder if Drew Havens and Cara Sobieski have ever spoken to each other or, better yet, if they've ever met?

3

Newark

He calls Miranda from the back of a cab.

"Where are you?"

"Road trip. Where are you?"

"Out. I spoke to Deborah."

"And?"

"She thinks he's capable of anything. But she's more interested in making sure she keeps her half of his fortune than in turning him in."

"Anything close to a motive?"

"He's not the patriot he leads us to believe. The government screwed his father way back when, and he's still raging and cheating and acting like an animal."

Havens thinks. This is nothing new.

"What's in Newark?"

"A piece," he tells her. "Enough to make me sure it's him, but not enough to stop him. You all right, Mir?"

"I'm fine. It's just . . . these are bad people, Drew. We basically . . ."

"I know. It was me. Not you."

"I've been thinking about what you said last night. I should have answered, but . . ."

"Not now, Mir. There's no need."

"I want to see you."

He looks out the window and takes two long breaths. One to silence the emotional response that's best for him and the other to formulate a rational answer that's best for her, and them. "I want to see you, too. I've wanted to see you every day. But I need to stay away, Mir. People are looking for me, and to be safe I think you should get out of your place for a while."

"Why don't I meet you in the city?"

"It . . . not a good idea."

"I want to. Drew."

"I do, too. More than anything. But this . . ."

"I know. We let them ruin us. I just don't want them to ruin the night."

Minutes after he hangs up, Tommy calls.

"You okay, Drew?"

"Splendid, Tommy. Peachy."

"The cops were here today. Talked to Rick. Talk to me."

"What do they think?"

"They think you killed Danny Weiss because you have it in for the fund and Rick. They think you've lost your shit because of your marriage and Erin."

"What'd you tell them?"

"I told 'em they were dead wrong. But dude . . ."

"What?"

"They have you on his phone. On surveillance vids outside his place. And of course Rick told them all about your visit. What are you gonna do? How can I . . ."

He thinks of all that Rourke did after Erin died. After Miranda left him. The long talks over dinner. Helping with his move and his guilt. "You've done enough, Tom."

"Where are you now?"

"In a cab. Somewhere in Newark."

"Dude, this is nuts. I'm worried about your state of mind."

"Me, too. But the more I dig the more I know that Salvado's attached to something bad, Tom. Scary bad."

"What? Let me help."

"He's gaming the market. Lining up shorts only to knock 'em down with something big and bad."

"Terrorism?"

"Call it whatever you want. It's pure evil."

"I'll see what I can find on my end. Where you wanna meet?"

"I'll call."

Minutes after getting off the phone with Rourke, on the outskirts of Newark, his phone rings again. An unfamiliar number with a Philly area code.

"Hello."

No reply, then: "Thought you might want to know. Just paid a visit to Springfield. Chuckie's gone." It's Laslow, he's sure of it.

4

The young man sitting alone surrounded by stacks of dusty pile manuscripts looks up. At first he seems pleased to see signs of life enter his solitary cavern of paper and unfortunate words.

Looking up and smiling, he says, "*Guten tag.*" The couple nods back, but upon seeing the woman's wire- and cable-bound hands, the young man's smile fades.

Heinrich raises a finger to his lips and shushes him.

Sobieski turns to face the door, raises her hands behind her back, and jerks her wrists toward Heinrich. Soon after Heinrich has untied her, she turns and smiles at the young man at the desk. "*Guten tag,*" she whispers. But the young man, his face frozen with terror, doesn't reply. Pressing her ear to the door, she hears soft footsteps receding down the hall toward Siren Securities.

Slowly she cracks open the door and peeks out. Two dark-haired white men stop in front of the door at the other end of the hall. One reaches into his black leather waistcoat, removes a pistol, and waits for the other to open the door. Sobieski turns to Heinrich, who is peeking over her shoulder, and whispers, "Get ready."

She watches the man without the gun swing open the door to Siren while the other drops into a shooting stance. They remain in the hallway for several moments before the shooter straightens and they cautiously move inside.

As soon as the men disappear from view, Sobieski grabs Heinrich by the elbow and fully opens the door. She bends her head out and looks down the hall one last time before pulling Heinrich into the hall. Five steps away she quietly opens the door to the emergency fire stairway. After Heinrich is through, she gently pulls the door closed behind her and they start down the first of nine flights of stairs.

The sky above Gendarmenmarkt Square is no longer a robin's egg shade of blue. It's been transformed into the ash gray she'd expected from the city of Berlin.

They turn right as soon as they leave the building. The lunchtime sidewalks are busy. Men and women in suits briskly passing, running errands, bringing bags of takeout back to their cubes. They are all walking with a sense of urgency, Sobieski thinks, but not a sense of purpose. The urgency of a hamster on a wheel rather than a person headed toward a fixed destination.

She's walking fast, with urgency and purpose, passing even the quickest pedestrians.

"Can you slow down a bit, please, my ribs . . ."

"You want to die? Then move."

Heinrich jogs to catch up. "Where to?"

Sobieski answers without looking. "First, away from here," she says. "Then, I have no idea."

"Where did you learn the kung fu?"

"It's not kung fu. It's nothing. Those men. Were they the ones who gave you the orders . . . your employers?"

"No," answers Heinrich. "I've seen them once before, but they were not my employers."

"When was that?"

Heinrich thinks. "Yesterday, actually. Only yesterday for the first time."

"What about your employers?"

"Employer, actually. One man."

"Right. Ever see him?"

"No. He's in the States. Strictly phone and text."

"What was his name?"

"His last name, at least I think it was his last name, was Homer."

They turn left, away from the busy square and the palatial walls of the financial institutions. They walk past a lunch shop and a pharmacy and an electronics store. As they near a *Biersalon*, she nudges Heinrich and says, "In here."

A waiter begins to lead them to a window table, but Sobieski tells Heinrich to ask him to sit them near the back of the dining area. In a booth, once seated, Sobieski asks for a pitcher and Heinrich gives the waiter a lengthy order.

She shakes him off. "Tell me about Homer. How did you initiate the contact with him? When did he recruit you?"

"I was contacted by one of his associates. This is embarrassing, but I met him at a beer hall about, I'd say, two months ago. Not as quiet as this. It's near the Square, and after work it is filled with traders and brokers and investment bankers. I had recently gotten my trading license and had been looking for work and—"

"What was he like?"

"His name is English, or perhaps American, but he clearly isn't. My guess is that he is Russian, perhaps Croat. He claimed to be an extremely wealthy person who needed an accredited broker to work for his firm."

"Siren?"

"Exactly. I started within a week of our meeting."

"And when you went to work for him and saw what this extremely wealthy financier's headquarters looked like, you didn't even think of . . ."

The waiter brings their drinks. Heinrich nods thanks, then finishes Sobieski's sentence. "Questioning it?" He sips his Berliner Weisse and nods approval. "No, I did not. I needed the job. I had been unemployed for almost a year and I was broke. Did I suspect that he was a criminal?" He shrugs. "You know what the economy has been like."

"So it's okay to work for terrorists in a bad economy. Do you think it was an accident that he found you at that bar?"

Heinrich scratches his chin, look away. He knows the answer, but isn't sure if he wants to give it to Sobieski. "I want, what's the word, immunity?"

"What do you think, I'm district attorney for planet earth? I saved your life, now you want immunity?"

They don't speak for a minute. Sobieski runs her fingers over the keypad on her phone. She knows she should check in with Michaud, who she sees has left her two messages, but she doesn't because she defied him and she doesn't know what to say. Right after this, she thinks. Looking around the restaurant, filled with young professionals, laughing, drinking in the middle of the day, she thinks of Marco Nello, who has also left her two messages in the past hour and a half, and wonders what he's doing right now.

"I don't think they found me by accident," Heinrich says. "I think they identified me as a potential employee, talented yet desperate enough to ignore certain things, and sought me out."

"Because you were an unemployed broker?"

"That," he answers. "But mostly because of my skills as a hacker, which, if I must say so, are substantial."

"What did you hack?"

"The trading accounts in the U.S., the brokerage houses and personal accounts of the traders in Hong Kong, Dubai, et cetera. The corporate sites and private accounts of the CEOs of the companies whose securities we later targeted for the trades. The shorts. Plus, the sequential thing, the multiple trades, that was my idea."

"Were there other trades that you performed for him besides the big ones?"

"Yes. Much smaller. But yes."

"How much longer? How many more do you think they're doing?"

"Not sure. They didn't say, but my guess, from the activity pattern since I began, is that this is their big week."

Sobieski straightens up. "By any chance did you, did you hack into . . . Homer's account?"

Heinrich's eyes go dead. Of course he did, Sobieski thinks. Then I've got to call Michaud and find a place to take this guy to break this open. But who knows if he'll freak and clam up under more intense *scrutiny*? For now, she thinks, while he's talking so freely, it's best to let him go.

"Look," Heinrich continues, "I knew that something criminal was going on. I knew that Homer wasn't legitimate and that the nature of these transactions . . . the short positions . . . the specific transactions . . . spread them out over time . . . I knew that they were done in this manner to avoid drawing unwanted attention to all parties. But I really was broke and they were offering me a *lot of money* for a few months' work. And the murders . . . Do you really think they will kill me?"

"When they're through with you?" Sobieski dips a spoon into her tea, twirls it counterclockwise, and arches her brow. "If they cleared out because they perceived some kind of threat yesterday . . ."

"Which I detected. I detected several actually. From Hong Kong and an IP address in New York City."

"Then why did you go back today?"

He pauses, takes another drink of his juice beer. "Because I kept the tracking software and a backup of everything I did there on a flash I'd hidden."

"A flash drive? That's a little crude for a hacker with substantial skills."

"I thought about floating it into my cloud, but then someone would have been able to make the connection."

"What software? Promis?"

He smiles. "You know Promis? I'm impressed. No, I made my own. Better than Promis. Promis on steroids. For kicks."

"Did they know about this?"

"No." He shakes his head. "No."

"Did you get it?"

Another head shake. "I was distracted."

"Where was it?"

"Stuck to the underside of a radiator with electrical tape."

The waiter arrives with Heinrich's fried meatballs. Sobieski takes a look at the dish and pulls her chair back. Her head aches from the concussion and her stomach is fluttering with nausea. "Where . . ." she begins, "what location were you going to work out of next? You were going to continue working for them, right?"

"Yes."

"Where?"

"They didn't say. But for the time being, today, I was to work out of my flat. I took one of their computers with me last night."

"Can we go there?"

"It's in Prenzlauer Berg, near Mitte. Sure. But don't you imagine they'll be looking for me?"

Sobieski doesn't answer. As she stares at him, she sips the tea for the first time but lets it trickle back into the cup because it has a coffee aftertaste. What else? "Did they give you orders to initiate any transactions today?"

As soon as he begins to nod, she sits up and leans closer, despite the smell of the meatballs.

"Where?"

"Ireland."

She tilts her head.

"Dublin," he continues. "They didn't tell me the name of the security yet, or the type of transaction."

"How would they contact you?"

"Coded messages. Cryptic. Greek stuff. I was to hear from them at two o'clock."

"If we get on your computer, it still might be there on the Siren account."

"If I go back, isn't it likely they'll kill me?"

"Take me there and I'll go up."

"Plus, it's not Siren anymore."

"Okay . . ."

"They closed that down yesterday when they broke down the office. Starting at two o'clock it's Ithaka. With a K."

"We have to go."

He ~~swallowed a mouthful into his mouth~~. "You sure you don't want ~~this~~?"

"Yes. Absolutely."

He ~~stands and wipes his mouth~~. "Okay, I'll take you there, but I'm not going in." She waits for the check while he puts his napkin on the table and holds up a finger, motioning himself to head to the bathroom in the back.

While she waits, Sobieski pushes Heinrich's plate to the far side of their table and tries to gather her thoughts. She's only been gone from her hotel for a few hours, but it feels like days. She knows she has to check to see if Sawa Luhabe has responded to her message, but first, she realizes, she has to call Michaud to tell him about Heinrich, to figure out what is going to happen in Dublin, to try, for once, to save a life.

For the first time in weeks the son of a bitch isn't there to pick up. "It's Sobieski," she begins her message, "and I have to talk to you ASAP about the next trade, which I've just been told is gonna go down in Dublin, with a connection to Siren's replacement firm, Ithaka. With a K. But Jesus, call me, Michaud. I need a secure place to take someone for interrogation."

She clicks off and begins drumming her fingers on the table. After two minutes, and still no sign of Heinrich, the once and former employee of Siren Securities and, briefly, Ithaka with a K, she stands up, spooked, overcome with the sense that something has gone disastrously wrong. She rushes to a waiter, grabs his sleeve, and says, "Bathroom! *Wo ist die Toilette?*"

The waiter points to a narrow hall in the back of the *Biersalon*. She runs past the other diners, followed by the waiter. She pounds on the door of the men's room with her open palms, but no one answers. She tries to push it open it, but it is locked.

As she takes two steps back, the waiter, sensing what's coming, calls, "Miss!" But it's too late. She lunges with her left leg toward the locked door while her right foot swings back and already begins to swivel above her waist.

The cheap interior bolt lock gives way beneath the impact of the bottom of her foot, and the door bursts open. Sobieski doesn't have to step inside to conclude that Heinrich is gone. The wide-open window that leads onto an alleyway tells her all she needs to know.

5

This is not how Rhonda had planned on spending her day. Having lunch with a deposed billionairess. Hopping around on behalf of her fugitive ex-husband. Rethinking everything about him and their marriage and divorce. And now this. Coming home to an apartment that has been visited by a stranger who may still be inside.

She knows someone has been here because she had left her *to do* list, a yellow legal pad, where she always did before going out, on the small oak table in the entry hall, next to a crystal vase of dried hydrangeas. Standing in the door frame, she takes a quick look into the apartment, scanning from left to right, and finally sees the yellow pad, facedown on the easy chair.

"Oh, shit," she says, to no one and perhaps someone. "The mail." Stepping backward out of the door and onto the front stoop, she wonders if Deborah Salvado had snitched on her so soon. And how could someone have gotten here so quickly? Or had someone been watching her long before this? She closes the door and walks slowly down the front path. At the mailbox she makes a show of inspecting each letter and piece of junk mail, in case someone is watching. Then she tilts her head back as if one of the envelopes has reminded her of something, shuts the mailbox door, clicks her key holder to unlock the Prius, and slides into the still-warm front seat.

She drives north on Bedford Road, then right onto Route 35, and then quickly onto the on-ramp for I-684 North. Looking into the rear-view to see if anyone is tailing her, she drives as fast as the Prius can manage. She hops off the interstate after one exit and winds her way along a series of stone wall–lined, wooded back roads. She stops in the parking lot of a pizza joint in the village/train station of Croton Falls. She wants to call Drew again, but she doesn't want to upset him about the visitor at her apartment, and he's right, until this is resolved it's best if they stay apart.

At one point last night, he told her, "Money didn't ruin us. I did." She didn't answer and wishes she had. You should have told him that a lot of things ruined us. Not just money, or the fund. A lack of judgment ruined us, she concludes. Allowing ourselves to be transfixed by a lifestyle that never should have been. The guilt, the self-loathing, the blaming—those were all collateral damage from the initial lack of judgment.

She opens her laptop and taps into one of the stores' wireless signals. You should have told him, she thinks, searching through the text of a poem nearly three thousand years old, that something that still exists cannot have been ruined. While seeking connections between past art and present evil, Homer and Salvado, scouring some twelve thousand lines written in dactylic hexameter, she can't help but note that for all of its focus on the epic adventures of Ulysses, it's the women of the story who make its most important and heroic choices. And that the ancient hero's homeward journey is not at all unlike the homeward journey Drew is in the midst of right now.

It begins to make sense in a cryptic, if not fully explicit way. Each of the first four passages from *The Odyssey* are somehow linked to one of the cities where a short occurred and an attempt was made on the trader's life. It's easy to find the link after the fact, when she knows both the city and the passage. But it's harder on upcoming days on which Weiss marked a passage but there is no information about the securities to be traded or the city. If she could find that out, the meaning of Weiss's glyphs for Thursday and Friday, perhaps she and Drew could save a life and find a way to catch Salvado in the act. The lines, from Book 24, refer to the "home of Ulysses." She thinks of Troy, or Ithaka. She thinks of every major city in the Mediterranean, but then it occurs to her that perhaps they are referring to a different Ulysses. What if they mean the home of the other famous literary Ulysses—the great novel by James Joyce, set not in Troy or Ithaka, but Dublin?

A half-block from her house she dims the lights and rolls to a stop. She turns off the car and looks across the street at her apartment. The porch light is on, probably turned on by Nikki, the disloyal other tenant upstairs who never has any visitors but says leaving the light on makes her feel safe. Otherwise the rest of the house, including Miranda's first-floor apartment, is dark.

She doesn't know what to do. At the very least she'd like to grab some things and leave. But she isn't sure if whoever was there earlier was looking for something or waiting for her. She wraps her arms around herself to fight the creeping night chill. Half the leaves are down, she notes, watching the silhouettes of backyard maples tilt in the breeze. In a few days they'll be empty. In ten minutes, she'll make a decision.

But first, she wants to close her eyes. They didn't sleep much last night. First talking. Then fighting the inevitable and then making love with an exhausting and exhilarating combination of ferocity, passion and rage, bliss and regret. Then reaching over and feeling the place he had just been.

Within minutes her head tilts back against the driver's seat. Soon after that a man's knuckles rap against her window. She's startled, but she doesn't scream. A tall, thin white man in jeans and a pullover sweatshirt bends to look at her. She reaches to turn the key, but the man is already opening her door. She lurches across the front seat to try to exit from the passenger side but stops when she sees a second man outside that door, bent at the waist, looking in.

The man on the driver's side asks, "Miranda Havens?"

No answer.

"We need to talk."

Her eyes dart back at the second man, who is opening the passenger side door and getting in. She lowers her head and closes her eyes.

"About your husband."

Have they killed him? she thinks. Or do they want me to tell them where he is so they can kill him later?

After moment she reopens her eyes and says to the steering wheel, "I don't have a husband."

6

Only three types of people jet each at the Newark Hilton: some one about to have an affair, embark on an ill-considered fling, or commit suicide. Havens wonders which type the woman at reception thinks he is.

In the corridor heading to the elevator he sees an open conference room. It's set up for a morning function, more than a dozen long tables broken into three rows, dotted with brochures and water bottles, name tags laid out in alphabetical order.

Four types, he thinks. Terrorists pay cash, too.

Next to the podium in the front of the room is exactly what he was hoping for: an easel with a two-foot by three-foot sketchpad. He takes the pad and a black Magic Marker and heads up to his room on the sixth floor.

His window overlooks a dark and vast industrial wasteland. Factory stacks and warehouses beneath a pale green and yellow haze of particulate clouds. He pulls the curtains, bolt-locks the door, kicks off his shoes, and turns on CNBC with the sound muted. The "host" bounces around a set with rolled-up sleeves, a financial expert with the soul of a carny. It's no surprise that Salvado was a regular, a trusted "friend of the show."

If enough people validate the reputations of enough people, every-one wins. Until, of course, they don't. Just ask the ratings experts.

He thinks of his late-night talk with Miranda. There is no mad or bad money, he thinks. Only mad or bad people with mad or bad intentions.

The markets were up today. Way up. Led by tech, supported by good job numbers, encouraging advance data out of Asia, and a somewhat stable liquid universe credit spread over benchmarks. It also doesn't hurt that no sovereign European nation appears to be on the brink of collapse today. He opens his laptop and gets onto the hotel wireless. While the home page loads, it occurs to him that he hasn't eaten all day. He calls room service and orders a cheeseburger and fries. Not the healthiest choice, but when someone is trying to kill you, cholesterol levels take a backseat to primal desire.

The first thing he checks is e-mail. There's a follow-up note from Rourke:

> Dude, there's absolutely something to your theory. The big guy is in full sociopath mode. Ate a young trader alive in the big room today, made him leave in tears, fired without so much as a shoebox full of belongings. We need to talk ASAP. Be safe.—TR

Then there's this, from an anonymous sender on a Hotmail account. The subject heading is: *DUBLIN*.

> I think a trade and a trader are about to be executed in Dublin, and here is why: The first passage about the Sirens activated the trading account at Siren in Berlin. The second passage about "brotherly" signaled which U.S. account to use in Philly. Each of the next three passages link in some way, often obscurely, to the place in which the trades took place that day. For instance, Wednesday, 11.106-7, mentions the beggar Iros,

which is a pun on Iris, who is (I kid you not) the god of rainbows. South Africa = the Rainbow Nation. The passage that aligns with the Dubai (oil country) movement on Tuesday mentions "a golden cruse of oil." For today, it mentions "the home of Ulysses," which I believe is the home of my favorite novel, James Joyce's *Ulysses*, set in Dublin. Cryptic and obscure to be sure, clearly they're using a shared code, but it seems that cryptic and obscure work to their advantage for acts of this nature. I tried calling, but your phone, like mine, is a POS. Be

to hack.

In less than five minutes he has something. A firm out of Dublin called Celtic Tiger Redux. A middleman out of Berlin at a firm called Ithaka, with a link to a U.S. trading account out of Philly, presumably one of Chuck's skells. The Dublin trader's name is Dempsey, and the short activity this time is in the insurance sector, specifically and exclusively a U.S.-based company called CGI that, of course, the Rising Fund loves as a long. His next search is for the international calling code for Ireland.

7

Dublin

Liam Dempsey believes that there is a fortune to be made in anxiety.

So it makes perfect sense that first thing each morning, rather than checking the major indexes that 99.9 percent of the financial world relies on, Dempsey goes right for his personally customized, self-titled Anxiety Index, a number derived from a complex combination of more than a dozen global indicators, each of which is a reflection of the world's most potentially catastrophic scenarios.

Considered are such things as Spanish debt, the London Interbank Overnight Index (LIBOR), the price of lumber, war dead in Afghanistan, Greek debt, the Baltic Dry Index (shipping), the price of oil, the number of and potential damages from natural disasters (earthquake, tsunami, hurricane, flooding) in play, Portuguese debt, political assassinations, credit default info for dozens of markets worldwide. And much, much more.

No one knows about the Anxiety Index except Dempsey, an anxious man who treats his condition not with meditation or prescription drugs, but by reveling in it and hoping to eventually leverage anxiety into some sort of spectacular personal financial gain.

One day he hopes that circumstances will prompt the Anxiety Index to climb above 9.0, that some doomsday sequence of acts or numbers will send it over the edge, serving as the canary in a coal mine indicating that everything will come crashing down, and that he will be among the very first to recognize its coming and exploit the situation. Dempsey has a plan in place for how to mine gold from a river of blood in a post–9.0 AI world. He calls it "Operation Higher Anxiety."

But today, his index hovers just below 8, far from the fifty-two-week high of 8.3, when things exploded in Egypt, Libya, and Yemen. Or the all-time high from when everything went down with AIG and Lehman and Bear Stearns and the U.S. subprime market. He was ready to implement Operation Higher Anxiety then, but somehow the world recoiled. So for now he carries on as a trader, formerly of Citibank, formerly of Commerzbank, formerly of Sumitomo, and now hanging on by a thread with the upstart firm Tiger Redux, a not-so-subtle nod to Dublin's late 1990s boom days, when it was known as the Celtic Tiger.

Dempsey's last official act at Tiger Redux is fitting: a major short play against a global insurance giant. A quarter-billion-dollar bet on the failure of a company that makes billions insuring against the failure of others. The call came out of a Berlin middleman at a firm called Ithaka Investments, via a Morgan Stanley trading account in Philadelphia. Because of the number of firms involved and the specific set of instructions laid out by the caller (mostly involving the meted out placement of a number of transactions as opposed to one large, attention-gathering play, as well as a promise of confidentiality), it's complicated. But far from too complicated for a veteran, albeit one of modest success, such as Dempsey.

As he begins to set the transactions in motion, he can't help but wonder what the client knows. What horrible thing could have prompted someone to place a quarter-billion-dollar bet on the imminent decline, if not the fall, of one of the world's largest insurance conglomerates? And how will it affect the rest of the world and, of course, the Anxiety Index? So he defies a mandate from the client and digs deeper into the stock, looking for clues and a reason to get involved in its downfall.

At one o'clock he tells his desk mate O'Dell that he's heading out to grab a bite for lunch, but O'Dell barely acknowledges him. O'Dell is twenty-seven, eight years Dempsey's junior, and has all the answers. According to O'Dell, if you're thirty-five and still working a desk at the likes of Tiger Redux, you are not worth knowing, or long for the financial world. Halfway to the door Dempsey hears his phone ring. He stops, stares, and then walks on. He's hungry. He's having a good day. Whatever it is, he decides, can only botch it up.

Dublin's International Financial Services Centre is the home to some 430 financial services companies, including Tiger Redux, and more than fourteen thousand workers, many of whom are out on the sidewalks on this warm and cloudy Wednesday. Dempsey walks across the street and buys a take-out ham and cheese sandwich in a restored structure that was once a tobacco store.

On the way to his regular bench on the north bank of the River Liffey, Dempsey stops, as he does almost every day, to consider the life-sized line of forlorn figures of the bronze Famine Memorial. His family history is defined by famine and war, expatriation and wanting. To Dempsey, the sculptures of so many ruined individuals are timeless symbols of economic despair, and the bronze mangy dog straggling behind the others could be the mascot, the corporate logo for everything his Anxiety Index represents.

He passes the tourist pubs and ambles farther north along Custom House Quay. At a bench in a quiet space just beyond the Custom House, he takes a seat and looks at the slate gray chop of the river. The sandwich is forgettable, which is fine. Dempsey eats the same sandwich every day for a reason. He doesn't want choice. He wants to fill his stomach, and the brief thirty minutes before he goes back to his desk and his screens and his numbers.

Part of the reason he hasn't been more successful, he realizes, isn't

a lack of financial acuity, but the lack of a personal touch with coworkers and clients. He's never been good at cold calls and client lunches
and sucking up to his supervisors. What he's been good at is predicting
failure, qualifying it and quantifying it and intuiting it.

And right now, Liam Dempsey senses a sort of epic failure, coursing
through his entire being, a disaster meme pulsing through the
industry, the culture, the moment, charged with stomach-churning
electricity. He's not yet sure why, but this insurance stock feels charged
with danger, ticking like a bomb in the center of a much larger environ-

always. The stranger jogs up from behind, catching his attention at
the last second, but it is too late to run or fight or scream. He doesn't see
or feel the seven-inch blade of the Ka-Bar military knife that slashes
deep into his windpipe with a backhand swipe. He thinks it is a punch,
or a shove. Dempsey briefly flails as he crumbles to the ground and sees
the blood jetting from his neck onto the cold cobblestones. He realizes
now that he wasn't punched, but he's incapable of making noise or
resisting. He hears the footsteps of his assailant running back the way
they came, and he hears air sucking through the wet hole that gapes
across his neck. He's still grasping his phone, the small screen frozen
on the latest numbers from the ascendant Anxiety Index, as he unfolds
upon the stone, his blood already pooling and running down the lip of
a storm drain, beginning a slow drift toward the city's edge and the
entrance to the North Sea.

8

Berlin

Rushing along a foreign sidewalk, looking for a glimpse of Heinrich Shultz's blond head. The weight of multiple failures sucking the breath out of her. She's defied her boss, rejected a seemingly good man, lost consciousness, and lost a witness and/or suspect. She stops at a corner and looks in all four directions for a miracle. Bending at the waist, gasping from hyperventilation, she fights off a wave of nausea.

Outside of romance, she's not used to failure.

Her phone rings. Now fucking Michaud calls. She stares at the screen but doesn't answer. Until she fixes this, she can't. A cab passes. She considers flagging it, but where would she go? The only place to go, she realizes, is Heinrich's apartment. But where in Berlin is that? Prenz-something district, if he was telling the truth, and there's no reason to think he was. Plus, she doesn't even know his last name. Heinrich something from the Prenz-something district. Even Michaud would laugh.

She asks a passing woman to point her toward the gate, back toward her hotel. Within minutes, the central arch comes into view, and as she approaches she can't help but think of the Gate's history, the people who passed beneath, died before it, and railed at it, from Napoleon and Hitler to Reagan.

And, of course, Kennedy. *Ich bin ein Berliner!*

Ich bin Schultz. As clearly as she remembers Kennedy's classic sound bite, she remembers the voice that pulled her back to consciousness back in Siren's office. Heinrich's voice on the phone. Heinrich Schultz. She cups her phone in her palm and wonders what to do, whom to call. Michaud would be best, but she's not ready to admit failure and to face the consequences. The alert light is flashing. Someone sent a text while she was walking. Marco.

Dinner tonight?

Rather than text back, she calls Marco Nello.

"I thought I'd somehow blown it."

"That's my job today," she answers.

"What do you think? What do you feel like eating?"

"I can't. I'm having a really bad day."

"Oh, I'm sorry. Perhaps . . ."

"Marco, could you help me find an address here in Berlin?"

"Sure, anything."

She tells him Heinrich Schultz's name and the partial neighborhood address. "Near Mitte?"

"Near Mitte . . . Prenzlauer Berg?"

"Yes."

"Bohemian neighborhood, gradually succumbing to gentrification. Give me a few minutes."

Two minutes later Marco Nello calls Sobieski with two addresses, the second of which is closer to Mitte. "Are you all right? You sound distressed."

"Yes," she answers. "I am distressed, but I'll be all right."

"Will I see you later?"

"I don't know, Marco. That depends upon how this goes."

"Call at any time, Cara. For anything. I'd love to see you."

In the taxi en route to the first Heinrich Shultz address, Sobieski's phone rings three times. The first two are Michaud and the third is Marco. All three times she chooses not to answer, not to speak with the two men in her life who care about her more than anyone else. Her boss and a man she just met. She decides not to think about what that means.

The cab stops outside a quaint sidewalk café on Eberwalder Strasse. She pays the driver and gets out. The length of the entry level of the home in which this Heinrich Shultz lives is covered with a gorgeous mural of trees and flowers. The stone of the upper three floors is a vivid pink. Looking both ways at the colors and murals and gardens real and imagined, she thinks, even the lowest level of criminal lives in a cooler neighborhood than me.

The striking imagery of the building momentarily took her eye away from the crowd circling on the sidewalk. Some are running away from the gathering, others toward it. Every other person seems to be talking frantically into a phone. As she draws closer, the crowd parts enough for her to glimpse the narrow leg and then the white-blond hair. And then the blood.

Her phone rings. Hong Kong. Not Michaud, but Cheung the criminal. She doesn't pick up.

When she sees that it is Shultz, she steps back and covers her mouth with her left hand. Her phone rings again. Michaud, again.

She picks up this time.

"Where the fuck have you been?"

"Michaud . . . I had to go in. . . . It was empty and, well, he surprised me."

"Who surprised you? I sent a six-man backup team to Siren. You couldn't wait fifteen minutes? What the hell were you thinking? Do you know how big this is?"

The crowd peels away from the body as the first policeman arrives.

"Let me go talk to the cops," she tells Michaud.

"No," he says.

"What?"

"Stay out of it."

In the distance, Sobieski can make out the wail of an ambulance. While the police begin directing the crowd to push back, to give them

room, a young woman bursts out of the front door of Shultz's apartment. Michaud drops the phone from her ear to watch. Halfway to the body the young woman is intercepted by one of the cops. He wraps his arms around her. When she tries her off the ground her feet thrash in kicking and flailing.

Finally the woman lets out a primal wail when she gets her first look at the still body of Heinrich Shultz, master hacker, financial advisor, accomplice to terrorists, failed fugitive, and a man she must have loved.

9

Newark

Dempsey is not in, and no one knows how to reach him.

Havens hangs up, grabs the large pad, and tears off a page. He smooths the page's sticky back against the wall behind the bed. He removes a framed watercolor print of a beach scene from a hook and then affixes four more sheets along the same wall.

The burger arrives. He devours it with one hand and writes in black marker with the other. "HONG KONG" atop the first sheet, then "DUBAI" atop the second, "JOHANNESBURG" atop the third, "RIO" atop the fourth, and atop the fifth he writes "DUBLIN." Next, on each sheet, he writes the date, the securities and approximate dollar value involved in the transaction, the name of the foreign/soon-to-be-murdered broker in that city, the name of the firm in Berlin that served as middle man, the name of the U.S.-based account that initiated the transactions, and the name of the U.S. citizen to whom the account supposedly belonged.

He rips off a sixth sheet, sticks it on the mirrored closet door, and writes "NOTES" atop it. Copying off Danny Weiss's whiteboard and Miranda's e-mail, he writes the corresponding book and line numbers from *The Odyssey*. Miranda's right: To figure this out, he'll need to be a human as well as a quant.

Rapidly, he scrawls a list of the sectors:

—TECH
—OLD MEDIA (publishing, TV, Hollywood, mags, newspapers)
—NEW MEDIA (social nets, digital entertainment, gaming, search, browser, etc.)

It's not difficult to make a connection between old and new media, technology and advertising. They're all, to some degree, in bed with one another, trying to figure out how to make a buck in a constantly evolving, digitized universe. Every day there's news of some new alliance between tech, entertainment, and branding. A slew of books have already been written about the age of convergence. But this insurance company's place on his wall makes no sense at all to Havens. What does CGI have to do with the others?

He does a search to see if there's a connection between one of the world's largest insurance companies and the other trades. Nothing. It doesn't insure any of the other companies or the buildings in which they are headquartered. Even the ad agency of record for CGI has nothing to do with the others.

Next he loses himself in data mining and model building, employing not just the considerable skills of the statistical arbitrage quant, but the skills of every type of relevant quant and theorist he knows. Normally his job is to determine the probable short-term success or failure of a security or sector, but in this instance it's about more than running numbers through a program and letting an algorithm determine the next step. This time he also must solve a behavioral problem. What does all of these trades and killings lead to? What goal, event, or catastrophe?

He strips down each trade and stock and looks at it in discrete and continuous time. He employs the tenets of basic probability theory, stochastic calculus, and builds and implements models in C++. He uses the martingale approach to analyze the effect of asset prices on the change of information flow, specifically how a piece of speculative or hypothetical information—for instance, a rumored terrorist act, or the death of a broker—can influence the price of an asset. Within two hours the walls and floor are littered with sheets covered with equations and notes.

An interesting pattern emerges. In addition to the Rising Fund longs and the huge matching international shorts, a growing supplemental short market has taken root. With each day, each ensuing trade/assault, the volume of the additional shorts placed on each security increases. At first gradually but now almost exponentially. Havens concludes that someone has been leaking information on the criminal end, and others around the world are copycatting the moves in smaller batches.

Next he turns to history. He takes the sequences that are occurring with these five stocks now and applies them to Weiss's historical models constructed to detect volatile stock movement before and after some of the worst disasters of recent times. The Mumbai shootings. The Bali nightclub bombing. The Spanish train bombing. The London Metro explosions. The attack on the USS *Cole*. The triple disaster in Japan. The first attack on the World Trade Center. And, of course, the last.

The most interesting irregularities occurred prior to the 9/11 attacks on the World Trade Center. According to the *9/11 Report* and analytics that have emerged since, in early September of 2001 five times as many shorts as normal were placed on stock for American

Airlines, United Airlines, Boeing, and Morgan Stanley Dean Witter, which occupied more than twenty-two floors of the Trade Center. Havens tries to imagine if, assuming there was a connection, he could have predicted what was coming if he had had foreknowledge of the 2001 trades; if he could have gathered enough information and presented a strong enough case to prevent the terrorists from ever getting off the ground that day.

Finally, exhausted, he flops onto the bed, closes his eyes, and thinks of Miranda and Danny Weiss and the five trades. And he wonders if there is to be a sixth, and will it be? What trader will die? And . . . why?

10

Berlin

"I've been relieved of my duties."

Marco Nello looks across the table at Sobieski. He had offered to take her to the finest restaurant in Berlin, anywhere she wanted. But here they are in a bakery at 9 P.M. Not having dinner, having strudel. It's what she wanted.

"I have to go back to Hong Kong."

He looks down.

"Not us. It's work."

"Why don't you stay a few extra days here?"

She shakes her head. "I have to make things right." She wants to tell him everything. That she went to a casino rather than get to know him, that she defied her boss, that she was assaulted as a result of her defiance, that a young man died this evening because she failed to properly do her job, and that somewhere in South Africa a woman might be dead—all because she lacked discipline and willpower. And whatever act of financial terrorism she's been investigating gets closer to happening by the minute.

Nello puts down his fork, holds up his hands. "You're right. I don't understand. And I'm guessing it's for the best that I don't. It was wrong of me to . . ."

"It wasn't wrong, Marco. It's just, right now, *I'm* what's wrong."

"You take your job seriously, which I admire. And it seems that you've made some kind of mistake. But if it was unintentional, if your reasons were pure, they'll forgive you."

"They may," she answers. "I won't. Not when lives are on the line."

"Look, without revealing state secrets, tell me what's going on."

She takes a bite of strudel, stares at him, and decides to tell him about everything, except the gambling. She tells him about Hong Kong, Dubai, Rio, and Johannesburg, Michaud and Mo, Lau, Al Mar, Valverde, and Sawa Luhabe. She tells him about Heinrich and Dublin, the abuse in U.S.-based new and old media, advertising and tech. That, besides it feels so good to have someone who cares to listen, she finds herself telling him why. Why she took this job, why she can't stop caring about it. Why her father's fifteen-year-old murder still consume, drive, and haunt her. "In other words, why I'm really a deeply flawed, extremely poor choice for you to enter into a relationship with."

Nello smiles. "We're all flawed."

"What should I do?"

"Go to Hong Kong, do what you need to. If you don't, we'll never have a chance."

"Really?"

"Then come back. Please. And stay for a while."

She twists the corners of her napkin and thinks of past boyfriends who refused to put her priorities first. Maybe that's because they knew that no matter where they lived or how much they agreed to accommodate her, she would always put her job before everything. Why should Marco Nello be any different?

"Or," he continues, "I can go to Hong Kong."

"Really?"

"Sure. When you're ready, I can take some time and visit you."

"Or," she says, allowing a smile, "maybe we can go someplace else."

The taxi stops in front of her hotel. They kiss briefly and hold each other close until the driver clears his throat.

"Do you want to come up?"

"Of course I do," Nello answers. "But you're leaving when—dawn? And I imagine you want to work, to start your comeback."

She opens the door, takes his hand, and pulls. "Come."

He pulls her against him in the empty elevator and they kiss. As the doors slide open, they back out onto her floor, still kissing. He brushes his lips against the back of her neck while she fumbles with the key card and unlocks her door. Inside they attempt to undress each other but quickly lose patience and strip off their own clothes. In bed her intensity is all-consuming and her release is almost primal, charged with visceral desire and, for the first time in too long, pure romantic attraction. Not sadomasochistic punishment, or the alleviation of guilt, or escape.

She's on her stomach, sweating, catching her breath, when he rises and looks out the window. It's late, close to three in the morning. "You'll stay, won't you?"

He comes back and sits on the edge of the bed, looks at her, and traces the back of his left hand against her hair.

"What about Fiji?" she asks.

"Fiji?"

"Our trip. Rent a bungalow . . . surf . . . read."

He puts on his underwear and reaches for his pants. "So," he says, buttoning his pants, then grabbing his dress shirt, "why do you think they're making those short trades and killing those traders?"

She rises up on an elbow. "That's what we were trying to find out. They're obviously gaming the market, hoping that some event will happen naturally, or they'll make it happen so they can cash in."

"You mentioned the categories, the—what do you call it—sectors they've shorted, but not the specific stocks. Do you know those?"

She sits up with her back against the headboard. "Yeah, Marco. Of course I do. Why?"

He buttons the last button on his shirt and looks for his suit jacket. Fully dressed, he turns to her with an expression on his face she hasn't seen before. "Because we have a mutual acquaintance who would very much like to know."

11

Newark

His cell phone buzzes and he lurches awake. He sits up and scans the room, trying to remember where he is. When he is. The silent TV and the hotel décor don't help, but when he looks at the wall above the bed and sees the writing on the wall, the giant pages filled with data but still no story, he remembers.

He scrambles off the bed and grabs the phone on the desk beside the TV remote. "Mir?"

"Yup."

He rubs his eyes, looks at the hotel clock radio flashing midnight. "What time is it, Mir?"

"Late. I don't know. Tomorrow late."

"Are you all right?"

She blows the air out of her lungs, sniffles some back through her nose.

"What's going on, Mir? You crying?"

"Uh-huh."

"Are you home? Because I can . . ."

"No," Miranda answers. "I'm not home. I won't go back, and no, Drew, you can't."

"Where are—"

She interrupts. "It's not important. I'm safe. For now. Okay?"

It's not okay, but Havens knows that voice. The topic is closed. "Tell me what happened, Mir."

He listens to her fill, then slowly empty her lungs. "Should I start with the midday break-in at my house, what I've learned about Salvado, or the two men who forced their way into my car while I was parked in front of the apartment?"

"Awww, shit . . ." He paces toward the door, then back to the window. He touches the slender break in the curtains but leaves them closed.

"Fill this."

"Salvado's people."

"I thought it at first, but now I'm pretty sure they only did the break-in."

"Then who?"

"Cops, Drew. NYPD homicide detectives, wanting to talk to me about Danny Weiss and, of course, you."

"I spoke to Rourke. They think I did it."

"Of course they think you did it. How does it feel to be a person of interest?"

"Danny Weiss was right. Salvado's panicking because he knows I can hurt him. Otherwise there was no need to point the police to me."

"Maybe they figured it on their own. They said without a doubt they can place you in Weiss's apartment the night he died. Phone records. Security camera at the nail salon next door. The cabbie who drove you there. All kinds of stuff, Drew."

"I shouldn't have gotten you involved."

"Then they asked if I'd seen you and I told them that I had."

"You should have."

"I mean, they found me half-asleep in my car, so who knows what else they know?"

"Don't lie on my behalf."

"I told them I didn't know anything about Weiss, including the fact that he had been murdered. I said that you didn't mention him to me and that I was not at all happy to see you."

"Did you tell them I stayed?"

"I did. I told them that you begged; said you were having some kind of emotional breakdown and had nowhere else to go. I said I let you stay on the couch. And when I got up this morning, you were gone; where, I have no idea."

"No mention of Salvado?"

"By the police? Other than the fact that he's your famous boss and that they'd spoken to him and, they hinted, he ratted you out, and that he's promised his full cooperation and he's extremely saddened and upset by the loss of a young talent like Weiss . . . no. I wasn't going to get into it with them because I didn't think it would help. Because of who he is and because he's the one who has them locked in on you."

He looks at the incomplete sheets of information covering the walls, trying to think of what to say, what to do next.

"My God, Drew, this is bad. Salvado is . . ."

"I'm going to fix this."

"You can't *fix* this! This is much more than a mathematical problem. It's life. Death. *Criminals*, Drew. If you try to fix this, you're going to get killed. And, you know, I kind of don't want that to happen."

"This is an encouraging development. The caring."

She doesn't answer.

"I'm gonna be fine, Mir."

"Well," she begins, steeling herself, all business now. "Did you get my Dublin message?"

"I did. I was too late."

"Well, I found out some things about your sociopath boss."

"From his sociopath wife?"

"That, plus I took the info she gave me and did some digging."

"And?"

"Your boy Salvado is more dangerous than you ever imagined."

For the next ten minutes Miranda reveals what Deborah Salvado told her this afternoon, plus what she's since discovered. This includes revelations of incidents that occurred before Salvado's comeback as an all-American financial success story, most notably a series of on-campus antigovernment arrests in college, angry letters to the editor of the *Wall Street Journal* and the *New York Times*, and dozens of bitter and inflammatory antigovernment, anticorporate, anti-American quotes he made prior to his first go-round in the hedge business.

"The thing is," Miranda explains, "back then, because he was just starting out, no one paid any attention. By the time he came back and got successful, everyone had forgotten his more radical views and looked at all what he was saying now that the money was starting to roll in.

"But," she says, "something happened in that period that broke the started The Rising, where he flipped the switch that changed him from hate to love, loss to profit, rabble rouser to patriot."

"Greed defeated revenge," Havens says. "Funny how no one cares about the past if there's money to be had in the present."

"I think there's more," Miranda offers. "Something that turned him into this monster."

He has no reply.

"How bad do you think this might be?"

"Bad enough to kill a bunch of innocent people, to take down companies."

"Don't you know anyone with the police, Drew? The SEC? I'll go with you."

"Whoever I know he knows better. Unless we can figure it all out, no one will believe it. Shit, we barely do. And it's more than just coming forward to say I'm innocent. If I do, I'll have to abandon this. Then no one will be around to try to stop it."

"You can walk away."

"It's going to be bad."

"I bet if you told him, he'd let you walk."

"Bad as in catastrophic. He already offered me the chance to walk. You really want me to walk away from that? For years I've screwed us up, Mir. This can't fix what was, but it's a chance for me to finally get something right."

Neither speaks for a while. They used to do this when they first started dating, not speaking for minutes at a time in the middle of a phone conversation. And those silences were magical. He felt that he grew more connected to her with each passing second during those silences. Then, later, after Erin died, before the divorce, their phone conversations were also often punctuated by long silences, though of an entirely different type. It was as if the process was being reversed during those calls, their connection fraying more with each passing second. Now this. He wonders what type of silence this is.

"You promise you're safe, Mir?"

"I promise."

He doesn't answer. Doesn't want to hang up.

"I'm gonna go now, Drew. We'll talk in the morning, okay?"

"Yeah, sure. Mir?"

"Uh-huh."

"Where are you?"

At first she doesn't answer. Then, while smoothing the cool white top sheet on her queen bed in the Chelsea Hotel, she says, "I'm fine, Drew. I'm in a good place."

12

S Luhabe uses the notes of Cara Sobieski and Drew Havens as a
jumping off point and discovers enough to make her cry. The
trades in Hong Kong, Dubai, Rio, and now Dublin. All shorts. All out of
Berlin. All except hers ending with the death of the trader. Somehow
they didn't get her. Somehow, for the time being, she's managed to
survive.

It's obvious that these are not random coincidences, but as hard as
she tries to make a connection, she can't find a motive or any clue as to
where this is all going, to what happens next.

It's after 9 P.M. She slept through the afternoon and woke at 6:45 to
see her brother sitting on her bed. They had a snack in her room, and
clearly he wanted to talk, to have some sort of confessional moment
with her, but even while freeloading in his gangster compound, she
refused to indulge him. "I have work to do, Muntukayise," she said.

"My name is Jolly."

"I don't know any Jolly."

"Yet you're willing to sleep under Jolly's roof, with the protection of
Jolly's guns."

"I have work to do."

He reached out and stroked her cheek. "It is good to see you, sister. I hope you will stay and see that I am a better man than the people you work with, the criminals who hide behind the shields of corporate logos."

When she runs out of leads she decides to make a list. A memo, called *What I Know Now*. She describes everything that has happened to her in the last forty-eight hours, from when she left for work Tuesday morning through all that she has discovered up until now. Of course, she leaves out the part about taking her family to Swaziland, and staying with her gangster brother here in Hillbrow. At the end of the note she cuts and pastes the e-mails that she has received from agent Cara Sobieski and Drew Havens.

After rereading it, she decides she should share it with them. Why not? She's researched both and they both appear to be who they said they are. She's typing the first address, Sobieski's, when she hears the initial gunshots in front of the house.

She rolls off the bed and rushes to her window. The armed guard in the back courtyard moves in a crouch along the edge of the concrete wall and then out of view, toward the front entrance.

Seconds later she hears more gunfire. The staccato bursts of automatic weapons. The roar of a shotgun blast. The same guard has scrambled back into the courtyard and stooped behind a stone barbecue chimney, when a single pistol shot tears into his hip and takes him down. She abandons the window and jogs to the door. Cups an ear to listen before opening it. Men shouting, also in bursts. Then more gunfire.

Inside the house the guns sound different. A deeper register, like guns that kill rather than toys.

Above the gunfire she hears the voice of her brother. He's at the base of the stairs.

"Come on!" he yells. "Come and get it!"

These people may think that they are gangsters, but they didn't know that they were raiding the house of the gangster Jolly Luhabe. She steps across the room and opens the door. Through the railing posts at the bottom of the stairs she sees his legs bending and straightening. When they straighten he reels off a burst of gunfire. When they bend he takes cover behind the stairway. "Jolly!" she calls.

"Go, sister!" he calls. "Back stair." He looks up the stairs, and when he sees her, he smiles. Sensing that this will be the last she'll see of her brother, she smiles back.

"Jolly, come . . ."

"Go!" he yells. "You can't stay here after this. Go now!" He punctuates the last word with another machine gun burst.

As she heads back to the bed by the computer, she hears a wounded man groaning downstairs, she guesses in the living room. After a short volley, the groaning stops. Then, more gunfire from other parts of the house, inside and out.

She scrolls up to the top of the document and clicks on SEND. Then she quickly snaps shut the laptop and shoves it inside her bag. When her hand comes out of the bag it is holding her husband's gun.

Halfway down the hall to the back stairway she stops. Jolly is still shooting and shouting at the bottom of the main stairway. She carefully steps down three stairs during another exchange of gunfire. Jolly has moved behind the edge of a doorway and is still aiming at one or more assailants in the living room.

Jolly looks up and sees his sister again. His eyes widen and a smile begins to form until he sees her raise the pistol in his direction. He ducks as she squeezes off the first of nine shots. Three find their mark, one in the temple of the man who had come in through the back door and was about to kill her brother.

13

Berlin

This time, when Sobieski goes back to Siren, she brings her gun.

At first, the night guard isn't going to let her pass. He asks for ID and when she reaches for her badge, she realizes that she never got it back from Heinrich Schultz. One more thing to explain to Michaud once she goes back to Hong Kong for phase one of her worldwide mea culpa tour.

"I am a law enforcement agent of the United States. A cop. Police." She tries to remember how to say it in German, but it's no use.

He shakes his head: "ID."

She pulls a fifty-euro bill out of the front pocket of her jeans and slaps it on his podium. "Five minutes," she says, holding up five fingers. "Okay?"

He takes the money, puts it in his own front pocket, and looks the other way.

After Nello left, with the names of the securities and her assurance that she would provide more, she went into the bathroom and vomited. Back in her room she sat naked on the hotel bed, the linens barely ruffled, and thought about suicide. It wouldn't have been for drama, or to show some guy that she meant it, or to get her family's attention.

That's because there is no guy, and no family to give or withhold attention. It would be just you, she thought. You'd be doing it to punish you. To end you.

"Cheung sent you all this way just to follow me?"

Nello nodded. "He saw immense potential in you. Rightfully, it turns out."

"What does he want?"

"Everything you know. What you owe him, in a sense, plus interest."

"Or else?"

"Not much. A gradual dismantling of your reputation and your life. Or a rather quick one."

"What about the book?"

He gave her a blank look.

"On the phone, you managed to all but tell me not to have read the book in the future."

He shrugged. "I looked it up on the Internet while you were reading it. We had a lot of time. By the way, I thought it sucked."

The door is still unlocked. She twists the knob, pushes it open, and flips on the overhead fluorescents. When she sees that the office is empty, she turns the lights back off, closes the door, and walks across the room. The glow of the surrounding buildings and streets provide enough light for her to see. On hands and knees she crawls the length of the bank of windows, dragging her left hand along the underside of the radiator cover.

Beneath the last window her fingers come to rest upon the electrical tape, and the lump beneath it. It doesn't take much to peel away one end of tape. Heinrich probably did the same almost every day. Since they searched him on the way out it was the only way he could have a hard copy of his transactions. She holds it up to the window for a better look. Red, small. Nothing special on the outside, but presumably powerful enough to take down a man, a company, or a government on the inside. She feels bad for Heinrich Shultz, but the son of a bitch had to know.

She walks back to her hotel along the night sidewalks of the financial district. She passes beneath the glass and steel towers and the ornate stone edifices that once housed royalty and are now home to the kings and queens of the financial kingdom. The progression makes sense, she thinks, which leads to another question: After monarchs and money, whom will we worship, to whom or what will we bow next?

In her coat pocket is her phone, which she has on mute. She doesn't want to hear from Michaud again, or Nello, or Cheung.

It's after 5 A.M. when she walks back into the lobby of her hotel. At six she's scheduled to go to the airport to head back to Hong Kong and Michaud and judgment.

Packing takes minutes. Primarily because she never unpacked the little she brought to begin with. When she's finished, she sits on the edge of the bed and rubs her face. It's too late to sleep, too early to do much else. She never thought she'd want to, but she wishes she could cry. When her father got arrested when she was in high school, she wouldn't allow it. Wouldn't even allow it when her mother passed away. She didn't cry then and hasn't cried since.

She thinks of the piece-of-shit Nello reprimanding her for living her life to atone for the imperfections of another and thinks, Even a liar and a criminal can see it. She wonders, When will it be okay to walk away? When will it be all right to abandon a career in law enforcement and leave the financial world and her superhero revenge-and-reparation fantasy and move on to whatever it is that she was meant to do?

Soon, she tells herself. She can feel it. But not now. Not after compromising everything by giving away inside information to a man who is worse than a criminal. She could never move on or end it like this.

It's been more than four hours since she last checked her messages. Some kind of record. She scrolls through the contents of her inbox. Michaud. Michaud. Michaud. Marco. Michaud. Flight confirmation for tomorrow. Or today, really. Michaud. Marco.

Then this, less than an hour ago: Sawa Luhabe.

As soon as she finishes reading Luhabe's *What I Know Now* message, and Luhabe's suggestion that she immediately get in contact with this American quant analyst, she grabs her bag and leaves for the airport. In the cab en route she's already on the phone with the airlines, looking for the next flight to New York.

THURSDAY,
OCTOBER 26

1

R—————————————————————————————
in his office this morning. He doesn't bother to check the need
nights or the futures or any of that other bullshit.

From now on, he thinks, none of that matters. For the next thirty-six hours he *is* the market. He will make and break it.

It's 5:25 A.M. The call is in five minutes.

He walks to his window and looks out at the Hudson. A tug pulling a barge out of the harbor, past the Statue of Liberty. The lights of commuter ferries blinking back and forth from Hoboken and Weehawken and points north. He thinks of his first job, before he was married, before he became rich. On the Mercantile Exchange, working for some douchenozzle who had a seat trading oil. "Light, sweet crude oil," the jackass told him on his first day, "the most wanted and valuable form of crude oil in the world."

For two years he took a bus from Fort Lee because he couldn't afford to live in the city. The moon and stars were out when he waited at his stop in the morning and again when he went home at night. For two years he lived and died by the fortunes of his boss, and light, sweet crude. Each contract was for one thousand barrels, or forty-two thousand gallons. The contracts were and still are traded for twenty-three hours and fifteen minutes each day from Monday to Friday (with a break from 5:15 P.M. to 6 P.M.), and from 9 A.M. until 2:30 P.M. in the open outcry, also called the pit session. He worked twelve-hour shifts, starting at 5:15 A.M., and discovered everything he needed to know about life and money in the pit, one of last places where buyers and sellers trade by hand signals and shouting. He found the primal, blood-thirsty competition nothing less than addicting. Often, when the guy working the late shift couldn't make it, he would volunteer to cover, working thirty-six straight hours.

When his boss got it right, young Salvado would sometimes get a spot bonus, nothing special, a few thousand here and there, and the occasional invite out for happy hour drinks. There he would pick at and probe every worthwhile quadrant of the greedy bastard's mind. And of course, when his boss got it wrong, when he'd lose big on the day or hit a prolonged slump, Salvado bore the brunt of his wrath.

It was those radical mood swings in his small, white, alternately generous and irascible boss that prompted Salvado to call him, behind his back, by the name of the commodity they traded: Light Sweet Crude.

For two years he helped make his boss tens of millions of dollars, only to be fired one brutal Friday afternoon in October. To this day, other than the fact that his boss was losing that week, he doesn't know why he was shit-canned. When he asked why, his boss said, "You should have seen the writing on the wall."

"The wall of what?" he answered. "A pit?"

In retrospect, he often thinks, after what happened to his father, he *should* have seen it coming. That day he vowed to do whatever it takes to succeed, and to never again be surprised by the markets and the people who control them.

At 5:30 the cell phone rings. He has a mobile for work, one for personal calls, and a phone just for this.

He answers: "Calypso."

"What if his great father came from the unknown world and rove these men like dead leaves through the place?"

"Right," Salvado replies. "Now I need to ask you a question."

"All right."

"What the fuck happened? Why so messy?"

"This is not a simple plan."

"Maybe it should have been," he says. "Maybe you got too cute."

"Cute?"

"Needless, unnecessarily complex. Killing . . ."

"We couldn't afford the risk."

"That's how you deal with risk?"

"We eliminate it, it's how . . ."

Salvado slams a hand on the desktop. "It's how things fail, it's how people get caught. What about the other guy? The fucking loose end?"

"We are working tirelessly to ensure that he is found."

Salvado looks back out the window. "So at lunch I do a tech walk-through. Everything in place?"

"Yes. And the transition?"

"Jesus. We went over this. It starts when the markets open here. Sometimes I think no one is paying attention to—"

"Just making sure."

"What about my cars? The flights. Because there's no way I'm sticking around—"

"It's all good."

Salvado sighs. "Listen. We need to find this fucking guy."

"You said he was a geek. Not much of a threat."

"I've upgraded him from geek to pain in the ass."

He sits on a couch facing the windows. First light touches the storm clouds from below before the sun breaks the horizon to the east, transforming black into eerie silver. The clouds roll low and fast across the still-dark river as if captured in time lapse. Four hours until the markets open. Then things will be better because then it will be all about work and execution. Cumulative steps toward a goal. There's no time to worry or second-guess or rage while the markets are open, or the cameras are rolling, or you have the attention of an auditorium. It's the downtime like now that has always been difficult. Memory lives in the downtime, as well as conscience and guilt.

At 7:15 the office phone rings. Caller ID announces it's Deborah. His ex. They haven't spoken in weeks, and it occurs to him that it's likely they will never speak again. While the office phone is still ringing, his personal cell also begins to ring. How the hell can she do that? he thinks. Harassing me in stereo. He takes the call on the cell.

"What, Deborah?"

"I want you and your attorneys to move it. I want this done as soon as possible."

"It will be done very soon, Deborah."

"Do me a favor: Try not to flush the rest of the fund down the toilet before we settle."

"The fund will turn around. Soon, Deborah."

"I hope. Because right now its vibe is not very positive at all."

"Oh, really?"

"Look at the numbers. I bet your clients are circling the wagons."

"If they're loyal, they'll be rewarded. Same goes for you."

"That sounds like some kind of threat."

"You'll know when I'm threatening, Deb."

"Really? Did Danny Weiss?"

"What?"

"Anyone else at The Rising fall this week?"

He stands again. It's light outside. He thinks, How'd I miss the sunrise? "What are you talking about?"

"The young guy. Weiss."

"How'd you know about Weiss?"

"I read the paper; I follow all things associated with the fund, Rick. Until we settle, it's kind of important that I do."

"I barely knew the guy."

"What about Drew Havens? How well do you know him?"

"Not very. Because apparently he's a suspect."

"Do you think Drew Havens is capable of murder, Rick? Because, you know, you told me he was probably the most decent person you've ever worked with."

"I'm never surprised by the things that people are capable of. Including Havens. Including murder."

"Why would Havens murder Danny Weiss?"

"How the fuck should I know?"

"You killed Weiss, Rick. Are you having another one of your epi..."

"To show why you called, to remind her."

"I called her to see what to pump her with before. To see if you're about to piss it all away."

He doesn't answer.

"I don't like it when people come to my house asking questions about your psychological makeup. I'm a good liar, but . . ."

"Who?"

"Miranda Havens."

"I thought they were through."

"Apparently not. She was snooping on his behalf."

"And you told her what?"

"Nothing of value. Like I said, darling, I want my money."

"You'll get your money."

"Maybe, in light of things, I should get more. You know, for keeping my mouth shut."

"Really? I thought our agreement has always been that you are to keep your mouth shut."

"That was about money. Murder . . . murder's different."

"You're right, Deb. That is different. That warrants a whole other sort of agreement, with a whole other set of rewards and penalties for anyone who threatens to break it."

She lets this register, wrestling with the fear of losing her fortune and the fear of losing her life. "What are you up to, Rick?"

"Setting things straight is what I'm up to. Settling karmic scores. By the way, where is Mrs. Havens these days? Still in Westchester—is it Katonah?"

"I'm gonna go now, Rick."

"And you're going to keep your formerly pretty mouth shut, correct?"

"Sure," Deborah Salvado answers. "Why change now?"

After his wife hangs up, he pockets the phone and slams his right palm against the window. He's watching the river but is thinking about Miranda Havens and Deborah, his wife, and how to make them go away.

A moment later his office landline rings. It's security.

"Gregory and Lisa from CNBC here to see you."

He looks at his watch: 7:35. He'd forgotten all about the interview, and he never forgets an interview. They want to do a quick teaser remote about tomorrow's inaugural DAVOS WEST (World Economic, Security, and Technology) Conference. "Sure," he answers, already arranging sound bites in his head. "Send them up."

He applies his own makeup. A touch of powder to his nose and forehead. A smidgen of gel to keep the graying curls on the side of his head from puffing out. He stares at himself in the mirror longer than usual, and usual is long to begin with. He wants to see what they'll see. If they can detect a chink in the armor. Instability in the eyes.

"Hey, hey!" he says, bounding across the office. "If it isn't the wacky morning crew."

Lisa and Greg laugh. They've done this with Salvado dozens of times before, and with each interview the line between journalism and patronage fades a shade lighter. "We're going on in five," says Lisa, the producer. "Simple Q and A with Ron in the studio."

"DAVOS WEST, right? The geek fest that's making Comic-Con look like it's halfway cool."

"Right."

"Live?"

"Actually, no. We're taping for a whole package that we're gonna air tonight. A conference-eve spectacular."

"Hmmm." Salvado thinks about what he'd say live now versus taped for later. Tonight. He thinks of one of the rules he actually believes from his best-selling book, *Confessions of a Market Mercenary*—Number 3: Context Is Everything.

"Between us, what I say now and what I would want to say tonight might be different."

She looked at Gregory, then Salvado. "You don't want to do it."

"Oh, I do want to do it, I just need your assurance, your word, that it won't air until tonight."

The producer and cameraman look at each other and shrug. "Sure," says Lisa.

"I say this because it will be a reflection of activities I'm going to execute today, you know?"

"Sure, gotcha."

Salvado continues. "Ron, too. No one back at the studio can use or comment or report until—"

"We won't even start putting it together until after the markets close, so no problem."

"Cool," Salvado answers, walking over to the set. Then to Gregory: "The sky's looking especially spectacular this morning. I was wondering if maybe you could shoot a bit more south, get the statue in frame just over my shoulder."

2

Darien, Connecticut

Miranda Havens picks up on the second ring. "Deb?"

"We need to talk."

"Well, sure. I can . . . whenever you want. Do you want me to come back up to Darien?"

"Not the best idea."

"What's going on?"

"When you have everything, you either get out or let the madness in."

"Deb?"

"Rick said this to me once during a fight. I'd just found receipts for a sex junket he took to Cuba. Receipts and photos, the asshole. Soon after that, after yet another string of his rages about the government-sponsored ruination of his family, the slights from the media, I gave up and let the madness in."

"I'm sorry about that, Deb, but . . ."

"In the days after he first moved out, before he came back to collect his belongings, I pored over his personal effects. Scrapbooks, letters, insurance papers, travel documents, and passports. Several. I was look-ing for evidence to use against him in our divorce trial, but what I found,

Miranda . . . That kid's murder—I'm terrified it's just the beginning . . . and you know, I don't want to be a part of the madness anymore."

"Where do you want to meet?"

"Are you at your—"

"No. It became, well . . . unsafe. I'm in the city. Chelsea."

"Hotel?"

Miranda pauses, at first reluctant to say exactly where she is.

"That's awfully sentimental of you."

"You know," Miranda says, surprised that Deborah remembers, "the police came to my place in Katonah yesterday. And I'm pretty sure someone else did, too. The police think Drew killed Danny Weiss."

"I know. It's not right. Is he okay? Is he safe?"

"I don't know. We haven't spoken."

Deborah doesn't believe this, but also doesn't blame Miranda for keeping quiet. "So, where?"

Miranda thinks. The rooftop of the Gansevoort. "What about our place? You know, where we went for your birthday, when we were still friends."

"Sure."

"I'm curious, what does your husband have to say about any of this?"

"That's why I want to meet. My husband is an animal."

3

Newark

His dream is a memory embedded in a dream.

He's with Miranda and Erin on a bright fall day, peak foliage season, roaming the grounds of Storm King, the vast outdoor sculpture park on the Hudson Highlands north of West Point. They are walking through a land sculpture called *Wavefield* by the artist Maya Lin. Acres and acres of grass-covered earth sculpted into the shape of the sea, of sets of waves up to fifteen feet high. Erin, who has recently begun to walk, trudges up one side of a wave and then rolls down the other. Over and over, giggling the entire time. For a while he stands atop the crest of a wave, shoulder to shoulder with Miranda, and watches Erin go two, three, four waves away. It's in the trough between the fourth and fifth wave that the girl turns to look for her parents but cannot find them. She calls his name—"Da?" then "Da!"—and he is overwhelmed with fear and panic, the sense that he's losing her, and he begins to sprint toward her. He bounds over one wave top and barrels down the next, calling her name, yelling that it's going to be all right. Even then, he knew it wasn't going to be all right. He and Miranda were having problems; in fact they were fighting that day, at the moment the girl walked away. It took less than a minute for him to catch up to her and pick her up in his arms, but in his dreams, in this dream, he never reaches her. She's always one wave away.

He awakens sweat-soaked and facedown on a large sheet of paper covered with mathematical scribbling, more questions than answers. He stares at the walls, hoping that thirty-five minutes of nightmare sleep will help him notice a clue that he missed. It doesn't. Five minutes later he's in the shower. He wants to be washed, dressed, and ready to run when he goes online with Danny Weiss's software.

He figures he has thirty to forty-five minutes before Salvado's hacking software picks up on him and alerts someone that he's poking around the universe of the Rising Fund. After that, probably another half hour before one of his guys makes his way out to the Newark bunker.

He watched the news and financial sites and is relieved that nothing horrible seems to have happened in the financial world while he was jamming overnight.

He checks the Rising Fund stocks and sees that they are down again, but nothing out of the ordinary.

He searches his own name and finds a dozen articles on Danny Weiss's death and sees that he's been upgraded from person of interest to murder suspect. The photo of him that accompanies many of the articles was taken at a company party at Cipriani in 2010. He has a flute of champagne in his right hand, and his left arm is around Danny Weiss, who, as usual, is smiling. The picture reminds him that he hired Weiss because he thought he was qualified, but also because he was different. He knew that Weiss was something of an outlier on both an intellectual and ethical level, and that his idealistic qualities might ultimately conflict with the goals of the firm. But he hired him anyway, because he was selfish. He hired Weiss because he was everything that he himself no longer was yet should have been. He also hired him, he realizes now, because he knew on some level that Weiss might be the one who could blow up his career and convince him to abandon it once and for all. That, he concludes, is the narrative behind that business decision.

He's all but given up on hearing from Sawa Luhabe, so much so that he almost deletes her forwarded message, which has a South African URL, in part because he assumes it's some sort of identity-stealing spam from a fictional Nigerian prince. Only a second glance at the sender's name makes him reconsider. He reads her words. *What I Know Now*, which was what, eight hours ago? Besides confirming that she was still alive, her note validates much of his findings about the trades in play.

He reads her recap of what happened in Dublin, the death of the trader Dempsey, and then about the death of Heinrich Shultz in Berlin, employee of Ithaka Investments. Ithaka, with a K, Luhabe notes, was the firm that placed the order with Dempsey in Dublin. Ithaka with a K also shares the same IP address as Siren, the firm that placed the previous four orders.

Siren is now Ithaka.

Havens searches Siren and Ithaka.

The first response is the Wikipedia entry for Odysseus. *Odysseus,* Wiki tells him, *is the ugly King of Ithaka, and the hero of Homer's epic poem* The Odyssey.

And of course the sirens of *The Odyssey* were famous for luring passing sailors to their island of Faiakes with their seductive song, only to be condemned to stay on the island forever. Knowing that the bones of sailors were scattered about the island, Odysseus had his shipmates put wax in his ears and bind him to the ship's mast until they had safely passed.

Havens thinks of Salvado the other night at the club: "*We're on an epic journey, an epic tale that is still being written, and when it's all over, it will be remembered as one of the great ones.*"

He clicks back to read the last lines of Luhabe's note:

I am safe for the time being. But I will never be safe unless this is resolved. In the limited time I've had to model this I have seen evidence that points to another forthcoming trade similar to mine at a yet TBD firm in Toronto, for the security NYCRE. With this in mind I would like to introduce you to each other. Each has contacted me separately and each seems to have skills and knowledge that complements the other's. Drew Havens of the Rising Fund, meet Cara Sobieski of the U.S. government task force on terrorism and financial intelligence.

He immediately calls up Weiss's chart and checks the numbers for

sees that she's beaten him to the punch. Her message is brief.

> Sobieski here.
> Boarding LUFT #125 Berlin-Newark.
> Meet?

He replies, *Yes*, then leaves his number. Flight tracker reveals that Sobieski's plane lands at 11 A.M., and he makes a note of the terminal and gate. He takes another look at Weiss's notes and sees further references to New York or Toronto, NYCRE, or what it all might be leading to. He imagines this is where Weiss's research suddenly ended, and he wonders how Luhabe, a woman on the run half a world away, found him.

Once again he looks at the sheets on the wall. All of Weiss's notes up to this point make sense. The stocks, the cities, and the dates align. What does not make sense is what they all mean, where they're heading. He hopes that agent Cara Sobieski, and perhaps Sawa Luhabe, wherever she is, can help him figure out what they mean, and fast.

Because there is no city or stock symbol listed in the box for tomorrow. Other than the brief foreign number sequence, the only writing on Weiss's whiteboard square for tomorrow's date, Friday, October 21, and on the tiny Mets schedule from Weiss's desk is a set of red exclamation points.

4

"Tell me something that doesn't make me want to puke."

Salvado, staring at the celeb handshake photos on his office wall, is disgusted by his presence in each of them.

"Okay. You're still a multibillionaire."

"Funny."

"And we're still alive."

"Fine. What about the others? Any luck?"

"We have a bead on him in Jersey. The wife bailed on the Katonah apartment. We were waiting last night, but the police found her first."

Salvado asks, "Where in Jersey?"

"Newark. The Hilton. Someone's en route."

"And I should be confident this will be taken care of because . . . ?"

"Because, to quote you, he's a social misfit not capable of functioning in a world beyond numbers. There's one more thing . . ."

"Yeah?"

"Your wife . . ."

"Right . . ."

"Well, she's heading into the city."

"Okay."

"And the trace . . . I'm waiting for playback, but they think she's been talking to the social misfit's ex-wife."

Salvado turns his back to the wall of photos and stares up at the monitors, a collage of talking heads and numbers, grim faces on trading floors staring at the large screens that control the future. "Well, I imagine that someone will have to . . ."

"So you agree . . . It has to be done?"

"Absolutely."

He puts the phone in his pocket, turns back to face the wall, and smashes his right fist into a photo of him, Alan Greenspan, and Alicia Keys.

"Everything all right, Rick?"

He turns. Roxanne, his executive assistant, stands at the threshold between her desk and the beginning of his suite. "Could be better, Rox. Do me a favor . . . get Ryan Connerly at Goldman on the phone, will ya?"

"Connerly."

"Yo. It's Rick Salvado."

"Captain America himself. What can I do for you?"

"I want to go long on NYCRE."

"More? What makes you so keen on the future of commercial real estate?"

"*New York* real estate. Manhattan real estate. Landmark real estate, you dumb mick."

"So you love New York and the USA is what you're saying."

"Almost as much as I love Brazilian ass and French wine."

Connerly laughs. Salvado's recent plays for The Rising make little sense to him, but since the fund is partially bankrolled by Goldman and somehow Salvado's plays helped save face for them in 2008 when the

Bear Stearns and Lehmans of the world sank, he knows not to ask too many questions of Rick Salvado.

"What's the problem?" Salvado asks.

"I'm just trying to figure out, you know, how exactly you're gonna fuck me over on this."

"Hah! Goldman should be thrilled to come along for the ride with the legendary Rising Fund."

"Right. It's an honor and a privilege, sir. Now, how long, how much, et cetera?"

"Just a buy," Salvado says. "Nothing major. But enough to make a statement."

"You speak and the market follows, right?"

"Used to," Salvado says. "But it will again. Can't you feel the market finally bottoming with people about little bet, Charlie?"

5

Toronto

"This is a lot of short," says Michel Loewen, of Smith Gable Limited, a small brokerage house on Yonge Street.

"You can't handle this? I'd think a house like yours could take on—"

"I can," Loewen replies. "We can . . . It's just . . ."

"I can make some other calls. I just thought you'd want in on the deal."

"No . . . No. I don't see why we can't make this work. How's the weather in Berlin?"

"Who knows? They keep me locked in a cubicle here, twenty-four seven."

Loewen calls up the profile of the security. "NYCRE, huh?"

"I don't even know what that stands for. I get the call, make a list of their quirky goddamn terms of execution, and, you know, try to find a market for it. It's a living, right?"

Loewen smiles as he clicks through screens, verifying the trading account that initiated the request, out of Philadelphia. "So," he says, satisfied with the on-paper authenticity of the account, "How exactly do you want me to execute this again, Mr. . . ."

"Homer."

6

taxis to the gate a mere two hours and twenty minutes later than expected, at 1:45 P.M. EST, she hears from Sawa Luhabe's American connection, the semi-famous hedge fund quant Drew Havens.

> -@ carousel 7.
> -With limo guys: holding sign w/yr name.

She responds:

> Me: Brown hoodie. Dark jeans.
> Tan sneaks.

The last to buy a ticket, stuck in the back row of a full flight, she's among the last to get off.

The immigration agent scans her passport and asks Sobieski if she has anything to declare.

"No."

"Well," the agent responds, slipping the stamped passport and declaration card through the half-moon hole in the glass, "welcome back."

Hopefully she'll soon be able to make a strong enough case that she'll have the courage to call Michaud and explain why she defied his orders and flew halfway around the world. Something major is about to go down, but she can't bring herself to call the man she respects and fears the most.

The woman in front of her has a cart overflowing with luggage, and the agents at the exit want to take a look. While Sobieski waits, she stretches her neck to see if she can spot Drew Havens on the other side. In a sea of limo drivers in black suits holding placards she sees him. Light blue T-shirt, a Mets cap, and jeans, holding the sign that bears her name. When they make eye contact, he waves.

"Next."

She steps up to the agents and smiles. Her right arm is halfway extended when a hand catches her elbow from behind. When she turns, another hand grabs her other elbow.

"Cara Sobieski?"

"Yes."

"We need you to come with us."

As soon as he sees the first agent reach for Sobieski's arm, Havens lowers the paper upon which her first name is written in Magic Marker. As they steer her one way, back into the secure part of the terminal, Havens turns toward the exit.

7

"I don't know. I'm waiting to hear from him." Miranda Havens rubs her arms with her hands. The rooftop of the Gansevoort is gorgeous, but out of the sun this late in the day in October it can be chilly.

"He might be better off getting himself arrested," Deborah Salvado says. "You know, safer."

"You're probably right. But he's more interested in . . . preventing whatever's about to happen than self-preservation."

"What do you think is in the works?"

Miranda takes a sip of Pinot Noir. She wasn't planning on drinking, but once Deb ordered a Bloody, she couldn't resist. "I don't know. From what I've heard from Drew, from what I've read, I'd have to say some kind of major market fraud; gaming it at the very least."

"What has Drew found out?"

Miranda pauses. "Deb, yesterday you practically threw me out of your house for asking too many questions, and now you're grilling me . . ."

"I was wrong. I was trying to protect my money. I gave him

everything, so many years, loveless, friendless, childless. Wealth became my child, the thing to which I paid the most attention and felt the most loyalty. It defined me, Mir, because nothing else did, and I was determined to walk away from it with something, even if it meant looking the other way when he did something to some other greedy bastard. . . ."

"Why the change?"

"Because this is different. He's different. I know you and Drew and you're not bad. I knew that young man, Weiss. He danced with me last year at the holiday party, and you could tell that the job was just part of a much larger life; he made me laugh."

"He was a good kid. Drew never spoke as fondly about anyone else his entire time at the fund. But still, you knew this all yesterday."

Deb nods. "I did. And a lot more than that. But yesterday I didn't think he would kill me."

"Today?"

She nods. "Today, I know he will. I could hear it in his voice. This morning. I told him you visited. It was a mistake. I did it as a ploy, because I was rattled by what you had said and I realized I could lose everything. But his reaction . . . I know how he gets."

Miranda takes another sip of wine. "We think he had Weiss killed because he discovered something he wasn't supposed to. Drew is twisted up over this because he hired Weiss and put him up to it. Not to uncover any crime, but because he couldn't understand what was happening with the fund. He never could have imagined what Weiss would find."

"What?"

"Bare minimum, Rick's had traders killed in at least four other cities around the world, all after executing trades he's linked to."

"Why?"

"As a lead-up to something bigger. That's the working model."

"Why not come forward?"

"You already said it. Rick's untouchable right now. Drew is wanted for murder. No one will believe him, unless he has all the answers."

Deborah Salvado looks for sun in the overcast sky ahead. Maybe the rooftop in mid-October was a bad idea after all. "You know, after all he's been through, he'll have us killed. Whatever he's up to, he will kill, or at least have someone do it for him, to protect his money and his legacy."

"I know." Miranda leans across the table. Her hands are trembling

safe. I hacked into his e-mail, his phone accounts . . . fifteen hundred texts to this one bimbo alone! Then, in a box in a closet, next to his childhood belongings, photo albums and scrapbooks and newspaper clippings about the alleged traumatic collapse of his family, I found things."

Miranda looks at the envelope but doesn't reach for it. "Things?"

"Travel documents to Russia. The northern Caucasus. Chechnya. Dagestan. In addition to his real passport, he has a second, under his mother's maiden name."

"How long ago did it start?"

"The trips began in 2002, just before he began The Rising. Once a year or so. Twice after he cashed in 2008. As you know, he made a fortune. I'm talking *billions*, Mir."

"Thanks to my husband."

"This is true. Drew created the model that uncovered the opportunity, but my husband put up the money. Anyway, in '02 someone stepped up and fronted him the liquidity to start over. He always said it was former clients, but based on this it looks like he struck up some kind of deal with these Russian . . . whatever they are. Anyway, after 2008, you'd think he'd have been at an all-time high. Fulfilled. Satisfied with his life. But if anything he became angrier, more hateful. At least privately. It's like he used his mind-blowing success as the jumping off point to . . . to destroy everything."

"Do you think he would have tried this if he hadn't made billions?"

She stares into Miranda's eyes while she considers the question. "I don't know. Maybe he didn't expect to make billions in 2008. Maybe the money and glory made it that much more difficult to cash out on his deal because, you now, he's an egomaniac. Because he became addicted to the attention." After another pause, eyes still fixed on Miranda's, Deborah Salvado says, "And of course he'd never have been able to operate on this scale, and had so much at his disposal, if your husband hadn't figured out a way to get those billions into his hands, to turn him into a superstar."

"So, do you think he's a terrorist, Deb?"

Deborah Salvado draws a long breath, then drinks deeply from the Bloody Mary glass. "It's semantics, but no, I don't," she says, stirring up the horseradish at the bottom with a celery stalk. "A terrorist acts for some kind of political or ideological gain, right? But Rick, he could care less about politics or policy, ideology or religion. Now, revenge? Vengeance? Hatred? That's what obsesses him. Always. His successes big or small were never about achievement or fulfillment; they were all about vindication and vengeance for something that he's permitted to fester in his brain, to twist him up and consume him.

"So, no, I don't think he's a terrorist." With a trembling hand she moves the envelope closer to Miranda and finishes. "What my husband is, is a sociopath."

8

They lead her through the ___ unmarked room adjacent to a Hudson News stand. Two TSA agents. Low-level, from the looks of it. A man and a woman. The man directs her to sit on a plastic chair with aluminum legs. There are three chairs in the room and nothing else. "Not sure if they told you, but I'm a federal agent," Sobieski says.

"We know," replies the woman, a stout redhead even younger than Sobieski. Unspoken: Big friggin' deal. Who isn't? "Our job is to do what they say and—"

"It's just that—"

The woman holds up her hand, interrupts right back. "Someone's getting in touch with someone about next steps. Overseas person, I think. So bear with us if it takes a bit."

"Do you know why they've decided to . . . ?"

"No. Your name came up and, well . . . here we are."

No one speaks for another fifteen minutes, until the man, a thin African-American who appears to be the redhead's supervisor, checks his watch, pronounces "Oh, shoot," and leaves. Transfixed by some mindless game on her smart phone, the woman barely acknowledges his departure.

While she waits, Sobieski wonders what will become of Havens. Will he hang around? Have they detained him as well? How will her failure to meet him change things? Maybe it's for the best, she thinks. Maybe this isn't worth throwing away what's left of her career. If she comes clean now, Michaud will understand. She shifts in her seat, stands. Not being allowed to move or act is killing her.

Her duffel bag, her phone, and her laptop are at the woman's feet. "Can I check my messages? I just got off a transatlantic flight."

The woman looks up. "Sorry. I'm not cleared for that."

Another forty minutes pass before the man returns. "They got her guy," he says to his partner. Then to Sobieski: "You got your phone?"

She points to her duffel at the woman's feet. The man sighs. More work. He walks across the room, picks the bag up with a grunt, and walks it over to her, pitched to one side as if the bag were filled with a bowling ball. Placing it at her feet, he says. "Your boss is gonna call . . . wants to talk to you." To his partner, he adds, "Hong Kong."

Sobieski reaches into the side pocket and removes the phone. She glances at her inbox while she waits for Michaud's call. Havens has left four messages. After she clicks on the first, the phone rings.

She answers, but keeps the text message on screen. "What am I supposed to do with you?"

"I'm sorry. I was about to get on a plane when I got a message from Luhabe. She said—"

"Stop. Sorry doesn't work with TFI. With disobeying orders. With a body turning up on a Berlin sidewalk where the deceased has your fucking badge in his back pocket."

She rocks her head back and closes her eyes. She'd forgotten about the badge.

"He took it while I was—"

"I've been on the phone with Berlin for the last five hours. Things like this, they end careers, Sobes."

She watches the male agent head back out into the terminal. She thinks about saying sorry, but sorry sounds weak, and would not be entirely true. "I had no time. Sawa Luhabe, she knows about Siren. And Ithaka. And Dublin . . . did you hear what happened in—"

"I knew about Dublin before Dublin knew about Dublin," Michaud says.

"Right. Of course you did . . . but the thing is, why I came, is she told me, late—*late*-late, while I was just about to board—she told me about

"Send the note."

"Okay."

"What happened with Nello?"

She grimaces. Of course he knows about Nello. She wonders how much. "He was a mistake. Too good to be true."

"That's it?"

She pauses, can't bring herself to mention the gambling and the breach. "Yeah, Boss. That's it."

"You're done, Sobes. You screwed up and I know this is killing you, but you're just making it worse, desperately trying to fix it." She rocks her head back, looks at the ceiling, then at the female agent staring at the game on her phone. "Come back and we'll see what happens next, but my word only goes so far. Sit tight. They're gonna put you on the next plane."

"Then what?"

"*Then* someone will meet you at the airport, take you to the office, and we'll go from there."

"What about my lead . . . this information?"

"Believe it or not, there are agents in New York, too. And D.C. And they don't disobey their boss. Send it. Then get on a fucking plane." Michaud hangs up.

Sobieski glances at the distracted agent.

"Twenty-four hours is all I need, Boss," she says, to no one, already changing her tone from defiant and desperate to compromising and conciliatory. "Then it's right back to Hong Kong."

She reads Drew Havens's latest text while continuing the fake conversation with Michaud.

Where R U? she reads.

"Uh, huh . . . Okay . . . I can do that . . . ," she fake says to fake Michaud, loud enough for the red-haired agent to hear.

Detained, she writes to Havens. *Want to send me back.*

U can't. Havens replies. *Tomorrow!*

"Good," she says out loud to no one. "I'm so glad you agree." Then she looks at the TSA agent, who's finally beginning to pay attention to her performance.

Havens continues with two quick bursts:

Friday—Last of 7 Trades . . .
1st six = murder . . . 7th = tragedy.

She looks at the guard, who is checking her watch, the door. "Of course I will," Sobieski says into the phone. "Is there anything else I can do for you while I'm here?"

Then she texts this to Havens: *OK . . . Meet me . . . where?*

Outside door 2, Havens texts. *Taxi stand. When?*

"Okay . . . I will. I promise."

Another look at the agent, who is standing, shifting her weight from foot to foot, impatiently rolling her neck. *Soon?*

"So wait . . . I can stay? Excellent," she shouts, standing. This time the agent turns and looks. "Cool," she continues, finishing her fake conversation. "I'll call when I get into midtown."

She makes a show of pushing off and putting her phone back into her pocket and then zipping her bag closed. Then she sits back straight in her chair with a thin smile, feigning excitement, but not excited enough to share. The agent bites:

"What's up?"

"Oh, there was a misunderstanding. My boss is fixing it as we speak. He wanted me to go to Philly first, but now I'll hit that on the way home."

"Huh." The agent looks down, ready to go back to her game.

The agent, fingers working the keyboard, shakes her head. "...terminal."

"Shit. Would you mind . . . or I can . . . I'll leave my bag . . . my stuff if you promise to keep an eye on it."

The agent hits pause, looks up, and gives Sobieski a look.

"I'd really appreciate it."

She lifts her chin toward the door. "On the right, like ten feet down."

Sobieski stands, hops from foot to foot, says, "*Thank you*," then, "You want anything from Starbucks?"

9

New York City

"**M**oney doesn't wait. Money doesn't have a pause button that will wait for you to come back to it after you've gotten your shit together. You told me to be here at three. It is now three and you are telling me you aren't ready?"

Salvado sits in his limo outside the Transmediant! Theater in midtown, barking through an open rear window at the head AV engineer for DAVOS WEST 2011. "You said three o'clock and now it is what—three-ten, three-fifteen—and you're telling me ten more minutes?"

"I'm incredibly sorry, Mr. Salvado. We've been having some issues with the sound system."

"Beautiful. We're gonna have the most powerful and influential people in the world of finance, security, and tech here in fifteen hours—heads of state, finance ministers, founders of the world's largest tech companies—to talk about the glittering new interconnected, seamlessly converged world of the future and you can't hook up the fucking speakers?"

"Minutes away, sir. If you'd like to come inside and wait . . ."

"No." He presses the window control, and a black shade rises up between him and the engineer. He calls Laslow. Laslow was to meet him here, but when Salvado heard about his wife and Havens's wife, he redirected him. "Anything?"

"No. But we think we've got an address."

Salvado snorts. "Find them."

He clicks off the call. On his BlackBerry he looks up the latest activity involving the fund and then goes to a program tracking each of the first six trades. "Shit," he says to himself. There is increasing short activity taking place, beyond the plays his people made, around the

There is no way to stop the momentum of a marketplace

the scent of blood. However, he thinks, maybe this isn't the worst thing. Maybe the more players piling on, the deeper these companies, markets, and economies will plummet, and it will be that much more difficult for authorities to unravel the aftermath and connect him to any of it. He just wishes it hadn't happened so soon. With the sub-prime shorts in 2008 it seemed for a while that The Rising was one of the only firms to get it. At first they grabbed up as much action as the risk managers at the banks would allow. But at a certain point the short opportunities were few and far between. People saw what was coming and cut him off from the action, which is too bad because he would have taken as much as they would have allowed. But it didn't matter. By then, he was positioned to make a killing of mythological proportions. Without Havens's quant wizardry and the people who entered into an agreement to bail him out and put him back on his feet after his disgrace in the wake the crash of 2001, the killing of 2008 would never have happened. Havens. The irony isn't lost on him that the man who made him obscenely rich is trying to take him down. That a man who couldn't save his own wife and kid suddenly thinks he can save the world. Someone taps on his window and mouths the words "We're ready."

The Transmediant! Theater is on the ground floor of the fifty-eight-story Transmediant! Tower on West 42nd Street, a stone's throw from the *New York Times* building. This afternoon the security check is cursory. Salvado's escort flashes his ID badge, and the guards at the lobby turnstile wave them through. Tomorrow, with Fortune 500 leaders, almost half of the G20 members, politicians, media moguls, and almost every A-list luminary in tech, media, and entertainment, it will be altogether different. "Tomorrow will be like a mashup of the G20, TED, and the Oscars," his escort boasts as he leads Salvado across the lobby and through the swinging doors at the rear of the theater.

Kinks in the sound system aside, Salvado is impressed by the theater, which is rumored to have cost more than a hundred million dollars at the time of its opening two years ago. It's both a technological showcase for all of the beta-level gadgets and platforms that represent the Transmediant! brand, and a living, breathing example of how money, politics, technology, and commerce can come together to form a cultural experience far greater than the sum of its parts.

This is also why, less than a year after Salvado proposed the event at a 9/11 anniversary, as a way to put New York back in the center of the financial and cultural universe, DAVOS WEST has supplanted the Allen & Company Conference in Sun Valley, the original DAVOS, and TED as *the* place to make the deals that will shape the future of global finance and commerce. It's also why, at 10 A.M. tomorrow, Rick Salvado, the most colorful pro-American financial figure in the world, will be delivering the keynote kickoff address on the main stage.

Salvado is led through more than a hundred rows of state-of-the-art seats, each a small media center unto itself. They stop at the foot of the stage, a massive modular platform that sits beneath the world's largest HD 3-D screen.

"The mayor will introduce you at ten sharp. He has something prepared, but if there's anything you'd like him to add or mention, let us know and we'll get word to him."

"No. I trust the mayor. Maybe not with the schools' budget, but . . ."

"Great. You'll have thirty-five minutes, but it's okay if you're over or under by a few. You'll come out of stage left, rigged with a wireless mic, plus there will be several backup mics available. Will you be using

"And then the giveaway."

Salvado raises an eyebrow.

"The book, right after you're done, which is what Mr. . . . . Laslow told us?"

"Oh," Salvado says. "Right. Yeah. The book. Whatever Laslow says."

The conference escort says, "Great. Your people are offloading now. I told them we can slip one under each seat, or put it in the swag bag, but they want it to be a surprise."

Salvado shrugs. "Whatever they think is best."

"Laslow's having them stacked in the back, unmarked, unopened. He says your hospitality people will be on hand tomorrow to open the boxes and hand them out, right after the keynote."

"Sounds good to me," says Salvado.

"Want to take a look?"

"Sure." They walk away from the stage to the back of the theater. Four of Laslow's guys, each with his own hand truck, are wheeling in and unloading six boxes at a time. They start in the right rear corner, stacking them in a row four boxes deep and five feet high. Already they're more than a third of the way across the room.

"How does that look, Mr. Salvado? Is that sort of the way you'd pictured it?"

Salvado stares at the boxes for a moment and smiles appreciatively. "Yes," he says. "It's exactly as I'd pictured it."

10

into the center of the terminal. Then she begins to jog through the mid-afternoon swarm of travelers, looking for the exit. As she weaves through the crowd, she takes off her sweatshirt, in case they've already put out word to look for a specific color. Then she reaches back and lets her hair down.

Rather than race along the front wall of the terminal from door number six to two she decides to get out on the sidewalk in case there's a sudden lockdown.

She tries to remember what he looks like, but it's a blur. She steps off the curb and hustles across the street, then the median, and then the second street. She wants to come up on Havens and the taxi stand from behind, to see what he's about. To see if someone's found him. Even without a physical description he's easy to spot. Tall, reasonably handsome in an uptight-white-money-guy kind of way. Definitely not a cop. He's also the only person outside the airport looking away from the taxi stands and rental car and hotel shuttles and toward the terminal. He's on his toes, craning and swiveling his neck, then pacing the length of the departure area. She'd like to wait longer. To make sure no one else is watching him, but a few seconds is all she's willing to give it. Every move from here on out will be a risk. Every second critical. How she manages and chooses to execute it all will determine everything.

He jumps when she taps him from behind. "Hey! Whoa. I—"

She interrupts by placing her arm on his elbow and turning him toward a waiting taxi. "We've got to get out of here, now."

They slide inside a cab and he shuts the door. He's about to speak again when the driver asks, "Where to?"

This throws them. Each looks at the other, each hoping the other has a better plan. When each sees that there is no better plan, that they're equally unprepared, they both say, "Manhattan."

"Do you have a computer?" she asks. "I had to leave mine behind back in the terminal."

"Yup," he says, tapping his travel bag. "They know that you've left?"

She half smiles. "Now they do."

"So where to?"

"Someplace where we can tell each other everything that Sawa Luhabe says we ought to know. Any thoughts?"

Havens looks out the window. They're almost out of the airport, within striking distance of the turnpike. "I'll think of something," he says. "But first," he says, lowering his voice to ensure that the driver doesn't hear, "you should know: I'm sort of wanted for murder."

"Well," Sobieski answers, not missing a beat, "at least we have that in common."

11

they met at the Gansevoort.

Neither feels like eating, or talking, or staying in the same place for long. There's hardly anything to celebrate today, plus it is too cold on the roof. Deborah Salvado pays. Even under these surreal circumstances, there's a protocol, a pecking order. They stand and smooth their clothes, brush back their hair, neither sure of the next step.

Miranda picks up the envelope and they begin to walk to the elevator.

"Where to now?" asks Deborah.

Miranda lifts her jaw to the north. "I'm gonna take a walk. Then I'm going up. Back to the Chelsea."

"That was your place. You and Drew. I remember."

"It was."

"Drew's there, isn't he?"

The elevator door opens and they get on. "No. I wish. But not now."

"Someday, right? You should."

"We should."

"You know," Deborah says as they descend to street level, alone in the car, "when he first started, when I first met you, I used to say terrible things about you to the other wives."

"You don't have to tell me this, Deb."

"It's because I was threatened. My queen bee status meant a lot to me, because it had an ugly power over the others. But not you. You . . . you and your husband were so comfortable with yourselves, and in love with each other. And I knew I would never have that."

The elevator door opens and they get off. The hotel lobby is quiet, and for a moment they stand, considering each other. Miranda has no answer for her.

"When your daughter died," Deborah continues, "and then you lost each other, I was ashamed of myself. But even then, when you came the other day, and I knew that you were trying to do the right thing, to prevent something awful from happening, I still resented you for being so good, and I hated myself for being willing to abide anything, to close my eyes to the worst, as long as I'd get my money."

"No one knows what anyone else really has or doesn't have, Deb."

They walk to the exit to the street and stop again. Dark so soon, Miranda thinks. Where'd the day go?

"Want me to walk with you a bit?"

Miranda thinks about it. She slides her fingers back and forth along the metal clasp of the envelope and thinks she should find some place to read it now. "No, Deb. I'm gonna sit here for a second and take a look at this. I want to make every minute count until he's out of trouble."

Deborah Salvado considers her again, and Miranda can see the conflict in the other woman's eyes, between resentment and respect, hate and affection. It's a frightening and sickening thing to see in someone. They hug for a moment and then Deborah Salvado pulls away.

"Good luck."

"Yeah. You, too," Miranda replies. Then she turns, takes a few steps into the middle of the lobby, and looks around, wondering if it's safe to remain here, to camp out on a couch and go through the details of Rick

Salvado's ghost life. Or if the smart thing is to keep moving in case someone is tracking her, or Deb Salvado.

Move on, she decides. Eliminate risk and assume the worst. Find a coffee shop or a park and read and call Drew and save him.

She walks back across the lobby and is halfway through the hotel door, already in the process of thanking the doorman, when she sees the man, the bald man, come up behind Deborah Salvado and grab her by the clavicle. The small-framed woman barely flinches under the much larger man's grasp. She turns to face him as if she's

She doesn't wait to see what his next move is before pivoting in the doorway and running back across the lobby.

12

New York

I n Bryant Park, in the shadow of the New York Public Library, two
fugitives hunch over a computer, jamming in the artificial light via
free Wi-Fi, exchanging intelligence and stories and fears.

In the cab from Newark and then over sandwiches at the bar of
the Half King on far West 23rd, he told her about Weiss and Salvado,
the brothers Jameson and his ex-wife, the seven trades, the twenty-
eight trades, *The Odyssey*, and the triple appearance of the Hindenburg
Omen.

She told him about Patrick Lau and Heinrich Shultz, Marco Nello,
and her failed investigation into Siren/Ithaka. They told each other
about Sawa Luhabe.

Then, as they walked, zigzagging east and west, slowly making
their way north, they switched from the human narrative to the
language of data and broke down the mechanics of the trades,
the health of the securities, the common and distinguishing factors.
The shorts. The odd way that the trades take the exact opposite position
on the same securities as the Rising Fund.

"Why?" They ask the same questions of each other at the same time,
and they share the same conclusions

"A diversion?"

"Really? But still . . . why?"

And, repeatedly, "What next?"

Different sounds from the city now: evening sirens, the hum of whirling tires on midtown streets taken over by taxis. Sobieski, in the same hooded sweatshirt she wore in the Berlin airport, shivers on the bench alongside Havens.

"You want to go someplace warm? Find a room?"

She shakes her head. "Soon. But this is good for now; let's figure

found nothing that led her to make the connection to Rick Salvado and the Rising Fund. She also came across a number of obscure references and data that she couldn't decipher. Watching Havens tear through the available data on his machine and the way in which he constructs and deconstructs models, she's convinced that he's gifted. But before she hands him Shultz's data, she wants to make sure she can trust him.

13

Miranda rushes across the lobby of the Gansevoort and exits through a fire door onto Ninth Avenue. Twice she stops to see if he is behind her and she doesn't see him. The bald man isn't keeping up with her, most likely because he's got Deborah in his car, but she continues to take extreme measures to make sure she is safe.

She walks and jogs quickly along Ninth, moving north, constantly checking over her shoulder. She slips in and out of several galleries between Tenth and Eleventh in Chelsea, pretending to look at the art while thinking the entire time about the envelope in her bag. She opens her phone and tries to call Drew, but it's dead. She didn't charge it after meeting with the police last night, and the charger is back in her apartment. Abandoning the galleries, she heads back east toward the hotel, but although it's past 9 P.M., she decides she isn't ready to go back. She doesn't want to be alone and she doesn't want to be with anyone. At 23rd she takes the 1 train uptown to Times Square. She walks north and west through the nighttime tourist clutter. It's after ten o'clock when she enters Joe Allen on 46th Street. The post-theater crowd is just beginning to congregate, but she's early enough to get a seat at a small corner table facing the door, near the bar.

She orders a glass of Sauvignon Blanc and wonders what has become of Drew and begins to convince herself that he's been killed. She waits for the waitress to bring her wine before opening the envelope. The contents are exactly what Deborah described: photocopies of the second passport, the news clippings about the father's suicide, the travel itineraries, the photos, including one of Salvado and three bearded men smiling in front of a Russian bank. But seen together, spread

hope for humanity. In her hands are the words and images that she sees assembled by the media after a grand and deadly event—Oswald posing with the carbine, Mohamed Atta jumpy and pixilated on an ATM security camera, McVeigh's yearbook pic—only this hasn't yet happened.

This dread feeling has pulsed beneath the surface of her thoughts since Drew called her the night Danny Weiss died. She immediately felt it, but didn't want to believe that someone she knew could be involved with this scale of evil. And worse, that she would be one of the few trying to prevent it. Now she feels and believes it all.

At eleven-thirty she places fifteen dollars on the table, stands, and departs. On Seventh Avenue she turns south, looking for a Kinko's. Soon she realizes that's not going to happen at this hour, so she settles for a bodega on 31st Street with a copy machine. Inside she makes a second set of the Salvado documents, folds them in half, and places them in her handbag. Then she walks the remaining eight blocks to the Chelsea, feeling more alone and numb than ever.

Inside she asks the woman at the front desk for another room key and an envelope. From her bag she removes the copied documents, refolds them, and slides them into the envelope with the room key. On a piece of hotel stationery she writes the room number and these words:

The bald man took Deborah today after she gave me this information.

I have tried to reach you, but my phone is dead.

I love you and hope to see you soon.

On the outside of the envelope she writes his name: Drew Havens. She hands the envelope to the woman and says, "My husband is supposed to meet me later. Please call my room if he comes, but if he happens to arrive while I'm out, would you please give him this."

Before closing the door, she hangs the DO NOT DISTURB sign on the knob.

As if that's going to stop anyone.

She turns the bolt lock and latches the chain. For good measure, she grabs a straight-backed chair from the desk near the TV and wedges it against the inside door handle, just as she used to do when she lived in the walkup on East Sixth, before she was married. Before she was rich.

After testing to make sure the chair is secure, she leans against the door and exhales. She looks at her watch. It's after midnight, but it feels much later. It feels as if she's been walking the streets of the city for days.

If I don't hear from him by the morning, she decides, still leaning against the closed and locked door of her room, attempting to regulate her breathing, I'm going to give the second envelope to the police.

When she's satisfied with the locks and the chair brace, she walks to the desk and takes her phone out of her bag. On a whim she tries once more, but it's indeed dead. She reaches for the hotel landline, telling herself, I'll call him all night if I have to.

The voice comes from the hall outside the bathroom and sucks the air out of her lungs. "What is it about this freaking hotel with you and your ex?" She drops the phone and stares at the blank wall. She doesn't turn. The bald man, she assumes, come to take her wherever he's taken Deb. "I mean," the voice continues, "sentimental value aside, this place, it really is kind of a shithole."

She cocks her head to the side. She recognizes that voice. When she turns, she sees not the bald man walking toward her, smiling, but her husband's oldest friend from the fund, Tommy Rourke.

14

After midnight and they're still searching.

Still on a park bench with a laptop and dozens of pieces of evidence yet no definitive answer. They're still using Havens's computer and Weiss's software. They know that it might give away their location, but they don't care. Technically, it's already Friday.

At 12:18 they get an alert that reveals more details on the sixth trade: NYCRE, short, out of Toronto with links to Berlin and Philly.

"New York City Real Estate," he tells her. "Salvado, of course, has a major long, and has been on the cable circuit recommending a buy on it. Not in any great numbers, but enough to make him amazingly popular with the Trumps and Donald Brens of the world."

Sobieski turns away, closes her eyes, then looks back at Havens. "The others make some sense. They're at least remotely linked, but this . . . I don't get it. It's a total outlier. Who gang-shorts some of the most consistently valuable properties in the world?"

Neither knows specifically who, but they both know the general answer: someone who thinks it's going to come crashing down.

"The account is listed under a different name in Philly," Havens says. "But all that means is it's the same middle man; just a different junky."

"Stealing the identities of junkies," Sobieski notes. "That's a first for me."

"Disposable income, disposable people."

Sobieski, who had been fading, inches closer to him on the bench. "Anything on the trader?" For instance, they both think, is he alive?

"Looking now."

While Havens searches for more on the Toronto trade, for anything on the whereabouts or condition of the trader Michael Loewen, Sobieski _____ _____ phone and begins to type a text for Michaud. She won't

yet released, but witnesses claim he was an employee in a nearby building." He looks up from the glow of the screen and stares across the park, toward the thinning traffic on Sixth Avenue. The wind has picked up, lifting leaves and the day's trash in a lazy swirl. The park is empty.

"What if you told your boss everything we know, right now? About me, and Weiss, and Salvado?"

Sobieski looks at him and rolls her eyes. "Sure," she says sarcastically. "Tell him that the fugitive employee who has twice defied him is basing her indictment of one of the world's most influential and beloved investors on the findings of one of *his* bitter ex-employees who also happens to be wanted for murdering one of his coworkers?"

"What do we have to do to get past that?"

"Figure it out. Come up with a motive. Evidence. Something that points to his next step."

"You think other people are tracking this in your agency? Or other agencies?"

Sobieski sighs. "Presently there are fifty-one different government organizations, many brand-new and flush with 9/11 dollars, charged with tracking the movement of terror-related money. In a perfect world they're omnipresent and omnipotent, all working together, exchanging leads and information, but my view of the world skews a little darker."

They stare back at the screen, each with the knowledge that there's only so much a computer can do. That, at some point people have to take action. But how? Where?

"What about your boss?" she asks. "Why don't we find him and squeeze him?"

"Salvado? We can try, but if he's in his town house, he'll be protected like a head of state, and if we don't have this completely figured out and we're caught, nothing will stop them from carrying out whatever they're up to."

"Why are you doing this?" Sobieski asks. "You made a fortune with Salvado. You must have everything. Why did you decide to go after him?"

"I wasn't going after him. I was looking for the truth. But not in a superhero way. I was looking for an explanation for some irrational movement going on in his fund, and . . . for the mess my life had become. I put him up to it, but Danny Weiss is the one who found this, the seven trades. He'd still be alive if I hadn't raised the red flags. The thing is I didn't put him up to it because I sensed an injustice, because I have a profound sense of right and wrong. I did it because of ego, more than anything. Which makes me guilty of something."

"So you're doing this for Weiss?"

"I'm doing this because I came to live a greedy, self-absorbed life. I've made millions along the way, but I lost my wife, and my daughter and my friend are dead, because I was obsessed with numbers and patterns and the culture of profit."

Sobieski considers this and decides she has nothing to say. She has little patience for the greedy. The laptop screen kicks into energy-saving mode and goes dark.

"What about you?" he asks. "With your training I bet you could've joined a fund or one of the big investment houses. Why'd you choose to be a cop instead?"

She stands. Even though they have no plan, no agreed upon next step, she's ready to move. "I chose to do this," she says, "because my father ruined our life; because he worked in finance and he was a lot worse than you."

They walk west across the park.

"Where is your ex-wife now?" asks Sobieski.

"Good question." He looks at his watch—1:39 A.M.—and stops at a

"You believe that?"

"She said she wasn't going back home."

"Then," Sobieski presses, "where?"

"Another good question." Havens looks across the park at the squared-off shadows of the library, silhouetted by the lights of the Pan Am building farther east. He doesn't believe that he spooked her at all. Instead he believes that the other night was the start of, if not new love, then at least redemption. He recalls Miranda's last words to him, *"I'm fine, Drew. I'm in a good place,"* and it finally occurs to him. Finally words make more sense than numbers.

"She's at the Chelsea Hotel." He turns and immediately starts walking toward Seventh and a south-bound cab.

"Where?"

"The Chelsea. We used to go there to get away, even after we were married."

Sobieski, jogging to keep up, asks, "She left a message?"

"No, I just know."

15

S he looks at the door, latched and blocked. Deduces, He was here first. Then, No way you'll make it out.

"Where have you been? I've been waiting awhile."

Miranda stares at him, "This figures. The only person besides Weiss whom he trusted is the bad guy."

"I always liked you, Miranda. Too bad your husband chose the wrong time to become human."

"What do you want?"

"Cooperation. Cooperate and you will live. If we wanted you dead right now, we wouldn't be having this little talk."

"What . . ."

"For starters, where is your husband?"

"Ex. You remember we're divorced, Tom. Drew said you were the only one at the firm who looked out for him after we split up, after we lost Erin."

"Can you think of a better time or way to gain his trust? So where is he?"

"Go to hell. I don't know."

He strikes her hard across the cheek with the back of his right hand. She stumbles back against the desk and stares at him. "I. Don't. Know."

"I know he's called you and that he visited you in Katonah. I also know you've been with Salvado's wife. Now, where?"

"He called because he found Weiss's body and he had no one to turn to. He came to Katonah for one night because he had nowhere to go. Last we spoke—and check my phone if you want, because it's dead—last we spoke he was on his way to Jersey to pursue some lead to impli-... When he never called back, I assumed something

down his boss, his company, and more."

"He's ten times the man you'll ever be."

He smacks her again. This time she doesn't flinch. "You forget where I'm coming from," she says, glaring at him. "I'm not one of the firm's pieces of arm candy who makes her money and moves on after the divorce, looking for her next victim. I'm a woman who lost the love of her life and her daughter because of you bastards. The only thing I want I can't have, so go ahead and kill me. Because without him I've got nothing."

Rourke stares at Miranda. He reaches in his jacket and pulls out a pistol. A Glock. "Okay," he says. "Get up."

16

"We're looking for a guest. Miranda Havens."

It's a different clerk from the woman Miranda spoke to a half hour ago. This one, a man in his sixties, in early for the start of the 2 A.M. shift, has never heard of her.

"You know the room number?"

Havens shakes his head. "No. She's my wife."

The man looks at Havens and Cara Sobieski and shrugs. He's seen kinkier over the years.

"She's here, right?"

The man looks at his computer. Doesn't say yes or no. "It's late. I guess I can call the room, but I can't give you the number."

Havens nods, but isn't optimistic. "I just tried her cell and she didn't pick up."

The clerk holds up his hands. "This is what I can do."

"Fine. Sure. Thanks."

The clerk dials and they wait. Clearly no one is picking up. The clerk holds out the still ringing phone. What now?

Havens tries a new approach: "Look. I was here two days ago. You can check my name in the system. Havens. Like hers. I have ID. I have my wedding picture with her."

The clerk squints, thinking, You carry a wedding photo of your ex? "Sorry. But they have rules. Otherwise people would be breaking into rooms all the time."

Sobieski leans on the counter and speaks for the first time. "Listen, this is important. We received an urgent message to meet her here."

The clerk moves his reading glasses toward the tip of his nose to get a better look at her. "You a cop?"

counter. She's wearing a brown suede jacket and a yellow beret. To avoid additional work she makes a point of keeping her head down and ignoring Havens and Sobieski. It's after 2 A.M. She's off duty and wants to go home.

"How about this," Havens pleads. "You take us up there. We go together and you open up the door and we take a quick look inside just to make sure everything's okay."

"I don't know," the male clerk says to the female clerk. "What do you think?" She still doesn't look up, but she does grab the computer monitor and tilts it her way for a better look. Only when she sees Miranda Havens's profile on the monitor does she look back at Havens. "What's your name again?"

"Havens. I was . . ."

She raises her hand to shush him. "I have something for you."

They all watch as she turns and removes the large envelope from the mail slot behind the counter.

He opens the envelope with his back turned to them and holds up the room key for the others to see. "Let's go," he says to Sobieski, moving toward the elevator.

On the way up he reads the short note from Miranda. "She says she's been trying to reach me. And that they took Salvado's wife away this afternoon."

They don't bother to knock. He inserts the key and swings open the door. He goes to the left, toward the bed and the sitting area, and Sobieski goes to the right, toward the bathroom. A moment later Sobieski joins him in the bedroom.

"I have no idea," he says, sitting on the edge of the bed.

"Maybe she'll come back."

"It's what, three o'clock?" He lies back and closes his eyes. Miranda's envelope is still in his left hand. He tries to think of where she might be but can only speculate on what happened to her.

Sobieski doesn't sit. She takes Havens's computer out of his bag and plugs it into an outlet next to the desk. Then she takes Heinrich Shultz's flash drive out of her pocket and plugs it into a USB port on the side of the laptop.

While she waits for the computer to load, Havens stares at Miranda's handwriting on the note and the outside of the envelope. He reaches inside and pulls out the pages. Fourteen in all. He stares at the first page for several seconds before moving on to the next and the next, allowing the breadth of information to register, and the hard data to inform the broader, increasingly troubling narrative.

"Come here," Sobieski says. "There's something I want to show you."

His silence draws Sobieski away from the computer.

"What?"

He hands her the pages and says, "We have to stop this bastard."

"You think he has your . . . wife?"

"One of his people has her. She knew someone was after her. That's why she left this at the desk."

The information revealed in the first file of Heinrich Shultz's drive is straightforward. It lists the details of the first four trades: Hong Kong, Dubai, Johannesburg, and Rio. "Dublin and Toronto happened after he was killed," Sobieski explains. They go over the list of the specific securities bundled within each trade, the amounts, and the instructions for how the trades were to be executed. In smaller, sub-ten-thousand-dollar "Smurfed" batches, to avoid detection by American authorities. Shultz's alias for the trades he executed was Homer.

"Homer Simpson?" Havens asks.

"don't stay too long away from home, leaving
your treasure there, and brazen suitors near;
they'll squander all you have or take it from you . . ."

"*The Odyssey?*"

"Very good. I Googled it. There are two more, all from the same book, and different from yours. I think these were activation cues for people in the trade cities to execute the traders because somehow their plan was compromised. For instance, I know that Lau in Hong Kong put down matching personal shorts out of his private account, and Al Mar placed calls to his broker brother-in-law, which must have pissed off the leaders of this enough to wipe out every loose end."

"Except Luhabe."

"This is true."

Havens leans in and reads:

10/18

"I stormed that place and killed the men who fought.
Plunder we took, and we enslaved the women,
To make division, equal shares to all."

10/19

"Stand clear, put up your sword;
let me but taste of blood. I shall speak true."

To Sobieski, he says, "Siren/Ithaka Securities. Mr. Homer."

The guy who killed Patrick Lau in Hong Kong had a Siren Securities logo on his briefcase. An ancient illustration of a woman.

Havens stands straight and reaches into his pocket. He pulls out the printout of Weiss's whiteboard and hands it to Sobieski without looking at it. "This is the board I saw in Weiss's apartment. He sent me the photo just before he was killed. Check out the unattached number sequences at the bottom of each page. I bet they match up to those passages. Chapter and page number."

"Book, more likely," Sobieski corrects. "Book and line numbers."

"Right—"

"Already doing it," she interrupts, typing. Two clicks later they have their first answer: "Yup: Book three, lines 340 to 346. Exact match. Then: Tuesday, 10/18. Book 6, lines 88 to 90."

"So they were used to activate each trade. When the code for each passage appears, somewhere, execute the trade?"

Sobieski nods. "Execute the trade, then the trader. Makes sense."

"What about the others?"

She searches online and then reads: "Rio: 'A pity you have more looks than heart. You'd grudge a pinch of salt from your own larder to your own handy man. You sit here fat on others' meat, and cannot bring yourself to rummage out a crust of bread for me.'"

Then, "Dublin. Eighteen, 55 to 57: 'So the great soldier took his bow and bent it for the bowstring effortlessly. He drilled the axe-heads clean, sprang, and decanted arrows on the door sill, glared, and drew again. This time he killed Antinous.' "

Then, "Toronto. Seventeen, 594 to 599: 'A guest remembers all of his days that host who makes provisions for him kindly.' "

They look at each other. "I get it. So there was a trade execution quote or clue that was somehow posted for the financial guy, then an _____ ____ ____ ____ _____ ___ _ ___ _ city. Somebody likes *The Odys-*

Havens rubs his eye_

ran, where else would she have gone? If someone has her, who? And where?

"Shit is happening overseas," Sobieski says. She's standing, leaning over the laptop.

"What shit?"

"Copycat plays. People copying the other trades even more than before. Either they know what's coming or they sense it and are going along for the ride."

"Where?"

"Eastern Europe. Moscow. Georgia. Ukraine. Mumbai. Paris . . ." Then she pauses. "And . . . Hong Kong. Actually, most of it's starting there." Nello and Cheung have wasted no time sharing her inside information, she thinks.

While Sobieski talks, Havens runs his fingers along the rest of the envelope.

"All stocks?"

"Yup, even NYCRE. Short money is moving on all of them. Money and chatter."

Havens thinks of Weiss. Thinks of 9/11 and the models he constructed the other night. How short money did indeed begin to move on airline, insurance, banking, and more than two dozen other securities in the days leading up to the attack. "Explain chatter."

"The volume and velocity that certain words and phrases appear in phone, cellular, and digital networks around the world. Sort of like the number one Twitter trending topics of the apocalypse."

"Trending the apocalypse," Havens says. "If they're onto it, and we're onto it, is it safe to assume some good guys are as well?"

Sobieski's mouth forms a grim frown. "Knowing something is up and knowing *what it is* are two different things, right?"

FRIDAY

1

As it turns out, fate was never particularly kind to the financial markets on Fridays, either. And, if one wants to get picky, Tues-
days, Wednesdays, and Thursdays haven't been much different from
the others.

Havens knows this, because he checked. At one point, four years
ago, he programmed a model that monitored the performance of
every day in the history of the New York Stock Exchange and found
that one was as likely to lose (or gain) everything on a Tuesday in April
as a Monday in October. The only real trend, he had to admit, was that
the biggest, most infamous crashes happened on autumn Mondays
and Fridays. Watching Sobieski pore over the Salvado documents,
Havens can't help but wonder if the Hindenburg Omen was correct,
and if today was destined to be one of those days.

He tries Miranda's phone again, but there's still no answer. He
checks his messages and e-mails, but nothing, only Rourke, checking
in, wishing him well, offering his help. They continue to look for clues
online, but they keep returning to the documents that Miranda left

him. "This is nuts," Havens says. "This is a guy who spent a million dollars on ads against building the mosque at Ground Zero."

Sobieski finishes, "and here we have a photo of him meeting with members of Tablighi Jamaat."

"How do you know?"

"It's my job. That's Taibur Rahman. Me knowing what terrorists look like is like you knowing who's the chairman of the Fed. Or the shortstop for the Yankees. If Salvado's not mujahideen, then he's certainly comfortable hanging out with them and, presumably, financing them."

"So what's his motive? He's a born-again radical Islamist?"

"In a way, yes," Sobieski says, handing him a copy of the news account of the events leading up to the suicide of Rick Salvado's father. "Whether he's radical Islam or not, his father's failures gave him enough of a connection to pursue when he realized that amassing unthinkable wealth and getting disgustingly rich weren't revenge enough."

Havens paces to the window and looks at the predawn street below. "I'm leaning toward tortured and insane versus ideological extremist, because this guy was the furthest from devout Muslim/Catholic/Jew I'd ever seen. Prostitutes. Drugs. Alcohol. Apparently the image of America's most patriotic investor was cultivated as a diversion."

Sobieski shrugs. No male behavior will ever surprise her again.

"Wait." Havens bends close to the computer. "What if he wasn't financing them, but they were the ones who have been financing him? What if someone in Chechnya was his guardian angel in 2002? Why not them, especially if they were willing to wait to call in their favor?"

"Go on . . ."

"What if, in 2001, when the market crashed and Salvado was disgraced and his shut-down Allegheny Fund was caught up in a fund mismanagement scandal, what if these people targeted him, approached him, and bailed him out? What if they gave him the money to start over again with the understanding that he would ultimately have to enact their financial will? I've always wondered how he got the money to come back after the NASDAQ bubble popped, but I never figured it out. He's claimed it was the loyalty of his investors that gave him new life, but I never saw anything to support that."

Sobieski pulls out her phone.

"What are you doing?"

"I'm calling my boss. He has to know."

Michaud answers with a threat. "I'm talking to a dead person."

While Sobieski tells Michaud about Rick Salvado's p... rorist connection, and his curious counter-connection to the deadly trades, Havens paces the floor and glances at the door every time a floorboard creaks in the hall outside. He turns on the TV with the sound off. CNBC.

It's been a horrific night overseas. Hong Kong. Tokyo. Europe's tanking. Bad. The futures are down. Why? He's tempted to turn up the volume, but he knows it won't matter. They don't know, either. Back on the computer, he returns to the models he constructed last night and slugs in the latest factor, the NYCRE trade out of Toronto. Every number registers. He can and does track minute shifts in the markets, fractional shifts in obscure securities. He builds models in his head in real time, and already he can see it, the coming crash, the wave heading west, before the programs and the press and the rest of the world. But he can't construct a model that will bring him to Miranda.

He hears Sobieski telling Michaud, "He *didn't* kill his coworker. . . . He's not a bitter former employee. . . ." It takes him a second to realize that she's talking about him. When she looks up, he smiles and waves at her. "Why do I know?" she continues. "Because he's right here and, well, I'm alive."

Havens grabs a pen, and on the back of one of the photocopies he starts to scribble the names of the trades again. If there are outliers, he decides, it's the insurance company CGI, and NYCRE, the New York landmark real estate firm. The other four, while not in the exact same industry, are in industries that often play together. New and old media, advertising and technology. He has a thought, but has to wait for Sobieski to get off the phone.

"I know I don't know what 'event' this is leading to," she rants, banging her fist close to the open laptop. "And I know he's the financial world's flavor of the month. . . . Would you rather I wait until after the fact? Do you need me to scan and fax this stuff to you? Do you think I'm inventing this? That I blew off a flight to Hong Kong because I wanted to act out a giant conspiracy? What else do you need? Well, that's not gonna happen. . . ."

She stares at the phone and then lays it down. Her five minutes with Michaud have apparently come to an end.

"So, what else do we need?" he asks.

"We need the 'it.' He said he'd look more closely at Salvado, but he's not going to have anyone approach him unless we give him the 'it.' He needs the *it* that makes sense of the *who*, *what*, and *why*. What does it all lead up to? He's been shamed. I've betrayed him and lied to him. I've been fired. You're wanted for murder, and Rick Salvado was just on the cover of *Businessweek* waving a little American flag in front of the fucking bull on Wall Street. So we have to be convincing beyond a doubt."

"Okay." Havens wants to tell her about his insurance and real estate hunch, but she's not through talking.

"Weiss's note, do you have it?"

He points to the desk. "Gave it to you."

"This lists a series of financial glyphs pointing to six securities, six trades, right?" Sobieski says, tapping a finger along the boxes for days of this week.

"Correct."

"But his text, the note Weiss sent you the night he was killed, said seven, right?"

Havens nods, quotes it: "This time: 7 Trades. Not 28."

With her right forefinger she draws a circle around the box for today's date, Friday, empty except for the two red exclamation points. "Any thoughts on what goes here? What's the seventh?"

2

New York City, 8:15 A.M.

It commences in a brokerage house in Sydney, with a fifty-million-dollar U.S. short position laid against Transmediant! placed by a firm in Berlin called Iliad on behalf of a Philadelphia-based client account.

Within minutes, dozens of other substantial but smaller shorts are placed on Transmediant!, from Tokyo to Mumbai, followed by many more even smaller positions heading east to west with the sun as markets open and others begin to close across the planet.

The Transmediant! plays are shadowed, almost without fail, by tens of thousands of other shorts on the other six securities that were alluded to on Danny Weiss's board. Most of the ancillary activity is originating in Hong Kong. And then, without any tangible link or reason, besides the fact that investors are smelling the scent of blood in the waters of a particular industry, sector, or an entire market, there commences frenzied shorting and across-the-board selling, starting in Asia, then Europe.

The Nikkei loses 5 percent in less than two hours of midday trading, London more than six before curbs kick in. Some exchanges and securities attribute their sell off to sovereign debt concerns or the bad set of numbers—employment, housing starts, confidence—du jour. But most of the panic, at first, never enters the human psyche. It's the by-product of an unprecedented volume of automated trading spreading virally across multiple market centers, across tens of thousands of computers capable of dumping in milliseconds what once took days.

Only when the cumulative effect begins to register with human beings, as the markets prep to open on the East Coast of the United States, does anxiety and fear begin to stir. Once awoken, that anxiety and fear spreads across the Atlantic like a tsunami. Like a plague. Like the fallout of a bomb.

One of Krupp's PR guys waves Salvado over to their group and explains the situation. Less than an hour before the market is to open, exchange officials and others at the Fed are discussing whether to implement trading curbs or circuit breakers to slow the velocity of a potential economic catastrophe. They're considering a one-hour trading halt in the cash market and a corresponding trading halt in the derivative markets, all of which are based on substantial movements in broad market indicators.

What everyone is trying to figure out, the man explains, is just what has triggered the seemingly random substantial movements. There's been no especially dismal set of jobs or production numbers released in the past twenty-four hours; no major corporation posted a significantly lower than expected earnings report; and despite what everyone is surmising, the major economies of most of the nations of the free world are, for the moment, relatively stable.

Inside a VIP lounge overlooking the trading floor, Salvado asks the head of communications for the NYSE, "Anyone know what's causing it?"

The man manages a gallows laugh. "You're asking me? Shit, I thought if anyone, you'd know."

A financial reporter for Reuters, tagged by a field producer with a video cam, asks, "Rick, can we get you on the record for a quick sound bite to discuss what we might be in store for today." Tommy Rourke gets between the reporter and Salvado.

"Give him a break, guys," Rourke says. "He just got here."

Under his breath Salvado whispers to Rourke, "What do I tell these people?"

"Gotta stay positive, Rick. Too late to change now."

Salvado turns to face the reporter. "Look," he says, "I'm here to talk about the biggest financial and business gathering in the history of New York, held in the coolest corporate public space in the world, owned by my pal Ben here," he says, pointing to Transmediant!'s Krupp, who teeters bug-eyed on the other side of the room in deep jittery conversation with a circle of advisors.

"Okay," replies the reporter. "How about we ask how you and Mr. Krupp feel about the fact that on the day you are to ring the bell, the day of a historic event, the world markets are tanking and the value of a share in his company has plummeted more than 40 percent?"

"How about you take your remote and go fuck yourself," Salvado answers, staring directly into the camera. Then, turning to Rourke and the NYSE communications guy, he says under his breath, "Transmediant! is already down by half?"

Rourke shrugs and says, "Everything's down half, pal." The PR guy claps his hand together and forces a smile. "This is a problem. Plus, how do you ring the opening bell for a market that, technically, if they impose curbs, will remain closed?"

Salvado's phone rings. He holds up a hand, excusing himself, and steps away. It's Roxanne. "Rick, I'm getting bombarded. The press. The conference people. Your investors are freaking. They want out now. Chilton at Goldman has called three times. He's worried about the fund, if it can handle this with all the longs. If we go under, he said it would not bode well for Goldman, either."

He hands the phone to Rourke. "Tell them I stand by my positions. No one even knows what's causing this. Say this could very well be some kind of market anomaly like a black box–induced flash crash. I don't know. Turn this into a statement with confidence. A smile. A steady hand. Give it to PR and make it an electronic release. Tell them that Rick Salvado still believes."

When he turns back around, a reporter from CNN is in front of

exchange, and the other two not far behind.

"What do you think, Rick? We have no info on this at all, other than, according to Treasury, a bunch of rumors and chatter. But it's bad. Like some kind of micro arms race is being waged. Computerized arbitrage."

Salvado squints, clicks his tongue. "Shit, you all know much more than me, and have much more information at your disposal, but my two cents? If it was me, and I had no hard evidence of anything, no overseas catastrophe, no explicit threat, no institution straddling the abyss, on the day of a major happening that transcends finance, after all we've been through, I'd open the goddamn thing. On freaking time. Last thing we need in this country is another collapse, or even a scare. Get a bunch of us to stand up, not just me and Ben, but some G20 guys, Trump, the mayor, and Zuckerberg go on camera and project confidence, downplay this and get things moving. I mean, the NYSE should be able to withstand a rumor storm, right?"

3

New York City, 8:39 A.M.

Miranda is led through the bowels of a midtown office building and into a storage room. A bearded man with an unholstered pistol and a thick Russian accent points to a straight-backed office chair and tells her to sit.

"I want to talk to Rourke," she says.

The man shoves her onto the seat and trains the pistol on her face. "Rourke," he says, mock laughing. "There is no Rourke."

After they took her out of the Chelsea, she was certain they were going to kill her and dump her somewhere on the west side, but they didn't. "You still have value," the Russian tells her. "Diminishing by the second, but if we reach your husband and he becomes a threat and he knows that we have you, we have leverage."

A welt has risen on her cheek. Her head throbs from a lack of sleep. To the dismay of the Russian, she begins to cry, overcome by the weight of what she's been through, what she knows, and the certainty that she and her husband and many others are about to die.

4

lack their usual swagger.

Havens and Sobieski watch it bearing down on them while frantically working to stop it.

The overnight dip. The approaching storm. The imminent crash.

One talking head wonders if black box algorithms have somehow overloaded the exchanges, if thousands of speed-of-light auto traders attempting to stay one step ahead of the meme have simultaneously placed a blizzard of sell orders. One anchor wonders about cyber warfare. A guest calls it, as if she's overheard the NYSE PR official, "computerized arbitrage."

Under his breath, Havens simply calls it "a disaster."

"What do you know about Transmediant!?" asks Sobieski.

"Beside the fact that it's another Salvado favorite? It claims to be the future of media and entertainment. Convergence specialists, bringing together new models and combinations of entertainment, content, branding, and tech. Decent numbers. Modest growth projections. Et cetera."

"So it fits in with the other six?"

"Yeah. No. Four of them, anyway." Havens remembers the point he wanted to make about the relationship between the real estate and insurance stocks. The outliers in the mix. "Hey," he asks, "is there a way with this program to track which NYCRE real estate holdings are insured by CGI?"

"With this? Yeah." She's already typing. Havens watches the TV. *POSSIBLE TRADING CURBS BEFORE THE BELL* scrawls across the bottom of the screen, followed by *COMPUTERIZED ARBITRAGE?* followed by *BLACK FRIDAY?* Then come the futures, a sea of red symbols.

Sobieski waves him over and jabs at the screen. "Here's a list of every company that's part of NYCRE. And here's a list of the companies from that group who are on record as having some level of an insurance relationship with CGI."

Havens leans in. "Of the seventy-eight real estate companies on the first list, at least nine are insured in some degree by CGI." As they look closer at the nine, one jumps out.

"Transmediant!" Sobieski says, straightening up and backing away from the screen as if it's on fire.

Havens moves to the keyboard and takes over while she paces, processing this new packet of information. He calls up the Transmediant! stock profile. "Down almost fifty percent before opening. Heavy volume. One of the ups that appeared all three times on Hindenburg Omen days in the past month." He opens the Wiki page, the Hoover profile. The company Web site. "Worldwide headquarters in midtown Manhattan," he reads aloud, "at the newly renovated, landmark Transmediant! Conference Center and Theater." Then, "A NYCRE property." Now he stands as well. "And look . . ." He points at the corporate logo at the head of the home page on the company Web site. She leans back in. "Transmediant!" Havens repeats.

"With an exclam, in red," Sobieski adds. "Just like Weiss's board."

They're hovering over the screen, shoulder to shoulder, looking for more. Sobieski says, "I had an English teacher in ninth grade who said a good writer never uses an exclamation point unless the world is on fire."

"Well, apparently, this one is especially well placed." Havens points at the screen, beneath the logo, at the copy under a headline that reads:

WHAT'S NEW AT TRANSMEDIANT!

the inaugural DAVOS WEST

Great Hall.

5

New York City, 9:10 A.M.

Twice the Russian's phone rings. Each time he leaves the room to take the call. Each time he turns to her at the door and says in broken English, "If you try to leave . . ." and finishes his thought with a wave of his pistol.

After the second call he returns with another chair and Deborah Salvado. He sets the chair down beside Miranda, looks at Deborah, and points at the chair. Deborah's hair hangs wild over the right side of her face, and her left cheek is also red and swollen. The women nod at each other but otherwise say nothing. What a strange fate, Miranda thinks, dying in this place alongside this woman.

Not until the man returns to the hallway to take a call does Deborah look up. She has tears in her eyes. "I'm sorry."

"We have to get out of here, Deb."

Deborah nods unconvincingly. With trembling fingers she brushes the loose strand of hair from her cheek.

Miranda stares at the man in the doorway. She considers rushing him and making a desperate dash to freedom, down the hall, up the stairs, onto the street. She imagines herself bursting out the front doors, flagging down a police car, and then what? Even though she knows she's about to die anyway, she knows such a move will also end in death, only sooner.

Deborah speaks as if reading her mind. "Don't even think of it. That pistol is an automatic weapon. They told me. You'd be torn to pieces before you got halfway to the stairs."

"Then what?"

Deborah whispers, "They're going to blow something up."

"This guy?"

"This guy, Rourke. My husband and whoever he's with."

heard my husband tell him to. On speaker phone.

6

"Michaud."

"My name is Sawa Luhabe. I am calling from Johannesburg, South Africa. Does this mean anything to you?"

Michaud sits up. He's in front of a bank of monitors, each displaying a different aspect of agent Cara Sobieski's story. He's smoking a cigarette, nursing a Chinese beer, and listening to Tony Bennett's "The Best Is Yet to Come." He lowers the music as his eyes track to the Jo'burg screen. "Ms. Luhabe. It is a pleasure to hear your voice. I've got people scouring the continent looking for you."

"I am presently in front of a TSI satellite office, prepared to surrender myself in exchange for your protection."

"You have my word. I'm sending a note to my colleague there as we speak and someone will come out to get you. I promise you'll be safe."

"Thank you."

"While you're waiting," he says. "By any chance have you recently spoken to our friend Sobieski?"

"Just via e-mail. While she was in flight, en route to New York."

7

Within five minutes the Dow falls off a five-hundred-point cliff. Stocks are down across the board. The seven securities of the seven trades fall the farthest, but programmed trading takes hundreds of others down with them. There are three thresholds, each of which represents a different level of decline in terms of points in the Dow Jones industrial average. Since it is before 2 P.M., the first halt will shut down the market for an hour. If threshold number two is breached before 1 P.M., the market will close for two hours.

They're in a cab, heading toward midtown, when Sobieski's phone rings. Michaud. "I just heard from your friend in Jo'burg. Tell me everything you know about Trans—"

"—mediant! We're heading there now."

"You think they're gonna hit the event?"

"Everything we've found points that way. Any way you can—"

"I'm already putting out word to clear it, but they won't unless I have something hard."

"How does that feel?" She looks out the window. Traffic on Sixth slows near the Garden. Havens rocks back and forth, glaring out the other window. Then, poking at her handheld, she says, "I'll forward what I have. . . . For starters, Transmediant!'s building is an NYCRE holding. CGI insures the building. CEOs for the other five stocks that were attached to the bloody short trades are going to be in the building today to hear Rick Salvado of The Rising give the keynote—"

"I just saw him on TV. Ringing the bell on crash day, telling everyone it's gonna be all right."

"Michaud, this is bad."

"You've got to wait for backup. I've already contacted Homeland, Treas—"

Sobieski interrupts: "We gotta go. . . ."

Michaud pauses. "Wait, Sobes. We've got to get the building shut down. Just wait, Cara. Wait until I get you backup."

Cara, she thinks. "You know I can't do that, Michaud. If it was just money, maybe."

"Jesus."

"Listen, Boss. I e-mailed you every passage we've found from *The Odyssey*. Someone somewhere is using them as a way to activate the trades and murders. Is there a way to run them all to see if they've shown up recently on a platform somewhere? A newspaper or blog or series of social media entries?"

"Sure. Already starting to look."

The cab turns left off the avenue.

"Here's something," Michaud says.

"Shoot."

"Crimson Classics: A Harvard Dude's Take on Greek Lit."

"Do you have an addy?"

"We're trying."

They see the logo on the side of the building up ahead. She clicks off.

Havens turns to her. "They found a blog?"

"Yup."

"Do you have a gun?"

She shakes her head, pounds her fist on her thigh. As soon as the traffic slows, she opens the door to the still moving cab.

"Do they have the blog guy?"

"They're tracking."

"What are we going to do when we get there?"

"Clear the building . . . take Salvado down," she answers, already three steps in front of him.

As they near the building, he asks one more question, "The blog—

8

In the limo uptown, Benjamin Krupp begins to cry.

Pathetic son of a bitch, thinks Salvado. A hundred million in the bank. Twenty-five-million-dollar bonus this year, with another twenty due in December, if he lives that long, and he's still crying. "Buck up, pal," he tells the Transmediant! CEO. "You've got about five minutes to get your shit together and give the most important speech of your life."

"I know," Krupp whimpers. "I know. But it's just that no one seems to have a goddamn clue."

"You do your part, Kruppy, and I promise, when I go on at ten, I will rock the place."

The limo slows as it turns off the avenue and heads toward the freight entrance. Salvado's BlackBerry vibrates. He holds it up with the screen facing away from Krupp.

At 9:39, despite Salvado's bold public proclamation at the Exchange, the first threshold of a crash was breached and a trading halt has automatically been triggered. You're powerful, Salvado thinks. But no one is powerful enough to override the automatic halts. In a few hours they'll give it another shot and try until the third threshold is breached, closing the market for the day. However, Salvado doesn't dwell on this. No way it's gonna get that far.

At 9:48 Krupp wipes his eyes, takes a stuttering breath, and opens his door. Media vans with satellites on their roofs line the street. Mic-toting correspondents scan the sidewalks for a notable willing to talk about the collapse. Two security guards step forward to greet Krupp at the loading dock on the side of the Transmediant! mail room. He looks back into the limo.

markets, shakes his head at the catastrophe in the making, and wonders how much of it is his fault, his doing.

The driver adjusts the mirror. "Sir?"

"Right. I'm going." He opens the door, then leans back inside. "You'll wait right here, front end pointing out, ready to roll?"

"Yes, sir." After Salvado closes the door, the driver pulls out his device and types,

The Lord of the Western Approaches, Approaches.

Which translates, in no less than four languages, for people in no less than seven countries, to *It's go time.*

9

They burst into the lobby, and Sobieski hustles across the marble floor, beneath the million-dollar murals and through the clustered billionaire conference-goers, toward the security desk. Two men are on top of her before she reaches the desk. "I'm a federal agent," she tells them as they close ranks upon her. "You've got to clear the building."

They grab her by the elbows and begin to steer her away from the others. "I'm agent Cara Sobieski of TSI, and you have got to believe me, there's a bomb in this building."

"Right," says one of the guards, pushing a button under his desk, motioning with a hand to another guard, "but you're gonna have to show us some kind of ID. . . ."

Seeing that time is wasting, Havens looks around the lobby, walks to a far wall near the banks of elevators, and pulls a fire alarm. As the alarm pierces the air, two businessmen who saw him yank the switch ask what's going on and he tells them, "There's a bomb in the building."

One of the men steps back and yells over his shoulder, just as Havens had hoped, "Says there's a bomb in the building."

Havens takes two steps back and watches. People heading inside turn around and head back out. Another alarm, set to a different pitch and rhythm, begins to sound. The two guards with Sobieski briefly let go of her arms and turn to look down the desk for information from their boss. At that instant, Sobieski slips away and runs toward the security turnstiles. Through the sea of conference-goers who have turned to leave she swims in, toward the theater.

Steps behind her once again, Havens follows.

10

New York City, 9:48 A.M.

"We're getting out of here," Deborah Salvado whispers to her. "You said . . ."

"It's only a matter of minutes before he kills us anyway, so I'm going to do something."

Miranda looks at her. She agrees.

"I'm going to try to get out first."

"He's in between us and the door. There's no—"

"The other way," Deborah whispers. "At the other end of the room, I'm not sure if there's a door, but next time he gets up, I'm going to try. When he follows . . . I want you to run out the other door through the hall as fast as you can."

"But . . ."

Deborah Salvado shakes her head. "This is the way it's supposed to happen. You didn't deserve this. And this . . . this is what I get. Plus, I feel lucky."

A few minutes later the bearded man's phone rings again.

11

financial and corporate elite and their broad-shouldered security guards. The blare of the alarms exponentially compounds
their market-related anxiety.

Ten years and a month since 9/11, and the fear rises back in an
instant.

Benjamin Krupp stands in the center of the stage, holding a Power-
Point clicker he'll never click, wondering how the day can possibly get
any worse. Over the PA system they are already playing the opening
bars to Rick Salvado's song, "The Rising," of course, by Bruce Springsteen. Or, the "other Boss," as Salvado likes to call him.

Sobieski crashes through the swinging doors at the rear of the
theater.

Havens is close behind. "Everyone out!" she screams. "There is a
bomb threat in this room." New York City PD foot patrol are first on the
scene, running onto both ends of the stage and directing the crowd
toward the exits. FDNY first responders, in full bunko gear, begin
entering from the rear. Sobieski continues to shout, "Everyone out!"
but she's not sure what to do next. She's scanning the crowd for

Salvado, whom she's never seen in person, and for anything that looks like it might be a bomb, but what does that look like, exactly? Right now, everything looks like a bomb.

Havens jumps onto a table in the back of the room, in part to get away from the stampede and in part to get a better view of the theater. He sees Laslow before Laslow sees him. The bald man is cursing at an uncooperative cell phone in his right hand and wearing a backpack. He looks even bulkier than usual and he's heading directly toward Havens.

Havens looks down at the tabletop and notices that it is covered with closed cardboard boxes stamped SALVADO MEMOIR. If anyone would know the status of Salvado's memoir, it's Havens. The guy never stopped talking about it, and its June publication date. He also knows that he's far from finished writing it. Terrorist or not, the egotistical son of a bitch couldn't keep his mouth shut over something like that. You're standing, Havens tells himself, on the fucking bomb. And Laslow, whose faulty phone was probably detonator number one, is detonator number two.

He leaps off the table and stumbles momentarily. When he looks back up, he can no longer see Laslow.

As he bounds through the side door near the stage, Salvado sees that he won't be delivering a keynote this morning. He sees the pile of books in the back of the room and hears people shouting "bomb" as they rush past, toward the exit. Only now does he realize the full extent of the pact he made in 2002. "What have I done?" he asks himself as he continues toward the stack of boxes. After three steps he sees the bald man and calls his name. "Laslow!"

Laslow turns and frowns. "What?"

"No one said anything about a bomb."

Laslow shrugs, quickly turns, then hustles away toward the boxes.

Havens is looking to his left as Laslow comes up on him from the right. Havens turns and reaches for Laslow, but the larger man recognizes him and punches him, glancing off his jaw, driving him back against the boxes. Havens straightens and surges forward, but Laslow steps back, pulls out a pistol, and points it at Havens. Havens stares at the gun, then directly at Laslow. "You don't know when to quit, do you, you fucking egghead?" Havens looks over Laslow's shoulder, where Salvado stands, panting and wild-eyed. Laslow glances back at Salvado, who nods, Do it. As Laslow turns, Havens braces himself for the shot, the close-range bullet to the head.

But as Laslow fires, Salvado's right fist slams down on his gun hand, knocking the pistol to the floor. Laslow turns and drives his left fist into Salvado's nose and a right uppercut that drops him to his knees. He

boxes. Before Laslow pitches face forward onto the theater floor, Havens grabs him and begins prying his dying hands away from anything that can set off the bomb that will take down the room, the building, and the economy.

When he looks up, he sees the man who made him rich and changed his life several times over, bleeding from the nose, on his knees staring at him with a look of terror in his eyes. Havens raises the gun but knows he won't fire it. He knows now that Salvado is an evil piece of trash, a criminal and a sociopath, but not a terrorist. Salvado takes a step back and slowly shakes his head while looking into Havens's eyes. The billionaire raises his arms in half apology, half surrender. "This was never part of the plan," he explains. Then, before Havens changes his mind, he turns and disappears into the crowd.

12

New York City, 9:59 A.M.

She hears the gunshot but doesn't bother to turn and see where it came from, or what it hit.

Instead she continues toward the stage and the pale and dumbstruck man she saw standing alongside Rick Salvado on TV this morning: the CEO of Transmediant!, Benjamin Krupp. She climbs the short flight of stairs two at a time and comes up on him from behind. He almost collapses under her touch.

"I'm a federal agent," she tells him. "Where's Salvado?"

Krupp stares at her, stunned, paralyzed with an array of fears. Personal. Professional. Universal. Plus, the realization, the confirmation of what he's always known, that he's a coward, not a leader. Sobieski almost smacks him, but she shakes him instead.

"Where?"

He turns to her. "Outside, in his limo, at the loading dock." He points toward the left rear exit. "That way."

As she turns to leave, she notices the teleprompter screen raised up out of the floor. The text, which will never be spoken, reads, "On behalf of Transmediant!, welcome to this great day in the history and the future of the new global economy."

Outside, most of those who have already left the building linger on the sidewalks. A SWAT team scrambles out the back doors of a truck, and dozens of agents from seemingly every law enforcement organization operating in the city are massing around the building's perimeter. Michaud got them to listen, she thinks, as she moves along the length of the concrete loading dock, looking for Salvado. She stops a building security guard. "You see a limo here?"

"What car ain't one this morning?"

"When did the last one pull out?"

edge of slow-moving traffic. Just before the corner she sees a limo stopped at a light with its right blinker flashing. She bears down on it and jerks open the rear passenger side door as the car begins to roll. Jogging to keep up, she looks inside. Rick Salvado is not there. Two stunned Japanese businessmen are. Without a word she slams the door and looks to the east and south. One limo is moving toward Madison on the other side of the intersection, and another, heading downtown, is stopped at a light a block away. She's about to head south, but one last glance at the eastbound vehicle reveals a vanity license plate that reads:

THE RI$ING

13

New York City, 10:01 A.M.

eborah nudges Miranda with her foot and Miranda nods. Together they watch the bearded man passionately talking, gesturing with the phone. He's taking short steps now, but not venturing into the hall and not beyond the edges of the doorjamb. Suddenly he kicks at the door, furious. When he momentarily disappears from view, Deborah rises and rushes toward the near exit.

At the same moment Miranda and the bearded man hear the door swing open on the other side of the room. The bearded man bursts back into the room. His mobile drops to the floor as he reaches to steady the gun. He runs right past Miranda, brushing against her leg and briefly looking at her before continuing past and through the far door.

As soon as he passes, Miranda is up and running out the near door toward an exit she's never seen but prays is close at hand. She pauses when she hears the first short burst of gunfire, back in Deborah's vicinity.

14

barrel of a policeman's gun. He lowers Laslow's gun and holds up his hands.

"All yours," he says, gesturing toward the gun. The cop bends and grabs it while keeping his gun fixed on Havens. Havens says, "Help me get this off him. It's some kind of bomb." When the cop, a tall, brawny redhead who looks about sixteen, hesitates, Havens unzips the top of the backpack, revealing a series of wires and the top of many blocks of C-4 explosive. The cop takes a step back as Havens peels off one shoulder strap, then swiftly but carefully shifts Laslow's weight to unsnap the other. He stands, holding the pack.

"What are you gonna do with it?" asks the cop.

"Get it away from those," Havens answers, pointing at the boxes.

"Follow me." The cop begins barreling through what's left of the crowd, holding his gun in the air. Havens tails him like a running back behind a pulling guard, holding the bag at arm's length, while the cop speaks into his radio, inquiring about the whereabouts of the bomb squad.

They burst out onto the street through a revolving door on the north side of the building and are greeted by two figures in full protective bomb gear. When they see the backpack in Havens's hand, they back off and point them toward the rear of an armored police vehicle parked half a block away. After Havens places the pack inside the truck, one of the bomb squad cops slams closed the hatch while another grabs him by the arm and rushes him out of range.

"In the theater . . . ," Havens explains as they near a makeshift NYPD command post, "there's a shitload of boxes in the back that are supposed to be filled with books but are filled with explosives."

A lieutenant tells him to sit tight and then rushes down the block with the bomb squad guys. Havens bends at the waist and puts his hands on his knees. He's wired and exhausted. His hands are shaking, and his entire body is spent. The past few days have been fueled by fear and adrenaline, and when the adrenaline ebbs it's all he can do to stay on his feet. He wonders what Sobieski is up to, and where Salvado has gone, but mostly he thinks of Miranda.

Hundreds of civilians from the upper floors continue to stream out of the building. The networks are setting up satellite trucks down the block, near Sixth, and he counts no fewer than four helicopters hovering over the tower. The redheaded cop stands ten feet away, talking to two members of a SWAT team. Havens reaches for his phone to try Miranda once again, but he's distracted by a familiar face, not heading out of the Transmediant! Building, but jogging back in. It's Tommy Rourke. Havens lowers the phone and watches. He's tempted to call out to Rourke, but Rourke is talking on his phone and gesturing frantically with his right hand. Over his left shoulder is a backpack not unlike the bag that Havens just stripped off Laslow.

In an instant it all becomes clear. The human narrative, the financial models, and the previously hidden truth. Rourke, who had been there since The Rising began, who delivered clients when no one wanted to touch Rick Salvado. Rourke, the Harvard Crimson grad and self-proclaimed humble classical literature major. The blog that's publishing the quotes that link back to Berlin, Hong Kong, Dubai, Rio,

Dublin, Toronto, and the whiteboard in Danny Weiss's apartment. The blog that runs the passages that activate it all:

Crimson Classics: A Harvard Dude's Take on Greek Lit

Rick Salvado may be a greedy, deceitful thief, but Tommy Rourke is a bona fide terrorist.

15

After the second burst of automatic gunfire, silence.

Miranda bounds up a flight of fire stairs but can't gain access to the lobby. As she starts up the next flight, she hears the door to the room below slam open, then the footsteps of the bearded man. The door to the next floor opens not on the lobby or office space she's hoping for, but another subterranean storage room. She steps inside, closes the door, and looks for a lock, but there is none. The room is filled with massive computer servers and HVAC apparatus. She runs along a row of servers, zigzagging in and out between gaps in the racks, looking for another exit, or anyplace to hide.

She drops to her knees when the stair door crashes open. Then she holds her breath and waits for the footsteps.

16

Salvado, it turns out, is

"Where'd he go?" Sobieski asks the driver through the open
rear door.

"Too much traffic. He got out and headed east. Asked for my
MetroCard."

She straightens, looks over the hood of the car, then leans back in.
"Where's the nearest subway?"

"Probably . . . Lex. Lex and 53rd, near Citicorp Center."

She runs. Across Madison. Through four lanes of moving traffic on
both sides of Park. Scanning the sidewalks as she moves, but she
doesn't see him. At 53rd and Lex, on a hunch, assuming he's headed
toward lower Manhattan or toward a connection out to the airport,
she goes down the downtown stairs. She skips through the turnstile
and bounds out onto the almost empty mid-morning platform. A quick
walk up and down. No Salvado. Then she looks across the tracks, at the
uptown side. It's him.

Since Salvado has no idea who she is, she figures she'll be able to
surprise him. But she realizes that by the time she goes back upstairs
and then down, he'll likely be gone. She stares at him for a moment,

coolly checking his BlackBerry while, for all he knows, thousands may be dying at this second, at his hand. She thinks of Patrick Lau and Sawa Luhabe and Heinrich and all of the others. And as she wells up with rage, she thinks of her father. The life he lived and the lie she can't live down.

She jumps.

Cara Sobieski's first journey on a New York City Subway track is across it. There's a collective gasp, first from the small group of travelers on her side, then from the group on the other, as she lands flat-footed on the gravel. She steps over the inside rail, the outside rail and then, carefully, over the third rail, before crossing over to the uptown track. She's watching the tracks, the tunnel, and Salvado at the same time. He notices her as the ground begins to shake and the glow of an approaching train's headlamp appears in the distance.

Perhaps he doesn't comprehend that she's following him, that she's after him, or perhaps he feels that she isn't going to make it. But he pauses for a moment and simply watches her as her eyes widen with urgency. She bounds over the uptown third rail and hoists her elbows onto the platform's edge. A young woman screams. A man in a suit, too far away to make a difference, starts to jog her way. She begins to muscle herself up as the train roars and takes shape at the end of the platform. But now Salvado steps forward, leans down as if to help her, then kicks at her face. She sees it coming and snaps her head back, rolls to the left with the force of the kick. Her left hand slips off the edge, and her right foot drops back onto the ground. As he rears back to kick her again, she pushes off the right leg and springs up with both hands, both arms.

This time she's ready for the kick, same foot and motion. She deflects it with her left arm as she rolls to her right. She rolls another full revolution on top of the platform deck and pops to her feet. Salvado lunges toward her, and realizing she has one chance to surprise him with her skills, she launches a vicious right spin kick. Her heel crushes against his right ear and rocks him back. While he regroups and readies to make another bull rush, she again surprises him by taking the offensive. She strikes his face with two straight left jabs and a right cross to his left temple. More stunned than injured, he staggers back. She kicks him hard in the balls and he flinches, but he still comes at her, pushing her to the lip of the platform. He lunges again. She sidesteps it, twists, and shoves him. The shove sends him to the edge but not quite over it. He teeters, trying to regain his balance.

There's a moment when she has an opportunity to deliver the death-____ ___ front of the train, or to reach out a

not enough to prevent

spins him away from her with a brute violence and drops ___ from a funnel cloud onto the concrete ten feet down the platform.

She watches him writhe, wounded but not fatally, and feels neither horrified nor ashamed nor satisfied. Not regretful or relieved. As the cars roll past, she looks at the faces pressed against doors, the heads bent over books, pushed together in a space filled with working people who will never see the inside of a limousine. People unaware of the fact that the blood of a billionaire almost ran beneath them. A billionaire about to be captured by a flawed and compromised and debauched individual. She watches and she doesn't know what to feel.

17

New York City, 10:08 A.M.

He sprints down the sidewalk and cuts sharply toward the entrance of the Transmediant! Tower.

Rourke is through the main entrance, moving against the seemingly endless stream of people filing out of the building from the upper floors. Havens follows. He pushes through the door and into the lobby. He can't see Tommy Rourke. He's lost somewhere in the chaos. Rourke, the only man to sit with him the night Erin died, the one who understood his moral qualms about the job and his growing distrust of Rick Salvado. Rourke was the only man on Wall Street he ever trusted, besides Danny Weiss.

He stops and looks for the entrance to the theater. Halfway across the lobby, some fifty feet away, he recognizes the top of Rourke's head and the pin-striped shoulders of his suit, heading toward the theater. Havens bolts toward him, trying to run, but every few steps he collides with an exiting person. One man shoves him out of the way, almost knocking him down before shouting, "Watch out, asshole!"

The stranger's shouts prompts Rourke to turn. When his eyes lock on Havens's, there is no uncertainty. He knows that Havens knows, and Havens has no doubt that Rourke is the one responsible for this.

Not Salvado. Rourke spins and begins to run toward the theater, shoving and stiff-arming people out of his way. Havens pursues, rushing for the hall outside the theater, the boxes of "books," the spot on the ground where Laslow lies dead beneath a sheet of black plastic, ten feet from more than a thousand pounds of explosives.

The backpack slows Rourke enough for Havens to close on him. Rourke turns as Havens leaves his feet and tackles him. They roll on the ground. Rourke thrashes and punches, more intent on escaping than

[text obscured] strap of the backpack, but Rourke

these two.

Rourke kicks at Havens's hands with the heel of his wingtip. Havens hangs on for two strikes but loses his grip on the third. Rourke breaks free and starts for the boxes of explosives, but a nearby cop sees him and starts toward him with his gun drawn. Rourke turns and runs up the main stairs toward the concourse, against traffic but not as much as in the lobby. Havens pursues, bounding up two stairs at a time. Rourke stops at the balcony, reaches into his pocket, and pulls out a phone. He's leaning over the railing, aiming the phone and jerking it toward the boxes below like a remote control for a set-top box, when Havens lowers his shoulder into him and drives him to the ground.

Havens dives on the larger man and they begin to wrestle again. With his free right hand Rourke punches his way back to his feet and again attempts to detonate the boxes with the phone. When Havens rises, Rourke grabs him and shoves him against the balcony rail. He's bent backward thirty feet in the air, grabbing at Rourke's throat with his right hand and clinging to the rail and his life with his left. He's squeezing Rourke's throat as hard as he can, but he's slipping. His feet are sliding out from under him and he's bent dangerously backward, close to toppling over the rail. "After I'm done killing you," Rourke says, "I'm going after your wife."

When Miranda comes out of the stairwell and into the lobby, she sees the chaos and knows that she is in the targeted building. Immediately she forgets about the man she managed to elude, still searching for her in the guts of the building, and she begins looking for Drew, first in the main theater, then in the lobby. Finally she sees Rourke trying to throw him off the balcony. She sprints upstairs and across the foyer. Two steps away she leaps and wraps her hands around Rourke's head and starts to gouge his eyes. He takes his hand off Havens and backhands Miranda in the face, knocking her to the ground.

This is enough of a break for Havens to regain his footing, but now Rourke is surging at him, intent on driving him off the balcony. Out of the corner of his eye Havens sees Rourke's phone rising up, and without hesitating he releases his left hand off the railing. With no hands on the rail to stabilize him he clenches his fist and throws a wild roundhouse not at Rourke, but his phone.

For a moment the phone seems to hang suspended in the air above the chaos of the lobby. Havens twists away from the rail. Rourke lunges for the phone instead of the stability of the railing. Without Havens's body to buttress him, his weight and the weight of the backpack begin to carry him over the edge. Rourke desperately reaches out and manages to catch the phone, but it's too late to save himself. He claws and thrashes as he plummets some fifty feet through the air of the building he aimed to topple, landing with a sickening wet thud on the cold marble floor.

Havens sprints back down the stairs. Bone shards stick out of a fracture on Rourke's left forearm, but in his left hand he still clutches the phone. Broken and on the verge of death, Rourke continues to pump the keypad. Havens steps on Rourke's wrist with one foot and kicks the phone out of his hand with the other. Rourke groans as Havens strips the backpack off him and slides it away. To the first cop, Havens says, pointing at the backpack, "Explosives"; to the second, pointing at the

18

...down the

...room in which she and Deborah Salvado had been held captive. The blood trail starts on the stairs past the far door. Deb was right, Miranda thinks, there was another way out. But was she fast enough?

"Deb!" No answer. But halfway up the steps they can hear labored breathing, a low, weak groaning. Lying on her back, bleeding profusely from a spot between her right chest and shoulder, is Deborah Salvado.

"Oh, shit, Deb," Havens says.

She looks up at them and manages a smile.

Havens yells back toward the cops for help. "She's alive!"

Deborah opens her mouth, mumbles, "Did he do it?"

Havens shakes his head. Miranda kneels down alongside her and takes her hand. "No, no, Deb. He didn't. I don't think he ever knew what they had planned."

Deborah Salvado looks at them both and smiles.

phone, "Detonator." Then he stoops and pats Rourke's jacket and trouser pockets. Before standing, he looks into Rourke's eyes.

"Why, Tommy?"

Rourke can't speak.

"The whole time. All these years you waited, to bring it down."

Before he dies, Rourke manages the weakest of nods.

FRIDAY

tion. The Flash Crash of October 21, 2011. And the fall of America's favorite hedge guy, Rick Salvado. No one will mention the fact that Exeter- and Harvard-educated Tommy Rourke was also a Chechnyan émigré who became radicalized against the West after being orphaned, a victim of Russian atrocities in 1994. His far-reaching terrorist plot that began in 1994, but took hold more than ten years ago, when he and his childhood friend and fellow terrorist Laslow first identified and approached the shamed and insolvent hedge guy Rick Salvado with an offer he couldn't refuse and would not fully understand until it was too late.

A decision was made at the executive level to keep it silo-ed, and silent. The economy couldn't sustain another crash. Another dip. The market systems couldn't be exposed to look so vulnerable. A landmark building in the center of Manhattan could never come that close to falling, let alone a building filled with the financial world's most powerful figures. Although the world has grown used to financial instability, bombs in a building filled with billionaires is a whole other story.

The crash was chalked up to market anomalies. Everything from computerized trading to double- and triple-dip fears to foreign debt concerns to a series of unexpectedly low quarterly reports in the tech sector.

A thorough study was promised and commissioned. Two studies, actually. Any significant short trade by which someone profited during the Flash Crash was labeled suspicious and would also be investigated. All this, of course, would take many months to conduct, by which time the public, consumed by new fears, would forget why or how any of it happened in the first place.

The incident at the Transmediant! Tower was deemed a false alarm. The explosives, which were quickly and subtly taken out of the building by NSA, TSI, and FBI operatives, were called harmless. Not really explosives after all, the story went. The bald man with the backpack acted alone. He was a disgruntled immigrant with a history of violence and mental illness. Rourke's death was collateral damage. Drew Havens's name was never associated with the fatal shooting of the would-be placebo bomber. In fact, no surveillance footage of the incident ever became available. It seems that the security cameras at the world's most sophisticated media and entertainment company were, apparently, on the fritz that morning.

The fall of Rick Salvado was just another in a long line of high-profile outrages in the financial industry. The Madoff du jour. Nothing surprised the public by the autumn of 2011 when it came to financial scandals. The story that was served up to the public was that Salvado was a fraud and a man who would do almost anything in the name of profit. What was truly scandalous was how many people believed him. His behavior on the subway platform late in the morning of October 21 was said to be the result of a market crash–driven psychotic episode. The acts of a man who had suddenly lost everything. The collapse of his fund was swift but not exactly shocking. Stars rise and burn out, and the collateral debris crushes millions every day on Wall Street.

In the end, Havens was convinced that Salvado was not a terrorist. Just a weak man who had made a pact at his most desperate and vulnerable moment and was willing to look the other way from everything for years. Even, eventually, terrorism, if it meant holding on to his money.

No one came forward to defend him at his trial. Not even his wife.

The markets survived. They quickly gained back some of the losses, but far from all. Because while the media and the authorities told one story, the markets themselves knew better. Deep down in the recesses of the patterns, in the calculations of the quants, the markets could

MONDAY,

1

only way to improve.

She asked Michaud for a week. He declined, but she took it anyway. And why stop at a week? She is trying to think long-term. Why not Brooklyn? Why not something different, away from money and terror and her past?

Her opponent snaps one, two, three straight left jabs at her, and she only manages to catch the third. She considers this progress. The only way to learn is from someone better than you. The only way to move on is to move on.

The second time Michaud called her, she did not pick up. The third time she threw away the phone.

Late one morning last week she spoke to Drew Havens. He was thrilled to hear from her. They discussed that day and clarified some of the events that had led up to it. At one point he asked her if she was all right. From their talks that night in Manhattan he remembered her issues with her father and Marco Nello, and her gambling.

"Is there anything I can do?" Havens asked, remembering their conversation on that night on the streets of Manhattan. "Because it would be my pleasure to—"

She cut him off. "No, everything's been resolved," she lied. "But thanks." She could not abide taking his money.

A few days after throwing out her phone, she got a call on her new one. From Cheung. He wanted to know how she was enjoying Brooklyn.

She doesn't have a big problem with the way the government handled things. She understands there are some things too dangerous for public consumption. She understands that at that level there are secrets on top of secrets, and she assumes that she only knows half of the facts and even less of the truth.

The same way with her family.

The same way in which those who think they know her only know half of the facts and even less of the truth.

Then today, just before she left for the gym, Michaud called on her new phone.

"How did you get this?"

"I think you'd be disappointed if I didn't."

"You gave my number to Cheung, didn't you?"

"A relationship with Cheung can have its privileges."

"I don't want to do this anymore, Michaud."

"Who cares about what we *want* to do? Want never enters the equation with this job, Sobes. We do it because we have to. And right now, you have to pay back some favors and get your ass back to work."

"Are you drinking?"

"Actually, yeah. But I'm karaoke-free for eight days. Taking it one song at a time. What about you? Staying away from the tables?"

She's so fixated on blocking the woman's lightning-fast punches that she doesn't see the leg sweep. She falls down face-first, barely catching herself with her gloved hands. The stale sweat smell of the canvas, the threat of defeat, feels good. It pushes her to her feet, more determined than ever to be ready for what's next.

She's spent quite a bit of time online these past few weeks. Looking into the case, but mostly looking into Rick Salvado. When discussing his fall, the media frequently wondered how one of the world's richest men could fall so hard, so fast. Because she knows more, she took it farther: She wondered how he ever became so complicit in destroying the system that made him. When she discovered his father's story, she understood. When she read more closely about the demise of Salvado's father, she realized they weren't so different after all.

He was the son of a hero.

She was the daughter of a criminal.

Each lived life as a response to the life of a father. The death of that

her feet, adjusts her headgear, and readies herself for her opponent's next move. This time she sees it coming before it even happens, and she has a response that surprises even her.

2

Katonah, New York

For the sixteenth consecutive day Drew Havens lives in a world without numbers.

When he wakes up, he doesn't bother to check the markets or his portfolio or even the scores on the sports pages.

In some regards he's doing this as an experiment, a deliberate act of will, but in others he's doing it out of necessity, to show Miranda that he's capable of change. That he will do whatever it takes to keep them together and in love.

Once the government debriefs ended and they told him how it was going to go down, what the agreed upon narrative would be for the press and the trials to come, he disappeared, taking a self-imposed sabbatical, refusing to talk to the press or anyone who had anything to do with his old life. Just Miranda.

She suggested they take a trip. St. Bart's or Fiji or Kauai. Some place far, to get away. But he didn't want to do anything lavish or remotely excessive. He wanted to stay in one place only: her rented apartment in Katonah.

In the mornings they walk around the corner for coffee at NoKa Joe's. Some days they set out for a hike through the trails at the Pound

Ridge Reservation or points farther north. Some days she runs errands and he hangs around the house. Once, while Miranda was out, he inquired about the house they almost bought when Erin was alive, and the Realtor told him she'd look into it.

They talk a lot, more than ever. But they don't talk about Erin, the past, or the future. They just do what feels right, moment by moment, and hope it lasts.

They're stretched out on the couch, watching a movie about a man whose job is to predict the future, when the phone rings. Miranda rises to answer it. Havens eavesdrops for a second, then loses interest and

He opens his eyes. "Sawa Luhabe?"

"Uh-huh. Sobieski gave her the number, though I imagine she could have found it on her own."

"What'd she say?"

"Well, we have a place to stay if we ever find ourselves in Johannesburg."

"Sweet."

After a moment, Miranda continues. "She also said to thank you. That you are a brave and decent man. And if not for you, she, and probably her daughter, wouldn't be alive."

Havens looks away from the TV and out the window and lets the words register. He wants to look up at Miranda but doesn't. To do so would make too much of the obvious, and still that might never be enough. Finally, he simply says it again:

"Sweet."

Acknowledgments

...........nt, counter-terrorism, and the financial services industry who took the time to share their own stories and stories about others not quite as hardworking and kind-hearted. Finally, thanks and love to Judy, Isabel, and Jamie.

About the Author